STAR TREK®
ARDEN OF KNOWLEDGE

STAR TREK®
BURDEN OF KNOWLEDGE

Written by **Scott & David Tipton**

Art by **Federica Manfredi**

Ink Assist by **Nicola Zanni** (Chapters 1-3) and **Riccardo Sisti** (Chapter 2)

Colors by **Andrea Priorini** and **Arianna Florean** (Chapters 3-4)

Color Assist by **Chiara Cinabro**

Letters by **Neil Uyetake, Chris Mowry,** and **Robbie Robbins**

Edits by **Scott Dunbier**

Collection Edits by **Justin Eisinger** • Collection Design by **Chris Mowry**

Cover Art by **Joe Corroney**

Special Thanks to Risa Kessler and John Van Citters at CBS Consumer Products.

www.IDWPUBLISHING.com   ISBN: 978-1-60010-803-7   13 12 11 10   1 2 3 4

IDW Publishing is: Operations: Ted Adams, CEO & Publisher • Greg Goldstein, Chief Operating Officer • Matthew Ruzicka, CPA, Chief Financial Officer • Alan Payne, VP of Sales • Lorelei Bunjes, Director of Digital Services • Jeff Webber, Director of ePublishing • AnnaMaria White, Dir, Marketing and Public Relations • Dirk Wood, Dir, Retail Marketing • Marci Hubbard, Executive Assistant • Alonzo Simon, Shipping Manager • Angela Loggins, Staff Accountant • Cherrie Go, Assistant Web Designer • Editorial: Chris Ryall, Chief Creative Officer, Editor-In-Chief • Scott Dunbier, Senior Editor, Special Projects • Andy Schmidt, Senior Editor • Bob Schreck, Senior Editor • Justin Eisinger, Senior Editor, Books • Kris Oprisko, Editor/Foreign Lic. • Denton J. Tipton, Editor • Tom Waltz, Editor • Mariah Huehner, Editor • Carlos Guzman, Assistant Editor • Bobby Curnow, Assistant Editor • Design: Robbie Robbins, EVP/Sr. Graphic Artist • Neil Uyetake, Senior Art Director • Chris Mowry, Senior Graphic Artist • Amauri Osorio, Graphic Artist • Gilberto Lazcano, Production Assistant • Shawn Lee, Graphic Artist

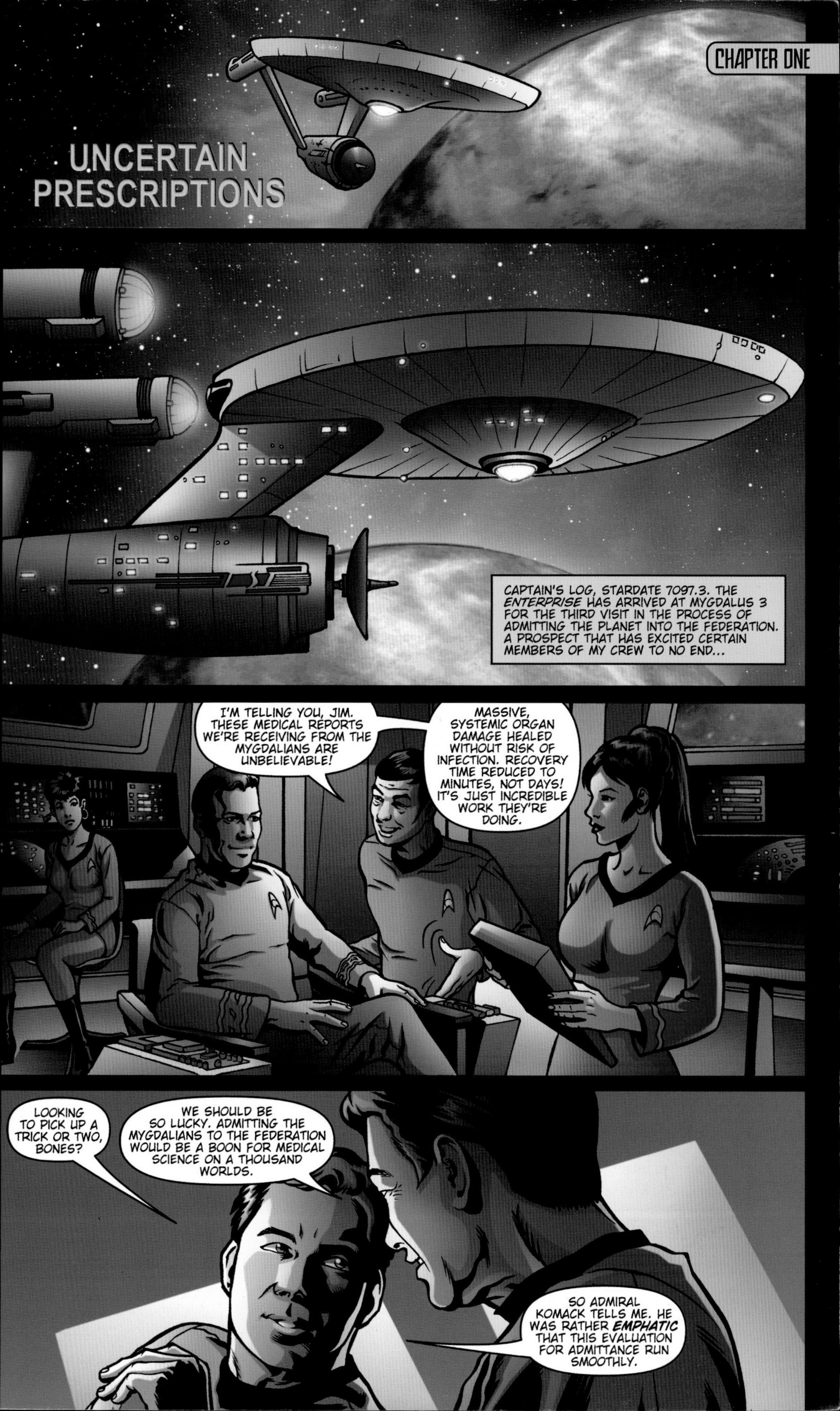
CHAPTER ONE
UNCERTAIN PRESCRIPTIONS
CAPTAIN'S LOG, STARDATE 7097.3. THE *ENTERPRISE* HAS ARRIVED AT MYGDALUS 3 FOR THE THIRD VISIT IN THE PROCESS OF ADMITTING THE PLANET INTO THE FEDERATION. A PROSPECT THAT HAS EXCITED CERTAIN MEMBERS OF MY CREW TO NO END...
I'M TELLING YOU, JIM. THESE MEDICAL REPORTS WE'RE RECEIVING FROM THE MYGDALIANS ARE UNBELIEVABLE!
MASSIVE, SYSTEMIC ORGAN DAMAGE HEALED WITHOUT RISK OF INFECTION. RECOVERY TIME REDUCED TO MINUTES, NOT DAYS! IT'S JUST INCREDIBLE WORK THEY'RE DOING.
LOOKING TO PICK UP A TRICK OR TWO, BONES?
WE SHOULD BE SO LUCKY. ADMITTING THE MYGDALIANS TO THE FEDERATION WOULD BE A BOON FOR MEDICAL SCIENCE ON A THOUSAND WORLDS.
SO ADMIRAL KOMACK TELLS ME. HE WAS RATHER ***EMPHATIC*** THAT THIS EVALUATION FOR ADMITTANCE RUN SMOOTHLY.

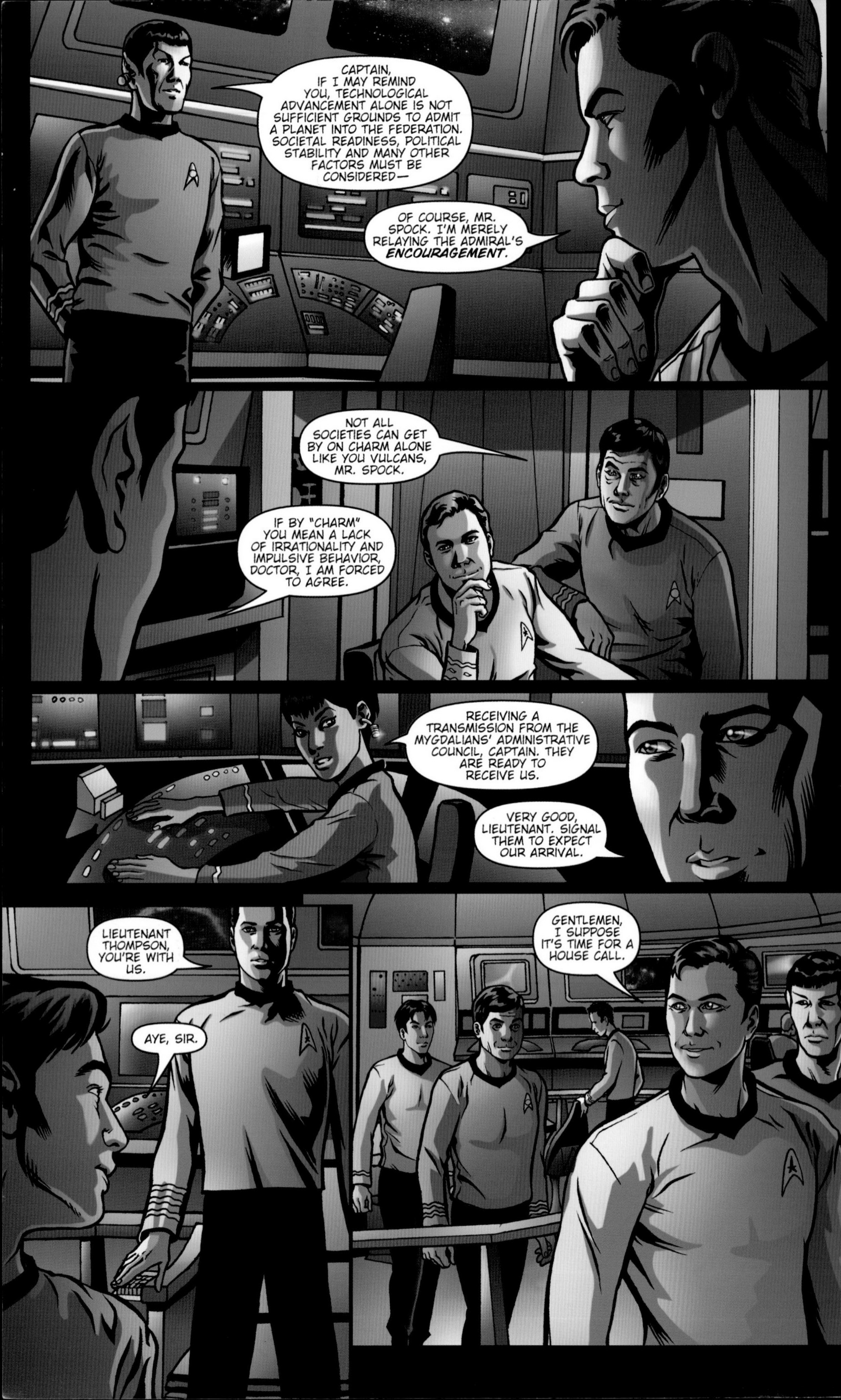

CAPTAIN, IF I MAY REMIND YOU, TECHNOLOGICAL ADVANCEMENT ALONE IS NOT SUFFICIENT GROUNDS TO ADMIT A PLANET INTO THE FEDERATION. SOCIETAL READINESS, POLITICAL STABILITY AND MANY OTHER FACTORS MUST BE CONSIDERED—
OF COURSE, MR. SPOCK. I'M MERELY RELAYING THE ADMIRAL'S *ENCOURAGEMENT*.
NOT ALL SOCIETIES CAN GET BY ON CHARM ALONE LIKE YOU VULCANS, MR. SPOCK.
IF BY "CHARM" YOU MEAN A LACK OF IRRATIONALITY AND IMPULSIVE BEHAVIOR, DOCTOR, I AM FORCED TO AGREE.
RECEIVING A TRANSMISSION FROM THE MYGDALIANS' ADMINISTRATIVE COUNCIL, CAPTAIN. THEY ARE READY TO RECEIVE US.
VERY GOOD, LIEUTENANT. SIGNAL THEM TO EXPECT OUR ARRIVAL.
LIEUTENANT THOMPSON, YOU'RE WITH US.
AYE, SIR.
GENTLEMEN, I SUPPOSE IT'S TIME FOR A HOUSE CALL.

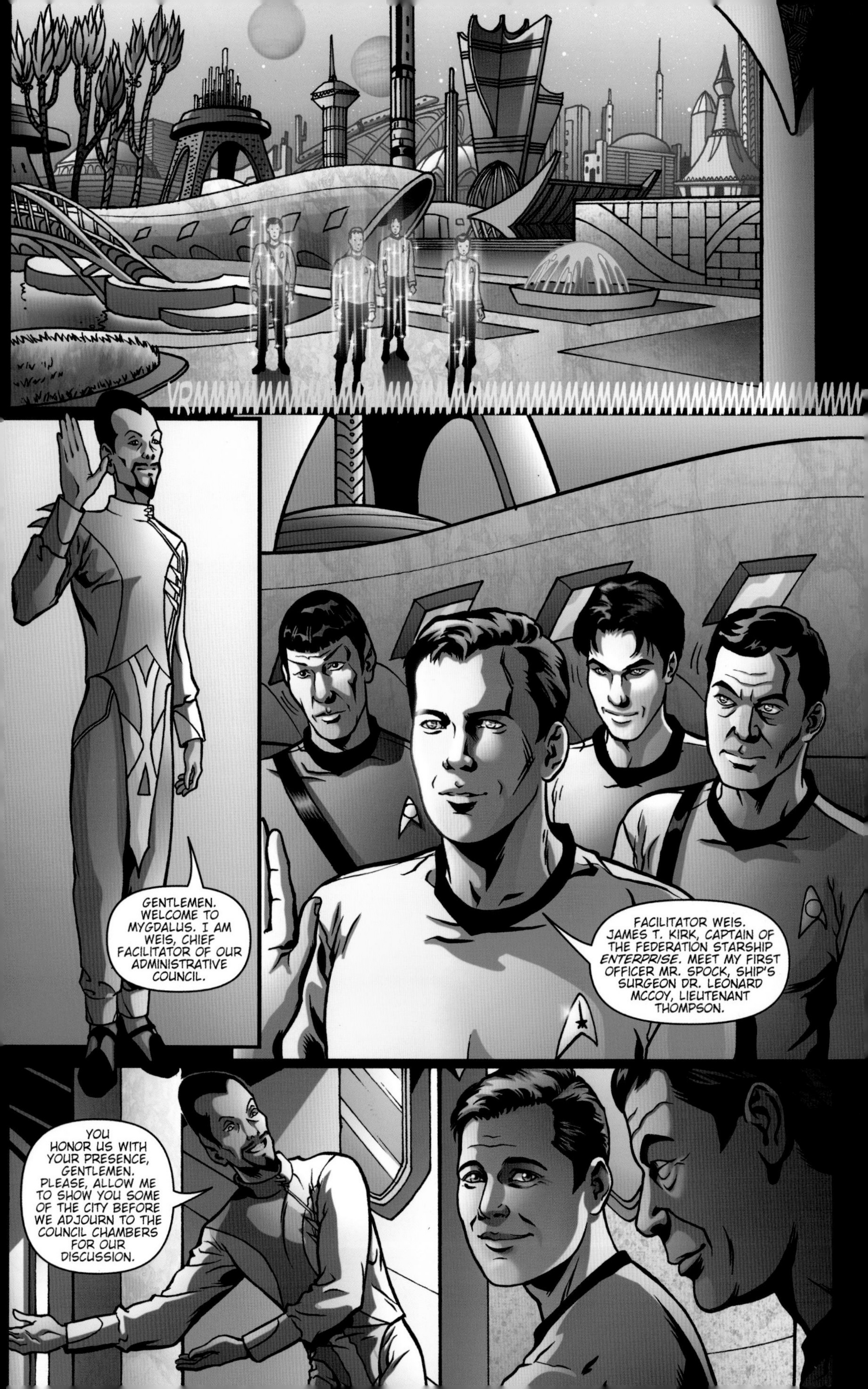
VRMMMMMMMMMMMMMMMMMMMMMMMMMMMMMMMMMMMMMMMMMMMMMMMMM
GENTLEMEN. WELCOME TO MYGDALUS. I AM WEIS, CHIEF FACILITATOR OF OUR ADMINISTRATIVE COUNCIL.
FACILITATOR WEIS. JAMES T. KIRK, CAPTAIN OF THE FEDERATION STARSHIP *ENTERPRISE*. MEET MY FIRST OFFICER MR. SPOCK, SHIP'S SURGEON DR. LEONARD MCCOY, LIEUTENANT THOMPSON.
YOU HONOR US WITH YOUR PRESENCE, GENTLEMEN. PLEASE, ALLOW ME TO SHOW YOU SOME OF THE CITY BEFORE WE ADJOURN TO THE COUNCIL CHAMBERS FOR OUR DISCUSSION.

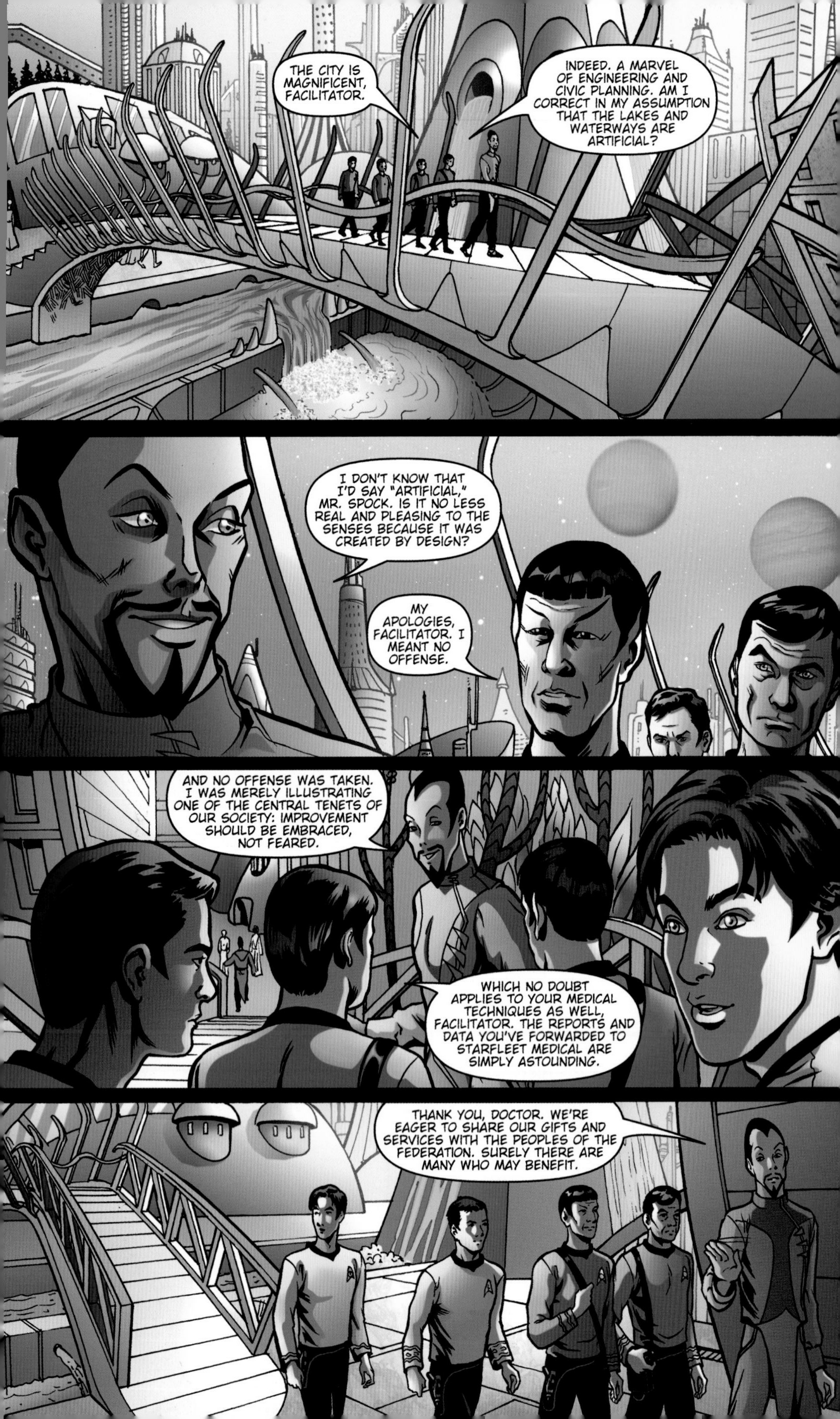
THE CITY IS MAGNIFICENT, FACILITATOR.
INDEED. A MARVEL OF ENGINEERING AND CIVIC PLANNING. AM I CORRECT IN MY ASSUMPTION THAT THE LAKES AND WATERWAYS ARE ARTIFICIAL?
I DON'T KNOW THAT I'D SAY "ARTIFICIAL," MR. SPOCK. IS IT NO LESS REAL AND PLEASING TO THE SENSES BECAUSE IT WAS CREATED BY DESIGN?
MY APOLOGIES, FACILITATOR. I MEANT NO OFFENSE.
AND NO OFFENSE WAS TAKEN. I WAS MERELY ILLUSTRATING ONE OF THE CENTRAL TENETS OF OUR SOCIETY: IMPROVEMENT SHOULD BE EMBRACED, NOT FEARED.
WHICH NO DOUBT APPLIES TO YOUR MEDICAL TECHNIQUES AS WELL, FACILITATOR. THE REPORTS AND DATA YOU'VE FORWARDED TO STARFLEET MEDICAL ARE SIMPLY ASTOUNDING.
THANK YOU, DOCTOR. WE'RE EAGER TO SHARE OUR GIFTS AND SERVICES WITH THE PEOPLES OF THE FEDERATION. SURELY THERE ARE MANY WHO MAY BENEFIT.

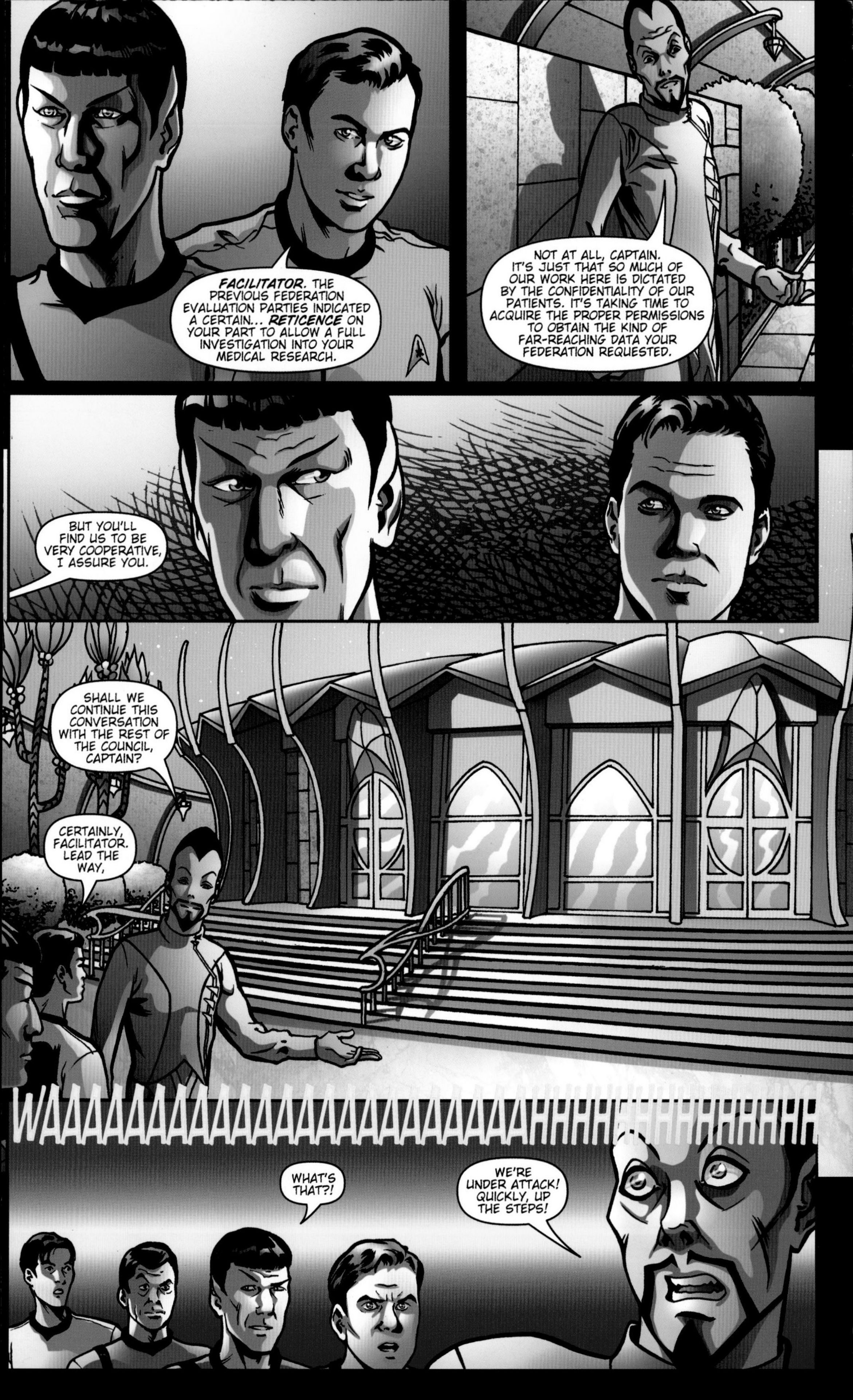

FACILITATOR. THE PREVIOUS FEDERATION EVALUATION PARTIES INDICATED A CERTAIN... *RETICENCE* ON YOUR PART TO ALLOW A FULL INVESTIGATION INTO YOUR MEDICAL RESEARCH.
NOT AT ALL, CAPTAIN. IT'S JUST THAT SO MUCH OF OUR WORK HERE IS DICTATED BY THE CONFIDENTIALITY OF OUR PATIENTS. IT'S TAKING TIME TO ACQUIRE THE PROPER PERMISSIONS TO OBTAIN THE KIND OF FAR-REACHING DATA YOUR FEDERATION REQUESTED.
BUT YOU'LL FIND US TO BE VERY COOPERATIVE, I ASSURE YOU.
SHALL WE CONTINUE THIS CONVERSATION WITH THE REST OF THE COUNCIL, CAPTAIN?
CERTAINLY, FACILITATOR. LEAD THE WAY,
WAAAAAAAAAAAAAAAAAAAAAAAAAAHHHHHHHHHHHHHHHH
WHAT'S THAT?!
WE'RE UNDER ATTACK! QUICKLY, UP THE STEPS!

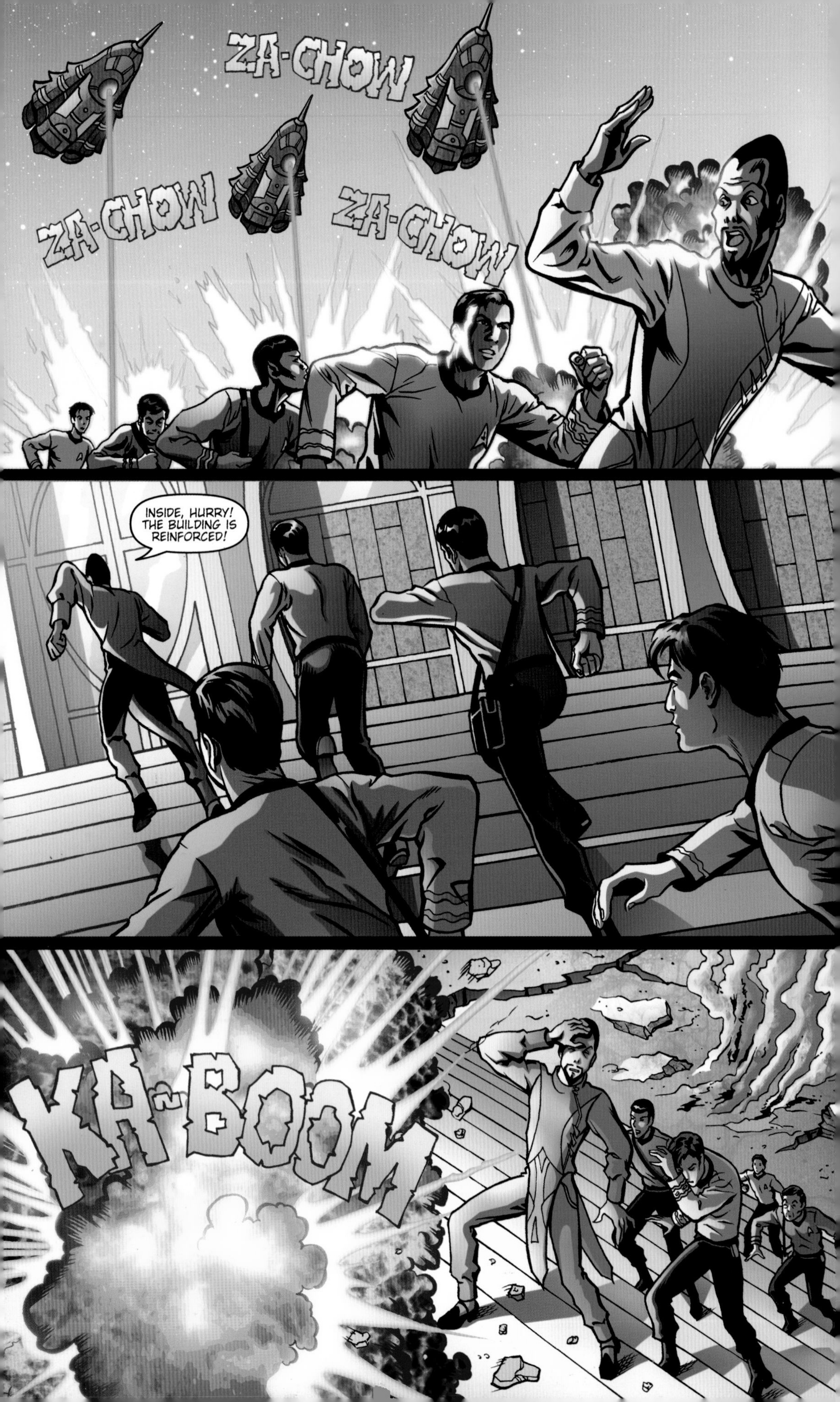
ZA-CHOW
ZA-CHOW
ZA-CHOW
INSIDE, HURRY! THE BUILDING IS REINFORCED!
KA-BOOM

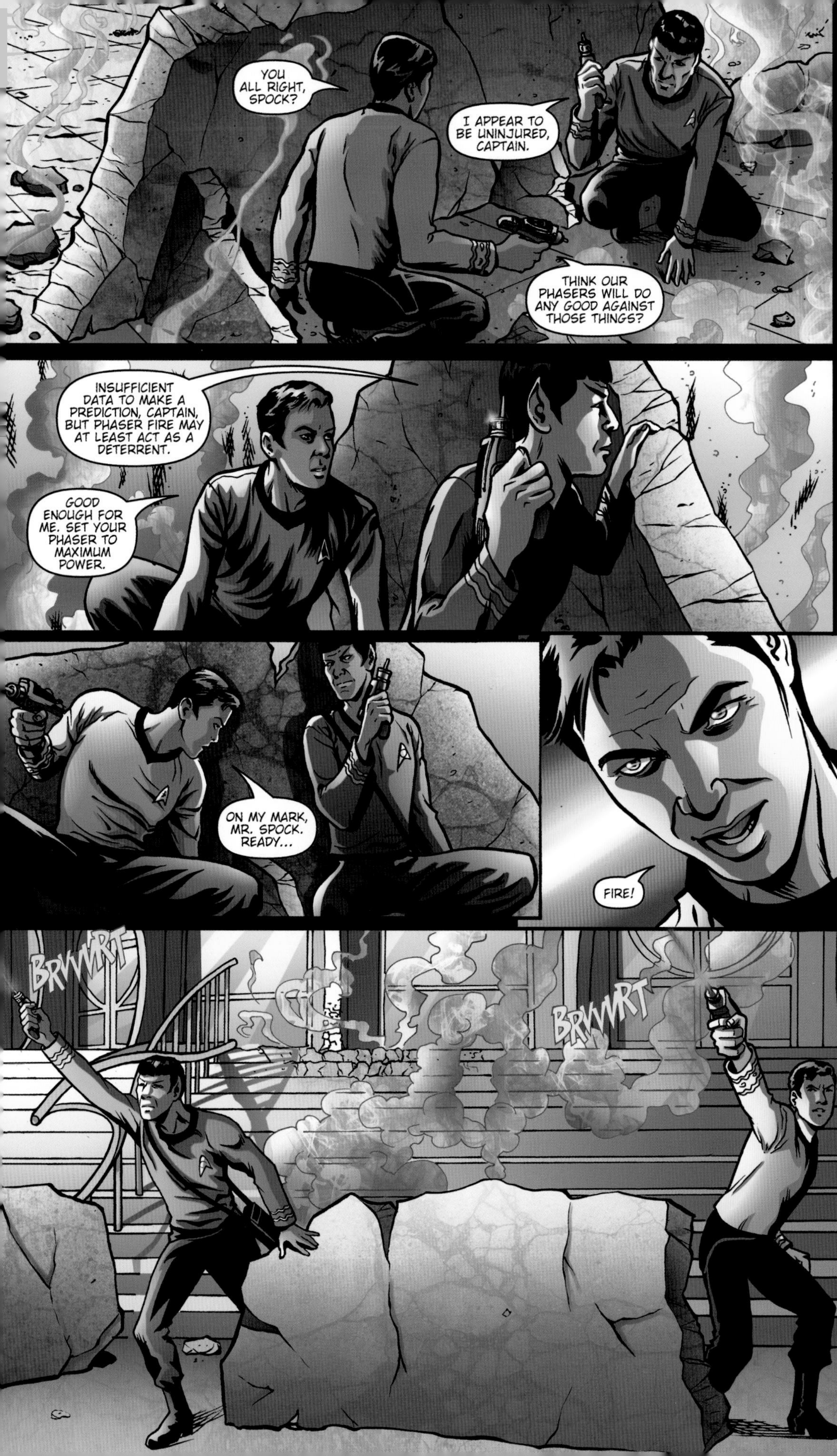
YOU ALL RIGHT, SPOCK?
I APPEAR TO BE UNINJURED, CAPTAIN.
THINK OUR PHASERS WILL DO ANY GOOD AGAINST THOSE THINGS?
INSUFFICIENT DATA TO MAKE A PREDICTION, CAPTAIN, BUT PHASER FIRE MAY AT LEAST ACT AS A DETERRENT.
GOOD ENOUGH FOR ME. SET YOUR PHASER TO MAXIMUM POWER.
ON MY MARK, MR. SPOCK. READY...
FIRE!
BRVVVRT
BRVVVRT

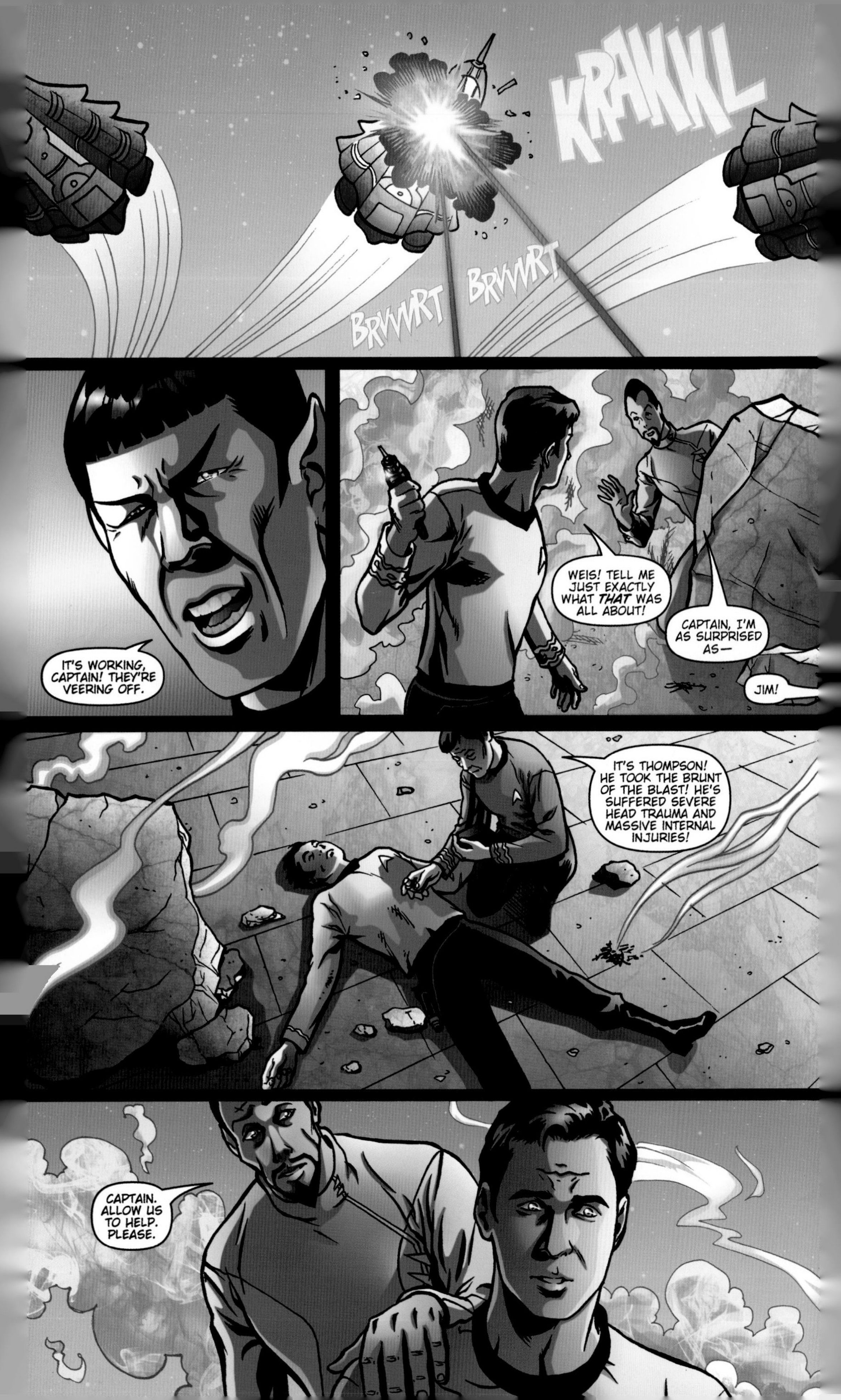
KRAKKL
BRVVVRT
BRVVVRT
IT'S WORKING, CAPTAIN! THEY'RE VEERING OFF.
WEIS! TELL ME JUST EXACTLY WHAT *THAT* WAS ALL ABOUT!
CAPTAIN, I'M AS SURPRISED AS—
JIM!
IT'S THOMPSON! HE TOOK THE BRUNT OF THE BLAST! HE'S SUFFERED SEVERE HEAD TRAUMA AND MASSIVE INTERNAL INJURIES!
CAPTAIN. ALLOW US TO HELP. PLEASE.

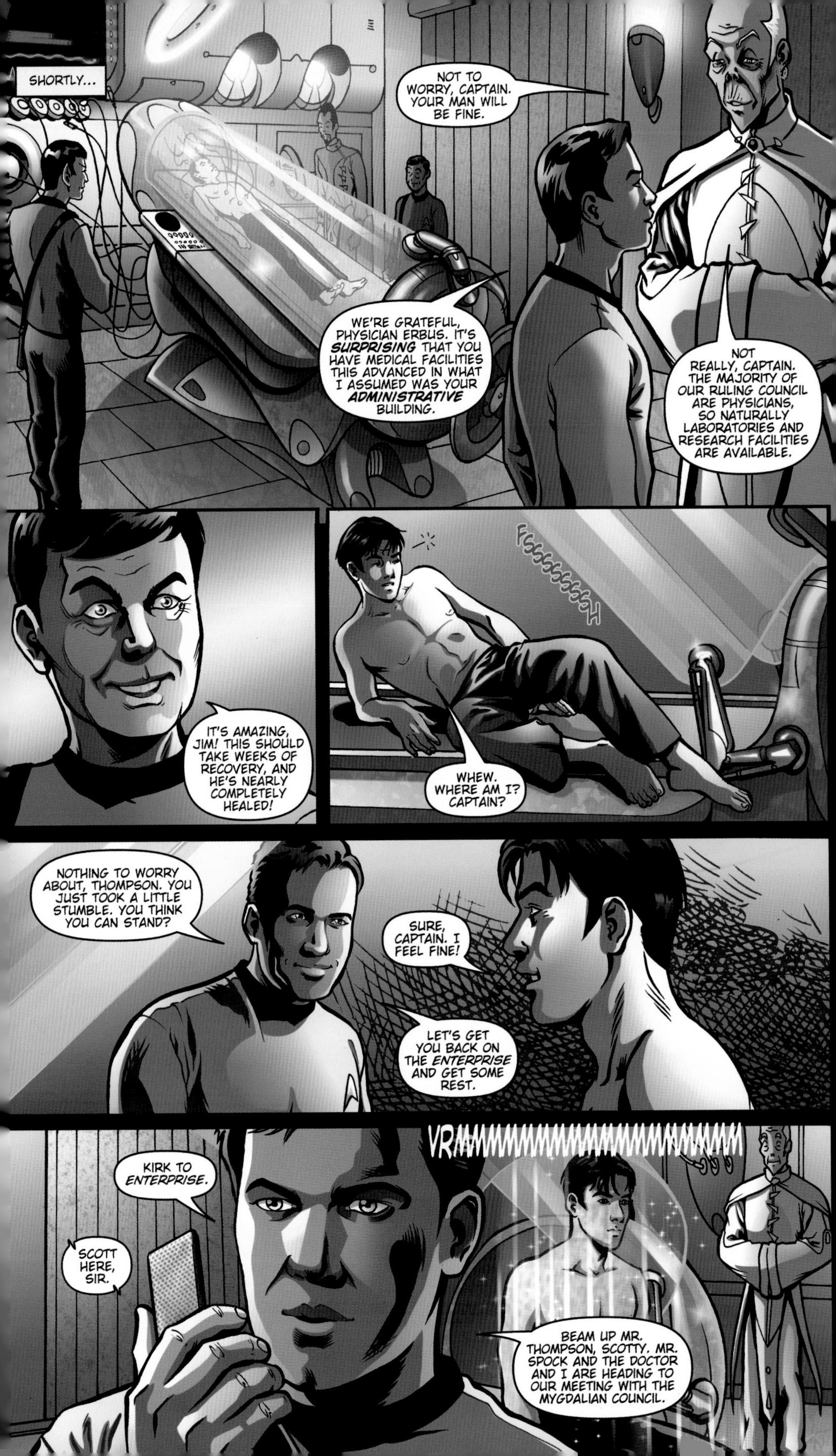
SHORTLY...
NOT TO WORRY, CAPTAIN. YOUR MAN WILL BE FINE.
WE'RE GRATEFUL, PHYSICIAN ERBUS. IT'S SURPRISING THAT YOU HAVE MEDICAL FACILITIES THIS ADVANCED IN WHAT I ASSUMED WAS YOUR ADMINISTRATIVE BUILDING.
NOT REALLY, CAPTAIN. THE MAJORITY OF OUR RULING COUNCIL ARE PHYSICIANS, SO NATURALLY LABORATORIES AND RESEARCH FACILITIES ARE AVAILABLE.
IT'S AMAZING, JIM! THIS SHOULD TAKE WEEKS OF RECOVERY, AND HE'S NEARLY COMPLETELY HEALED!
FSSSSSSSSSH
WHEW. WHERE AM I? CAPTAIN?
NOTHING TO WORRY ABOUT, THOMPSON. YOU JUST TOOK A LITTLE STUMBLE. YOU THINK YOU CAN STAND?
SURE, CAPTAIN. I FEEL FINE!
LET'S GET YOU BACK ON THE ENTERPRISE AND GET SOME REST.
VRMMMMMMMMMMMMMMMMMM
KIRK TO ENTERPRISE.
SCOTT HERE, SIR.
BEAM UP MR. THOMPSON, SCOTTY. MR. SPOCK AND THE DOCTOR AND I ARE HEADING TO OUR MEETING WITH THE MYGDALIAN COUNCIL.

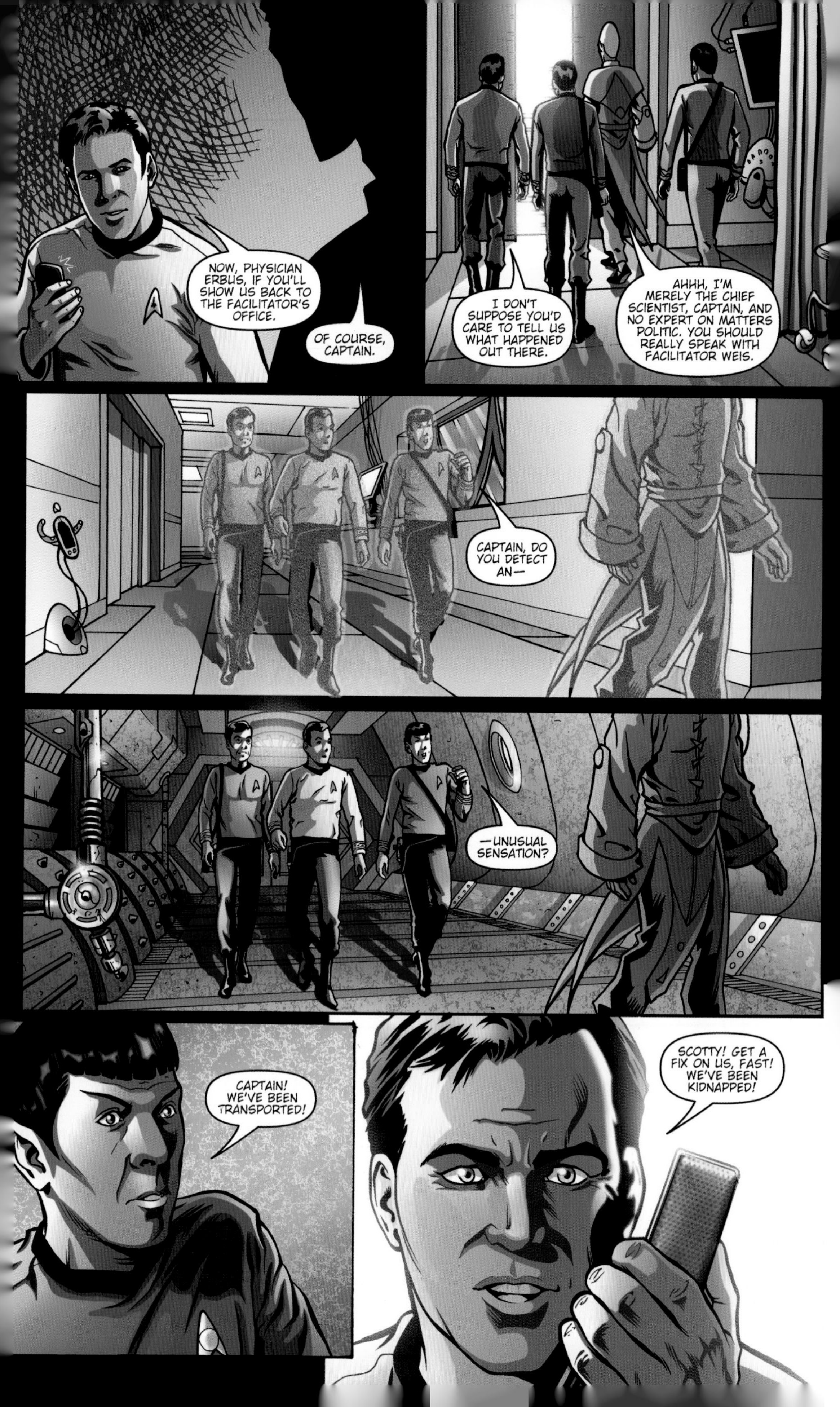
NOW, PHYSICIAN ERBUS, IF YOU'LL SHOW US BACK TO THE FACILITATOR'S OFFICE.
OF COURSE, CAPTAIN.
I DON'T SUPPOSE YOU'D CARE TO TELL US WHAT HAPPENED OUT THERE.
AHHH, I'M MERELY THE CHIEF SCIENTIST, CAPTAIN, AND NO EXPERT ON MATTERS POLITIC. YOU SHOULD REALLY SPEAK WITH FACILITATOR WEIS.
CAPTAIN, DO YOU DETECT AN—
—UNUSUAL SENSATION?
CAPTAIN! WE'VE BEEN TRANSPORTED!
SCOTTY! GET A FIX ON US, FAST! WE'VE BEEN KIDNAPPED!

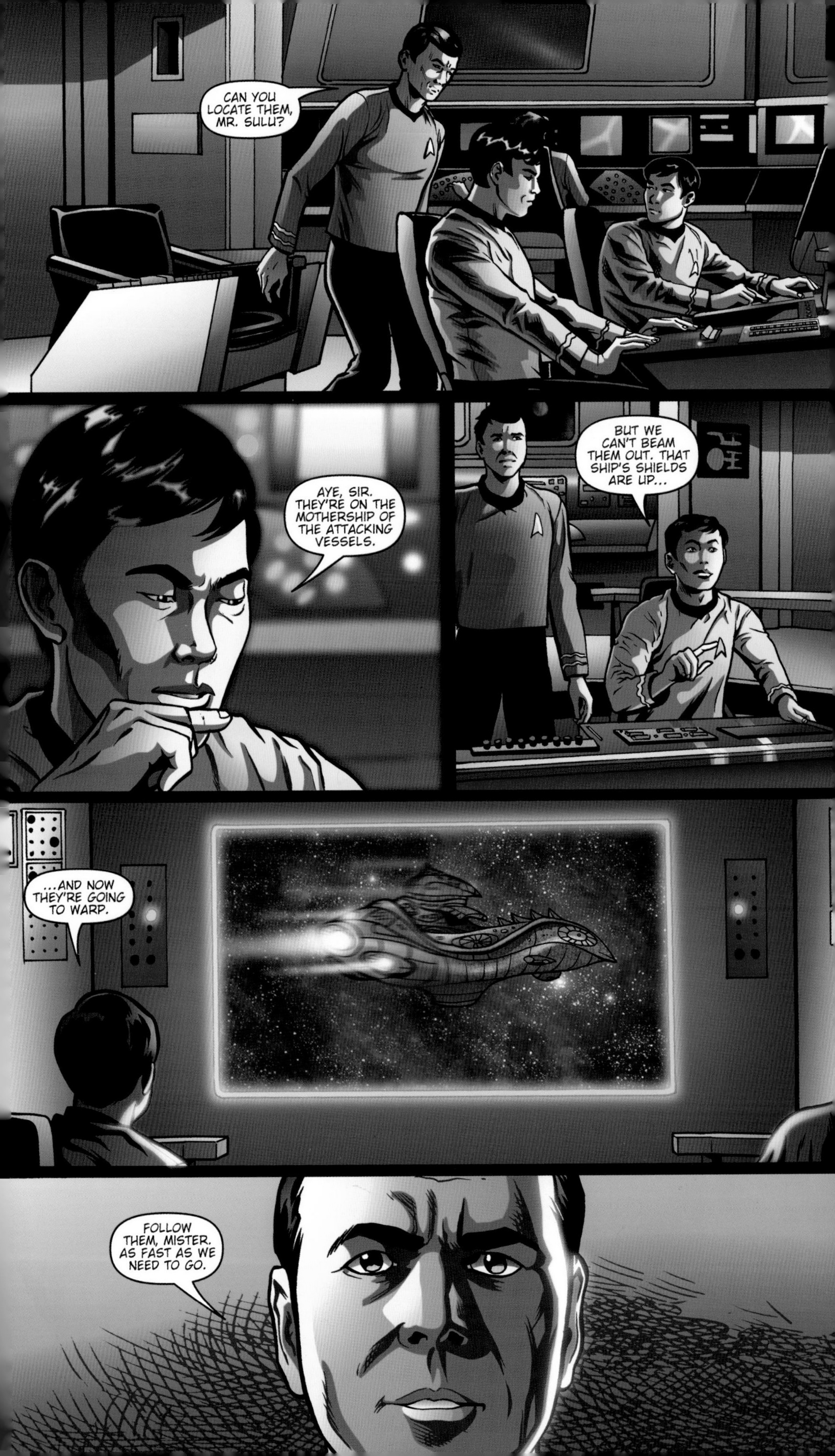
CAN YOU LOCATE THEM, MR. SULU?
AYE, SIR. THEY'RE ON THE MOTHERSHIP OF THE ATTACKING VESSELS.
BUT WE CAN'T BEAM THEM OUT. THAT SHIP'S SHIELDS ARE UP...
...AND NOW THEY'RE GOING TO WARP.
FOLLOW THEM, MISTER. AS FAST AS WE NEED TO GO.

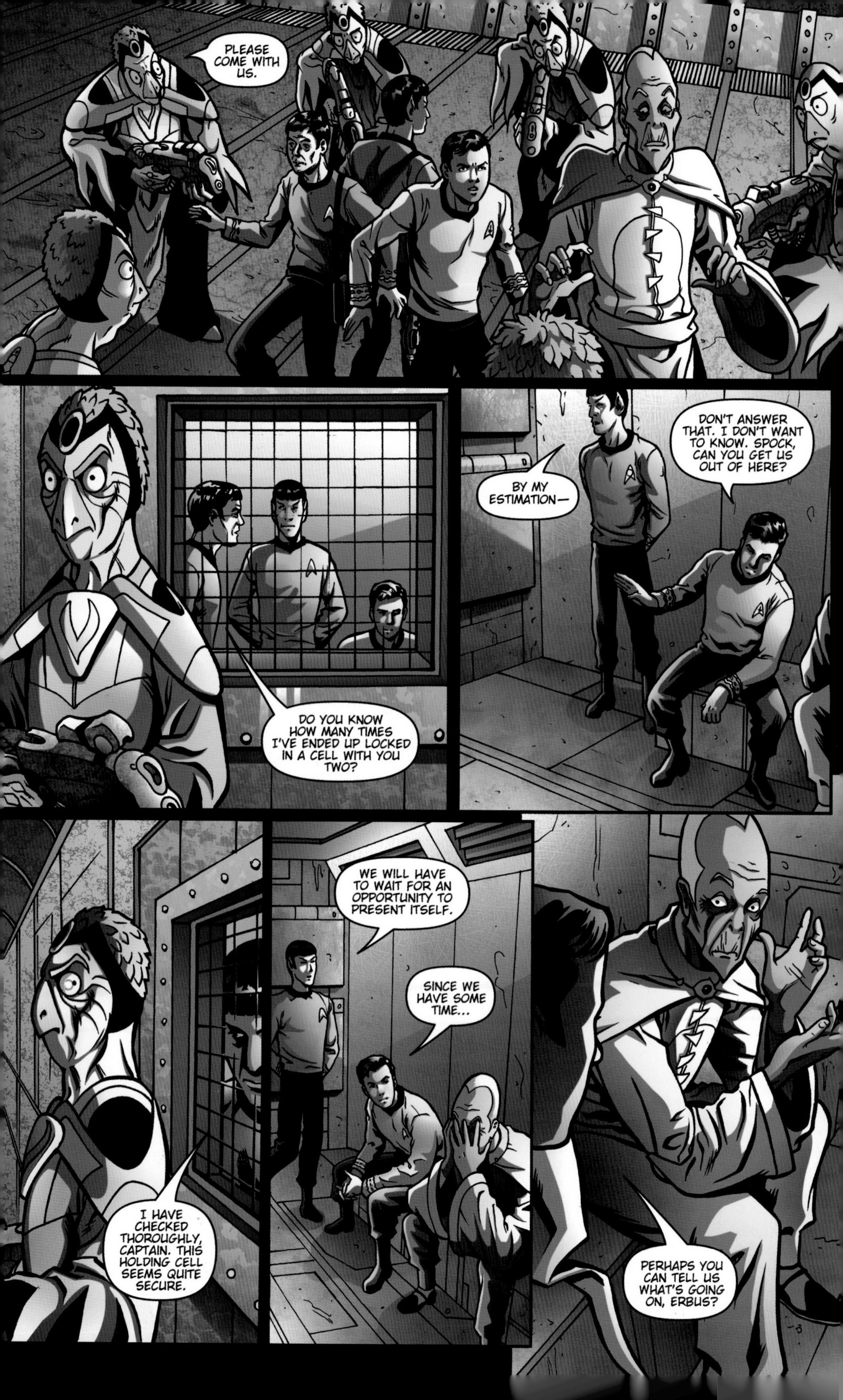

PLEASE COME WITH US.
DO YOU KNOW HOW MANY TIMES I'VE ENDED UP LOCKED IN A CELL WITH YOU TWO?
BY MY ESTIMATION—
DON'T ANSWER THAT. I DON'T WANT TO KNOW. SPOCK, CAN YOU GET US OUT OF HERE?
I HAVE CHECKED THOROUGHLY, CAPTAIN. THIS HOLDING CELL SEEMS QUITE SECURE.
WE WILL HAVE TO WAIT FOR AN OPPORTUNITY TO PRESENT ITSELF.
SINCE WE HAVE SOME TIME...
PERHAPS YOU CAN TELL US WHAT'S GOING ON, ERBUS?

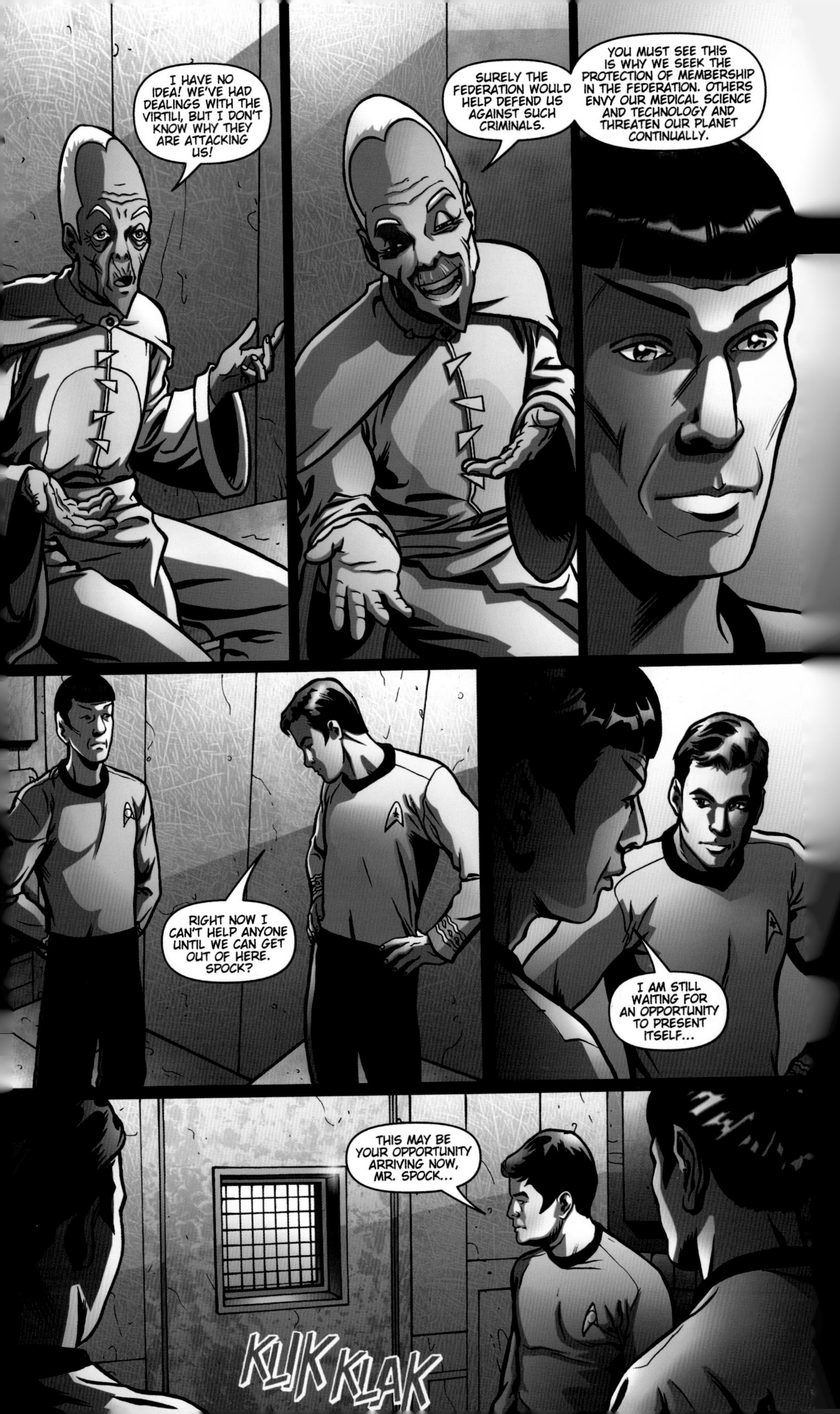
I HAVE NO IDEA! WE'VE HAD DEALINGS WITH THE VIRTILI, BUT I DON'T KNOW WHY THEY ARE ATTACKING US!
SURELY THE FEDERATION WOULD HELP DEFEND US AGAINST SUCH CRIMINALS.
YOU MUST SEE THIS IS WHY WE SEEK THE PROTECTION OF MEMBERSHIP IN THE FEDERATION. OTHERS ENVY OUR MEDICAL SCIENCE AND TECHNOLOGY AND THREATEN OUR PLANET CONTINUALLY.
RIGHT NOW I CAN'T HELP ANYONE UNTIL WE CAN GET OUT OF HERE. SPOCK?
I AM STILL WAITING FOR AN OPPORTUNITY TO PRESENT ITSELF...
THIS MAY BE YOUR OPPORTUNITY ARRIVING NOW, MR. SPOCK...
KLIK KLAK

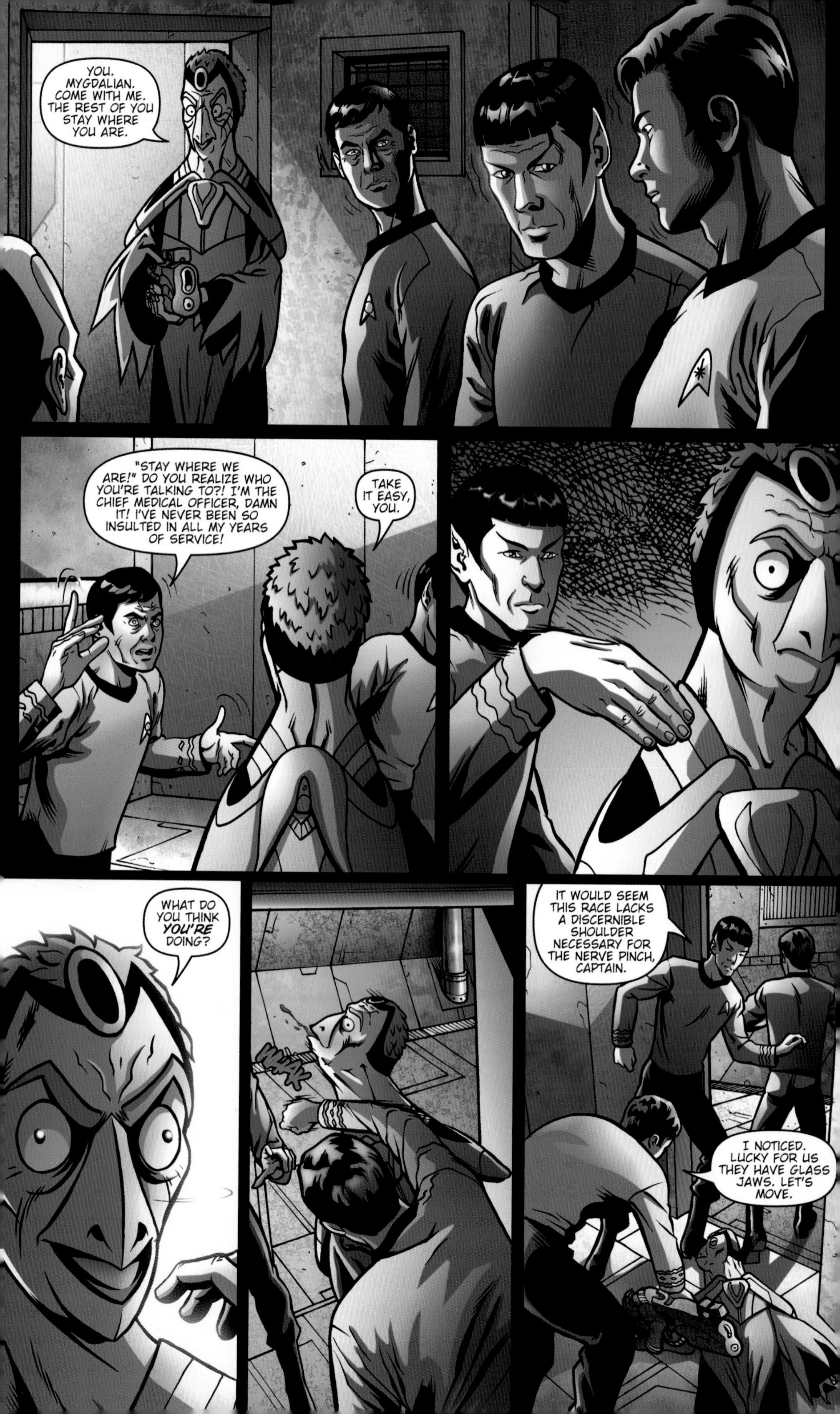
YOU. MYGDALIAN. COME WITH ME. THE REST OF YOU STAY WHERE YOU ARE.
"STAY WHERE WE ARE!" DO YOU REALIZE WHO YOU'RE TALKING TO?! I'M THE CHIEF MEDICAL OFFICER, DAMN IT! I'VE NEVER BEEN SO INSULTED IN ALL MY YEARS OF SERVICE!
TAKE IT EASY, YOU.
WHAT DO YOU THINK *YOU'RE* DOING?
IT WOULD SEEM THIS RACE LACKS A DISCERNIBLE SHOULDER NECESSARY FOR THE NERVE PINCH, CAPTAIN.
I NOTICED. LUCKY FOR US THEY HAVE GLASS JAWS. LET'S MOVE.

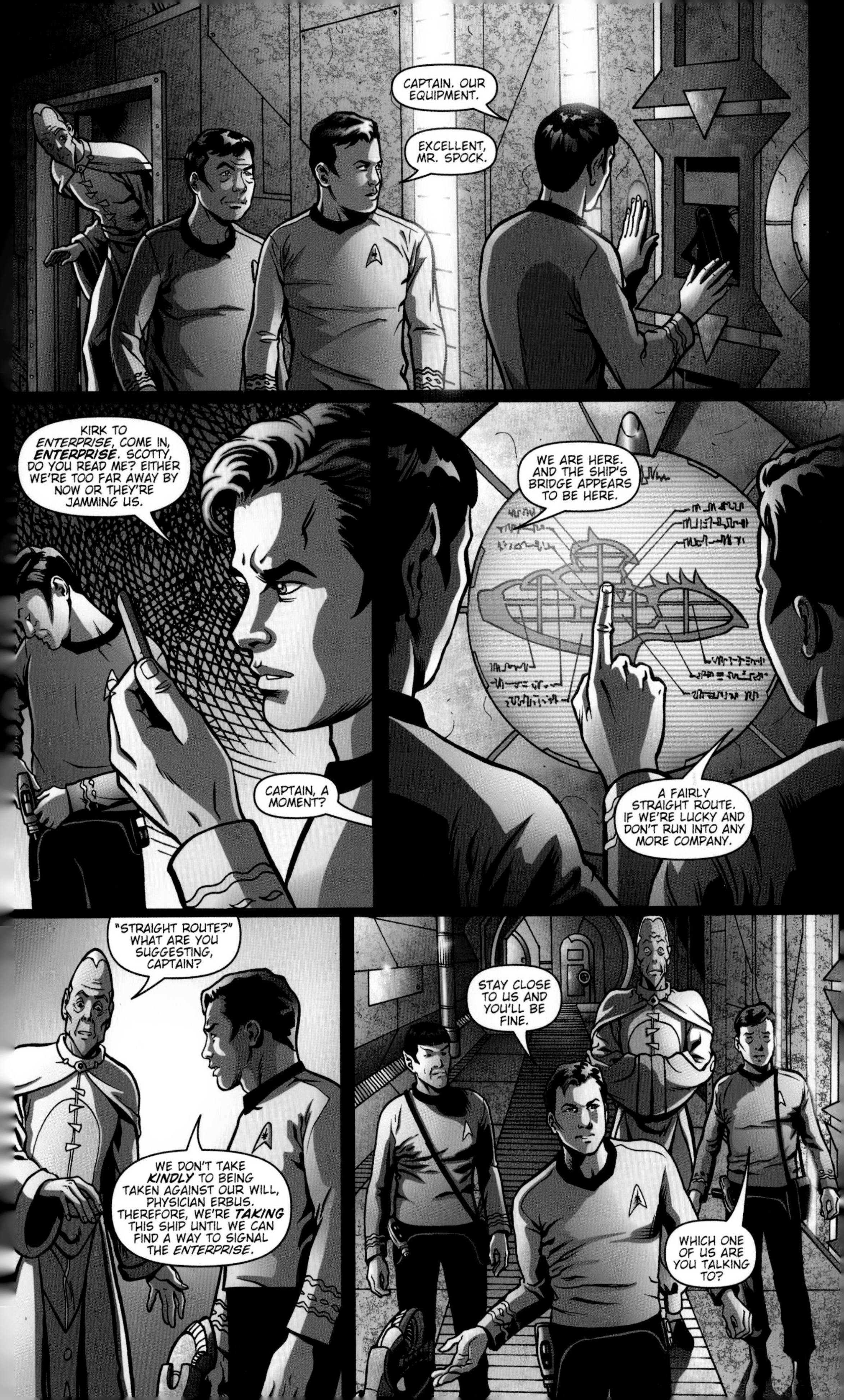
CAPTAIN. OUR EQUIPMENT.
EXCELLENT, MR. SPOCK.
KIRK TO *ENTERPRISE*, COME IN, ***ENTERPRISE***. SCOTTY, DO YOU READ ME? EITHER WE'RE TOO FAR AWAY BY NOW OR THEY'RE JAMMING US.
CAPTAIN, A MOMENT?
WE ARE HERE. AND THE SHIP'S BRIDGE APPEARS TO BE HERE.
A FAIRLY STRAIGHT ROUTE. IF WE'RE LUCKY AND DON'T RUN INTO ANY MORE COMPANY.
"STRAIGHT ROUTE?" WHAT ARE YOU SUGGESTING, CAPTAIN?
WE DON'T TAKE ***KINDLY*** TO BEING TAKEN AGAINST OUR WILL, PHYSICIAN ERBUS. THEREFORE, WE'RE ***TAKING*** THIS SHIP UNTIL WE CAN FIND A WAY TO SIGNAL THE *ENTERPRISE*.
STAY CLOSE TO US AND YOU'LL BE FINE.
WHICH ONE OF US ARE YOU TALKING TO?

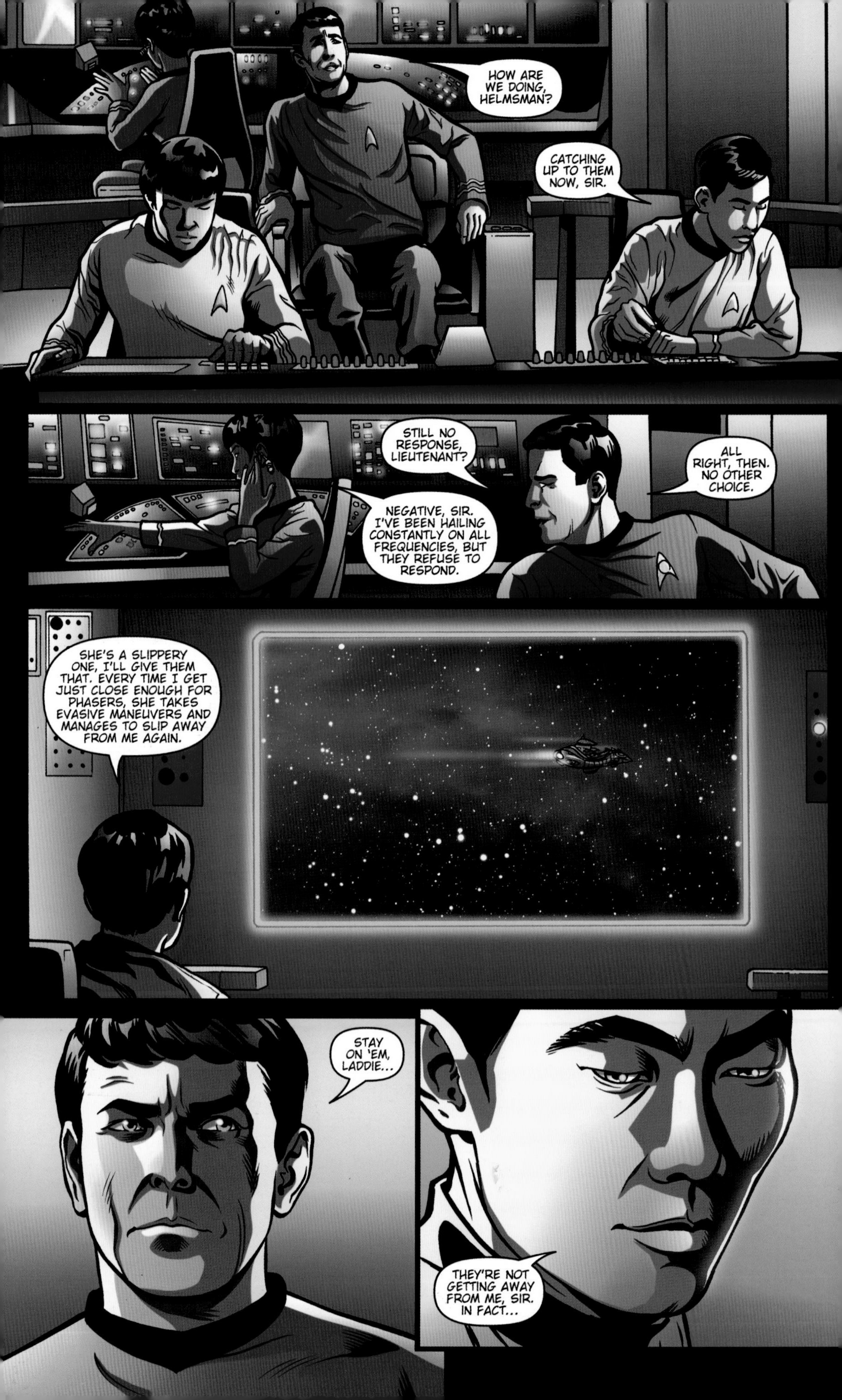
HOW ARE WE DOING, HELMSMAN?
CATCHING UP TO THEM NOW, SIR.
STILL NO RESPONSE, LIEUTENANT?
NEGATIVE, SIR. I'VE BEEN HAILING CONSTANTLY ON ALL FREQUENCIES, BUT THEY REFUSE TO RESPOND.
ALL RIGHT, THEN. NO OTHER CHOICE.
SHE'S A SLIPPERY ONE, I'LL GIVE THEM THAT. EVERY TIME I GET JUST CLOSE ENOUGH FOR PHASERS, SHE TAKES EVASIVE MANEUVERS AND MANAGES TO SLIP AWAY FROM ME AGAIN.
STAY ON 'EM, LADDIE...
THEY'RE NOT GETTING AWAY FROM ME, SIR. IN FACT...

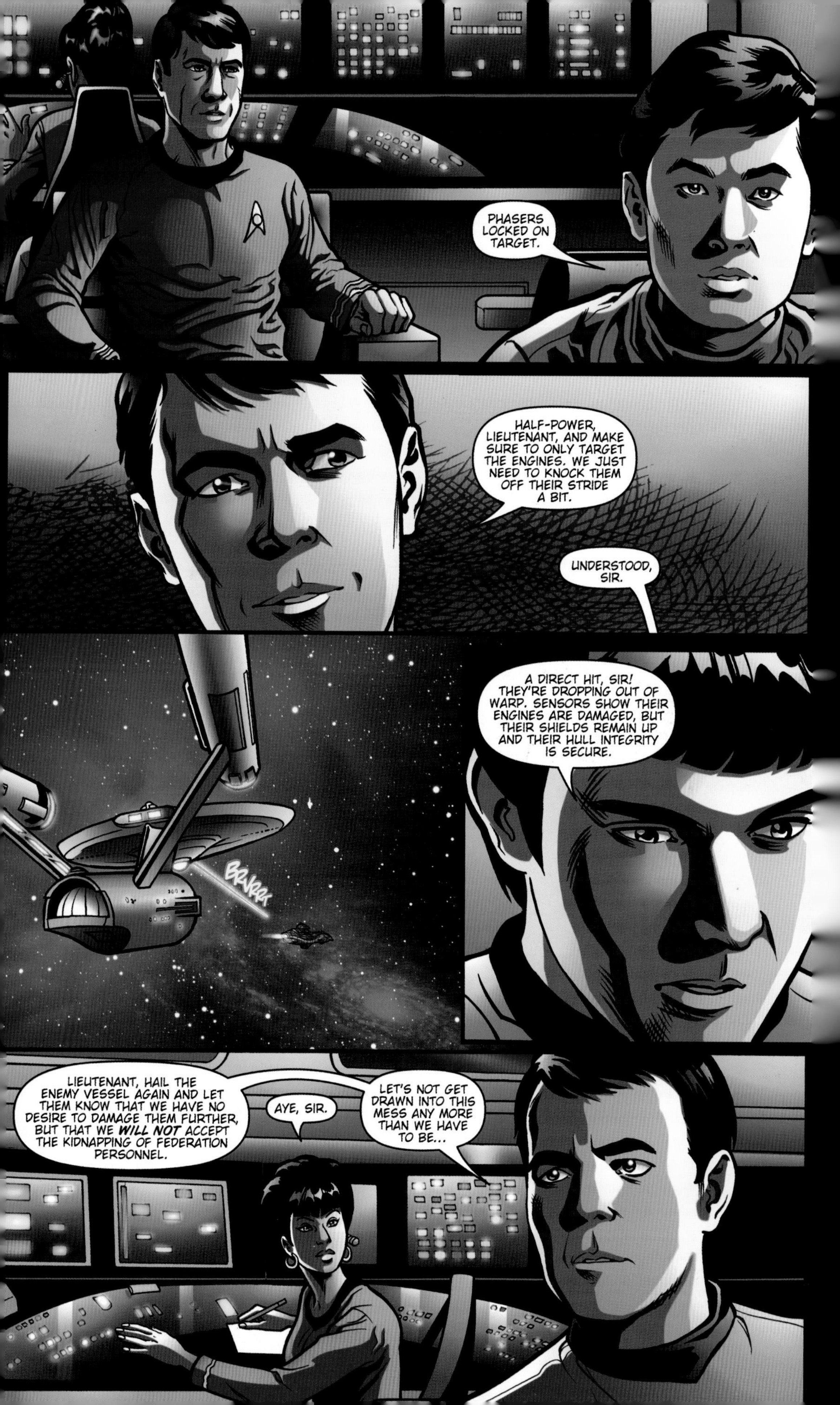
PHASERS LOCKED ON TARGET.
HALF-POWER, LIEUTENANT, AND MAKE SURE TO ONLY TARGET THE ENGINES. WE JUST NEED TO KNOCK THEM OFF THEIR STRIDE A BIT.
UNDERSTOOD, SIR.
BRVRRR
A DIRECT HIT, SIR! THEY'RE DROPPING OUT OF WARP. SENSORS SHOW THEIR ENGINES ARE DAMAGED, BUT THEIR SHIELDS REMAIN UP AND THEIR HULL INTEGRITY IS SECURE.
LIEUTENANT, HAIL THE ENEMY VESSEL AGAIN AND LET THEM KNOW THAT WE HAVE NO DESIRE TO DAMAGE THEM FURTHER, BUT THAT WE *WILL NOT* ACCEPT THE KIDNAPPING OF FEDERATION PERSONNEL.
AYE, SIR.
LET'S NOT GET DRAWN INTO THIS MESS ANY MORE THAN WE HAVE TO BE...

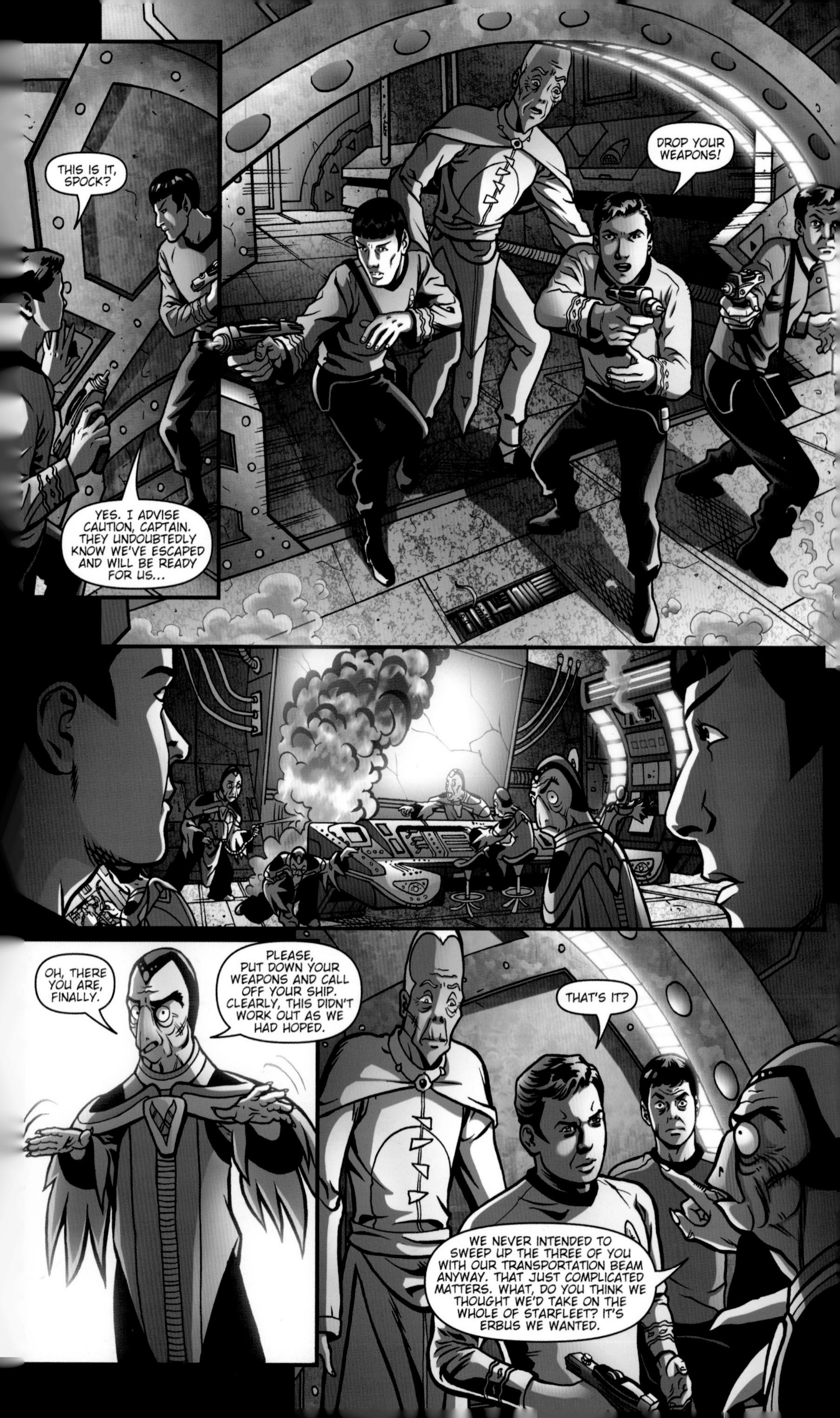
THIS IS IT, SPOCK?
YES. I ADVISE CAUTION, CAPTAIN. THEY UNDOUBTEDLY KNOW WE'VE ESCAPED AND WILL BE READY FOR US...
DROP YOUR WEAPONS!
OH, THERE YOU ARE, FINALLY.
PLEASE, PUT DOWN YOUR WEAPONS AND CALL OFF YOUR SHIP. CLEARLY, THIS DIDN'T WORK OUT AS WE HAD HOPED.
THAT'S IT?
WE NEVER INTENDED TO SWEEP UP THE THREE OF YOU WITH OUR TRANSPORTATION BEAM ANYWAY. THAT JUST COMPLICATED MATTERS. WHAT, DO YOU THINK WE THOUGHT WE'D TAKE ON THE WHOLE OF STARFLEET? IT'S ERBUS WE WANTED.

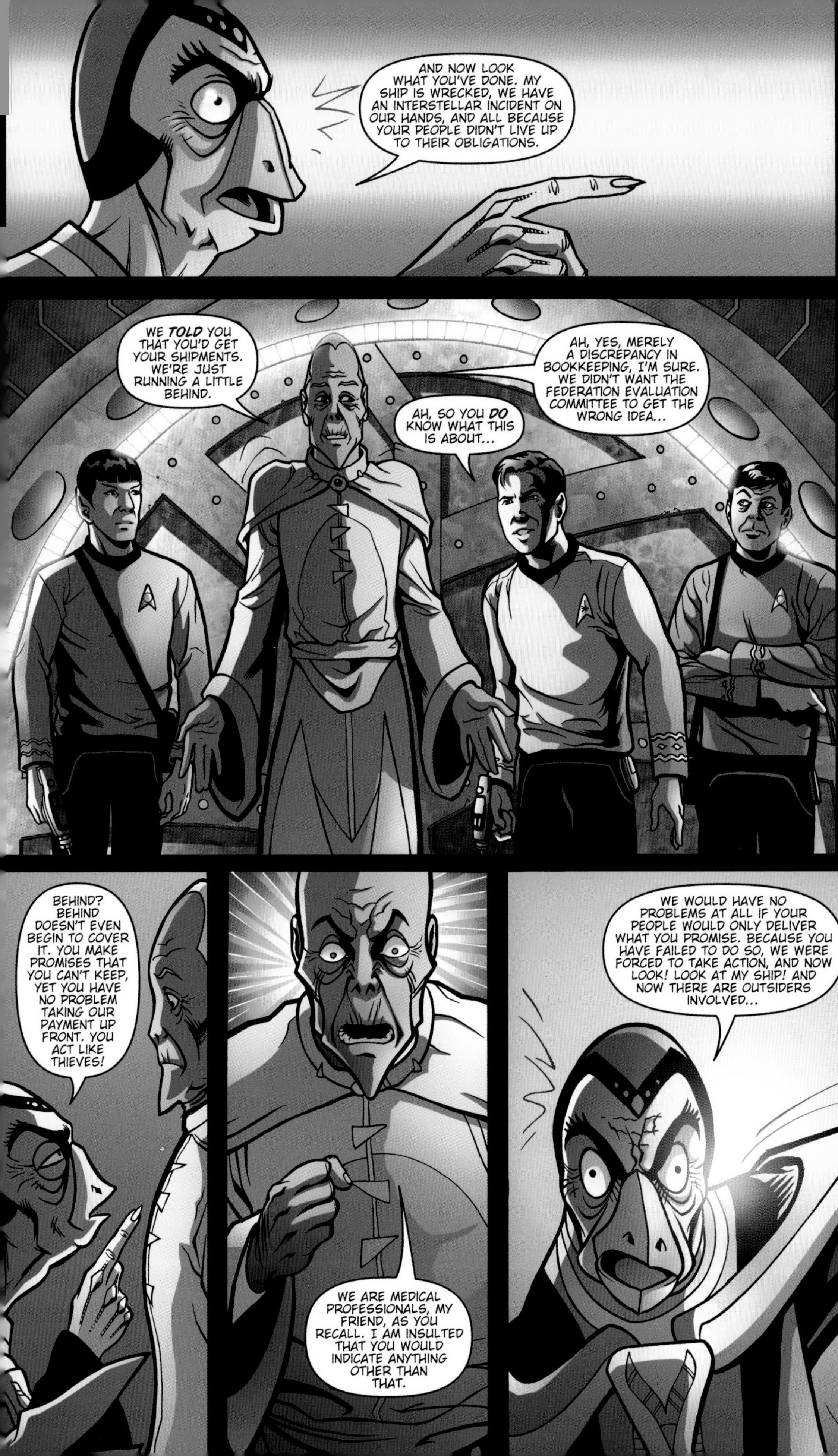
AND NOW LOOK WHAT YOU'VE DONE. MY SHIP IS WRECKED, WE HAVE AN INTERSTELLAR INCIDENT ON OUR HANDS, AND ALL BECAUSE YOUR PEOPLE DIDN'T LIVE UP TO THEIR OBLIGATIONS.
WE *TOLD* YOU THAT YOU'D GET YOUR SHIPMENTS. WE'RE JUST RUNNING A LITTLE BEHIND.
AH, SO YOU *DO* KNOW WHAT THIS IS ABOUT...
AH, YES, MERELY A DISCREPANCY IN BOOKKEEPING, I'M SURE. WE DIDN'T WANT THE FEDERATION EVALUATION COMMITTEE TO GET THE WRONG IDEA...
BEHIND? BEHIND DOESN'T EVEN BEGIN TO COVER IT. YOU MAKE PROMISES THAT YOU CAN'T KEEP, YET YOU HAVE NO PROBLEM TAKING OUR PAYMENT UP FRONT. YOU ACT LIKE THIEVES!
WE ARE MEDICAL PROFESSIONALS, MY FRIEND, AS YOU RECALL. I AM INSULTED THAT YOU WOULD INDICATE ANYTHING OTHER THAN THAT.
WE WOULD HAVE NO PROBLEMS AT ALL IF YOUR PEOPLE WOULD ONLY DELIVER WHAT YOU PROMISE. BECAUSE YOU HAVE FAILED TO DO SO, WE WERE FORCED TO TAKE ACTION, AND NOW LOOK! LOOK AT MY SHIP! AND NOW THERE ARE OUTSIDERS INVOLVED...

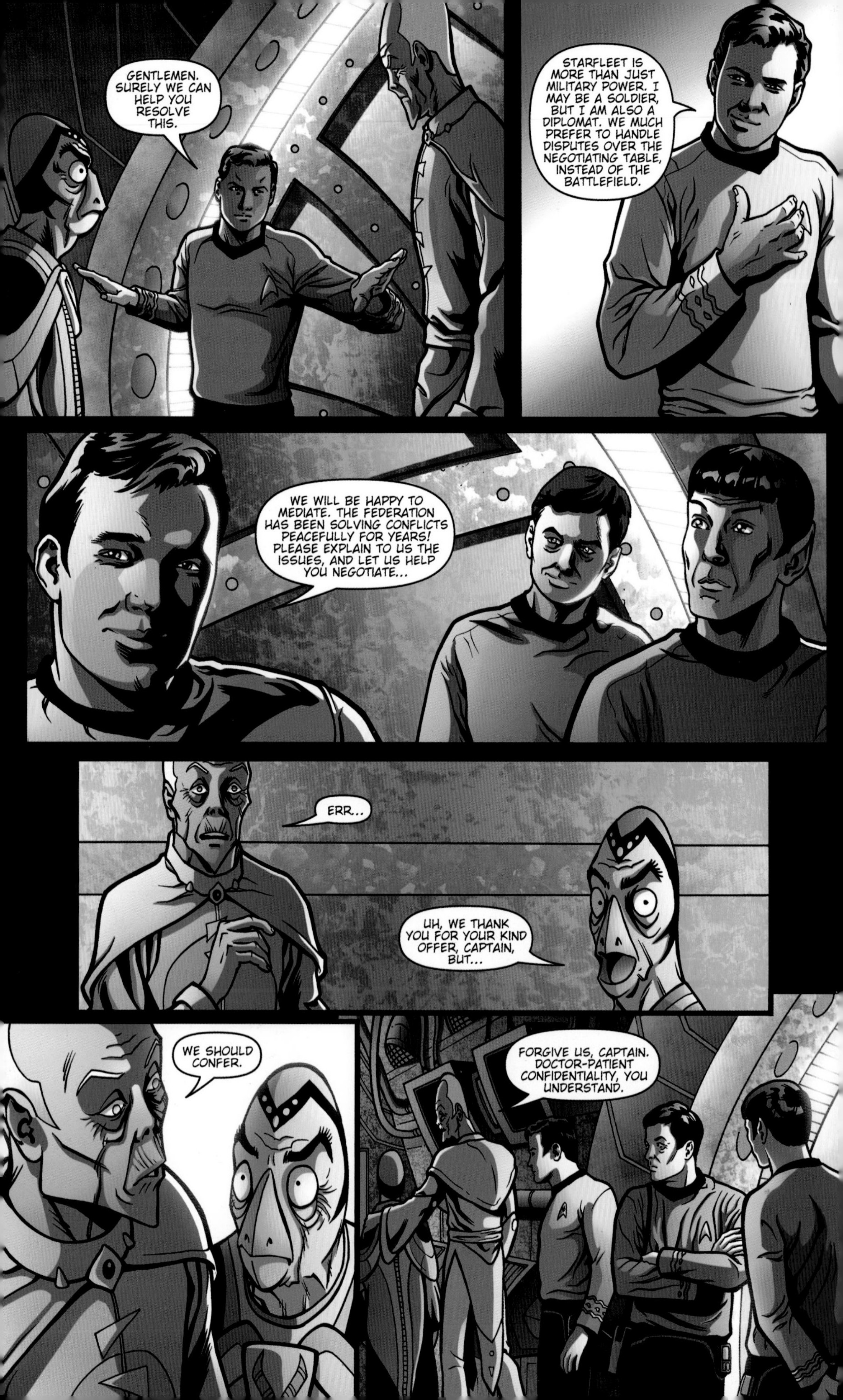
GENTLEMEN. SURELY WE CAN HELP YOU RESOLVE THIS.
STARFLEET IS MORE THAN JUST MILITARY POWER. I MAY BE A SOLDIER, BUT I AM ALSO A DIPLOMAT. WE MUCH PREFER TO HANDLE DISPUTES OVER THE NEGOTIATING TABLE, INSTEAD OF THE BATTLEFIELD.
WE WILL BE HAPPY TO MEDIATE. THE FEDERATION HAS BEEN SOLVING CONFLICTS PEACEFULLY FOR YEARS! PLEASE EXPLAIN TO US THE ISSUES, AND LET US HELP YOU NEGOTIATE...
ERR...
UH, WE THANK YOU FOR YOUR KIND OFFER, CAPTAIN, BUT...
WE SHOULD CONFER.
FORGIVE US, CAPTAIN. DOCTOR-PATIENT CONFIDENTIALITY, YOU UNDERSTAND.

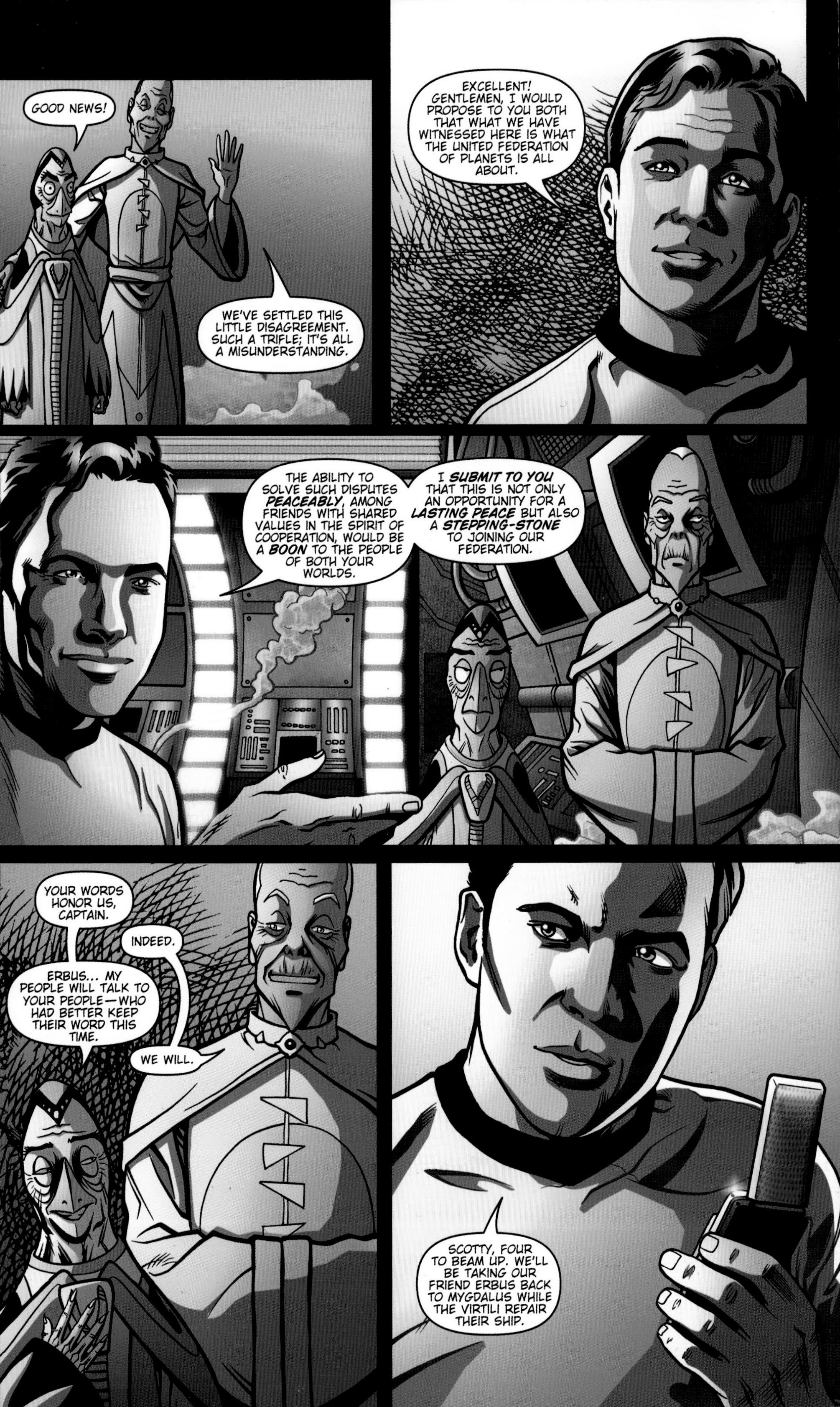

GOOD NEWS!
WE'VE SETTLED THIS LITTLE DISAGREEMENT. SUCH A TRIFLE; IT'S ALL A MISUNDERSTANDING.
EXCELLENT! GENTLEMEN, I WOULD PROPOSE TO YOU BOTH THAT WHAT WE HAVE WITNESSED HERE IS WHAT THE UNITED FEDERATION OF PLANETS IS ALL ABOUT.
THE ABILITY TO SOLVE SUCH DISPUTES PEACEABLY, AMONG FRIENDS WITH SHARED VALUES IN THE SPIRIT OF COOPERATION, WOULD BE A BOON TO THE PEOPLE OF BOTH YOUR WORLDS.
I SUBMIT TO YOU THAT THIS IS NOT ONLY AN OPPORTUNITY FOR A LASTING PEACE BUT ALSO A STEPPING-STONE TO JOINING OUR FEDERATION.
YOUR WORDS HONOR US, CAPTAIN.
INDEED.
ERBUS... MY PEOPLE WILL TALK TO YOUR PEOPLE—WHO HAD BETTER KEEP THEIR WORD THIS TIME.
WE WILL.
SCOTTY, FOUR TO BEAM UP. WE'LL BE TAKING OUR FRIEND ERBUS BACK TO MYGDALUS WHILE THE VIRTILI REPAIR THEIR SHIP.

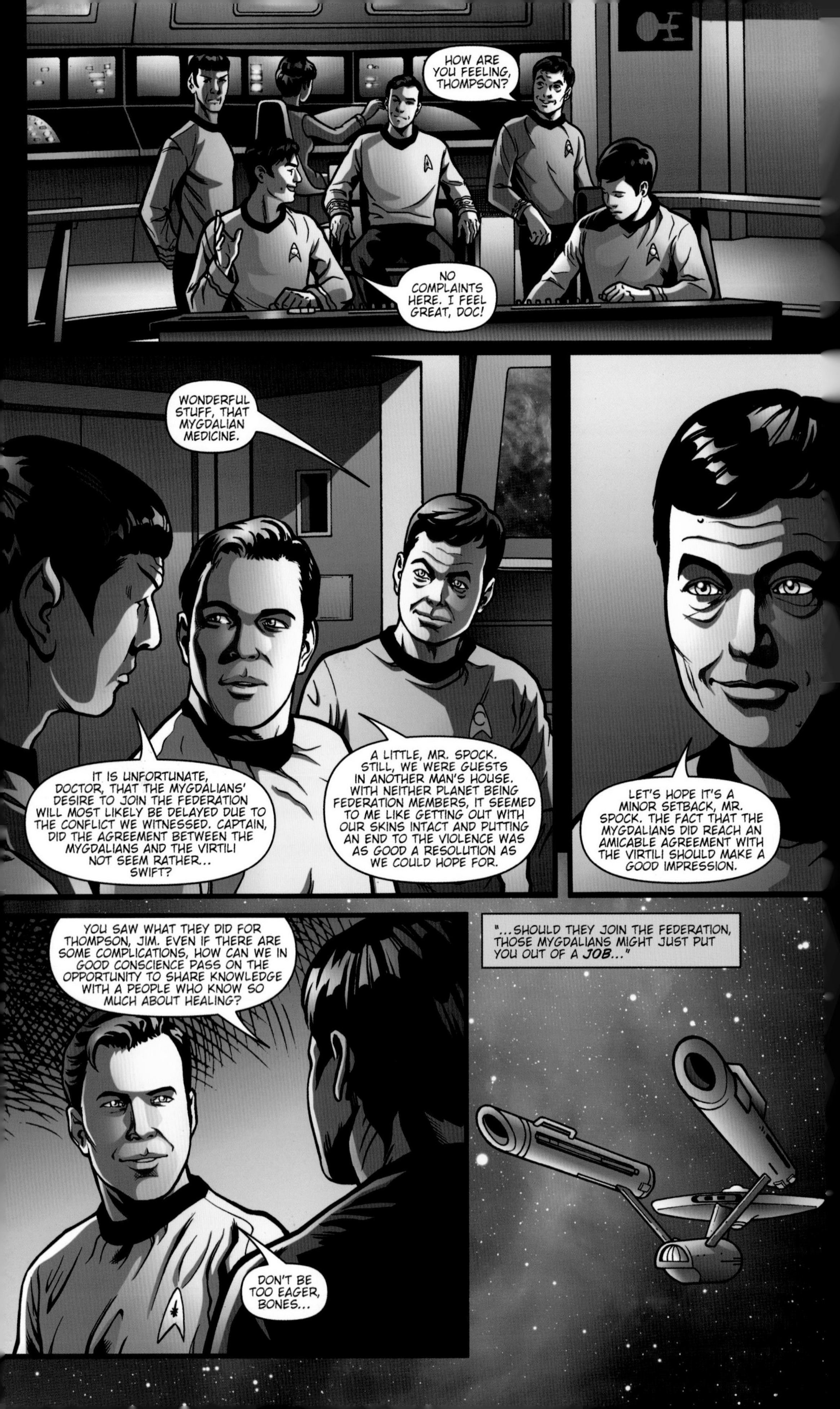
HOW ARE YOU FEELING, THOMPSON?
NO COMPLAINTS HERE. I FEEL GREAT, DOC!
WONDERFUL STUFF, THAT MYGDALIAN MEDICINE.
IT IS UNFORTUNATE, DOCTOR, THAT THE MYGDALIANS' DESIRE TO JOIN THE FEDERATION WILL MOST LIKELY BE DELAYED DUE TO THE CONFLICT WE WITNESSED. CAPTAIN, DID THE AGREEMENT BETWEEN THE MYGDALIANS AND THE VIRTILI NOT SEEM RATHER... SWIFT?
A LITTLE, MR. SPOCK. STILL, WE WERE GUESTS IN ANOTHER MAN'S HOUSE. WITH NEITHER PLANET BEING FEDERATION MEMBERS, IT SEEMED TO ME LIKE GETTING OUT WITH OUR SKINS INTACT AND PUTTING AN END TO THE VIOLENCE WAS AS GOOD A RESOLUTION AS WE COULD HOPE FOR.
LET'S HOPE IT'S A MINOR SETBACK, MR. SPOCK. THE FACT THAT THE MYGDALIANS DID REACH AN AMICABLE AGREEMENT WITH THE VIRTILI SHOULD MAKE A GOOD IMPRESSION.
YOU SAW WHAT THEY DID FOR THOMPSON, JIM. EVEN IF THERE ARE SOME COMPLICATIONS, HOW CAN WE IN GOOD CONSCIENCE PASS ON THE OPPORTUNITY TO SHARE KNOWLEDGE WITH A PEOPLE WHO KNOW SO MUCH ABOUT HEALING?
DON'T BE TOO EAGER, BONES...
"...SHOULD THEY JOIN THE FEDERATION, THOSE MYGDALIANS MIGHT JUST PUT YOU OUT OF A JOB..."

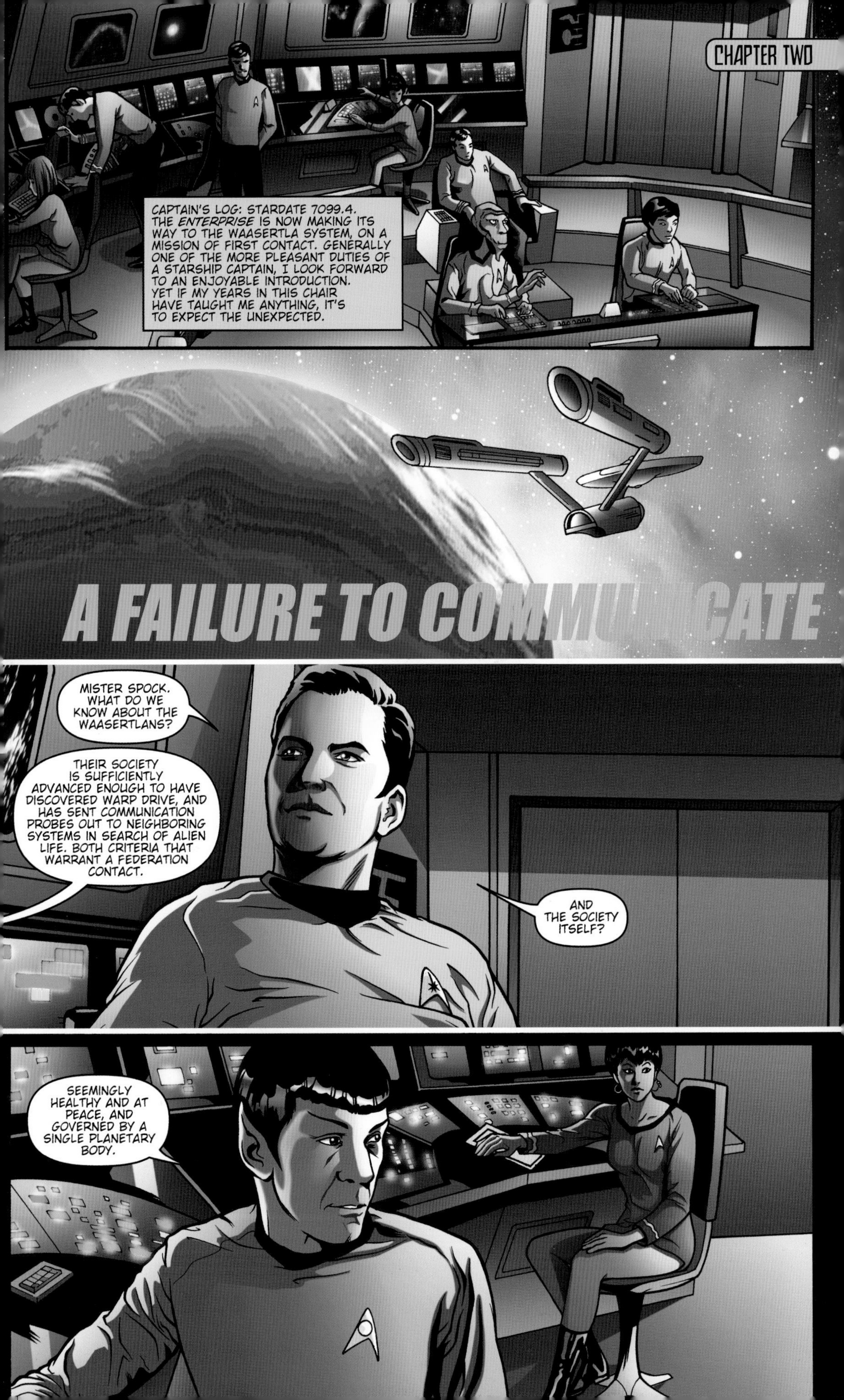
CHAPTER TWO
CAPTAIN'S LOG: STARDATE 7099.4. THE *ENTERPRISE* IS NOW MAKING ITS WAY TO THE WAASERTLA SYSTEM, ON A MISSION OF FIRST CONTACT. GENERALLY ONE OF THE MORE PLEASANT DUTIES OF A STARSHIP CAPTAIN, I LOOK FORWARD TO AN ENJOYABLE INTRODUCTION. YET IF MY YEARS IN THIS CHAIR HAVE TAUGHT ME ANYTHING, IT'S TO EXPECT THE UNEXPECTED.
A FAILURE TO COMMUNICATE
MISTER SPOCK. WHAT DO WE KNOW ABOUT THE WAASERTLANS?
THEIR SOCIETY IS SUFFICIENTLY ADVANCED ENOUGH TO HAVE DISCOVERED WARP DRIVE, AND HAS SENT COMMUNICATION PROBES OUT TO NEIGHBORING SYSTEMS IN SEARCH OF ALIEN LIFE. BOTH CRITERIA THAT WARRANT A FEDERATION CONTACT.
AND THE SOCIETY ITSELF?
SEEMINGLY HEALTHY AND AT PEACE, AND GOVERNED BY A SINGLE PLANETARY BODY.

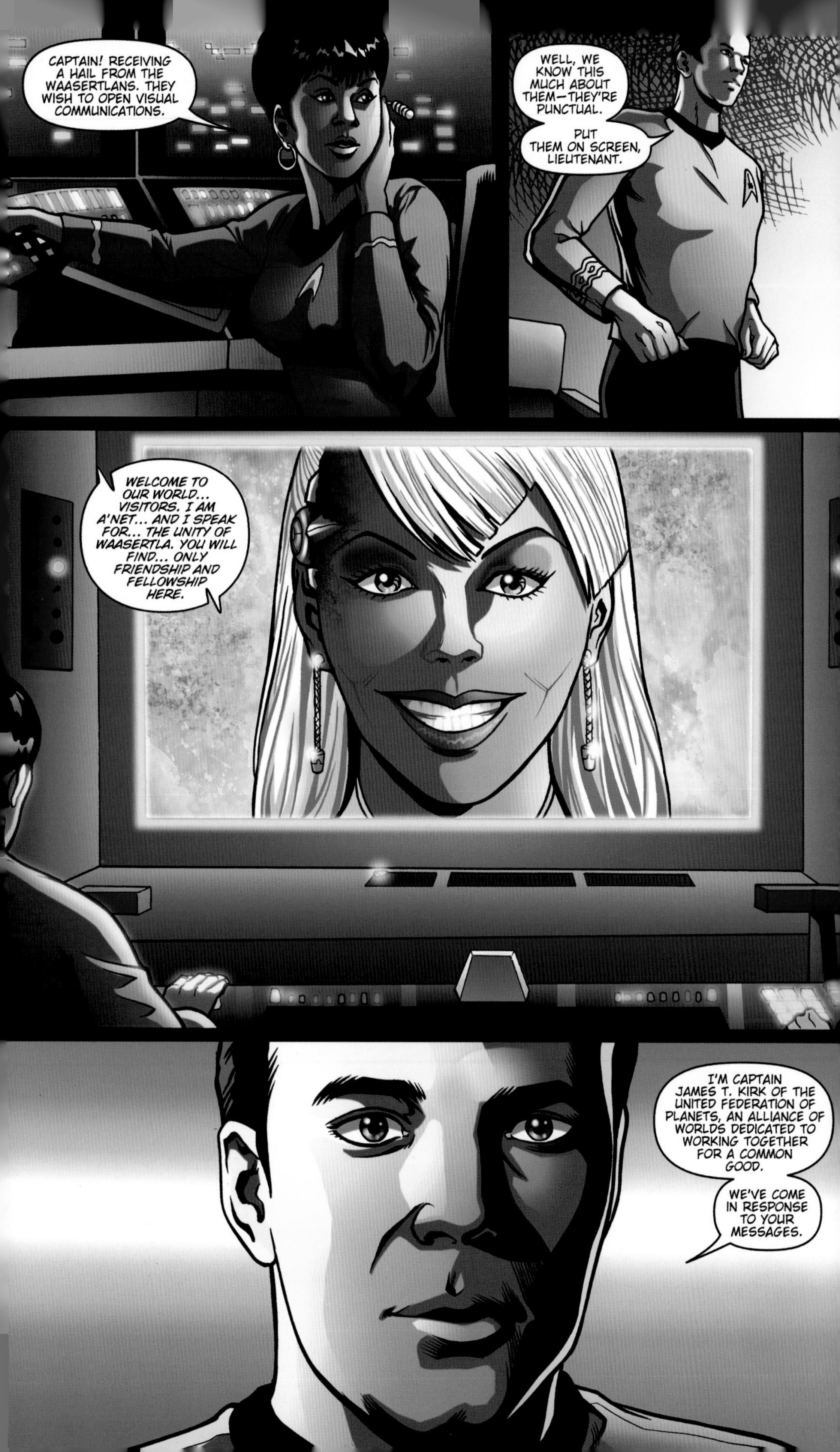
CAPTAIN! RECEIVING A HAIL FROM THE WAASERTLANS. THEY WISH TO OPEN VISUAL COMMUNICATIONS.
WELL, WE KNOW THIS MUCH ABOUT THEM—THEY'RE PUNCTUAL.
PUT THEM ON SCREEN, LIEUTENANT.
WELCOME TO OUR WORLD... VISITORS. I AM A'NET... AND I SPEAK FOR... THE UNITY OF WAASERTLA. YOU WILL FIND... ONLY FRIENDSHIP AND FELLOWSHIP HERE.
I'M CAPTAIN JAMES T. KIRK OF THE UNITED FEDERATION OF PLANETS, AN ALLIANCE OF WORLDS DEDICATED TO WORKING TOGETHER FOR A COMMON GOOD.
WE'VE COME IN RESPONSE TO YOUR MESSAGES.

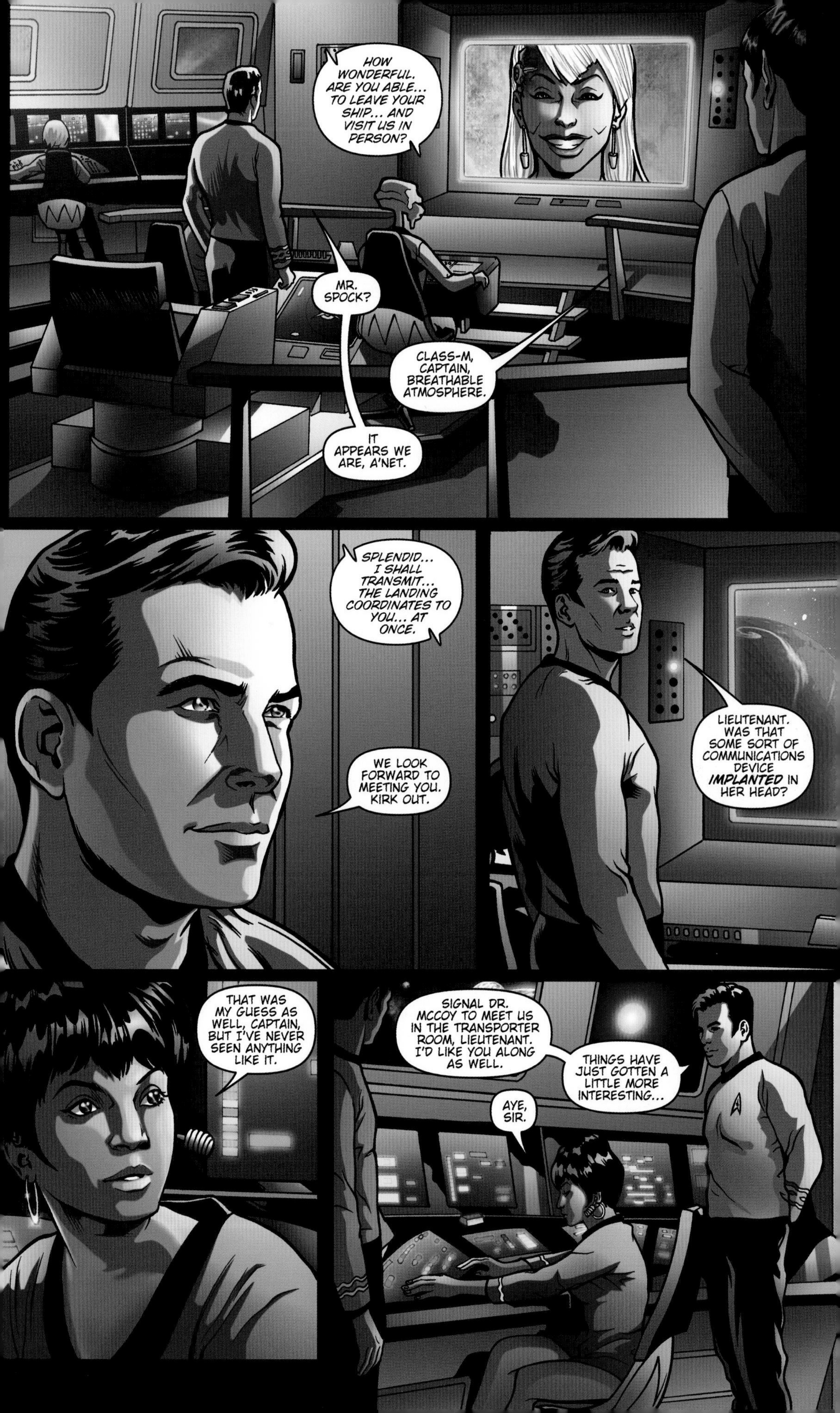
HOW WONDERFUL. ARE YOU ABLE... TO LEAVE YOUR SHIP... AND VISIT US IN PERSON?
MR. SPOCK?
CLASS-M, CAPTAIN, BREATHABLE ATMOSPHERE.
IT APPEARS WE ARE, A'NET.
SPLENDID... I SHALL TRANSMIT... THE LANDING COORDINATES TO YOU... AT ONCE.
WE LOOK FORWARD TO MEETING YOU. KIRK OUT.
LIEUTENANT. WAS THAT SOME SORT OF COMMUNICATIONS DEVICE IMPLANTED IN HER HEAD?
THAT WAS MY GUESS AS WELL, CAPTAIN, BUT I'VE NEVER SEEN ANYTHING LIKE IT.
SIGNAL DR. MCCOY TO MEET US IN THE TRANSPORTER ROOM, LIEUTENANT. I'D LIKE YOU ALONG AS WELL.
AYE, SIR.
THINGS HAVE JUST GOTTEN A LITTLE MORE INTERESTING...

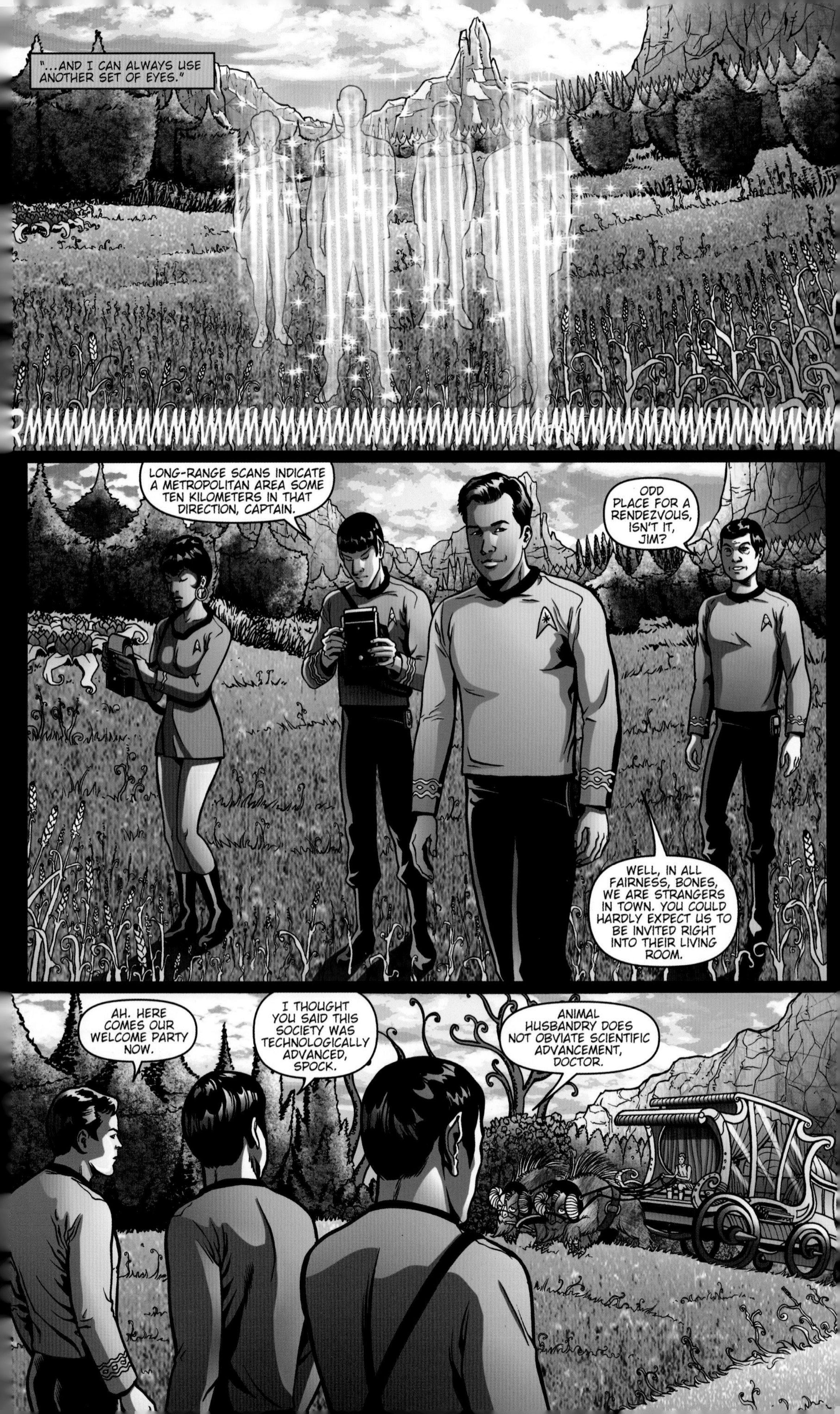
"...AND I CAN ALWAYS USE ANOTHER SET OF EYES."
RMMMMMMMMMMMMMMMMMMMMMMMMMMMMMMMMMM
LONG-RANGE SCANS INDICATE A METROPOLITAN AREA SOME TEN KILOMETERS IN THAT DIRECTION, CAPTAIN.
ODD PLACE FOR A RENDEZVOUS, ISN'T IT, JIM?
WELL, IN ALL FAIRNESS, BONES, WE ARE STRANGERS IN TOWN. YOU COULD HARDLY EXPECT US TO BE INVITED RIGHT INTO THEIR LIVING ROOM.
AH. HERE COMES OUR WELCOME PARTY NOW.
I THOUGHT YOU SAID THIS SOCIETY WAS TECHNOLOGICALLY ADVANCED, SPOCK.
ANIMAL HUSBANDRY DOES NOT OBVIATE SCIENTIFIC ADVANCEMENT, DOCTOR.

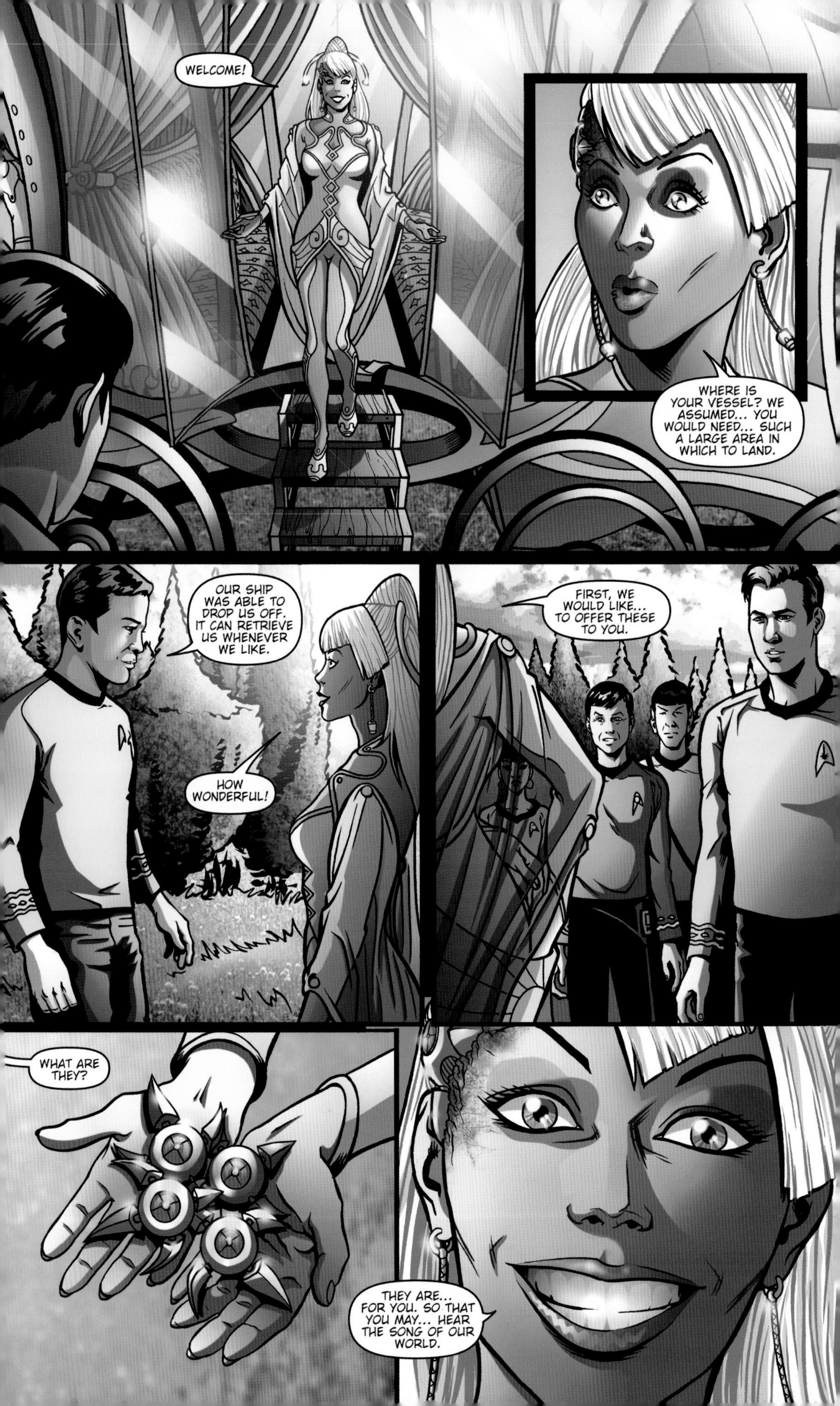
WELCOME!
WHERE IS YOUR VESSEL? WE ASSUMED... YOU WOULD NEED... SUCH A LARGE AREA IN WHICH TO LAND.
OUR SHIP WAS ABLE TO DROP US OFF. IT CAN RETRIEVE US WHENEVER WE LIKE.
HOW WONDERFUL!
FIRST, WE WOULD LIKE... TO OFFER THESE TO YOU.
WHAT ARE THEY?
THEY ARE... FOR YOU. SO THAT YOU MAY... HEAR THE SONG OF OUR WORLD.

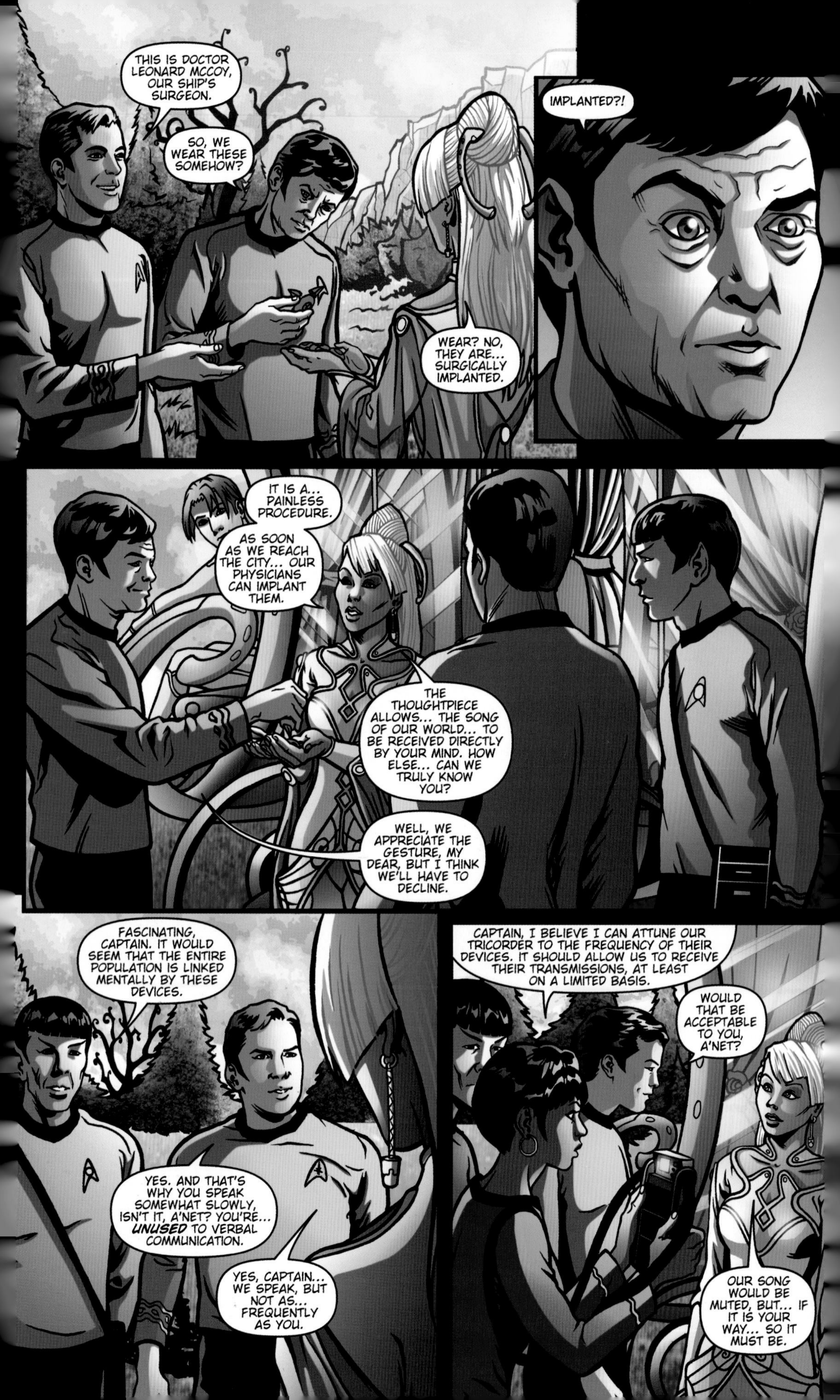
THIS IS DOCTOR LEONARD MCCOY, OUR SHIP'S SURGEON.
SO, WE WEAR THESE SOMEHOW?
WEAR? NO, THEY ARE... SURGICALLY IMPLANTED.
IMPLANTED?!
IT IS A... PAINLESS PROCEDURE.
AS SOON AS WE REACH THE CITY... OUR PHYSICIANS CAN IMPLANT THEM.
THE THOUGHTPIECE ALLOWS... THE SONG OF OUR WORLD... TO BE RECEIVED DIRECTLY BY YOUR MIND. HOW ELSE... CAN WE TRULY KNOW YOU?
WELL, WE APPRECIATE THE GESTURE, MY DEAR, BUT I THINK WE'LL HAVE TO DECLINE.
FASCINATING, CAPTAIN. IT WOULD SEEM THAT THE ENTIRE POPULATION IS LINKED MENTALLY BY THESE DEVICES.
YES. AND THAT'S WHY YOU SPEAK SOMEWHAT SLOWLY, ISN'T IT, A'NET? YOU'RE... ***UNUSED*** TO VERBAL COMMUNICATION.
YES, CAPTAIN... WE SPEAK, BUT NOT AS... FREQUENTLY AS YOU.
CAPTAIN, I BELIEVE I CAN ATTUNE OUR TRICORDER TO THE FREQUENCY OF THEIR DEVICES. IT SHOULD ALLOW US TO RECEIVE THEIR TRANSMISSIONS, AT LEAST ON A LIMITED BASIS.
WOULD THAT BE ACCEPTABLE TO YOU, A'NET?
OUR SONG WOULD BE MUTED, BUT... IF IT IS YOUR WAY... SO IT MUST BE.

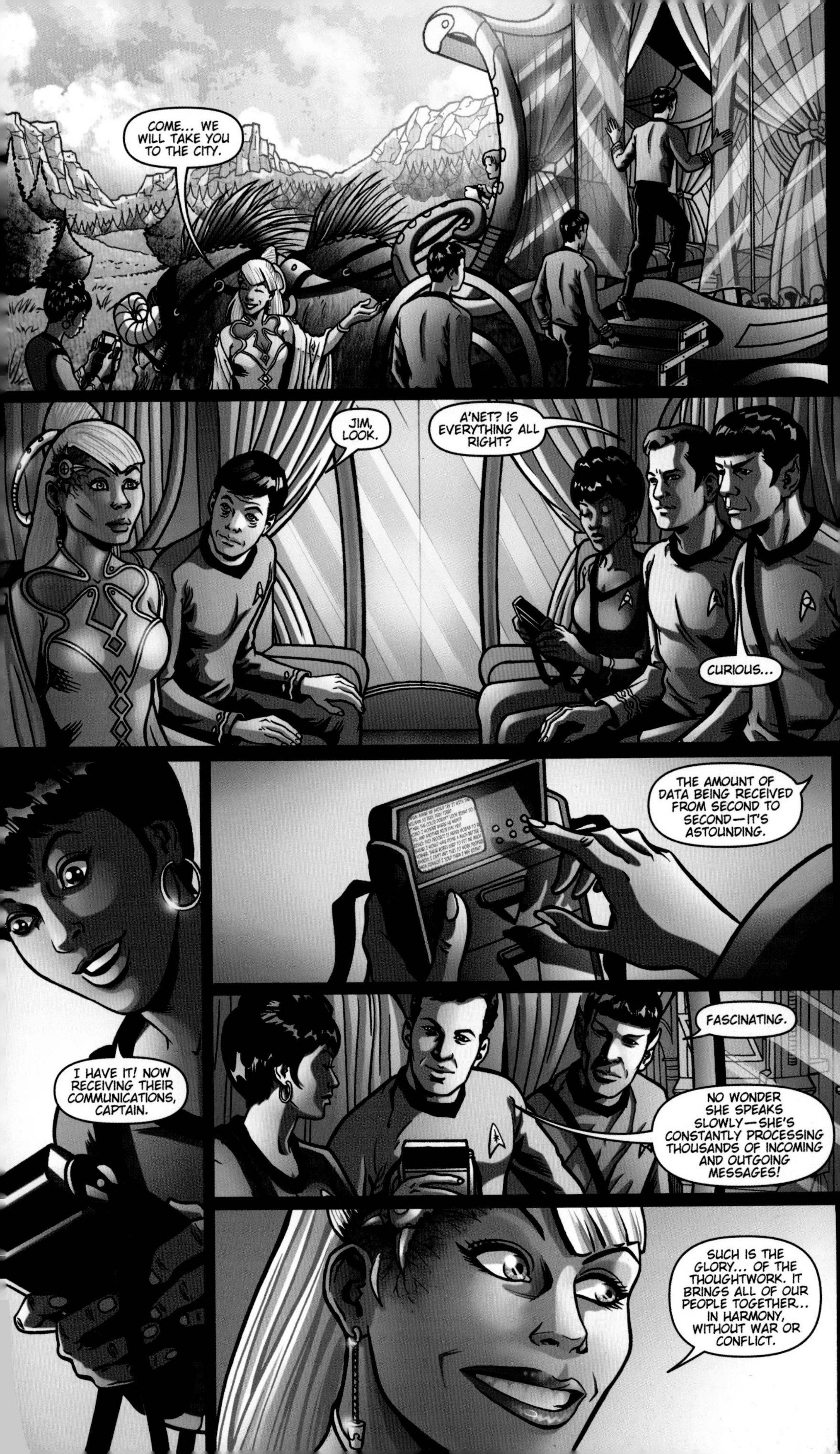
COME... WE WILL TAKE YOU TO THE CITY.
JIM, LOOK.
A'NET? IS EVERYTHING ALL RIGHT?
CURIOUS...
THE AMOUNT OF DATA BEING RECEIVED FROM SECOND TO SECOND—IT'S ASTOUNDING.
I HAVE IT! NOW RECEIVING THEIR COMMUNICATIONS, CAPTAIN.
FASCINATING.
NO WONDER SHE SPEAKS SLOWLY—SHE'S CONSTANTLY PROCESSING THOUSANDS OF INCOMING AND OUTGOING MESSAGES!
SUCH IS THE GLORY... OF THE THOUGHTWORK. IT BRINGS ALL OF OUR PEOPLE TOGETHER... IN HARMONY, WITHOUT WAR OR CONFLICT.

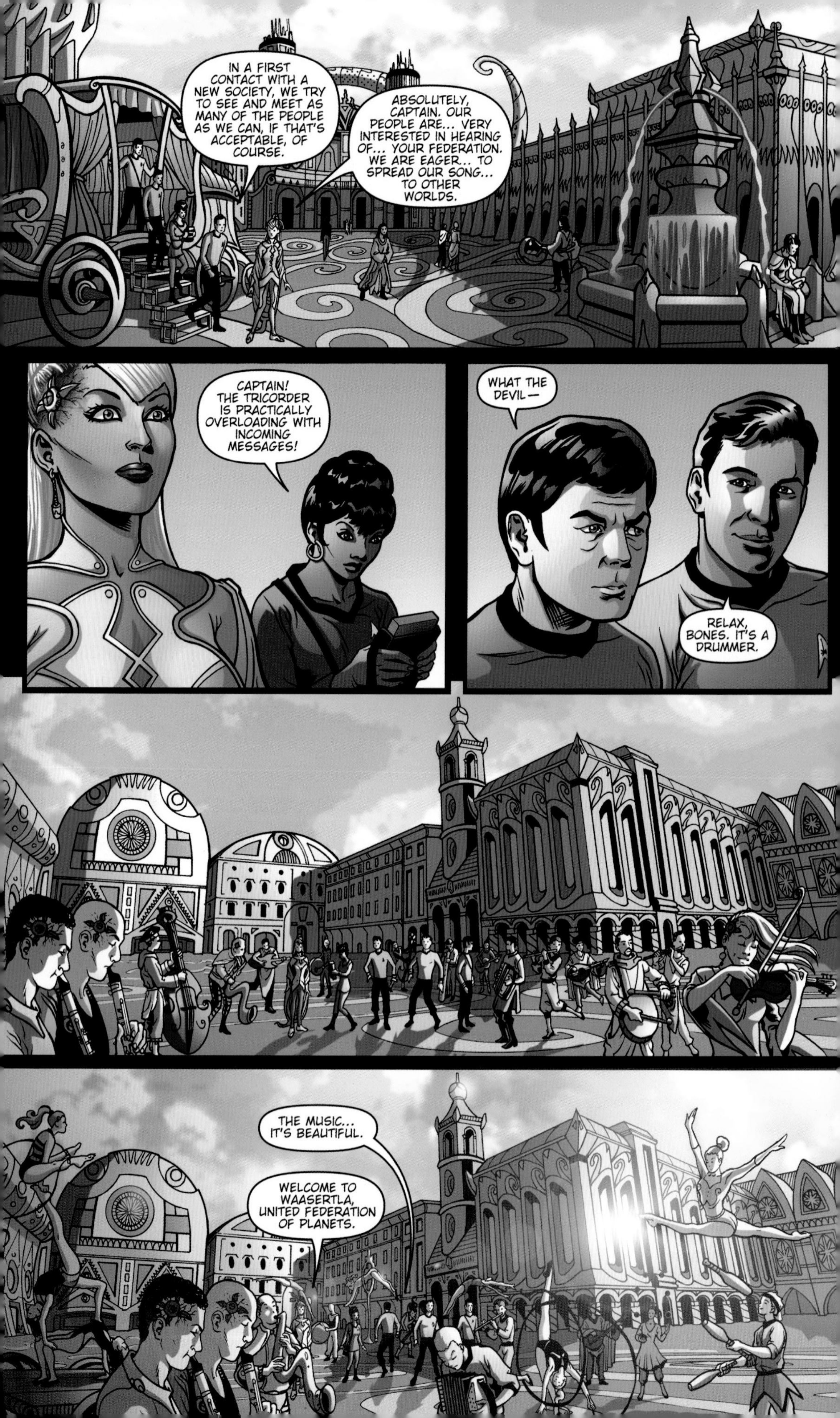

IN A FIRST CONTACT WITH A NEW SOCIETY, WE TRY TO SEE AND MEET AS MANY OF THE PEOPLE AS WE CAN, IF THAT'S ACCEPTABLE, OF COURSE.
ABSOLUTELY, CAPTAIN. OUR PEOPLE ARE... VERY INTERESTED IN HEARING OF... YOUR FEDERATION. WE ARE EAGER... TO SPREAD OUR SONG... TO OTHER WORLDS.
CAPTAIN! THE TRICORDER IS PRACTICALLY OVERLOADING WITH INCOMING MESSAGES!
WHAT THE DEVIL—
RELAX, BONES. IT'S A DRUMMER.
THE MUSIC... IT'S BEAUTIFUL.
WELCOME TO WAASERTLA, UNITED FEDERATION OF PLANETS.

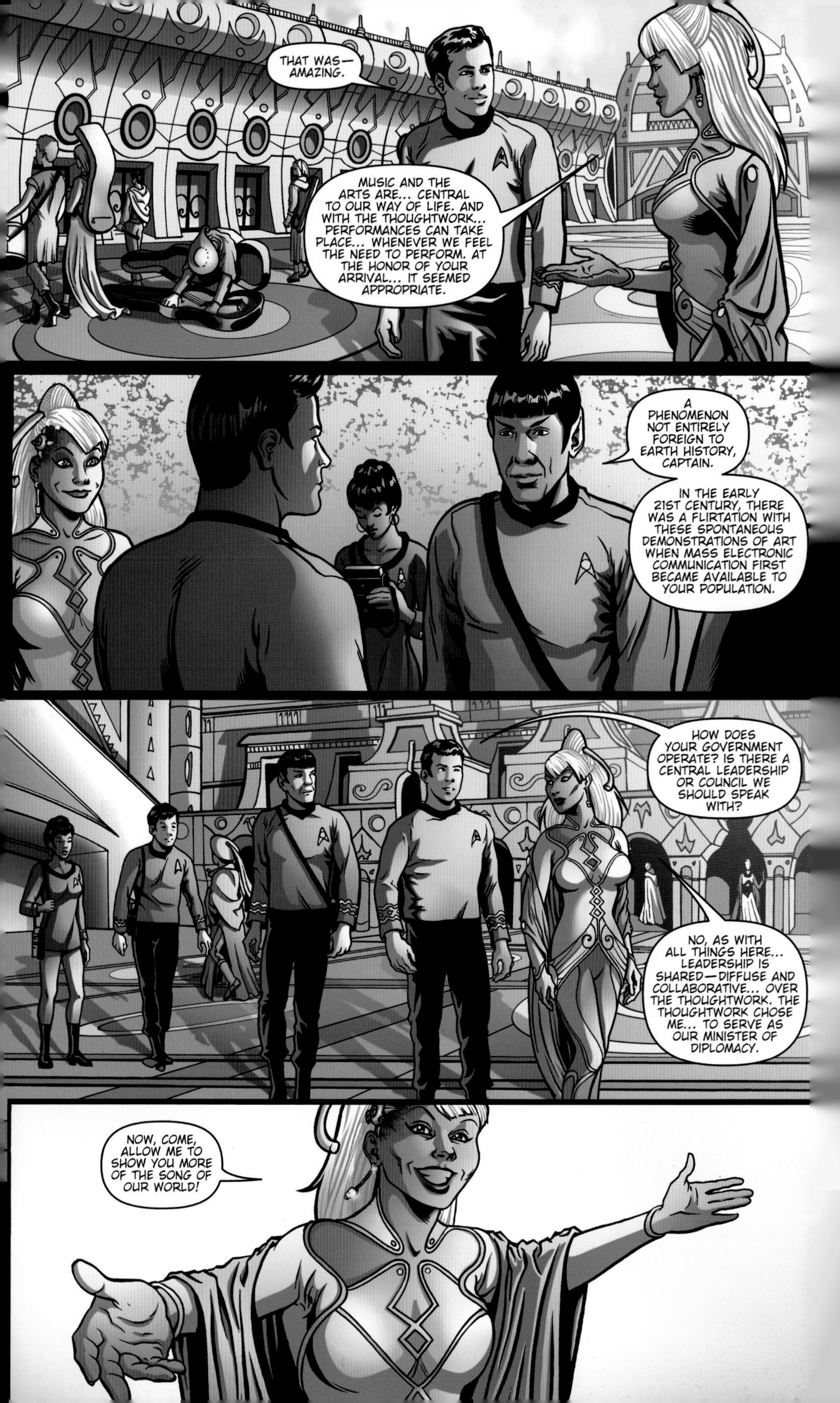
THAT WAS—AMAZING.
MUSIC AND THE ARTS ARE... CENTRAL TO OUR WAY OF LIFE. AND WITH THE THOUGHTWORK... PERFORMANCES CAN TAKE PLACE... WHENEVER WE FEEL THE NEED TO PERFORM. AT THE HONOR OF YOUR ARRIVAL... IT SEEMED APPROPRIATE.
A PHENOMENON NOT ENTIRELY FOREIGN TO EARTH HISTORY, CAPTAIN.
IN THE EARLY 21ST CENTURY, THERE WAS A FLIRTATION WITH THESE SPONTANEOUS DEMONSTRATIONS OF ART WHEN MASS ELECTRONIC COMMUNICATION FIRST BECAME AVAILABLE TO YOUR POPULATION.
HOW DOES YOUR GOVERNMENT OPERATE? IS THERE A CENTRAL LEADERSHIP OR COUNCIL WE SHOULD SPEAK WITH?
NO, AS WITH ALL THINGS HERE... LEADERSHIP IS SHARED—DIFFUSE AND COLLABORATIVE... OVER THE THOUGHTWORK. THE THOUGHTWORK CHOSE ME... TO SERVE AS OUR MINISTER OF DIPLOMACY.
NOW, COME, ALLOW ME TO SHOW YOU MORE OF THE SONG OF OUR WORLD!

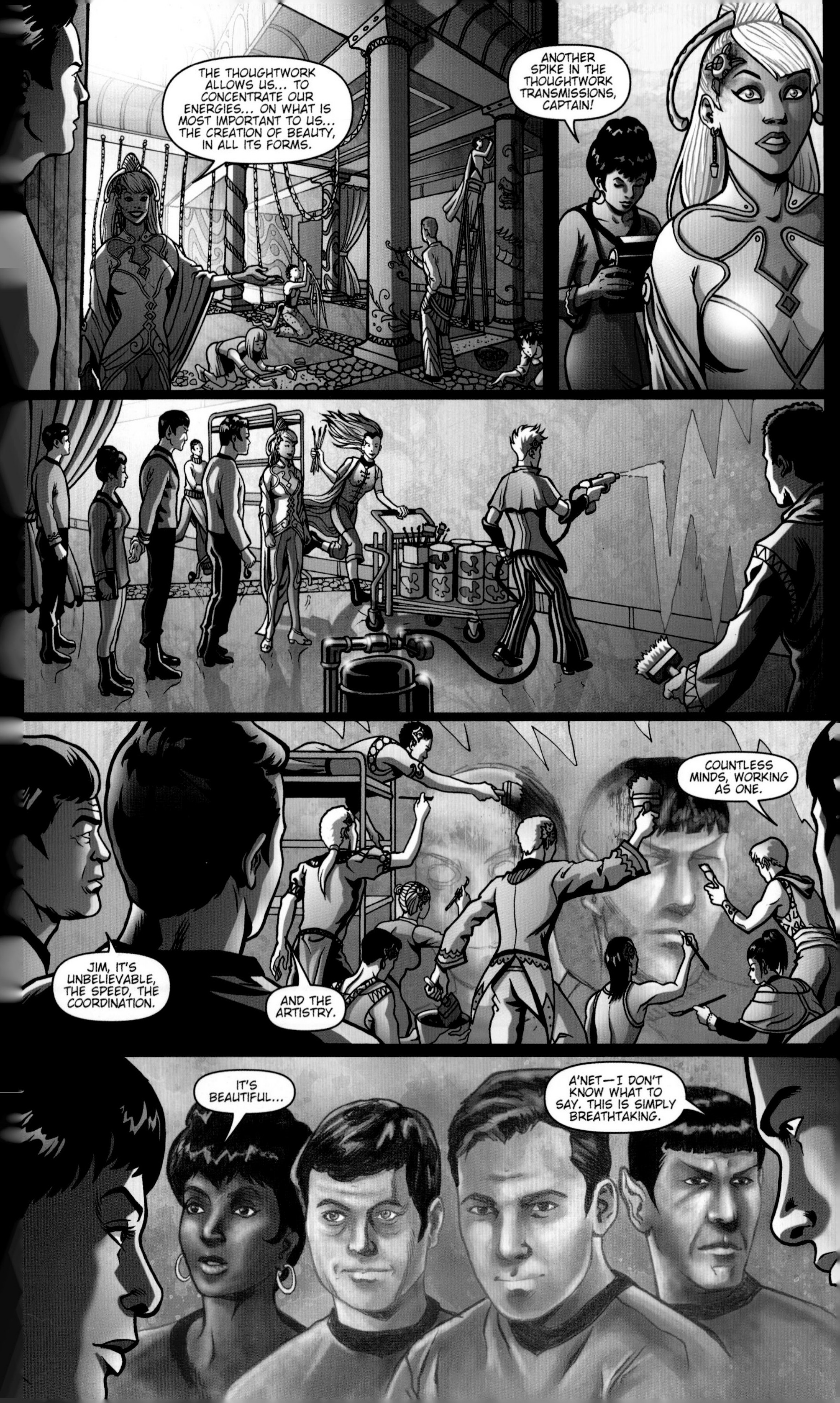
THE THOUGHTWORK ALLOWS US... TO CONCENTRATE OUR ENERGIES... ON WHAT IS MOST IMPORTANT TO US... THE CREATION OF BEAUTY, IN ALL ITS FORMS.
ANOTHER SPIKE IN THE THOUGHTWORK TRANSMISSIONS, CAPTAIN!
COUNTLESS MINDS, WORKING AS ONE.
JIM, IT'S UNBELIEVABLE, THE SPEED, THE COORDINATION.
AND THE ARTISTRY.
IT'S BEAUTIFUL...
A'NET—I DON'T KNOW WHAT TO SAY. THIS IS SIMPLY BREATHTAKING.

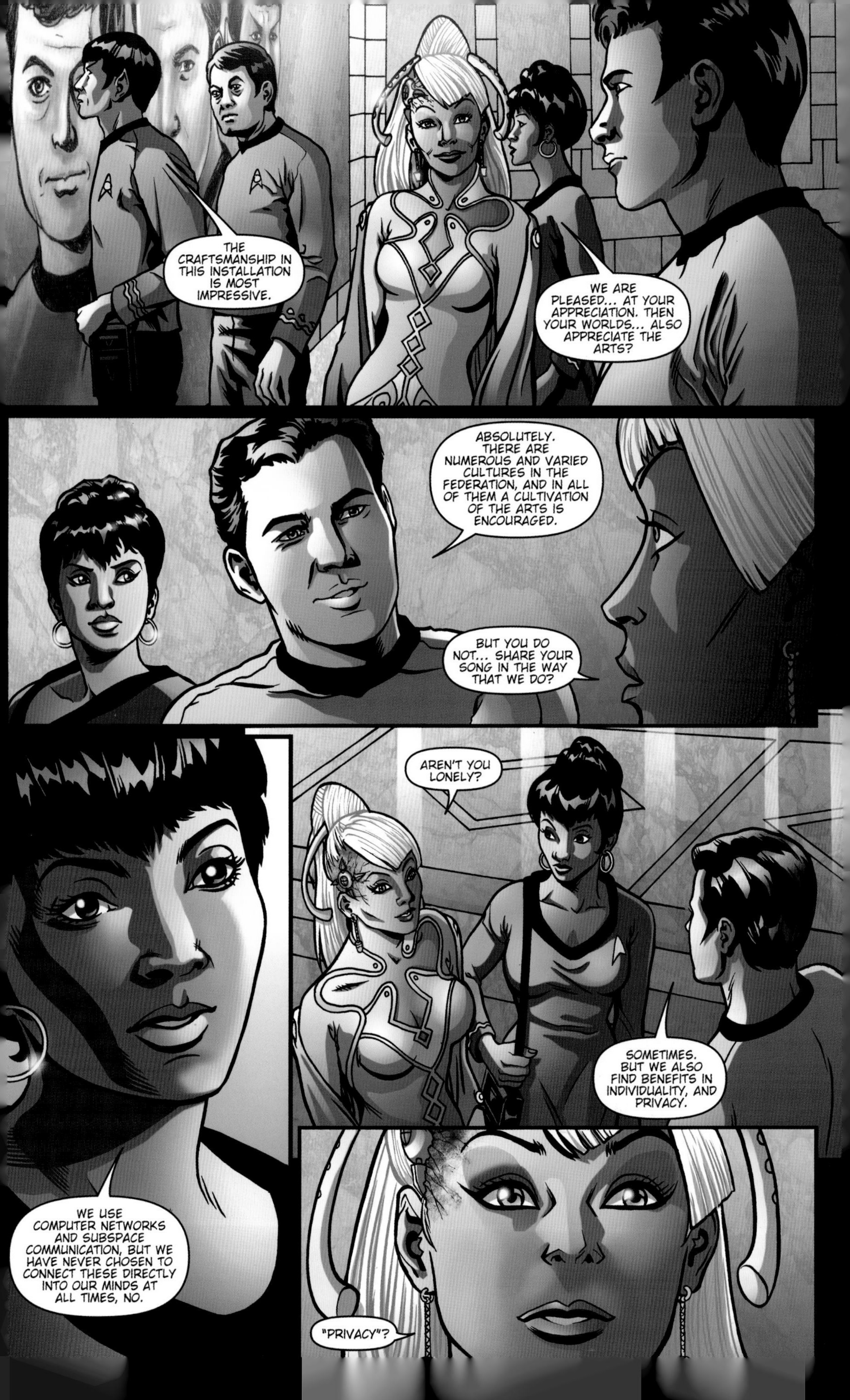
THE CRAFTSMANSHIP IN THIS INSTALLATION IS MOST IMPRESSIVE.
WE ARE PLEASED... AT YOUR APPRECIATION. THEN YOUR WORLDS... ALSO APPRECIATE THE ARTS?
ABSOLUTELY. THERE ARE NUMEROUS AND VARIED CULTURES IN THE FEDERATION, AND IN ALL OF THEM A CULTIVATION OF THE ARTS IS ENCOURAGED.
BUT YOU DO NOT... SHARE YOUR SONG IN THE WAY THAT WE DO?
WE USE COMPUTER NETWORKS AND SUBSPACE COMMUNICATION, BUT WE HAVE NEVER CHOSEN TO CONNECT THESE DIRECTLY INTO OUR MINDS AT ALL TIMES, NO.
AREN'T YOU LONELY?
SOMETIMES. BUT WE ALSO FIND BENEFITS IN INDIVIDUALITY, AND PRIVACY.
"PRIVACY"?

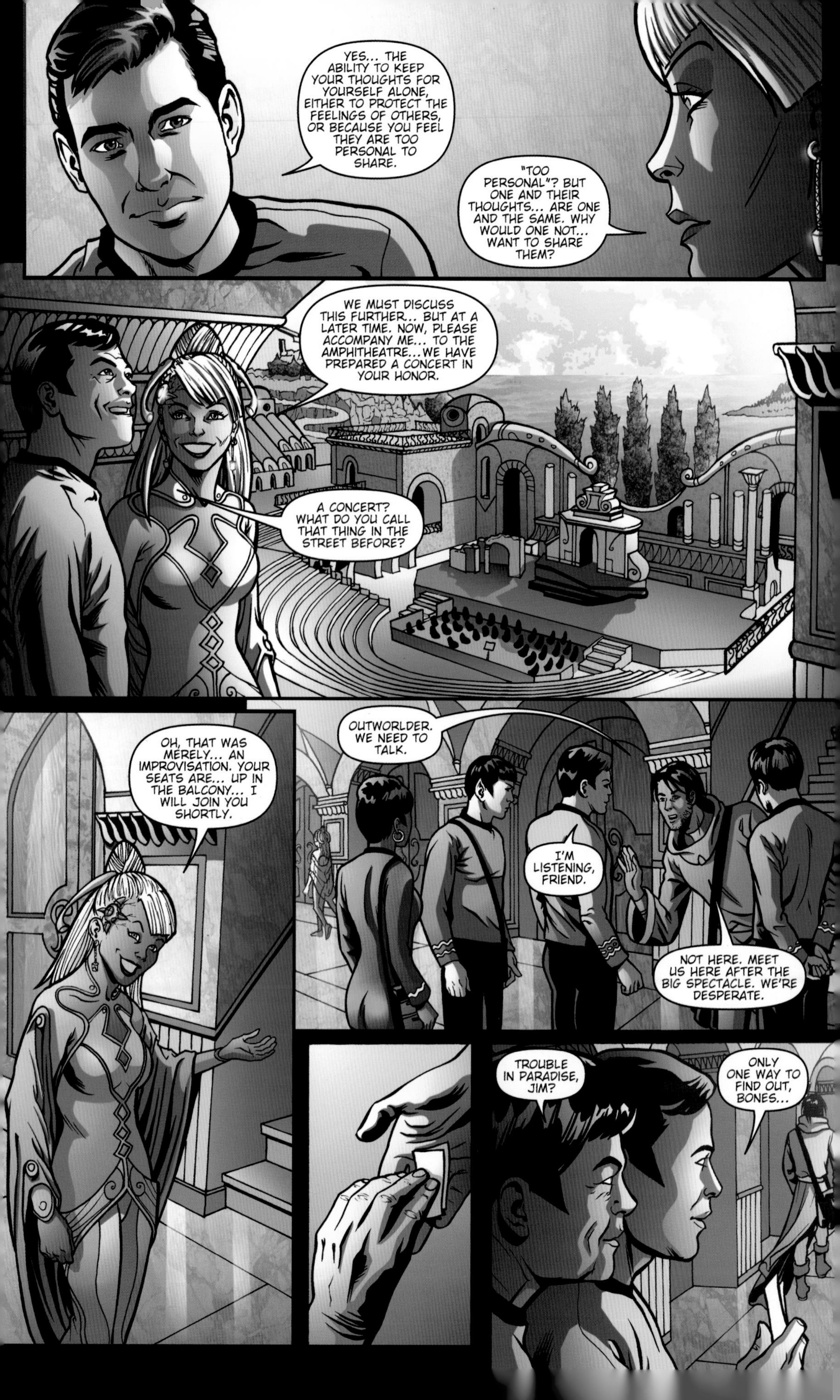
YES... THE ABILITY TO KEEP YOUR THOUGHTS FOR YOURSELF ALONE, EITHER TO PROTECT THE FEELINGS OF OTHERS, OR BECAUSE YOU FEEL THEY ARE TOO PERSONAL TO SHARE.
"TOO PERSONAL"? BUT ONE AND THEIR THOUGHTS... ARE ONE AND THE SAME. WHY WOULD ONE NOT... WANT TO SHARE THEM?
WE MUST DISCUSS THIS FURTHER... BUT AT A LATER TIME. NOW, PLEASE ACCOMPANY ME... TO THE AMPHITHEATRE... WE HAVE PREPARED A CONCERT IN YOUR HONOR.
A CONCERT? WHAT DO YOU CALL THAT THING IN THE STREET BEFORE?
OH, THAT WAS MERELY... AN IMPROVISATION. YOUR SEATS ARE... UP IN THE BALCONY... I WILL JOIN YOU SHORTLY.
OUTWORLDER. WE NEED TO TALK.
I'M LISTENING, FRIEND.
NOT HERE. MEET US HERE AFTER THE BIG SPECTACLE. WE'RE DESPERATE.
TROUBLE IN PARADISE, JIM?
ONLY ONE WAY TO FIND OUT, BONES...

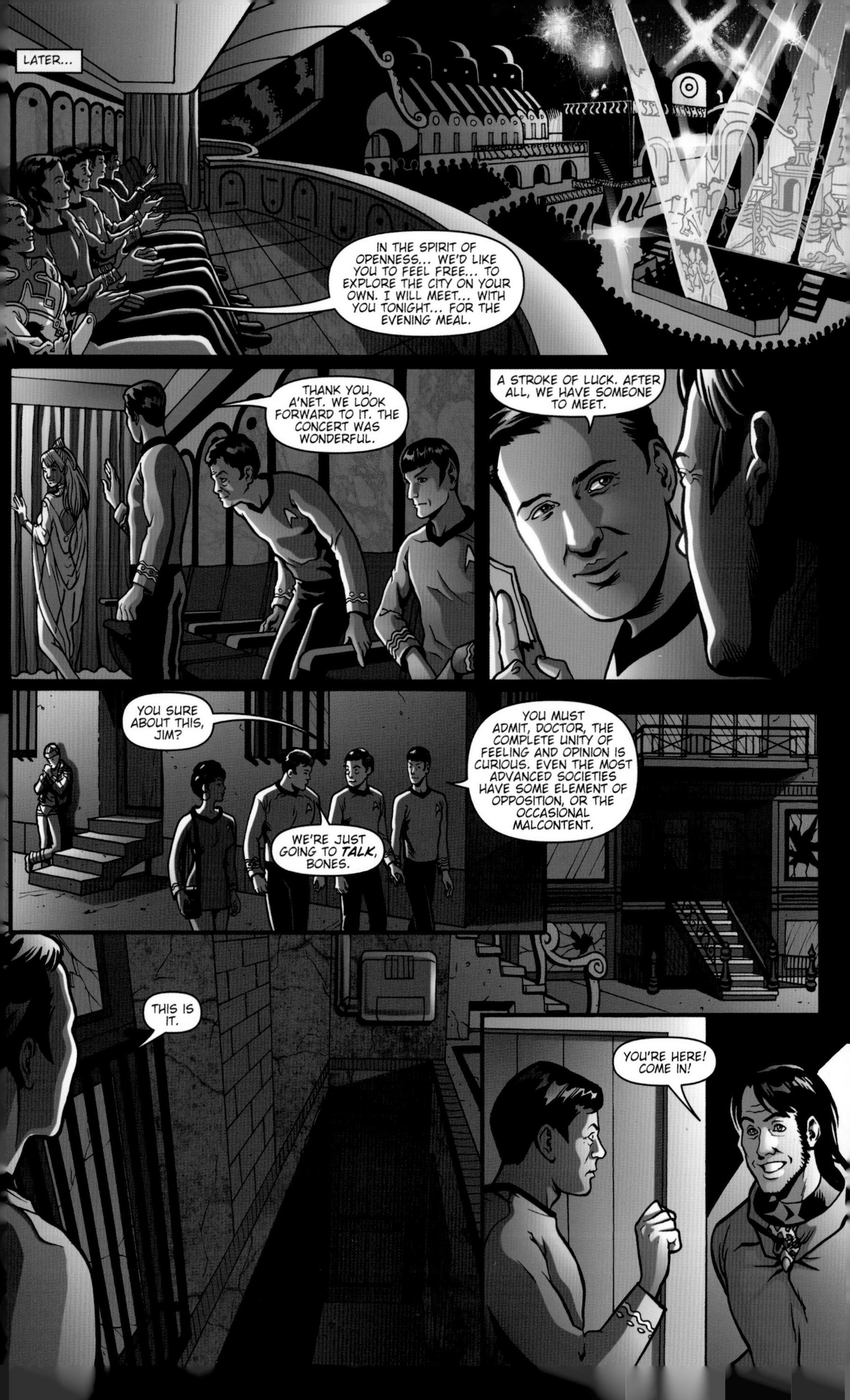
LATER...
IN THE SPIRIT OF OPENNESS... WE'D LIKE YOU TO FEEL FREE... TO EXPLORE THE CITY ON YOUR OWN. I WILL MEET... WITH YOU TONIGHT... FOR THE EVENING MEAL.
THANK YOU, A'NET. WE LOOK FORWARD TO IT. THE CONCERT WAS WONDERFUL.
A STROKE OF LUCK. AFTER ALL, WE HAVE SOMEONE TO MEET.
YOU SURE ABOUT THIS, JIM?
WE'RE JUST GOING TO TALK, BONES.
YOU MUST ADMIT, DOCTOR, THE COMPLETE UNITY OF FEELING AND OPINION IS CURIOUS. EVEN THE MOST ADVANCED SOCIETIES HAVE SOME ELEMENT OF OPPOSITION, OR THE OCCASIONAL MALCONTENT.
THIS IS IT.
YOU'RE HERE! COME IN!

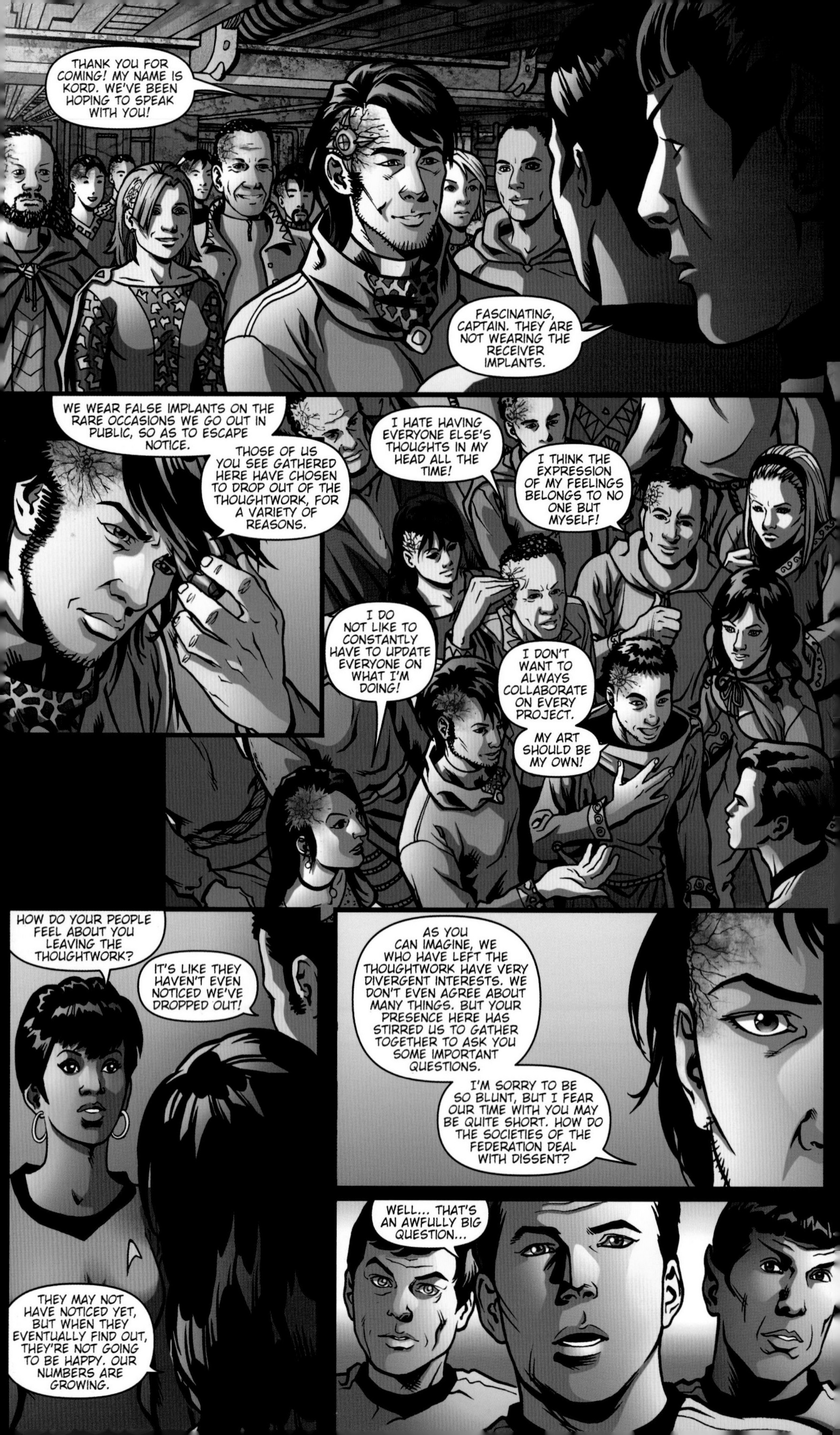
THANK YOU FOR COMING! MY NAME IS KORD. WE'VE BEEN HOPING TO SPEAK WITH YOU!
FASCINATING, CAPTAIN. THEY ARE NOT WEARING THE RECEIVER IMPLANTS.
WE WEAR FALSE IMPLANTS ON THE RARE OCCASIONS WE GO OUT IN PUBLIC, SO AS TO ESCAPE NOTICE.
THOSE OF US YOU SEE GATHERED HERE HAVE CHOSEN TO DROP OUT OF THE THOUGHTWORK, FOR A VARIETY OF REASONS.
I HATE HAVING EVERYONE ELSE'S THOUGHTS IN MY HEAD ALL THE TIME!
I THINK THE EXPRESSION OF MY FEELINGS BELONGS TO NO ONE BUT MYSELF!
I DO NOT LIKE TO CONSTANTLY HAVE TO UPDATE EVERYONE ON WHAT I'M DOING!
I DON'T WANT TO ALWAYS COLLABORATE ON EVERY PROJECT.
MY ART SHOULD BE MY OWN!
HOW DO YOUR PEOPLE FEEL ABOUT YOU LEAVING THE THOUGHTWORK?
IT'S LIKE THEY HAVEN'T EVEN NOTICED WE'VE DROPPED OUT!
THEY MAY NOT HAVE NOTICED YET, BUT WHEN THEY EVENTUALLY FIND OUT, THEY'RE NOT GOING TO BE HAPPY. OUR NUMBERS ARE GROWING.
AS YOU CAN IMAGINE, WE WHO HAVE LEFT THE THOUGHTWORK HAVE VERY DIVERGENT INTERESTS. WE DON'T EVEN AGREE ABOUT MANY THINGS. BUT YOUR PRESENCE HERE HAS STIRRED US TO GATHER TOGETHER TO ASK YOU SOME IMPORTANT QUESTIONS.
I'M SORRY TO BE SO BLUNT, BUT I FEAR OUR TIME WITH YOU MAY BE QUITE SHORT. HOW DO THE SOCIETIES OF THE FEDERATION DEAL WITH DISSENT?
WELL... THAT'S AN AWFULLY BIG QUESTION...

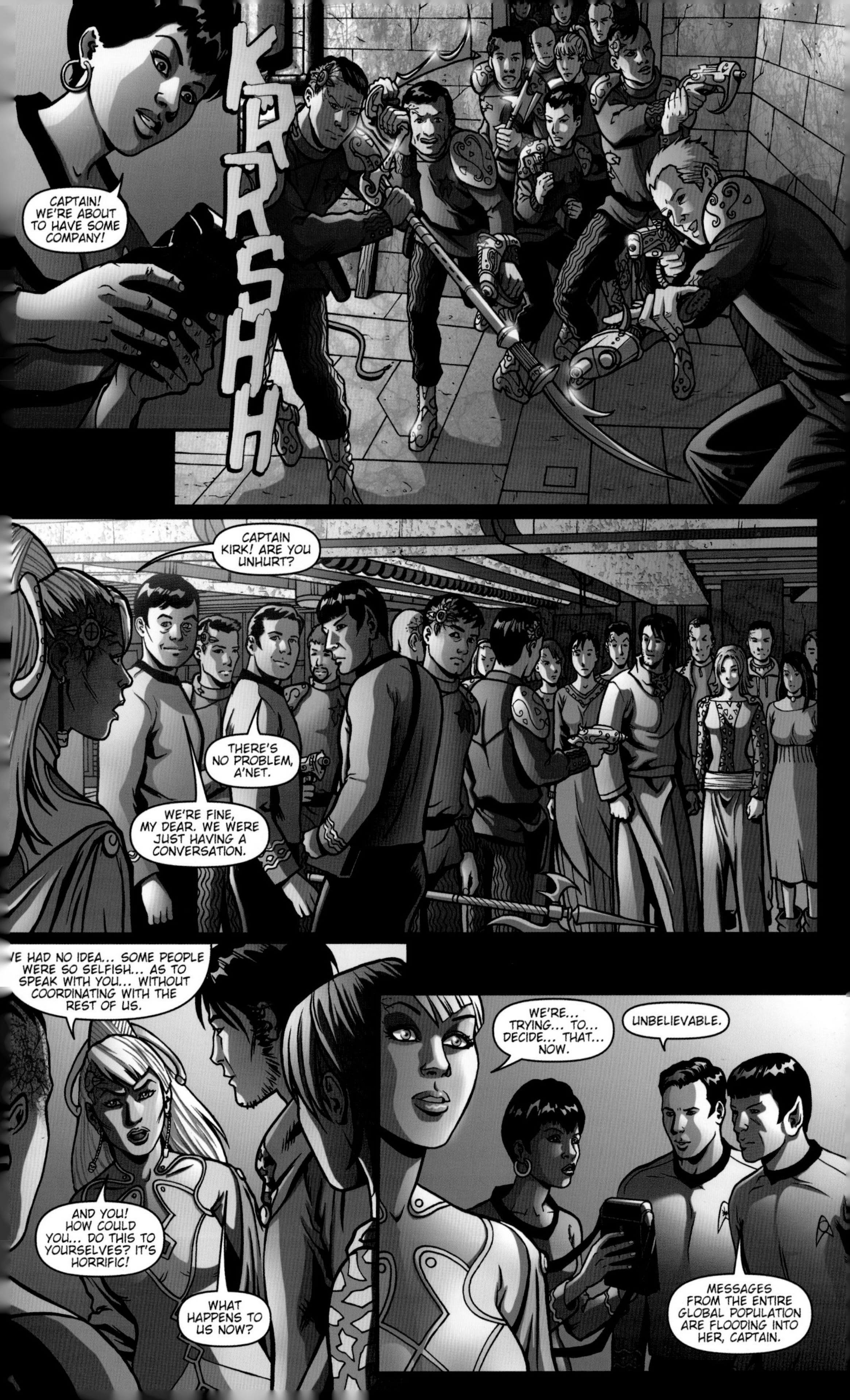
CAPTAIN! WE'RE ABOUT TO HAVE SOME COMPANY!
KRRSHH
CAPTAIN KIRK! ARE YOU UNHURT?
THERE'S NO PROBLEM, A'NET.
WE'RE FINE, MY DEAR. WE WERE JUST HAVING A CONVERSATION.
WE HAD NO IDEA... SOME PEOPLE WERE SO SELFISH... AS TO SPEAK WITH YOU... WITHOUT COORDINATING WITH THE REST OF US.
AND YOU! HOW COULD YOU... DO THIS TO YOURSELVES? IT'S HORRIFIC!
WHAT HAPPENS TO US NOW?
WE'RE... TRYING... TO... DECIDE... THAT... NOW.
UNBELIEVABLE.
MESSAGES FROM THE ENTIRE GLOBAL POPULATION ARE FLOODING INTO HER, CAPTAIN.

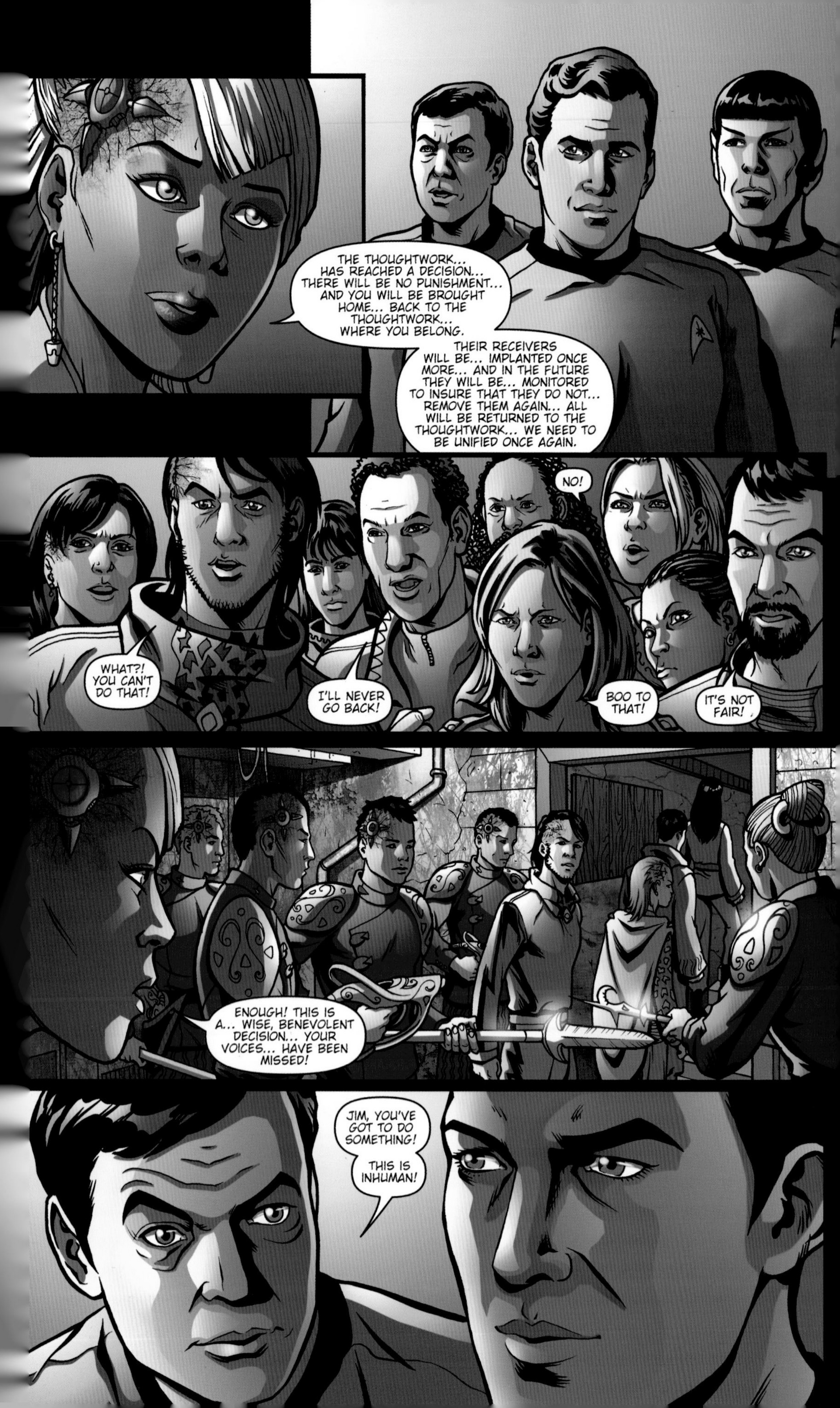
THE THOUGHTWORK... HAS REACHED A DECISION... THERE WILL BE NO PUNISHMENT... AND YOU WILL BE BROUGHT HOME... BACK TO THE THOUGHTWORK... WHERE YOU BELONG.
THEIR RECEIVERS WILL BE... IMPLANTED ONCE MORE... AND IN THE FUTURE THEY WILL BE... MONITORED TO INSURE THAT THEY DO NOT... REMOVE THEM AGAIN... ALL WILL BE RETURNED TO THE THOUGHTWORK... WE NEED TO BE UNIFIED ONCE AGAIN.
NO!
WHAT?! YOU CAN'T DO THAT!
I'LL NEVER GO BACK!
BOO TO THAT!
IT'S NOT FAIR!
ENOUGH! THIS IS A... WISE, BENEVOLENT DECISION... YOUR VOICES... HAVE BEEN MISSED!
JIM, YOU'VE GOT TO DO SOMETHING!
THIS IS INHUMAN!

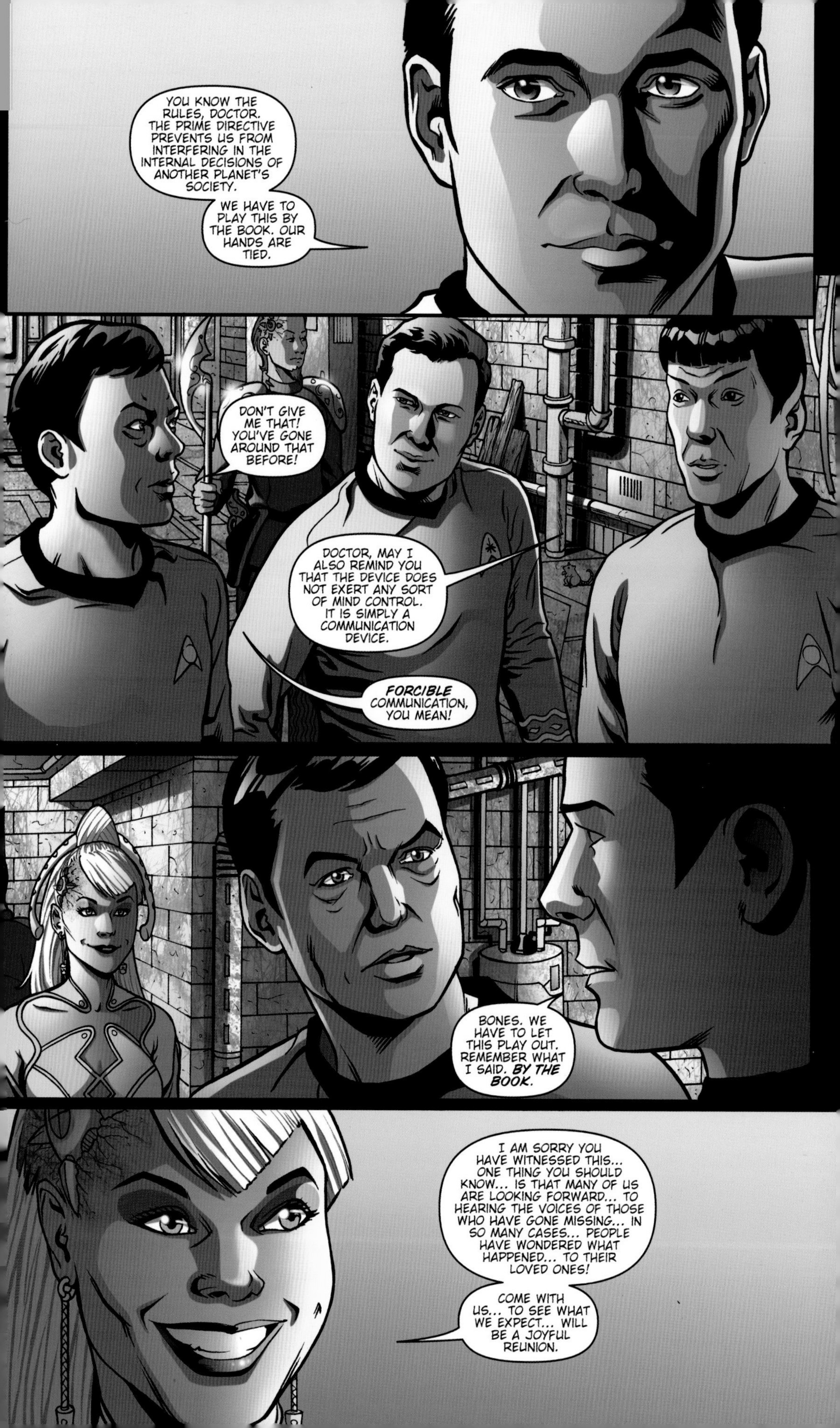
YOU KNOW THE RULES, DOCTOR. THE PRIME DIRECTIVE PREVENTS US FROM INTERFERING IN THE INTERNAL DECISIONS OF ANOTHER PLANET'S SOCIETY.
WE HAVE TO PLAY THIS BY THE BOOK. OUR HANDS ARE TIED.
DON'T GIVE ME THAT! YOU'VE GONE AROUND THAT BEFORE!
DOCTOR, MAY I ALSO REMIND YOU THAT THE DEVICE DOES NOT EXERT ANY SORT OF MIND CONTROL. IT IS SIMPLY A COMMUNICATION DEVICE.
FORCIBLE COMMUNICATION, YOU MEAN!
BONES. WE HAVE TO LET THIS PLAY OUT. REMEMBER WHAT I SAID. *BY THE BOOK*.
I AM SORRY YOU HAVE WITNESSED THIS... ONE THING YOU SHOULD KNOW... IS THAT MANY OF US ARE LOOKING FORWARD... TO HEARING THE VOICES OF THOSE WHO HAVE GONE MISSING... IN SO MANY CASES... PEOPLE HAVE WONDERED WHAT HAPPENED... TO THEIR LOVED ONES!
COME WITH US... TO SEE WHAT WE EXPECT... WILL BE A JOYFUL REUNION.

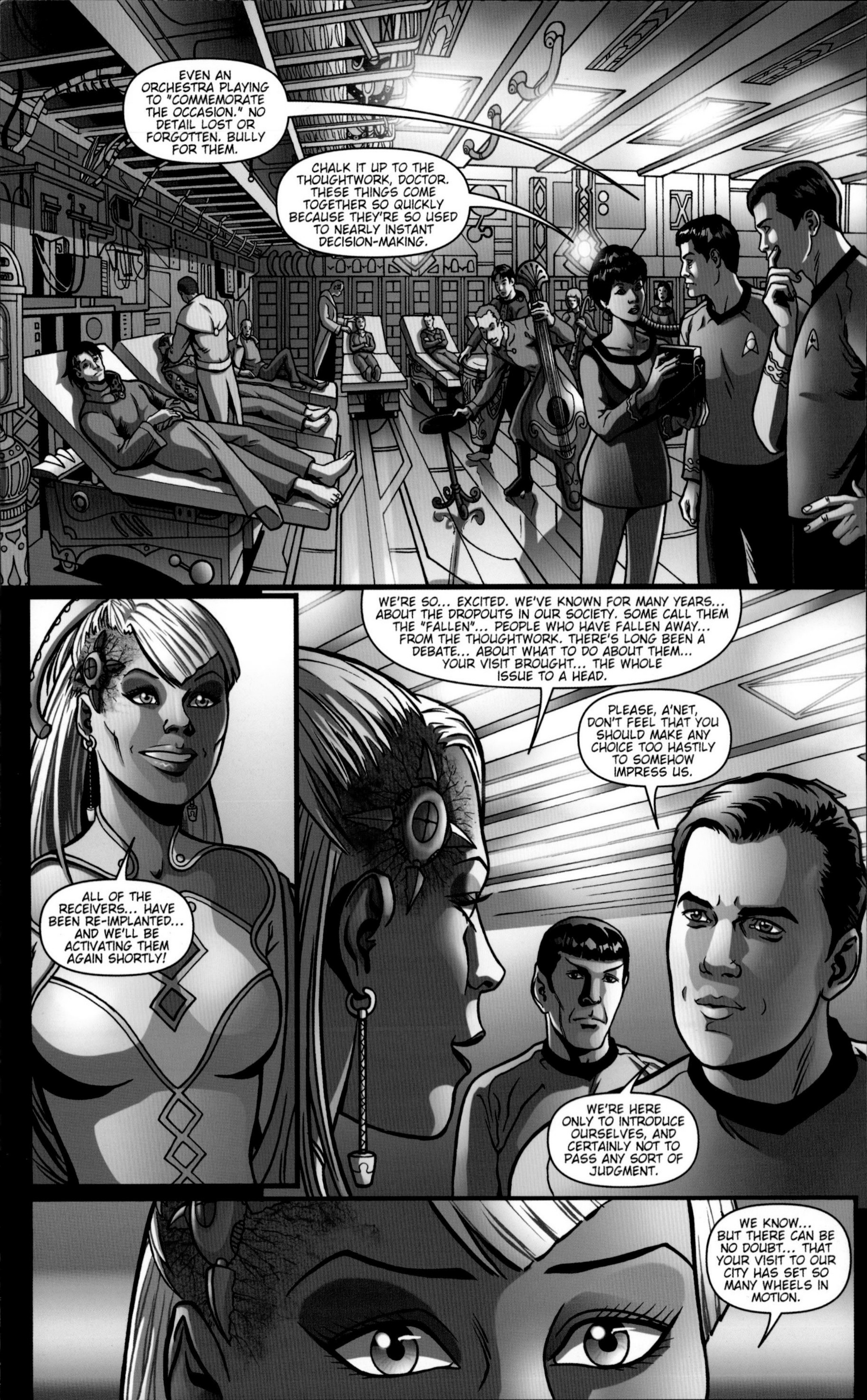
EVEN AN ORCHESTRA PLAYING TO "COMMEMORATE THE OCCASION." NO DETAIL LOST OR FORGOTTEN. BULLY FOR THEM.
CHALK IT UP TO THE THOUGHTWORK, DOCTOR. THESE THINGS COME TOGETHER SO QUICKLY BECAUSE THEY'RE SO USED TO NEARLY INSTANT DECISION-MAKING.
ALL OF THE RECEIVERS... HAVE BEEN RE-IMPLANTED... AND WE'LL BE ACTIVATING THEM AGAIN SHORTLY!
WE'RE SO... EXCITED. WE'VE KNOWN FOR MANY YEARS... ABOUT THE DROPOUTS IN OUR SOCIETY. SOME CALL THEM THE "FALLEN"... PEOPLE WHO HAVE FALLEN AWAY... FROM THE THOUGHTWORK. THERE'S LONG BEEN A DEBATE... ABOUT WHAT TO DO ABOUT THEM... YOUR VISIT BROUGHT... THE WHOLE ISSUE TO A HEAD.
PLEASE, A'NET, DON'T FEEL THAT YOU SHOULD MAKE ANY CHOICE TOO HASTILY TO SOMEHOW IMPRESS US.
WE'RE HERE ONLY TO INTRODUCE OURSELVES, AND CERTAINLY NOT TO PASS ANY SORT OF JUDGMENT.
WE KNOW... BUT THERE CAN BE NO DOUBT... THAT YOUR VISIT TO OUR CITY HAS SET SO MANY WHEELS IN MOTION.

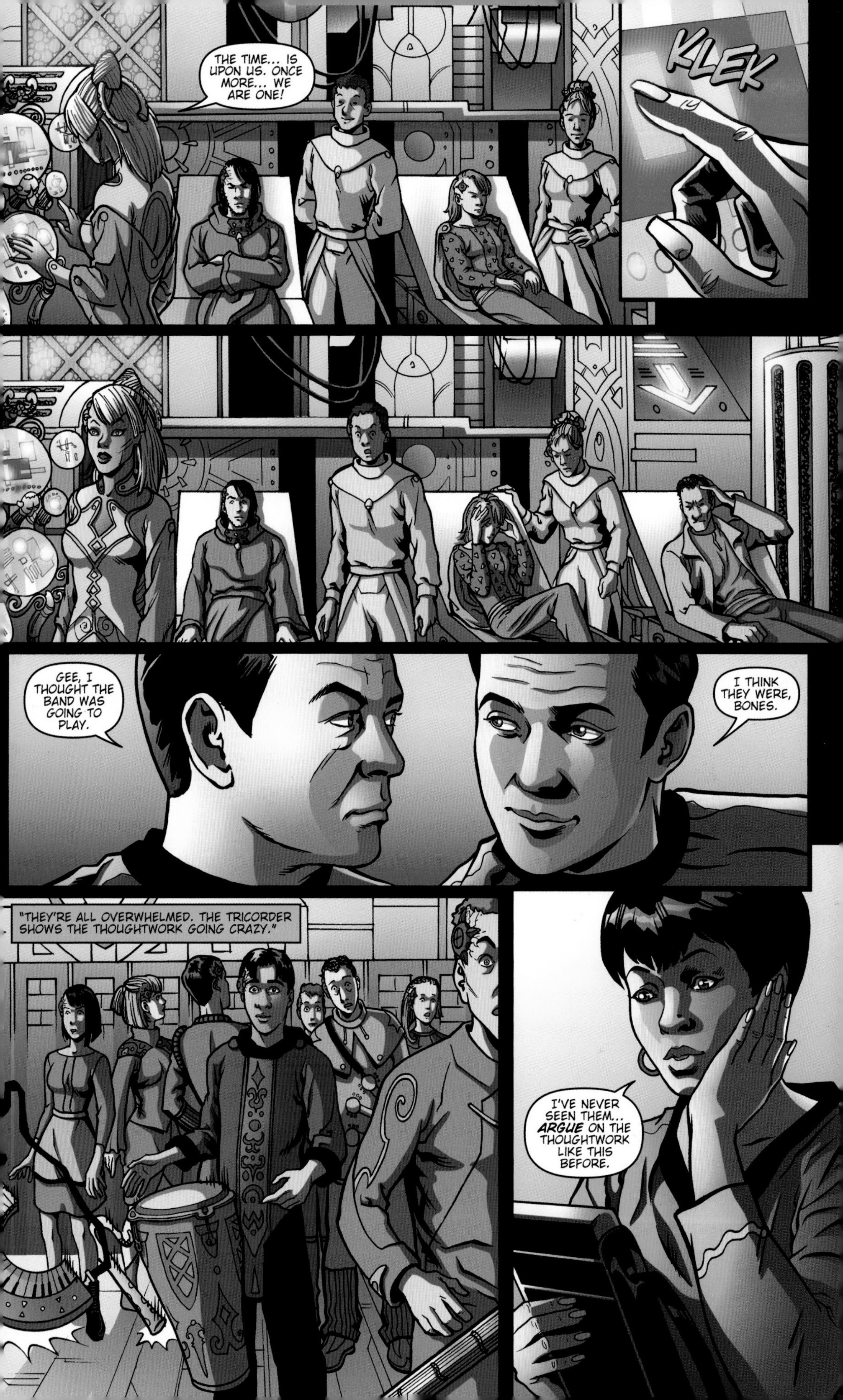
THE TIME... IS UPON US. ONCE MORE... WE ARE ONE!
KLEK
GEE, I THOUGHT THE BAND WAS GOING TO PLAY.
I THINK THEY WERE, BONES.
"THEY'RE ALL OVERWHELMED. THE TRICORDER SHOWS THE THOUGHTWORK GOING CRAZY."
I'VE NEVER SEEN THEM... ARGUE ON THE THOUGHTWORK LIKE THIS BEFORE.

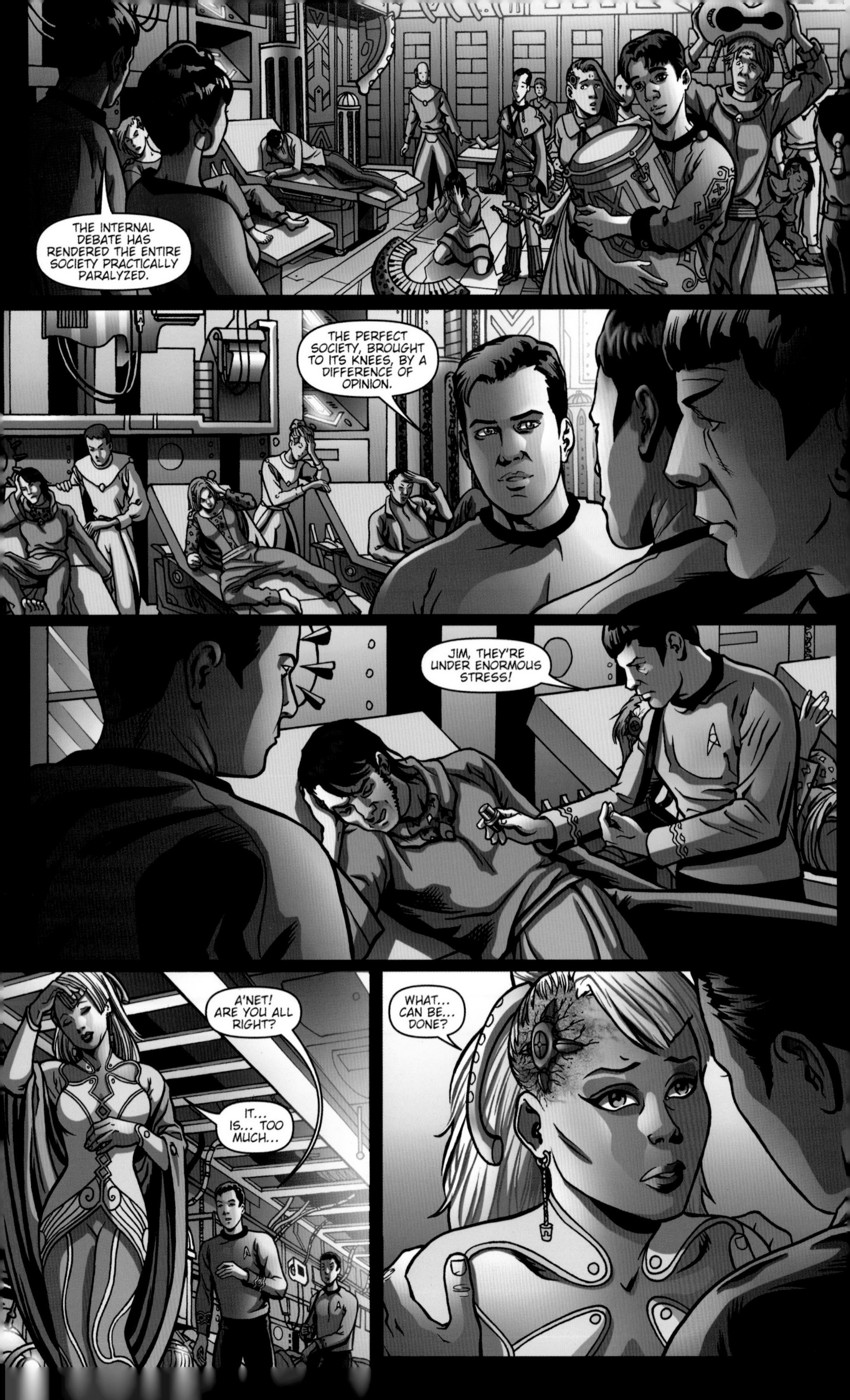
THE INTERNAL DEBATE HAS RENDERED THE ENTIRE SOCIETY PRACTICALLY PARALYZED.
THE PERFECT SOCIETY, BROUGHT TO ITS KNEES, BY A DIFFERENCE OF OPINION.
JIM, THEY'RE UNDER ENORMOUS STRESS!
A'NET! ARE YOU ALL RIGHT?
IT... IS... TOO MUCH...
WHAT... CAN BE... DONE?

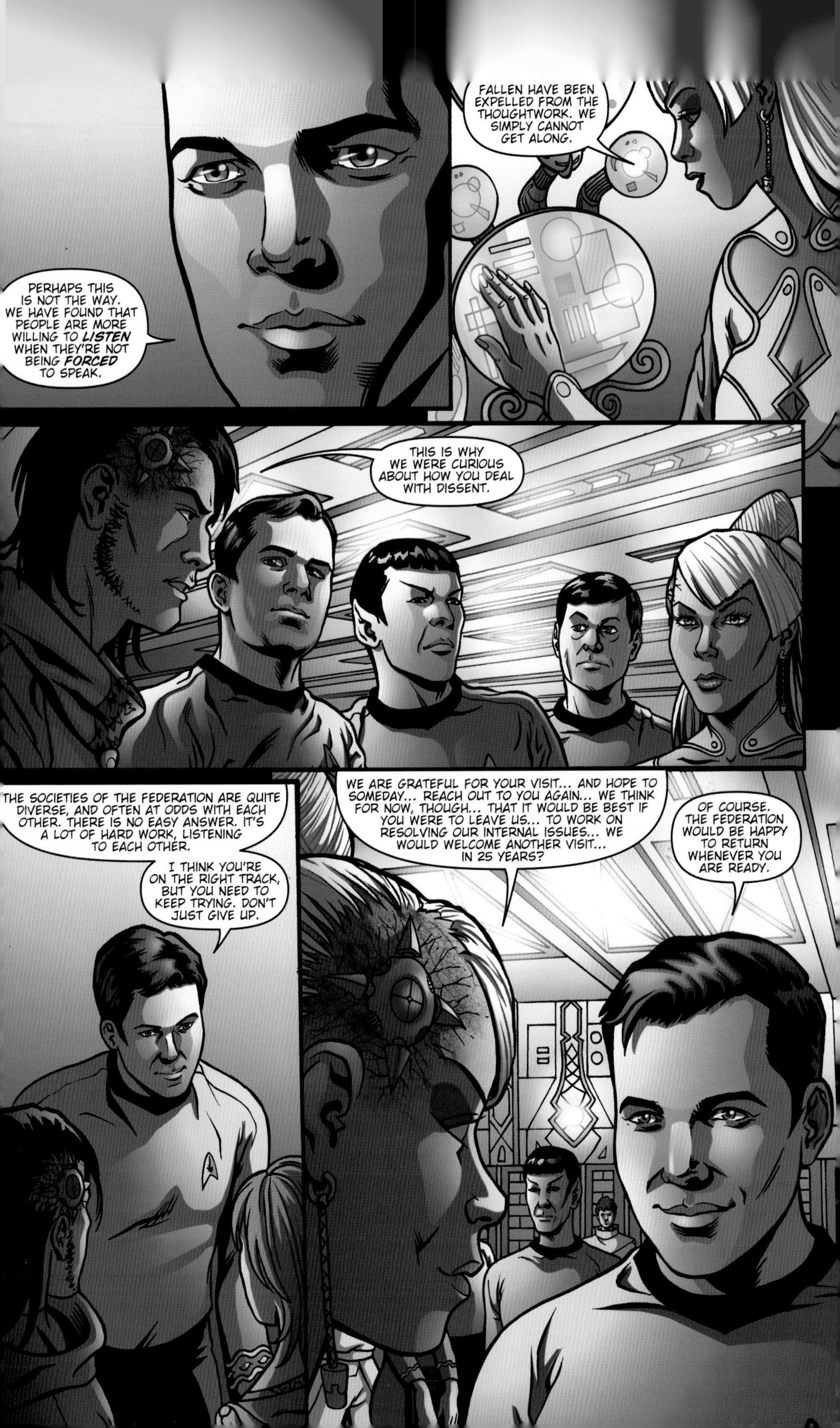
FALLEN HAVE BEEN EXPELLED FROM THE THOUGHTWORK. WE SIMPLY CANNOT GET ALONG.
PERHAPS THIS IS NOT THE WAY. WE HAVE FOUND THAT PEOPLE ARE MORE WILLING TO LISTEN WHEN THEY'RE NOT BEING FORCED TO SPEAK.
THIS IS WHY WE WERE CURIOUS ABOUT HOW YOU DEAL WITH DISSENT.
THE SOCIETIES OF THE FEDERATION ARE QUITE DIVERSE, AND OFTEN AT ODDS WITH EACH OTHER. THERE IS NO EASY ANSWER. IT'S A LOT OF HARD WORK, LISTENING TO EACH OTHER.
I THINK YOU'RE ON THE RIGHT TRACK, BUT YOU NEED TO KEEP TRYING. DON'T JUST GIVE UP.
WE ARE GRATEFUL FOR YOUR VISIT... AND HOPE TO SOMEDAY... REACH OUT TO YOU AGAIN... WE THINK FOR NOW, THOUGH... THAT IT WOULD BE BEST IF YOU WERE TO LEAVE US... TO WORK ON RESOLVING OUR INTERNAL ISSUES... WE WOULD WELCOME ANOTHER VISIT... IN 25 YEARS?
OF COURSE. THE FEDERATION WOULD BE HAPPY TO RETURN WHENEVER YOU ARE READY.

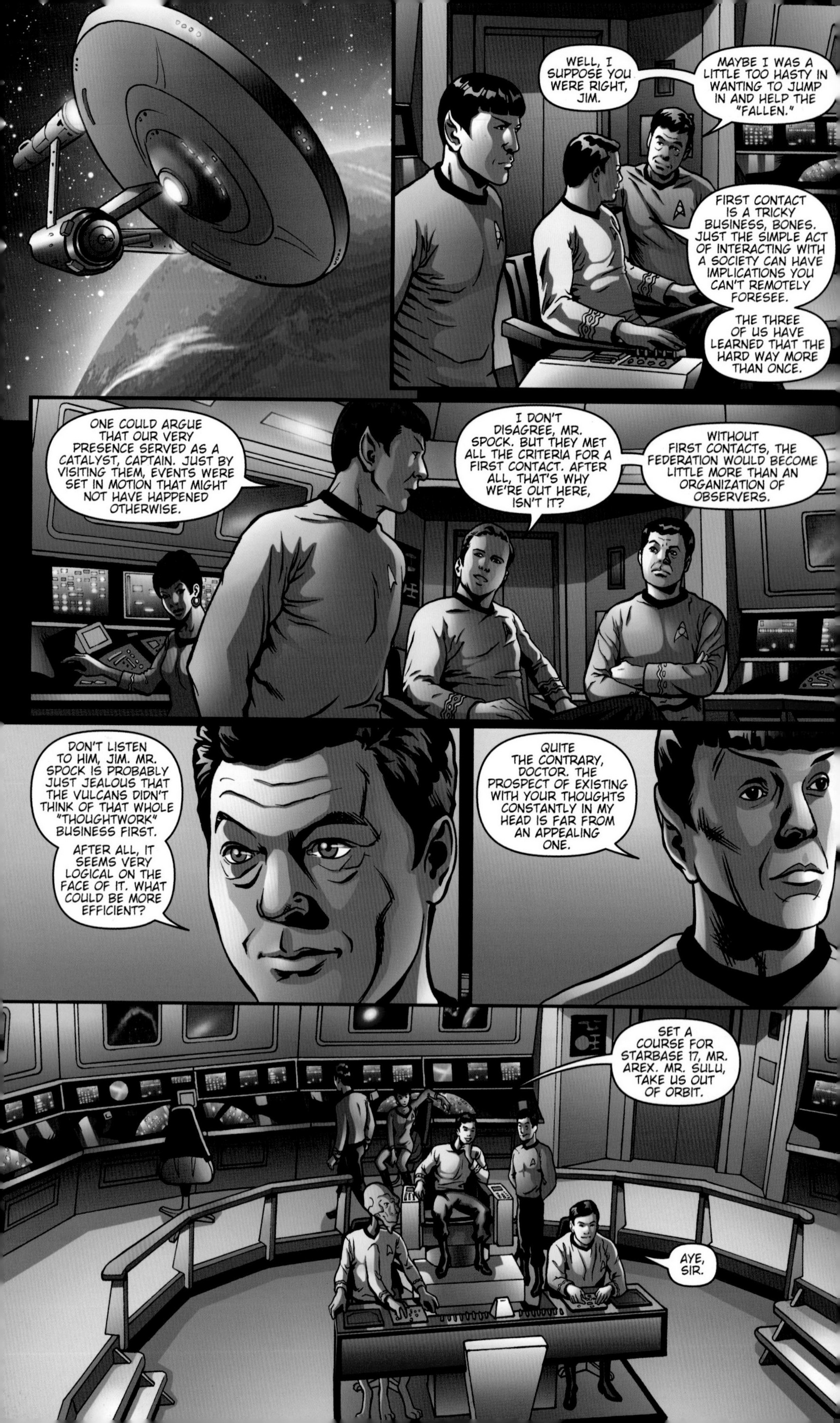
WELL, I SUPPOSE YOU WERE RIGHT, JIM.
MAYBE I WAS A LITTLE TOO HASTY IN WANTING TO JUMP IN AND HELP THE "FALLEN."
FIRST CONTACT IS A TRICKY BUSINESS, BONES. JUST THE SIMPLE ACT OF INTERACTING WITH A SOCIETY CAN HAVE IMPLICATIONS YOU CAN'T REMOTELY FORESEE.
THE THREE OF US HAVE LEARNED THAT THE HARD WAY MORE THAN ONCE.
ONE COULD ARGUE THAT OUR VERY PRESENCE SERVED AS A CATALYST, CAPTAIN. JUST BY VISITING THEM, EVENTS WERE SET IN MOTION THAT MIGHT NOT HAVE HAPPENED OTHERWISE.
I DON'T DISAGREE, MR. SPOCK. BUT THEY MET ALL THE CRITERIA FOR A FIRST CONTACT. AFTER ALL, THAT'S WHY WE'RE OUT HERE, ISN'T IT?
WITHOUT FIRST CONTACTS, THE FEDERATION WOULD BECOME LITTLE MORE THAN AN ORGANIZATION OF OBSERVERS.
DON'T LISTEN TO HIM, JIM. MR. SPOCK IS PROBABLY JUST JEALOUS THAT THE VULCANS DIDN'T THINK OF THAT WHOLE "THOUGHTWORK" BUSINESS FIRST.
AFTER ALL, IT SEEMS VERY LOGICAL ON THE FACE OF IT. WHAT COULD BE MORE EFFICIENT?
QUITE THE CONTRARY, DOCTOR. THE PROSPECT OF EXISTING WITH YOUR THOUGHTS CONSTANTLY IN MY HEAD IS FAR FROM AN APPEALING ONE.
SET A COURSE FOR STARBASE 17, MR. AREX. MR. SULU, TAKE US OUT OF ORBIT.
AYE, SIR.

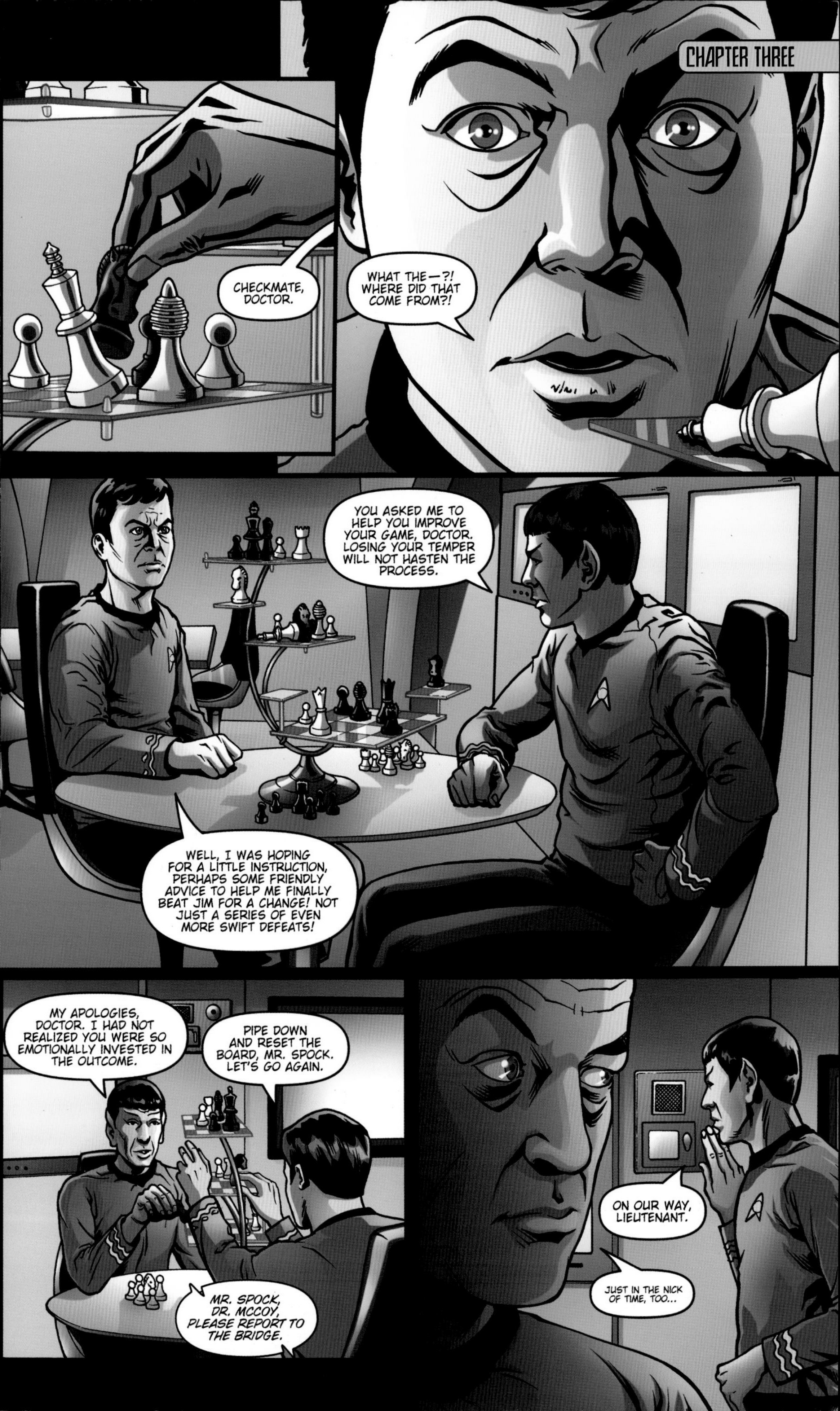
CHAPTER THREE
CHECKMATE, DOCTOR.
WHAT THE—?! WHERE DID THAT COME FROM?!
YOU ASKED ME TO HELP YOU IMPROVE YOUR GAME, DOCTOR. LOSING YOUR TEMPER WILL NOT HASTEN THE PROCESS.
WELL, I WAS HOPING FOR A LITTLE INSTRUCTION, PERHAPS SOME FRIENDLY ADVICE TO HELP ME FINALLY BEAT JIM FOR A CHANGE! NOT JUST A SERIES OF EVEN MORE SWIFT DEFEATS!
MY APOLOGIES, DOCTOR. I HAD NOT REALIZED YOU WERE SO EMOTIONALLY INVESTED IN THE OUTCOME.
PIPE DOWN AND RESET THE BOARD, MR. SPOCK. LET'S GO AGAIN.
MR. SPOCK, DR. MCCOY, PLEASE REPORT TO THE BRIDGE.
ON OUR WAY, LIEUTENANT.
JUST IN THE NICK OF TIME, TOO...

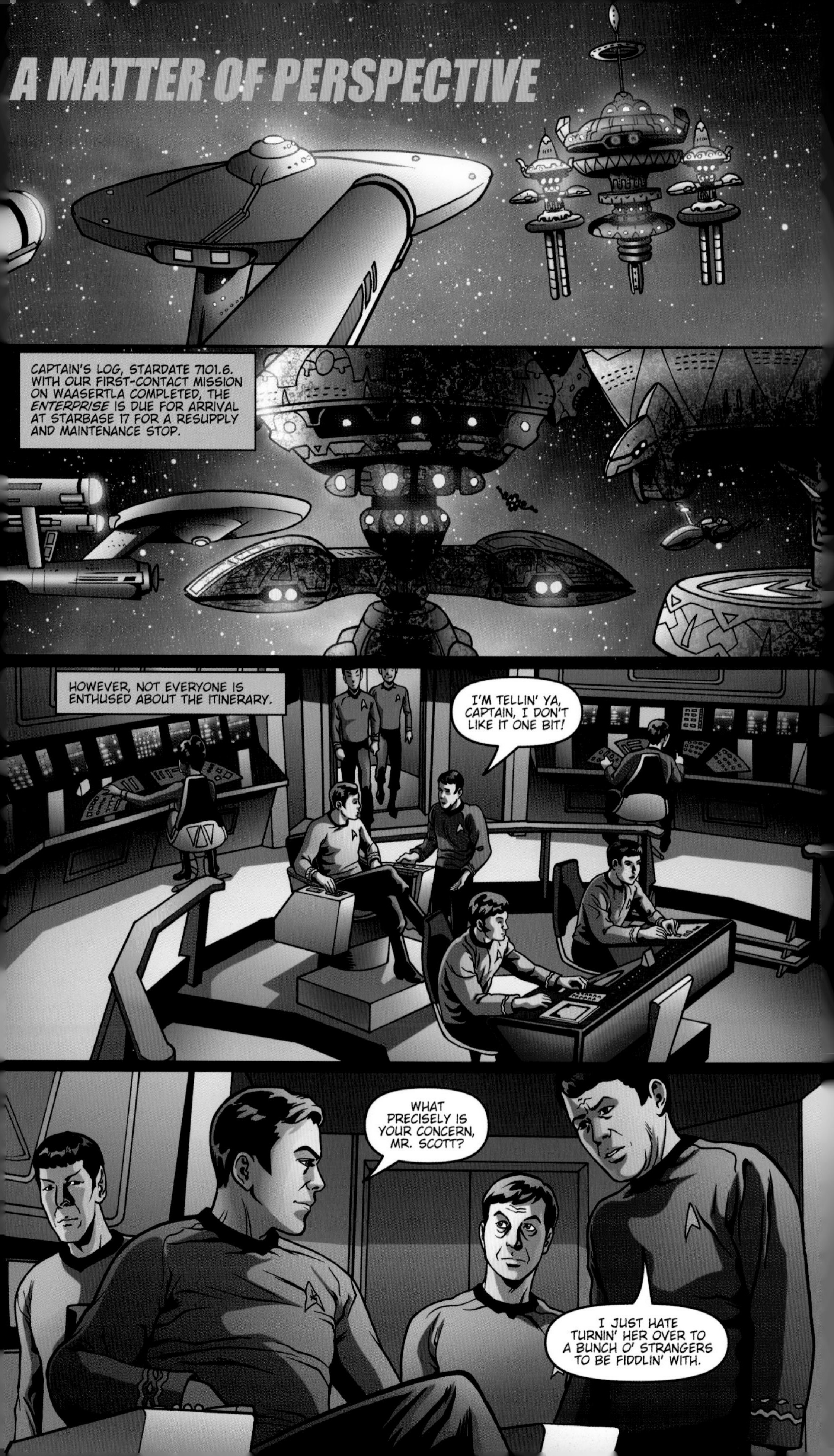
A MATTER OF PERSPECTIVE
CAPTAIN'S LOG, STARDATE 7101.6. WITH OUR FIRST-CONTACT MISSION ON WAASERTLA COMPLETED, THE *ENTERPRISE* IS DUE FOR ARRIVAL AT STARBASE 17 FOR A RESUPPLY AND MAINTENANCE STOP.
HOWEVER, NOT EVERYONE IS ENTHUSED ABOUT THE ITINERARY.
I'M TELLIN' YA, CAPTAIN, I DON'T LIKE IT ONE BIT!
WHAT PRECISELY IS YOUR CONCERN, MR. SCOTT?
I JUST HATE TURNIN' HER OVER TO A BUNCH O' STRANGERS TO BE FIDDLIN' WITH.

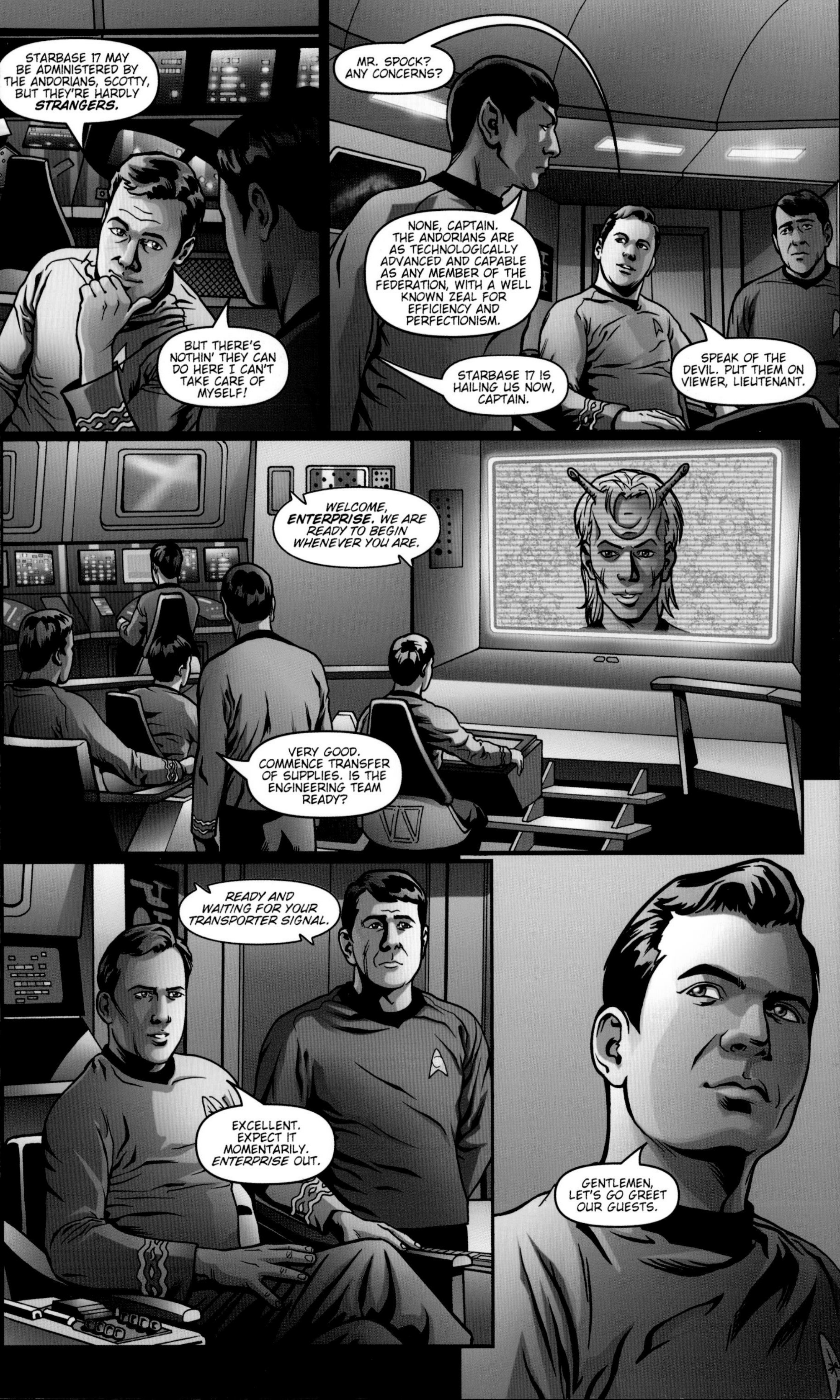
STARBASE 17 MAY BE ADMINISTERED BY THE ANDORIANS, SCOTTY, BUT THEY'RE HARDLY STRANGERS.
BUT THERE'S NOTHIN' THEY CAN DO HERE I CAN'T TAKE CARE OF MYSELF!
MR. SPOCK? ANY CONCERNS?
NONE, CAPTAIN. THE ANDORIANS ARE AS TECHNOLOGICALLY ADVANCED AND CAPABLE AS ANY MEMBER OF THE FEDERATION, WITH A WELL KNOWN ZEAL FOR EFFICIENCY AND PERFECTIONISM.
STARBASE 17 IS HAILING US NOW, CAPTAIN.
SPEAK OF THE DEVIL. PUT THEM ON VIEWER, LIEUTENANT.
WELCOME, ENTERPRISE. WE ARE READY TO BEGIN WHENEVER YOU ARE.
VERY GOOD. COMMENCE TRANSFER OF SUPPLIES. IS THE ENGINEERING TEAM READY?
READY AND WAITING FOR YOUR TRANSPORTER SIGNAL.
EXCELLENT. EXPECT IT MOMENTARILY. ENTERPRISE OUT.
GENTLEMEN, LET'S GO GREET OUR GUESTS.

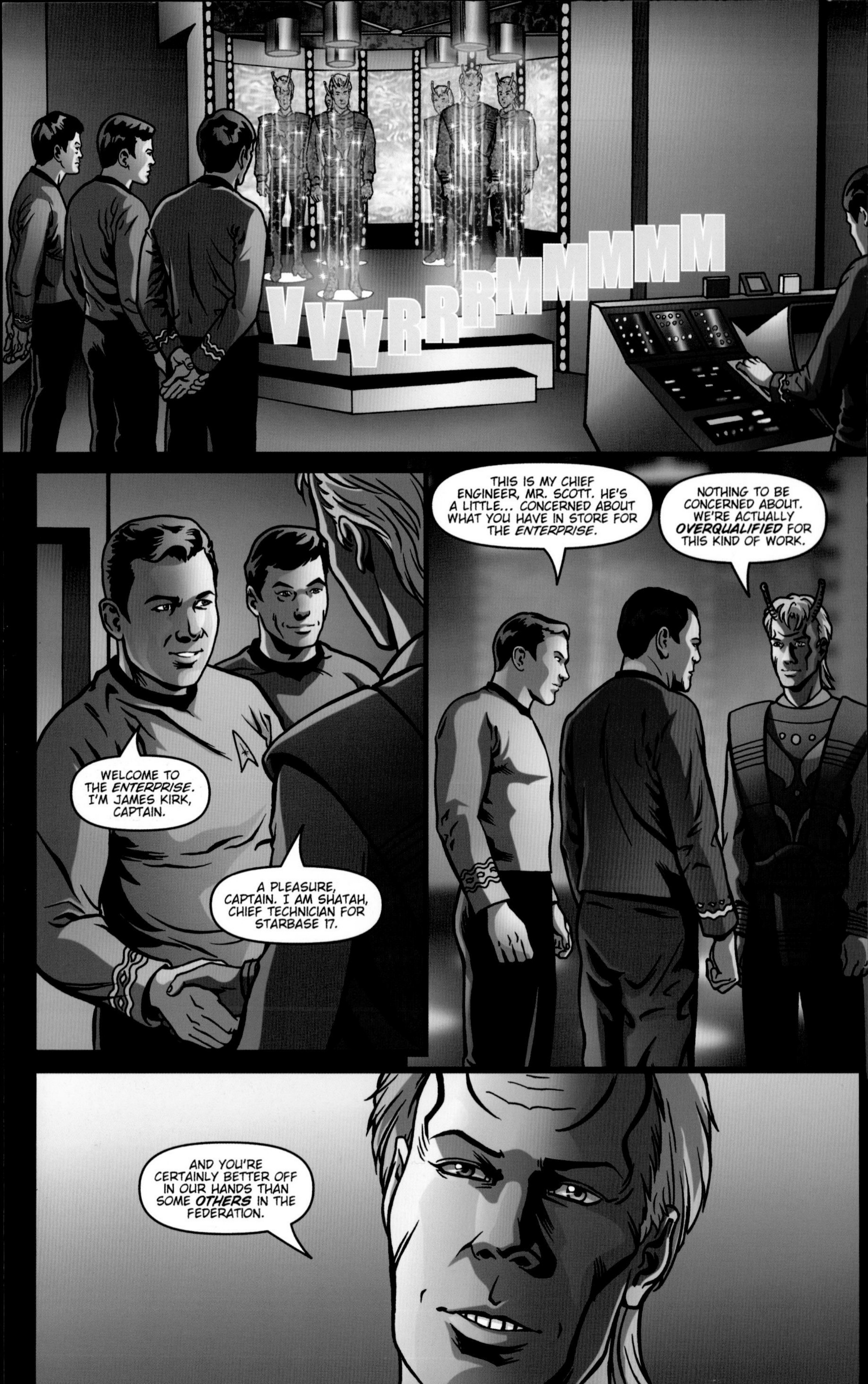
VVVRRRRMMMMMMM
WELCOME TO THE *ENTERPRISE*. I'M JAMES KIRK, CAPTAIN.
A PLEASURE, CAPTAIN. I AM SHATAH, CHIEF TECHNICIAN FOR STARBASE 17.
THIS IS MY CHIEF ENGINEER, MR. SCOTT. HE'S A LITTLE... CONCERNED ABOUT WHAT YOU HAVE IN STORE FOR THE *ENTERPRISE*.
NOTHING TO BE CONCERNED ABOUT. WE'RE ACTUALLY ***OVERQUALIFIED*** FOR THIS KIND OF WORK.
AND YOU'RE CERTAINLY BETTER OFF IN OUR HANDS THAN SOME ***OTHERS*** IN THE FEDERATION.

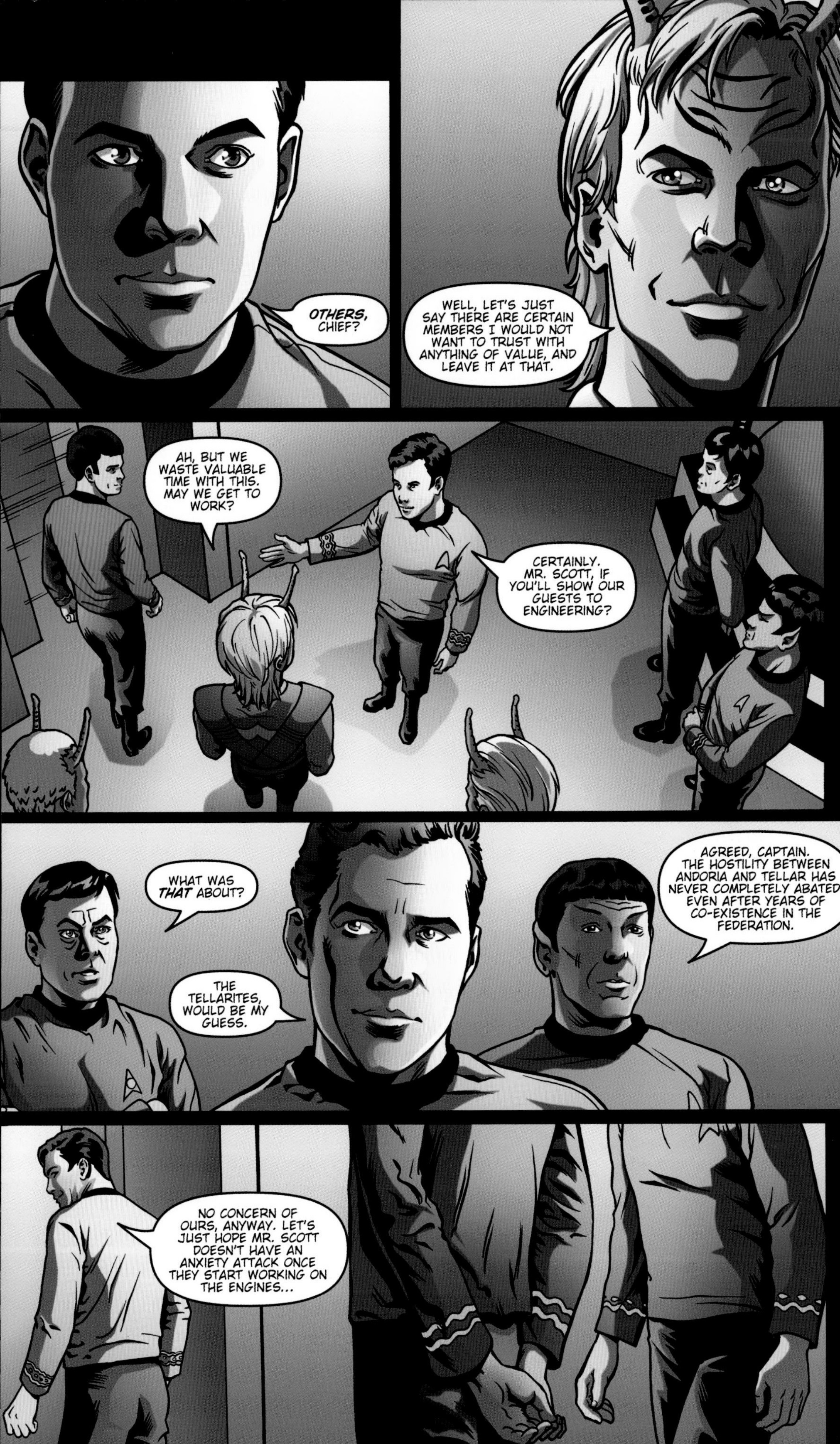
OTHERS, CHIEF?
WELL, LET'S JUST SAY THERE ARE CERTAIN MEMBERS I WOULD NOT WANT TO TRUST WITH ANYTHING OF VALUE, AND LEAVE IT AT THAT.
AH, BUT WE WASTE VALUABLE TIME WITH THIS. MAY WE GET TO WORK?
CERTAINLY. MR. SCOTT, IF YOU'LL SHOW OUR GUESTS TO ENGINEERING?
WHAT WAS *THAT* ABOUT?
THE TELLARITES, WOULD BE MY GUESS.
AGREED, CAPTAIN. THE HOSTILITY BETWEEN ANDORIA AND TELLAR HAS NEVER COMPLETELY ABATED EVEN AFTER YEARS OF CO-EXISTENCE IN THE FEDERATION.
NO CONCERN OF OURS, ANYWAY. LET'S JUST HOPE MR. SCOTT DOESN'T HAVE AN ANXIETY ATTACK ONCE THEY START WORKING ON THE ENGINES...

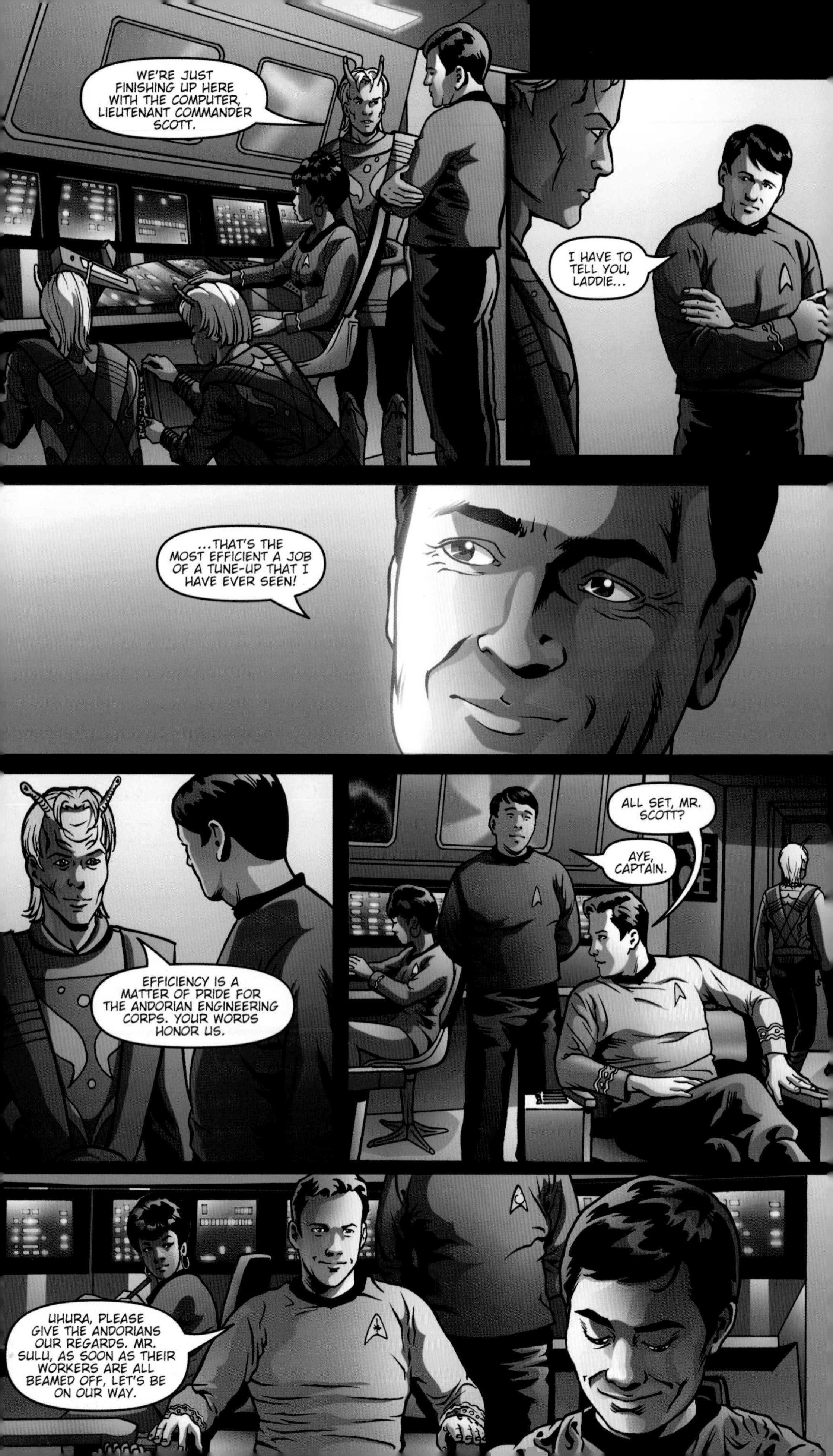
WE'RE JUST FINISHING UP HERE WITH THE COMPUTER, LIEUTENANT COMMANDER SCOTT.
I HAVE TO TELL YOU, LADDIE...
...THAT'S THE MOST EFFICIENT A JOB OF A TUNE-UP THAT I HAVE EVER SEEN!
EFFICIENCY IS A MATTER OF PRIDE FOR THE ANDORIAN ENGINEERING CORPS. YOUR WORDS HONOR US.
ALL SET, MR. SCOTT?
AYE, CAPTAIN.
UHURA, PLEASE GIVE THE ANDORIANS OUR REGARDS. MR. SULU, AS SOON AS THEIR WORKERS ARE ALL BEAMED OFF, LET'S BE ON OUR WAY.

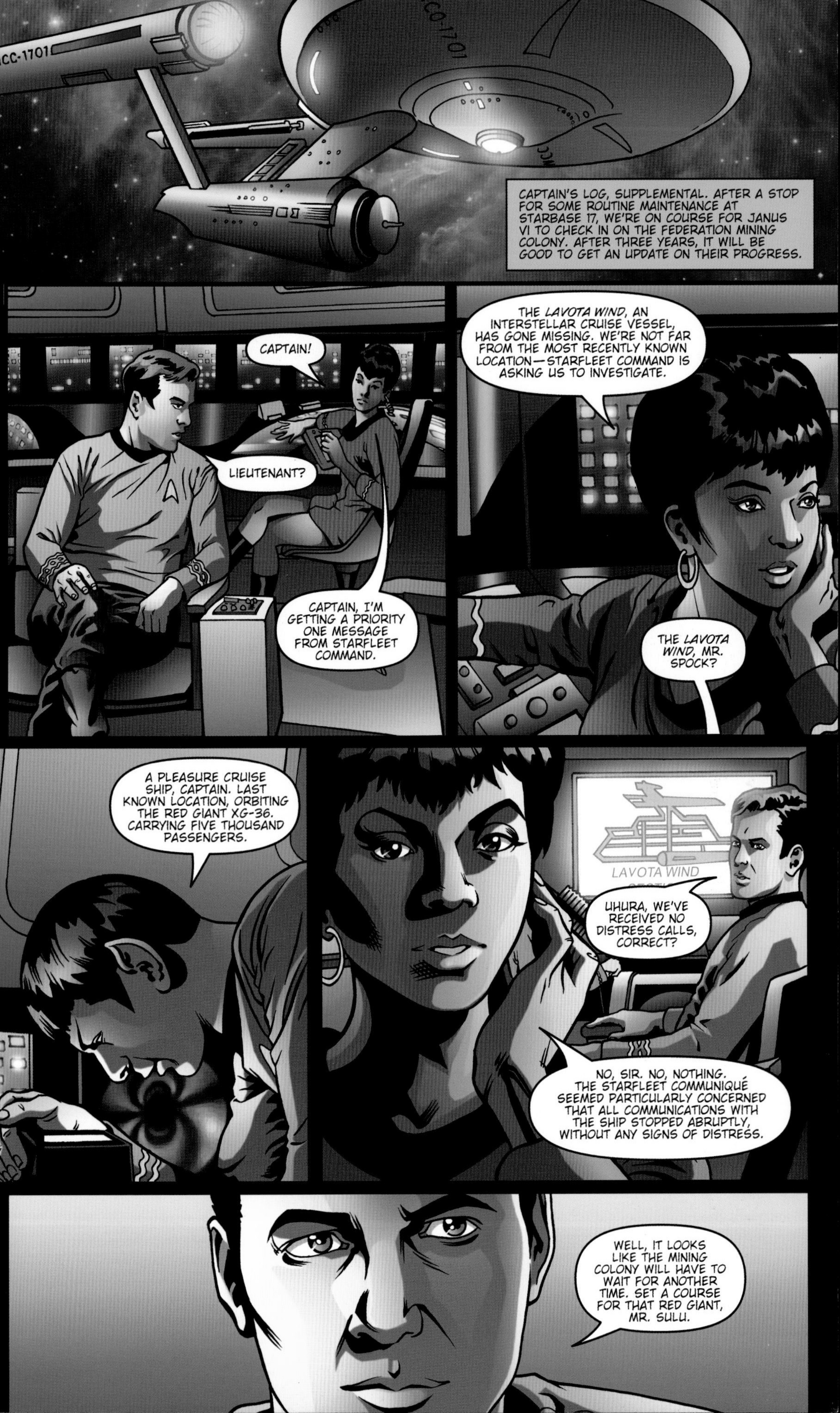
CAPTAIN'S LOG, SUPPLEMENTAL. AFTER A STOP FOR SOME ROUTINE MAINTENANCE AT STARBASE 17, WE'RE ON COURSE FOR JANUS VI TO CHECK IN ON THE FEDERATION MINING COLONY. AFTER THREE YEARS, IT WILL BE GOOD TO GET AN UPDATE ON THEIR PROGRESS.
CAPTAIN!
LIEUTENANT?
CAPTAIN, I'M GETTING A PRIORITY ONE MESSAGE FROM STARFLEET COMMAND.
THE *LAVOTA WIND*, AN INTERSTELLAR CRUISE VESSEL, HAS GONE MISSING. WE'RE NOT FAR FROM THE MOST RECENTLY KNOWN LOCATION—STARFLEET COMMAND IS ASKING US TO INVESTIGATE.
THE *LAVOTA WIND*, MR. SPOCK?
A PLEASURE CRUISE SHIP, CAPTAIN. LAST KNOWN LOCATION, ORBITING THE RED GIANT XG-36. CARRYING FIVE THOUSAND PASSENGERS.
LAVOTA WIND
UHURA, WE'VE RECEIVED NO DISTRESS CALLS, CORRECT?
NO, SIR. NO, NOTHING. THE STARFLEET COMMUNIQUÉ SEEMED PARTICULARLY CONCERNED THAT ALL COMMUNICATIONS WITH THE SHIP STOPPED ABRUPTLY, WITHOUT ANY SIGNS OF DISTRESS.
WELL, IT LOOKS LIKE THE MINING COLONY WILL HAVE TO WAIT FOR ANOTHER TIME. SET A COURSE FOR THAT RED GIANT, MR. SULU.

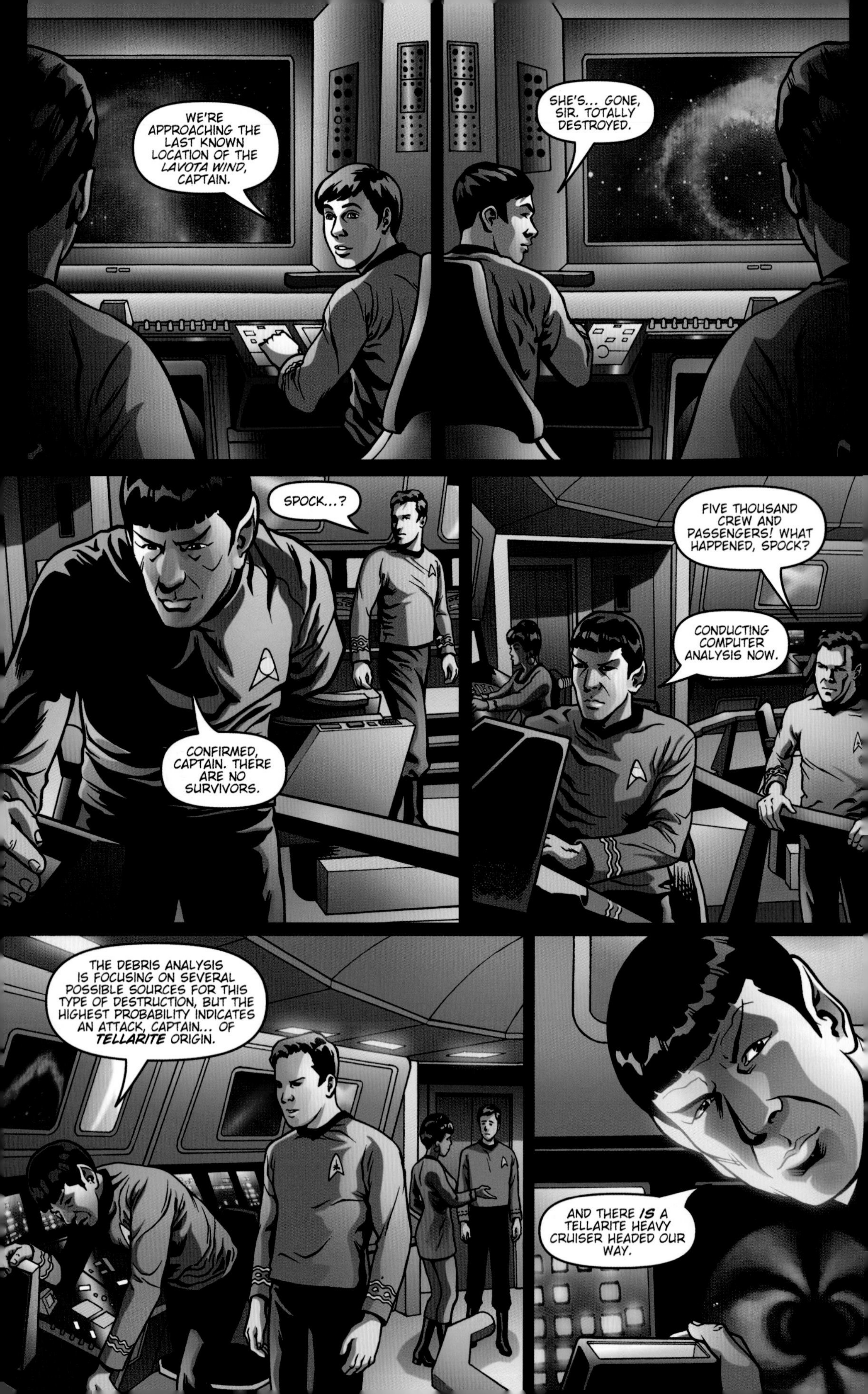
WE'RE APPROACHING THE LAST KNOWN LOCATION OF THE *LAVOTA WIND*, CAPTAIN.
SHE'S... GONE, SIR. TOTALLY DESTROYED.
SPOCK...?
CONFIRMED, CAPTAIN. THERE ARE NO SURVIVORS.
FIVE THOUSAND CREW AND PASSENGERS! WHAT HAPPENED, SPOCK?
CONDUCTING COMPUTER ANALYSIS NOW.
THE DEBRIS ANALYSIS IS FOCUSING ON SEVERAL POSSIBLE SOURCES FOR THIS TYPE OF DESTRUCTION, BUT THE HIGHEST PROBABILITY INDICATES AN ATTACK, CAPTAIN... OF ***TELLARITE*** ORIGIN.
AND THERE ***IS*** A TELLARITE HEAVY CRUISER HEADED OUR WAY.

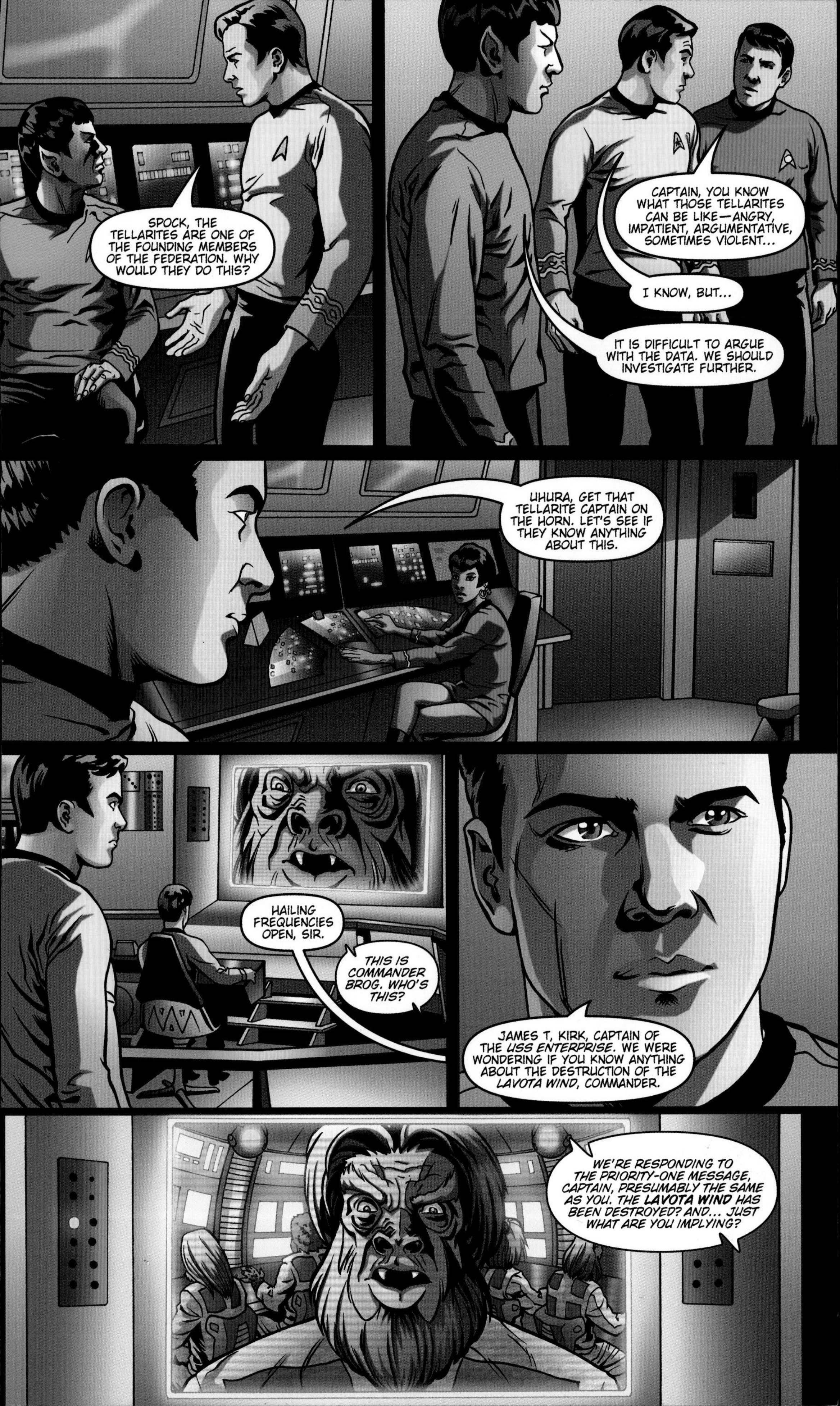
SPOCK, THE TELLARITES ARE ONE OF THE FOUNDING MEMBERS OF THE FEDERATION. WHY WOULD THEY DO THIS?
CAPTAIN, YOU KNOW WHAT THOSE TELLARITES CAN BE LIKE—ANGRY, IMPATIENT, ARGUMENTATIVE, SOMETIMES VIOLENT...
I KNOW, BUT...
IT IS DIFFICULT TO ARGUE WITH THE DATA. WE SHOULD INVESTIGATE FURTHER.
UHURA, GET THAT TELLARITE CAPTAIN ON THE HORN. LET'S SEE IF THEY KNOW ANYTHING ABOUT THIS.
HAILING FREQUENCIES OPEN, SIR.
THIS IS COMMANDER BROG. WHO'S THIS?
JAMES T, KIRK, CAPTAIN OF THE *USS ENTERPRISE*. WE WERE WONDERING IF YOU KNOW ANYTHING ABOUT THE DESTRUCTION OF THE *LAVOTA WIND*, COMMANDER.
WE'RE RESPONDING TO THE PRIORITY-ONE MESSAGE, CAPTAIN, PRESUMABLY THE SAME AS YOU. THE ***LAVOTA WIND*** *HAS BEEN DESTROYED? AND... JUST WHAT ARE YOU IMPLYING?*

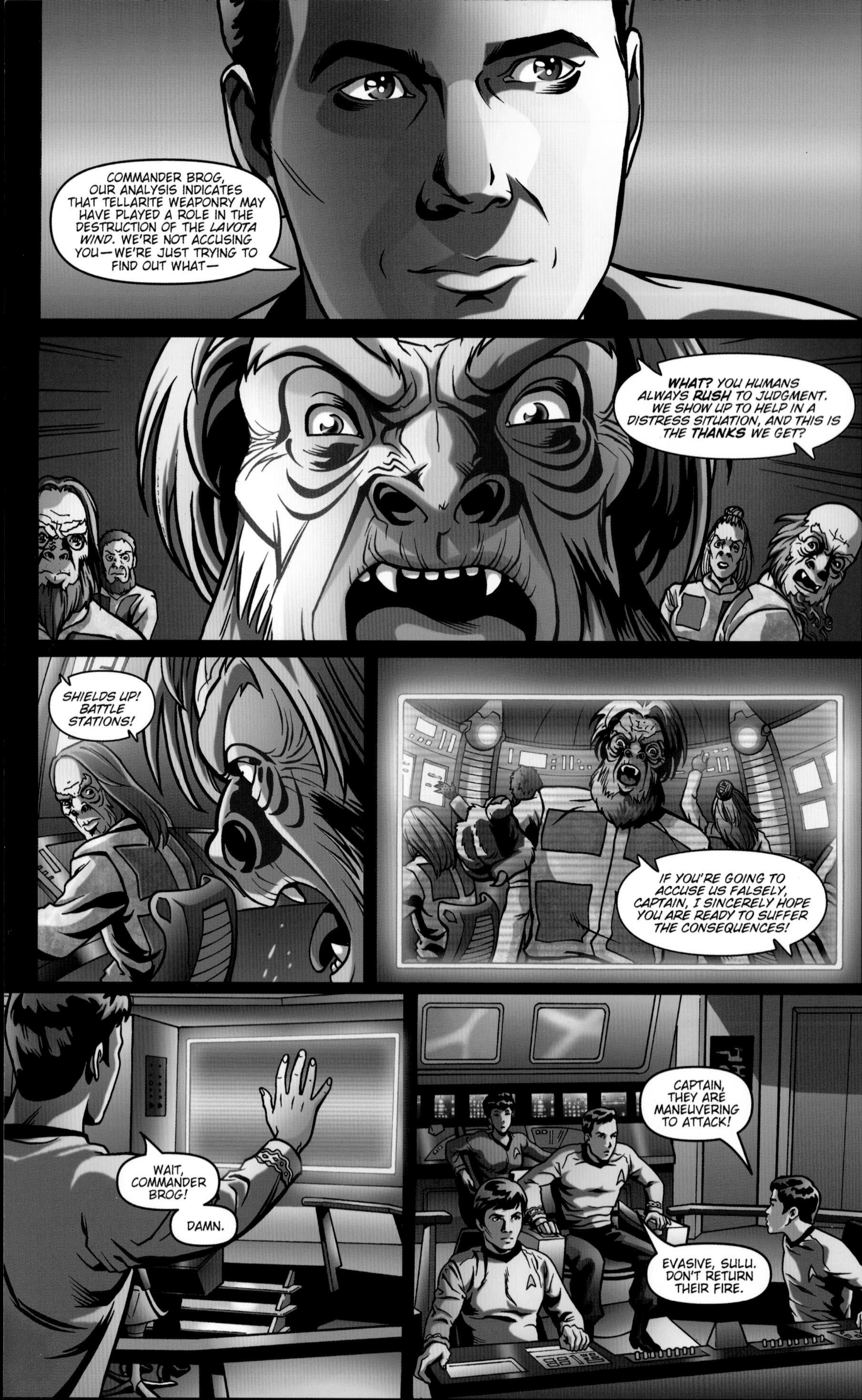
COMMANDER BROG, OUR ANALYSIS INDICATES THAT TELLARITE WEAPONRY MAY HAVE PLAYED A ROLE IN THE DESTRUCTION OF THE *LAVOTA WIND*. WE'RE NOT ACCUSING YOU—WE'RE JUST TRYING TO FIND OUT WHAT—
*WHAT? YOU HUMANS ALWAYS **RUSH** TO JUDGMENT. WE SHOW UP TO HELP IN A DISTRESS SITUATION, AND THIS IS THE **THANKS** WE GET?*
SHIELDS UP! BATTLE STATIONS!
IF YOU'RE GOING TO ACCUSE US FALSELY, CAPTAIN, I SINCERELY HOPE YOU ARE READY TO SUFFER THE CONSEQUENCES!
WAIT, COMMANDER BROG!
DAMN.
CAPTAIN, THEY ARE MANEUVERING TO ATTACK!
EVASIVE, SULU. DON'T RETURN THEIR FIRE.

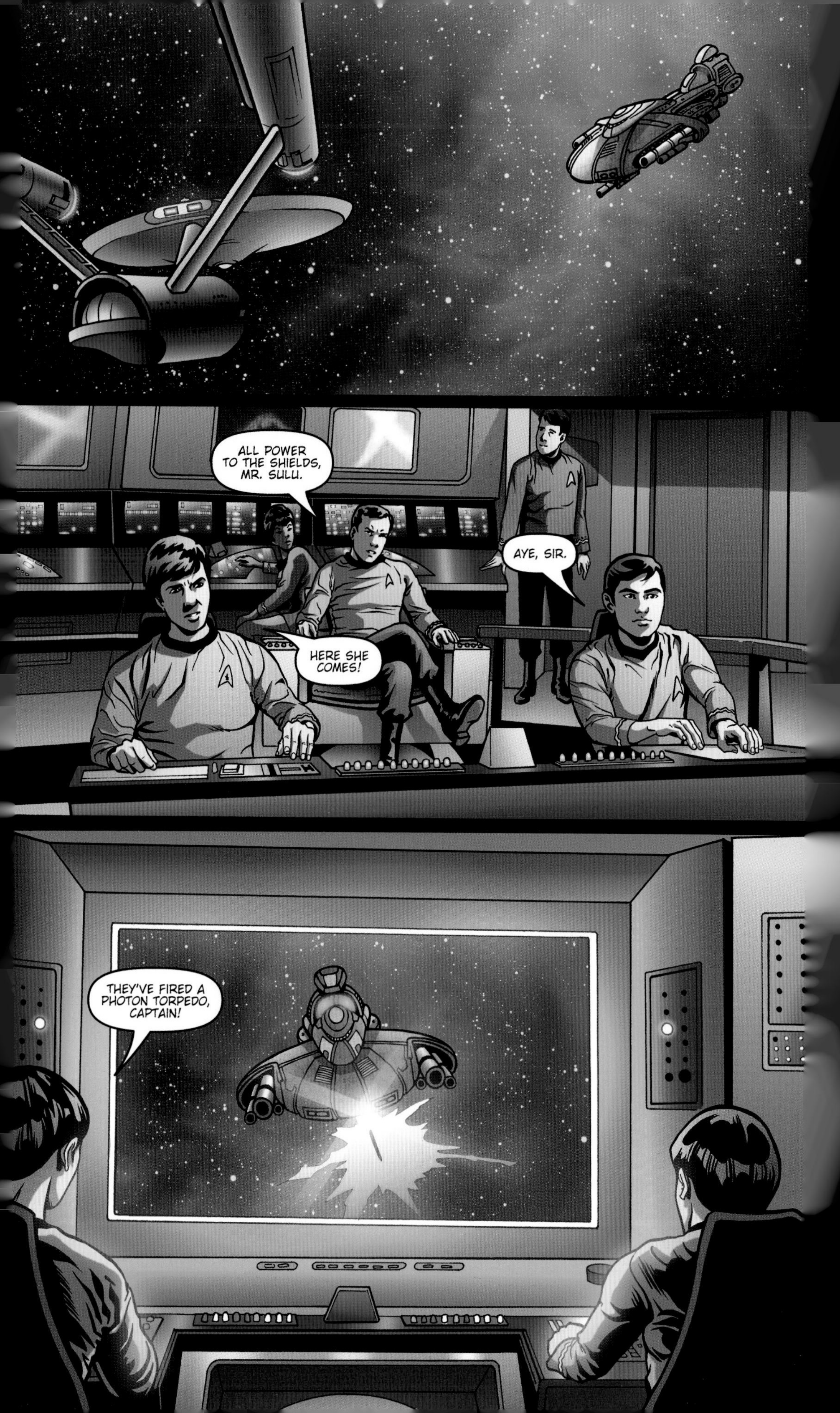
ALL POWER TO THE SHIELDS, MR. SULU.
AYE, SIR.
HERE SHE COMES!
THEY'VE FIRED A PHOTON TORPEDO, CAPTAIN!

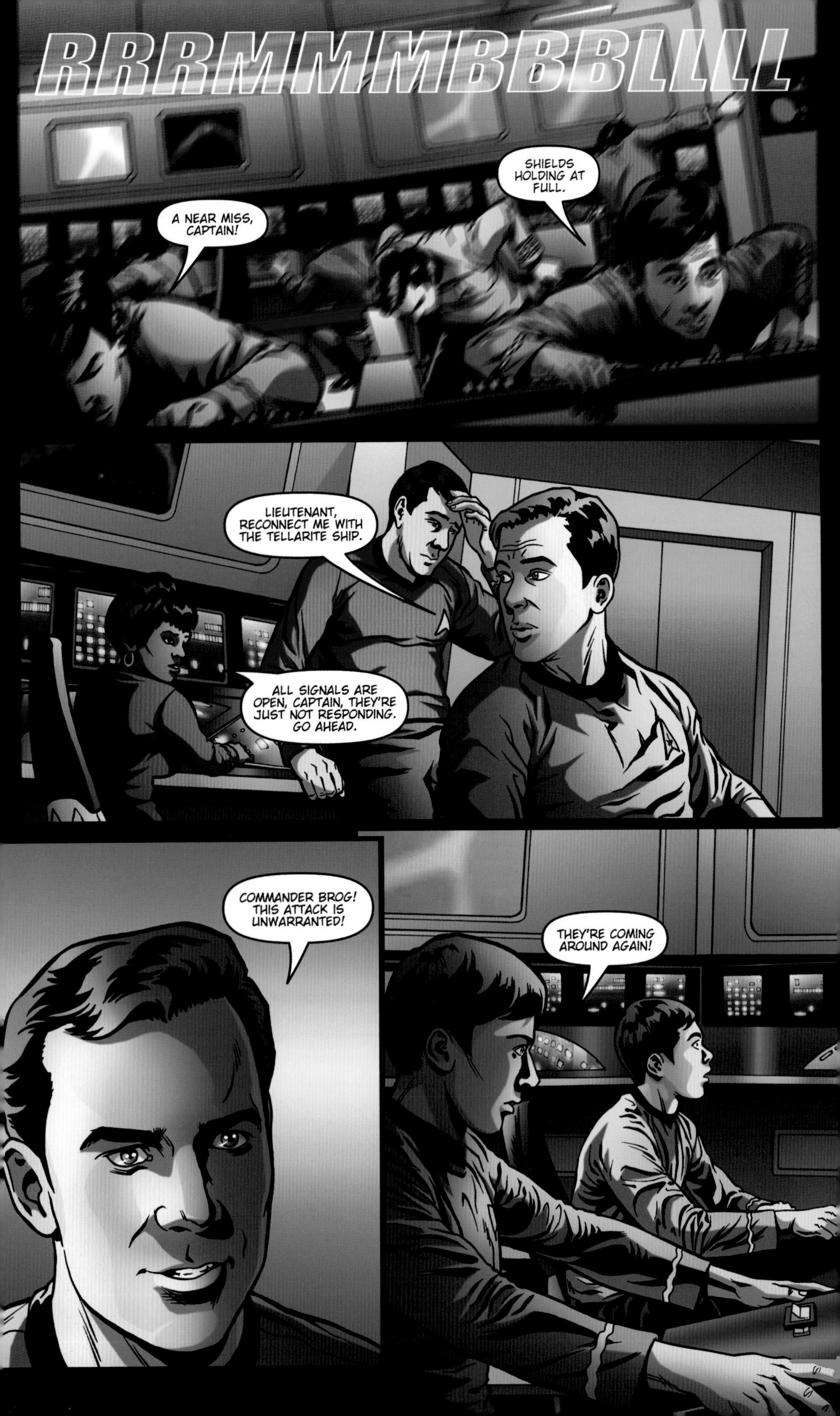
RRRMMMBBBLLLL
A NEAR MISS, CAPTAIN!
SHIELDS HOLDING AT FULL.
LIEUTENANT, RECONNECT ME WITH THE TELLARITE SHIP.
ALL SIGNALS ARE OPEN, CAPTAIN, THEY'RE JUST NOT RESPONDING. GO AHEAD.
COMMANDER BROG! THIS ATTACK IS UNWARRANTED!
THEY'RE COMING AROUND AGAIN!

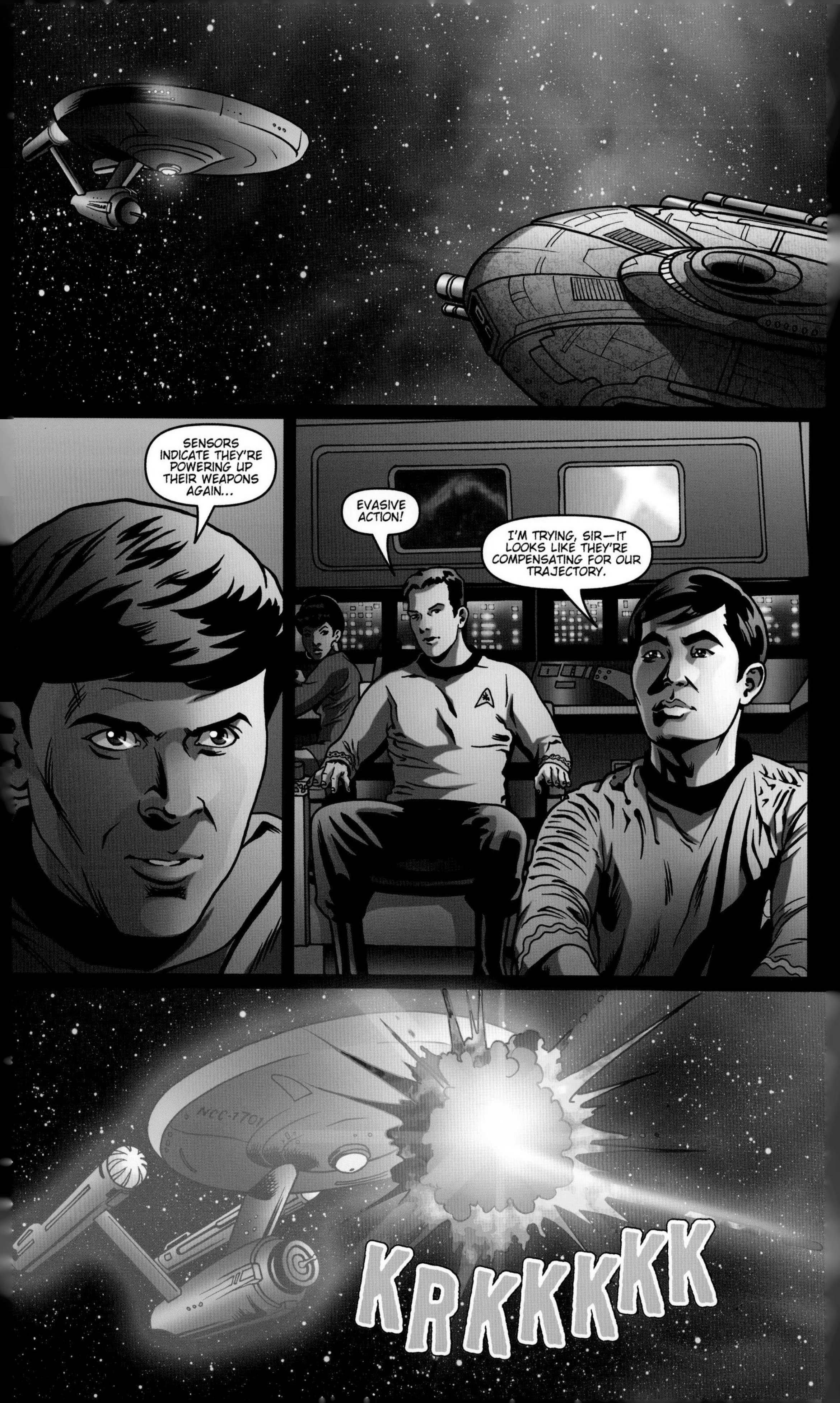
SENSORS INDICATE THEY'RE POWERING UP THEIR WEAPONS AGAIN...
EVASIVE ACTION!
I'M TRYING, SIR—IT LOOKS LIKE THEY'RE COMPENSATING FOR OUR TRAJECTORY.
NCC-1701
KRKKKKK

RRRRMMMMBBBBL

TORPEDO HIT TO THE SAUCER SECTION! SHIELDS HOLDING, CAPTAIN!

ALL RIGHT, THAT'S *ENOUGH*. SPOCK, WHAT HAVE WE GOT OUT THERE?

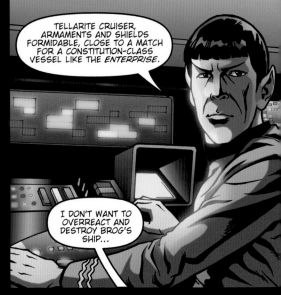

TELLARITE CRUISER, ARMAMENTS AND SHIELDS FORMIDABLE, CLOSE TO A MATCH FOR A CONSTITUTION-CLASS VESSEL LIKE THE *ENTERPRISE*.

I DON'T WANT TO OVERREACT AND DESTROY BROG'S SHIP...

ON THE OTHER HAND, THE *ENTERPRISE* CAN ONLY TAKE SO MUCH DAMAGE BEFORE I'M FORCED TO RESPOND. SPOCK, DO WE HAVE A LITTLE TIME?

AFFIRMATIVE. I ESTIMATE THAT OUR SHIELDS CAN SUSTAIN AT LEAST THREE MORE DIRECT HITS BEFORE EXHAUSTING AVAILABLE POWER.

SCOTTY, CAN YOU GIVE ME MORE THAN THAT IF WE NEED IT?

I'VE GOT CREWS WORKIN' ON IT NOW, CAPTAIN!

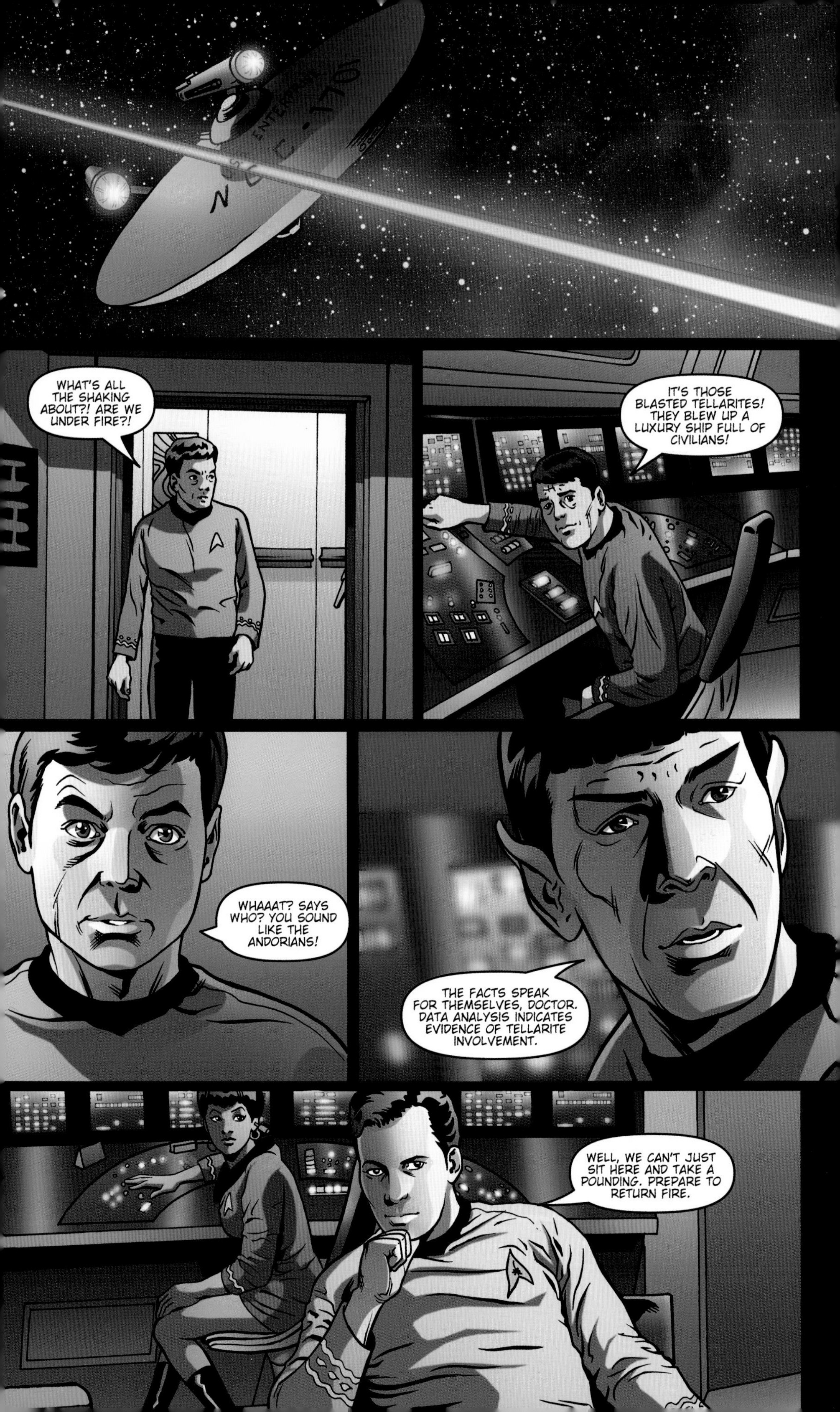
ENTERPRISE
NCC-1701
WHAT'S ALL THE SHAKING ABOUT?! ARE WE UNDER FIRE?!
IT'S THOSE BLASTED TELLARITES! THEY BLEW UP A LUXURY SHIP FULL OF CIVILIANS!
WHAAAT? SAYS WHO? YOU SOUND LIKE THE ANDORIANS!
THE FACTS SPEAK FOR THEMSELVES, DOCTOR. DATA ANALYSIS INDICATES EVIDENCE OF TELLARITE INVOLVEMENT.
WELL, WE CAN'T JUST SIT HERE AND TAKE A POUNDING. PREPARE TO RETURN FIRE.

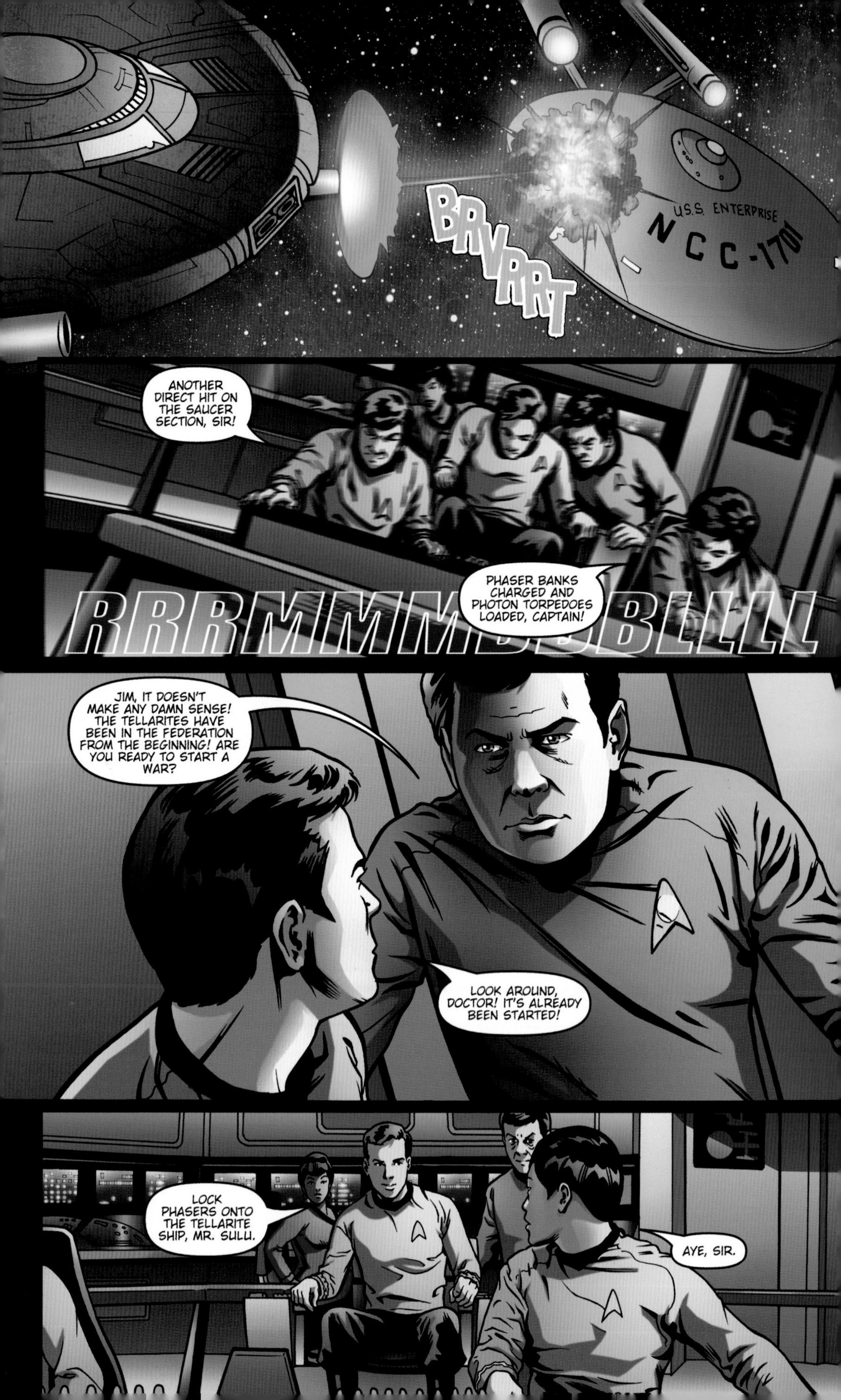
U.S.S. ENTERPRISE
NCC-1701
BRVRRRT
ANOTHER DIRECT HIT ON THE SAUCER SECTION, SIR!
RRRMMMMBBLLLL
PHASER BANKS CHARGED AND PHOTON TORPEDOES LOADED, CAPTAIN!
JIM, IT DOESN'T MAKE ANY DAMN SENSE! THE TELLARITES HAVE BEEN IN THE FEDERATION FROM THE BEGINNING! ARE YOU READY TO START A WAR?
LOOK AROUND, DOCTOR! IT'S ALREADY BEEN STARTED!
LOCK PHASERS ONTO THE TELLARITE SHIP, MR. SULU.
AYE, SIR.

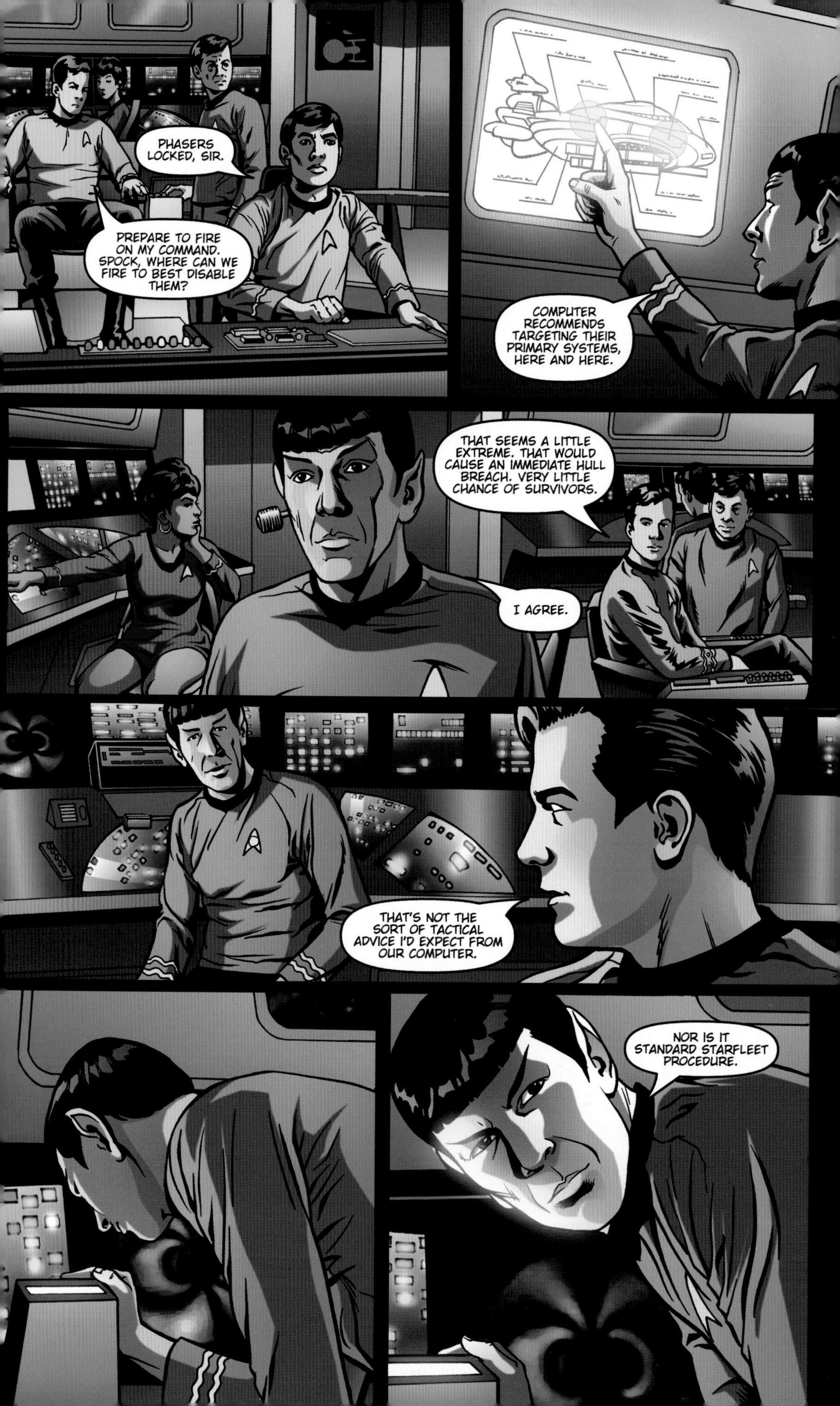
PHASERS LOCKED, SIR.
PREPARE TO FIRE ON MY COMMAND. SPOCK, WHERE CAN WE FIRE TO BEST DISABLE THEM?
COMPUTER RECOMMENDS TARGETING THEIR PRIMARY SYSTEMS, HERE AND HERE.
THAT SEEMS A LITTLE EXTREME. THAT WOULD CAUSE AN IMMEDIATE HULL BREACH. VERY LITTLE CHANCE OF SURVIVORS.
I AGREE.
THAT'S NOT THE SORT OF TACTICAL ADVICE I'D EXPECT FROM OUR COMPUTER.
NOR IS IT STANDARD STARFLEET PROCEDURE.

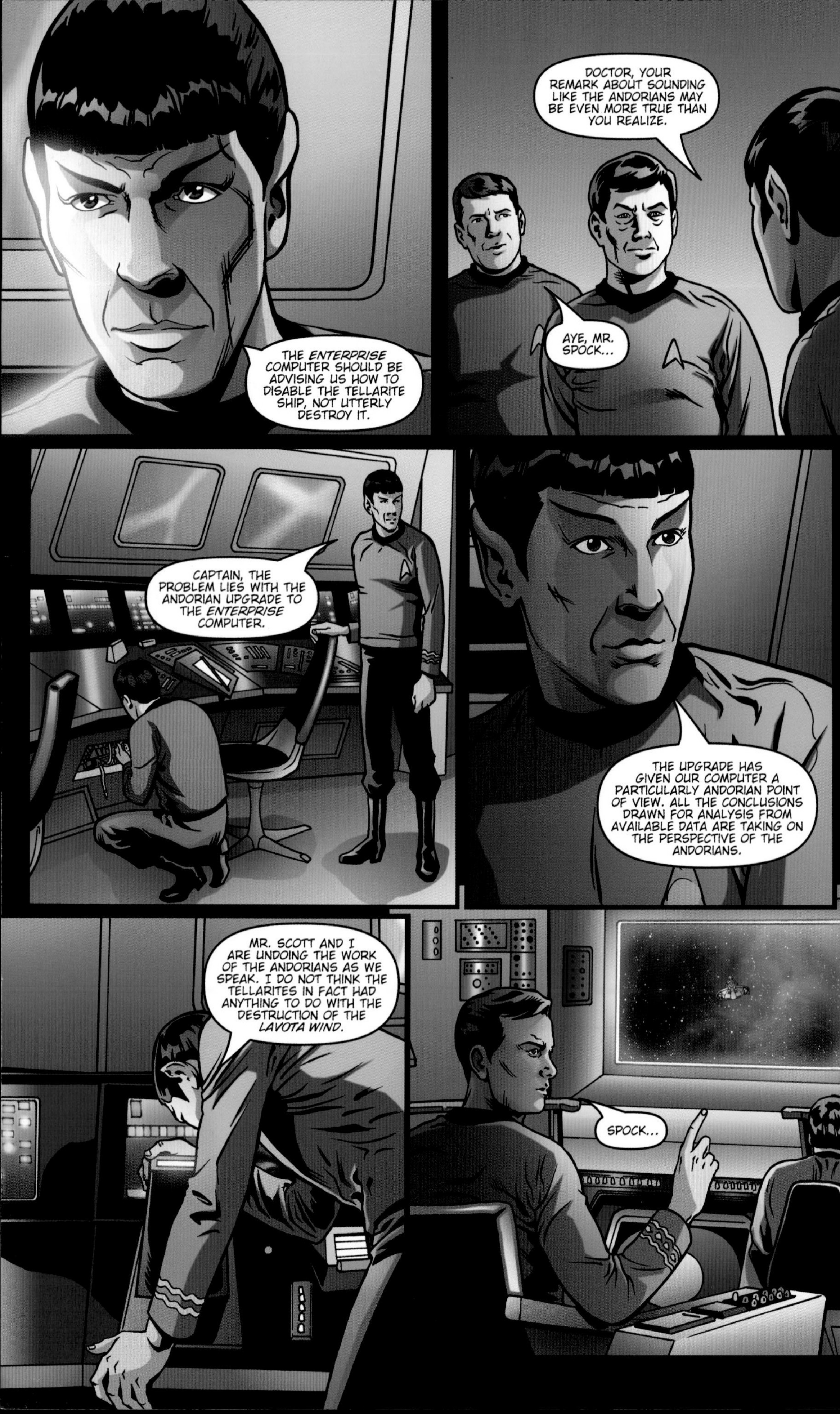
THE *ENTERPRISE* COMPUTER SHOULD BE ADVISING US HOW TO DISABLE THE TELLARITE SHIP, NOT UTTERLY DESTROY IT.
DOCTOR, YOUR REMARK ABOUT SOUNDING LIKE THE ANDORIANS MAY BE EVEN MORE TRUE THAN YOU REALIZE.
AYE, MR. SPOCK...
CAPTAIN, THE PROBLEM LIES WITH THE ANDORIAN UPGRADE TO THE *ENTERPRISE* COMPUTER.
THE UPGRADE HAS GIVEN OUR COMPUTER A PARTICULARLY ANDORIAN POINT OF VIEW. ALL THE CONCLUSIONS DRAWN FOR ANALYSIS FROM AVAILABLE DATA ARE TAKING ON THE PERSPECTIVE OF THE ANDORIANS.
MR. SCOTT AND I ARE UNDOING THE WORK OF THE ANDORIANS AS WE SPEAK. I DO NOT THINK THE TELLARITES IN FACT HAD ANYTHING TO DO WITH THE DESTRUCTION OF THE *LAVOTA WIND*.
SPOCK...

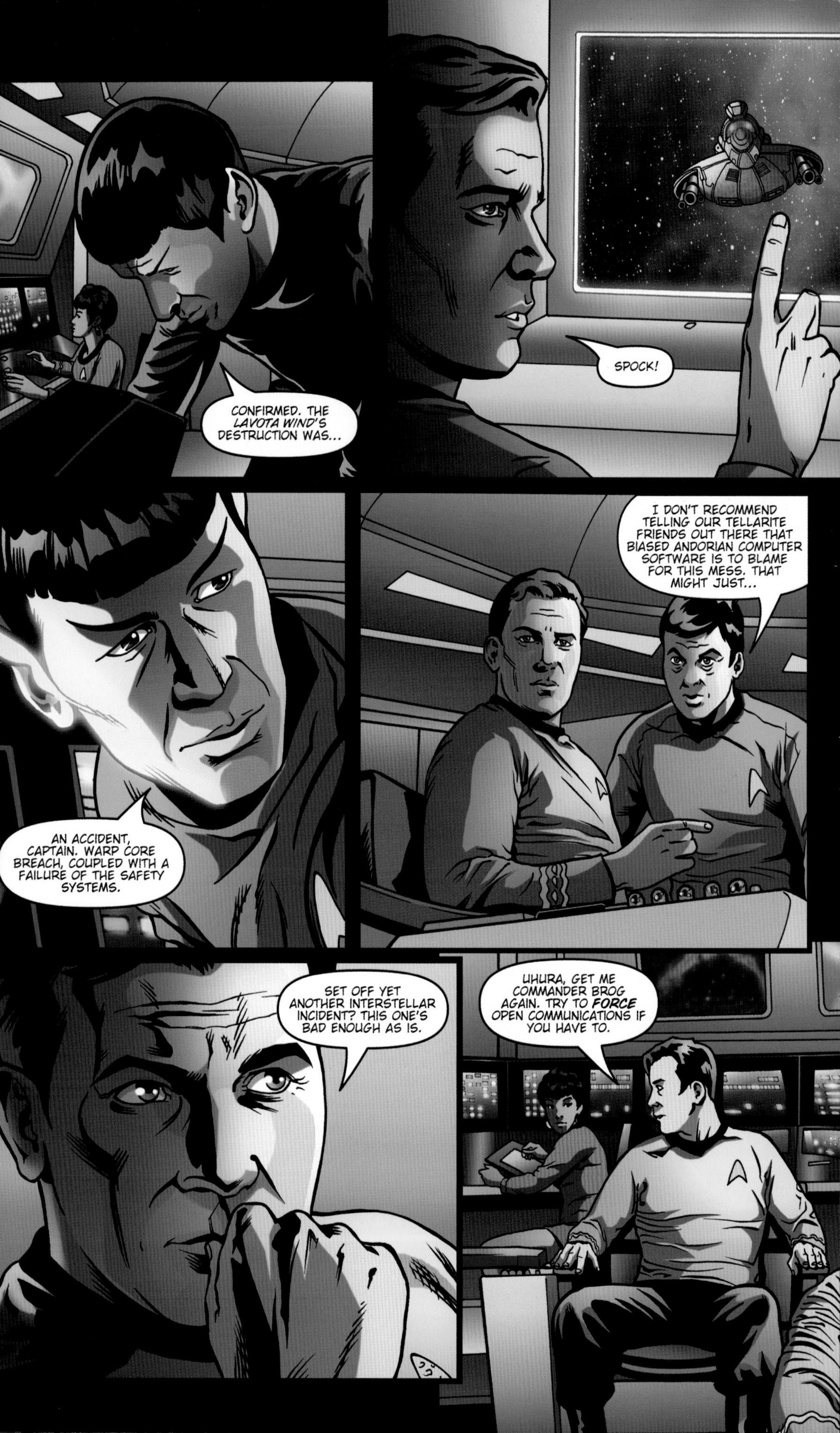
CONFIRMED. THE *LAVOTA WIND*'S DESTRUCTION WAS...
SPOCK!
AN ACCIDENT, CAPTAIN. WARP CORE BREACH, COUPLED WITH A FAILURE OF THE SAFETY SYSTEMS.
I DON'T RECOMMEND TELLING OUR TELLARITE FRIENDS OUT THERE THAT BIASED ANDORIAN COMPUTER SOFTWARE IS TO BLAME FOR THIS MESS. THAT MIGHT JUST...
SET OFF YET ANOTHER INTERSTELLAR INCIDENT? THIS ONE'S BAD ENOUGH AS IS.
UHURA, GET ME COMMANDER BROG AGAIN. TRY TO ***FORCE*** OPEN COMMUNICATIONS IF YOU HAVE TO.

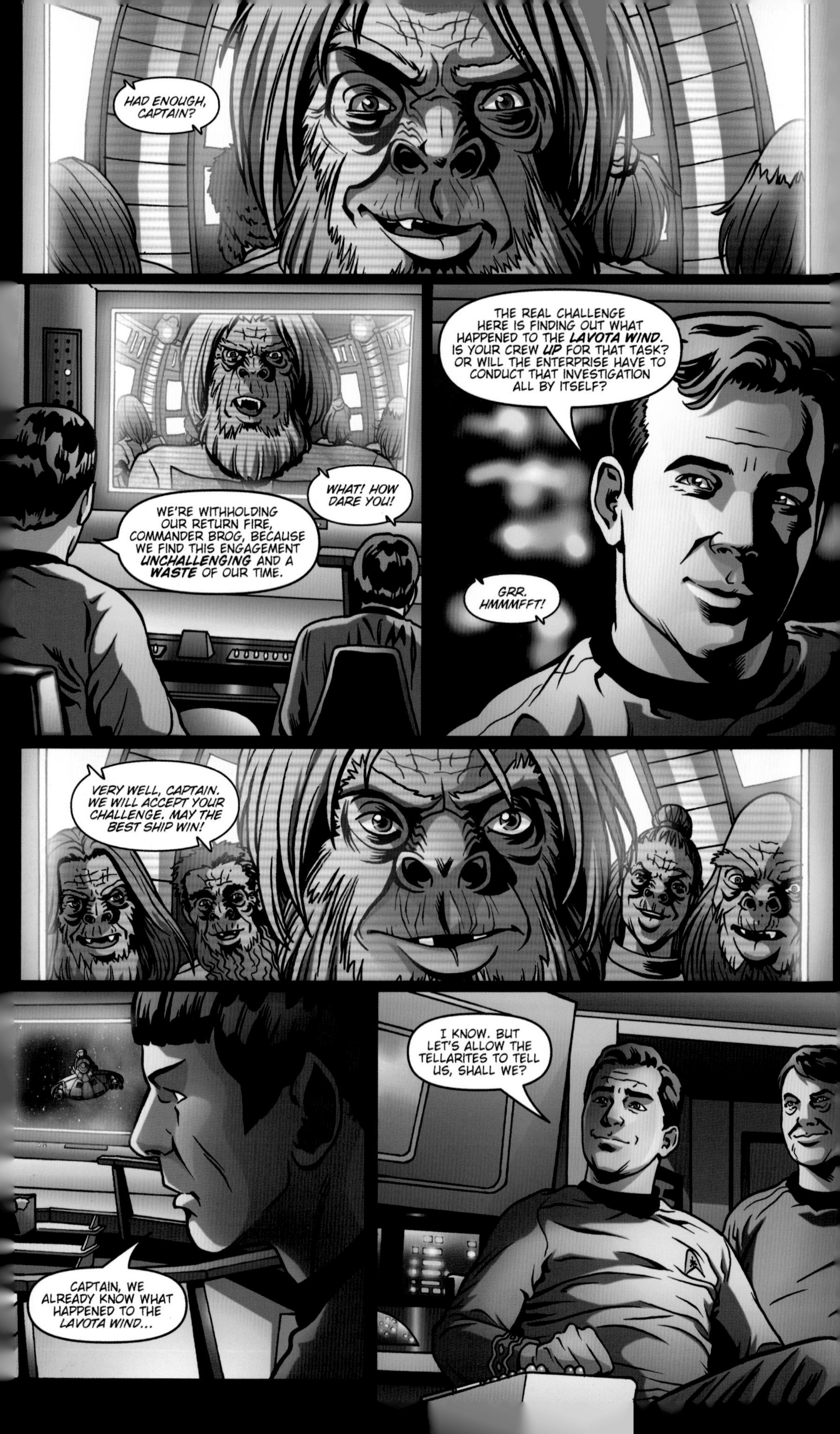
HAD ENOUGH, CAPTAIN?
WE'RE WITHHOLDING OUR RETURN FIRE, COMMANDER BROG, BECAUSE WE FIND THIS ENGAGEMENT UNCHALLENGING AND A WASTE OF OUR TIME.
WHAT! HOW DARE YOU!
THE REAL CHALLENGE HERE IS FINDING OUT WHAT HAPPENED TO THE LAVOTA WIND. IS YOUR CREW UP FOR THAT TASK? OR WILL THE ENTERPRISE HAVE TO CONDUCT THAT INVESTIGATION ALL BY ITSELF?
GRR. HMMMFFT!
VERY WELL, CAPTAIN. WE WILL ACCEPT YOUR CHALLENGE. MAY THE BEST SHIP WIN!
CAPTAIN, WE ALREADY KNOW WHAT HAPPENED TO THE LAVOTA WIND...
I KNOW. BUT LET'S ALLOW THE TELLARITES TO TELL US, SHALL WE?

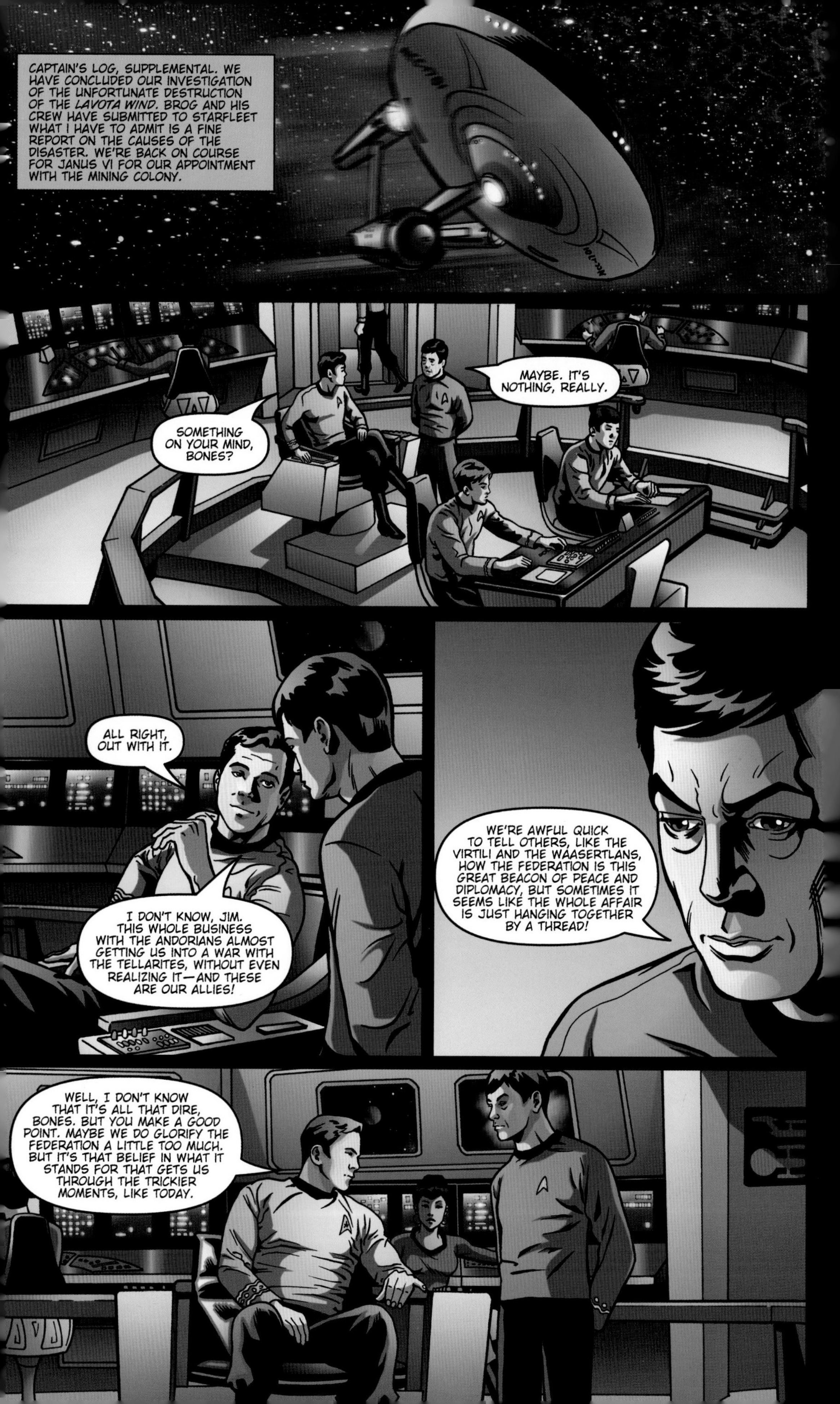
CAPTAIN'S LOG, SUPPLEMENTAL. WE HAVE CONCLUDED OUR INVESTIGATION OF THE UNFORTUNATE DESTRUCTION OF THE *LAVOTA WIND*. BROG AND HIS CREW HAVE SUBMITTED TO STARFLEET WHAT I HAVE TO ADMIT IS A FINE REPORT ON THE CAUSES OF THE DISASTER. WE'RE BACK ON COURSE FOR JANUS VI FOR OUR APPOINTMENT WITH THE MINING COLONY.
SOMETHING ON YOUR MIND, BONES?
MAYBE. IT'S NOTHING, REALLY.
ALL RIGHT, OUT WITH IT.
I DON'T KNOW, JIM. THIS WHOLE BUSINESS WITH THE ANDORIANS ALMOST GETTING US INTO A WAR WITH THE TELLARITES, WITHOUT EVEN REALIZING IT—AND THESE ARE OUR ALLIES!
WE'RE AWFUL QUICK TO TELL OTHERS, LIKE THE VIRTILI AND THE WAASERTLANS, HOW THE FEDERATION IS THIS GREAT BEACON OF PEACE AND DIPLOMACY, BUT SOMETIMES IT SEEMS LIKE THE WHOLE AFFAIR IS JUST HANGING TOGETHER BY A THREAD!
WELL, I DON'T KNOW THAT IT'S ALL THAT DIRE, BONES. BUT YOU MAKE A GOOD POINT. MAYBE WE DO GLORIFY THE FEDERATION A LITTLE TOO MUCH. BUT IT'S THAT BELIEF IN WHAT IT STANDS FOR THAT GETS US THROUGH THE TRICKIER MOMENTS, LIKE TODAY.

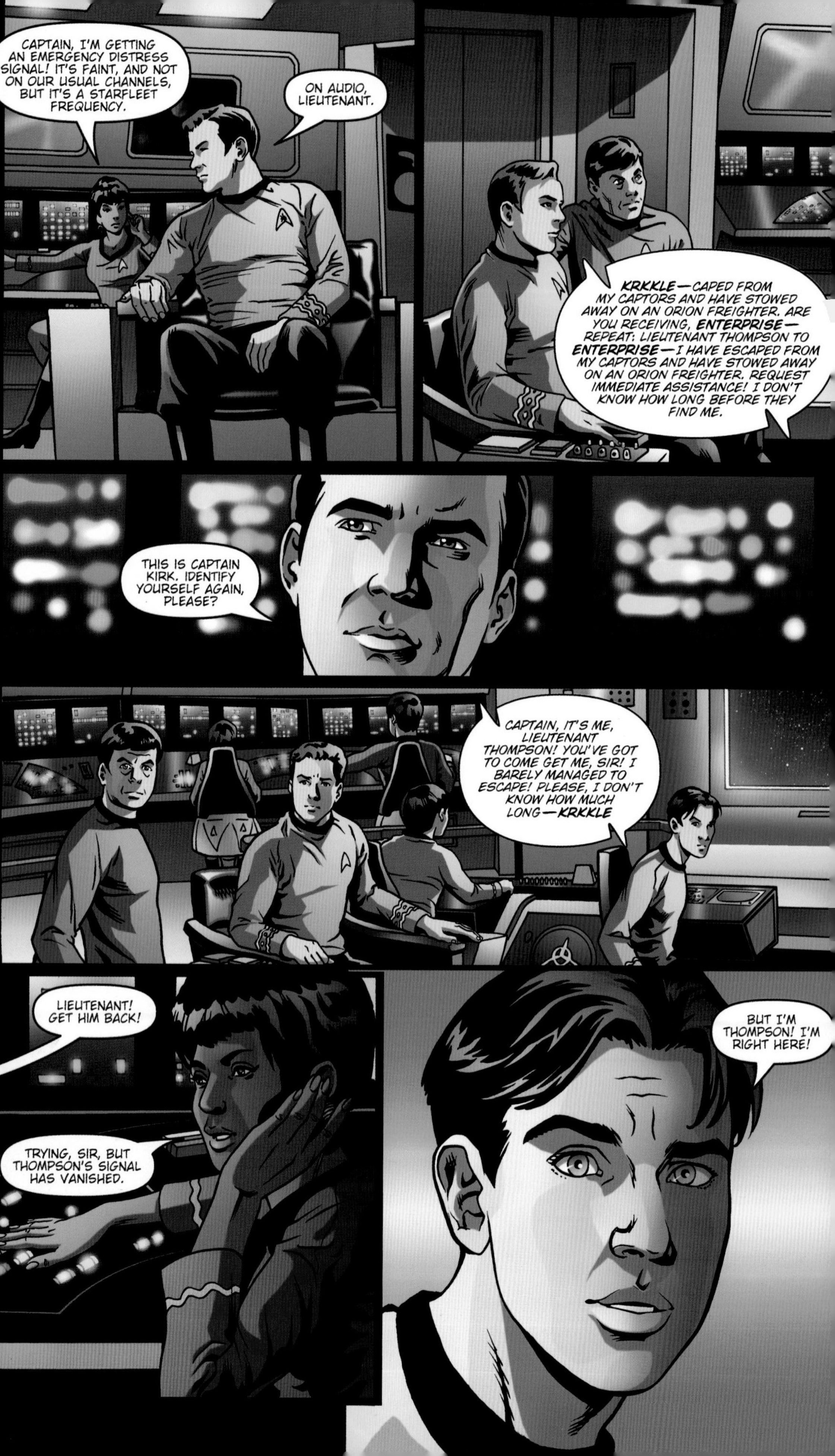

CAPTAIN, I'M GETTING AN EMERGENCY DISTRESS SIGNAL! IT'S FAINT, AND NOT ON OUR USUAL CHANNELS, BUT IT'S A STARFLEET FREQUENCY.
ON AUDIO, LIEUTENANT.
KRKKLE—CAPED FROM MY CAPTORS AND HAVE STOWED AWAY ON AN ORION FREIGHTER. ARE YOU RECEIVING, ENTERPRISE—REPEAT: LIEUTENANT THOMPSON TO ENTERPRISE—I HAVE ESCAPED FROM MY CAPTORS AND HAVE STOWED AWAY ON AN ORION FREIGHTER. REQUEST IMMEDIATE ASSISTANCE! I DON'T KNOW HOW LONG BEFORE THEY FIND ME.
THIS IS CAPTAIN KIRK. IDENTIFY YOURSELF AGAIN, PLEASE?
CAPTAIN, IT'S ME, LIEUTENANT THOMPSON! YOU'VE GOT TO COME GET ME, SIR! I BARELY MANAGED TO ESCAPE! PLEASE, I DON'T KNOW HOW MUCH LONG—KRKKLE
LIEUTENANT! GET HIM BACK!
TRYING, SIR, BUT THOMPSON'S SIGNAL HAS VANISHED.
BUT I'M THOMPSON! I'M RIGHT HERE!

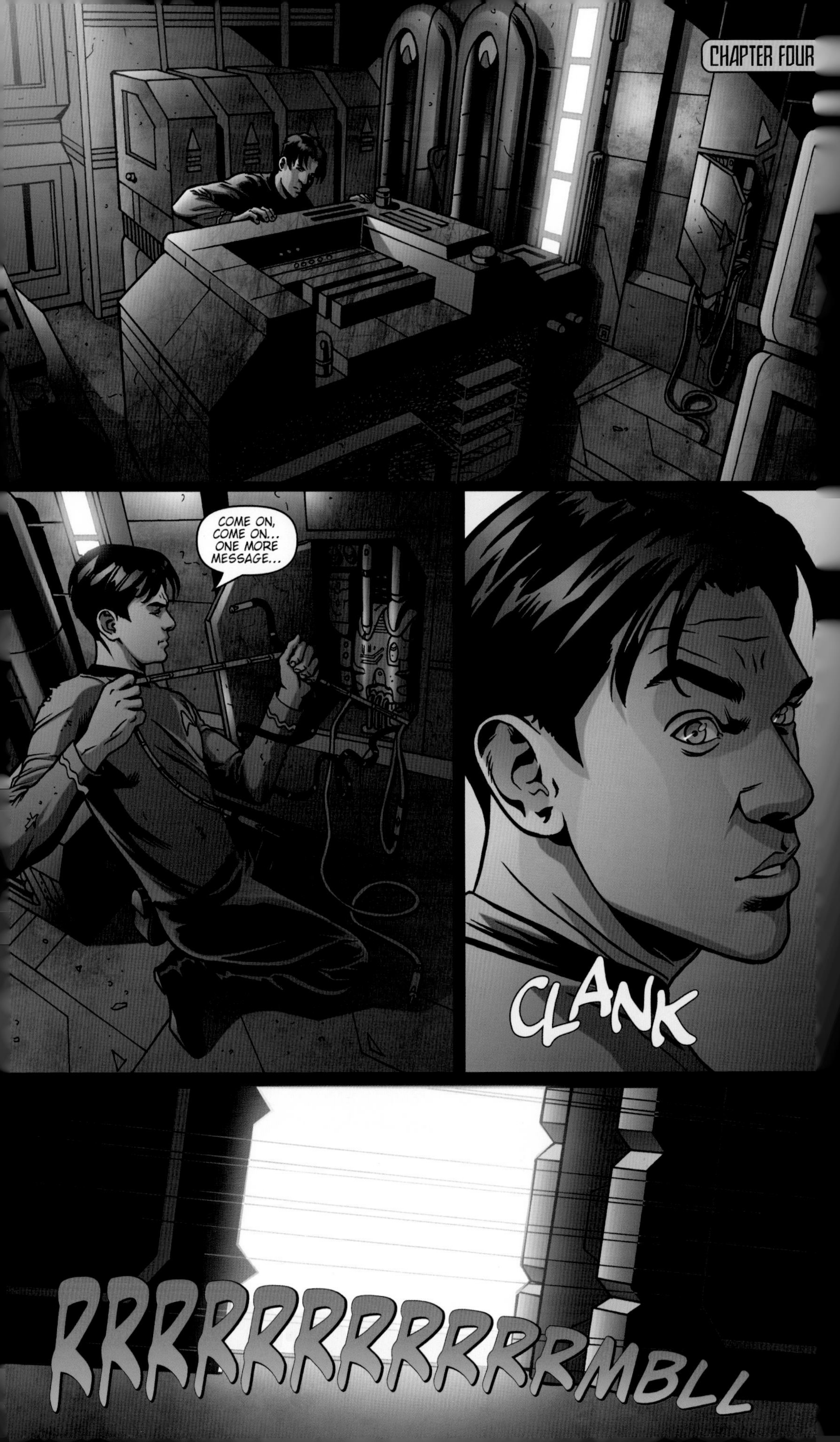
CHAPTER FOUR
COME ON, COME ON... ONE MORE MESSAGE...
CLANK
RRRRRRRRRRRRRMBLL

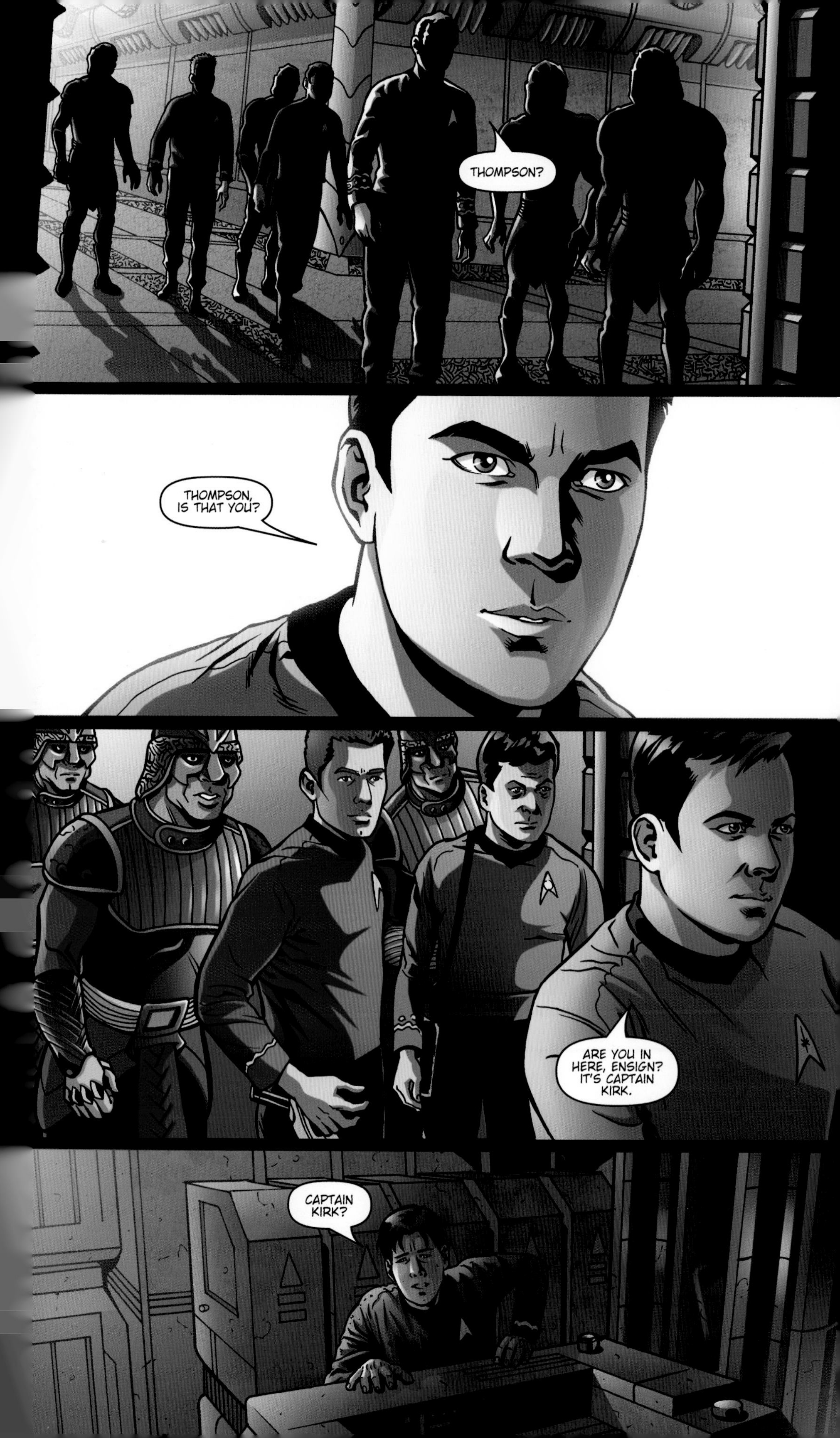
THOMPSON?
THOMPSON, IS THAT YOU?
ARE YOU IN HERE, ENSIGN? IT'S CAPTAIN KIRK.
CAPTAIN KIRK?

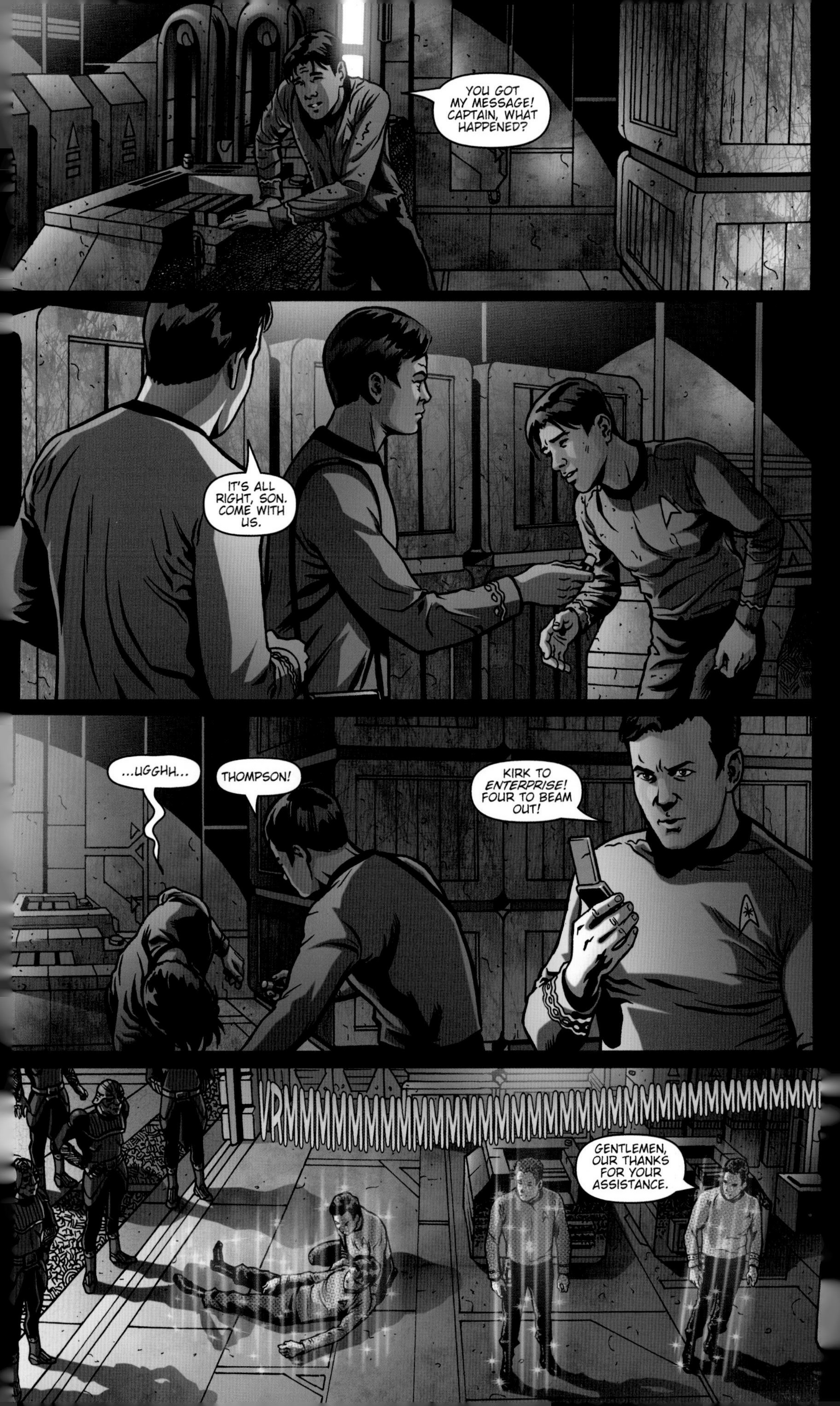

YOU GOT MY MESSAGE! CAPTAIN, WHAT HAPPENED?
IT'S ALL RIGHT, SON. COME WITH US.
...UGGHH...
THOMPSON!
KIRK TO *ENTERPRISE!* FOUR TO BEAM OUT!
VRMMMMMMMMMMMMMMMMMMMMMMMMMMMMMMMMMMMMMMMM
GENTLEMEN, OUR THANKS FOR YOUR ASSISTANCE.

THE BURDEN OF KNOWLEDGE

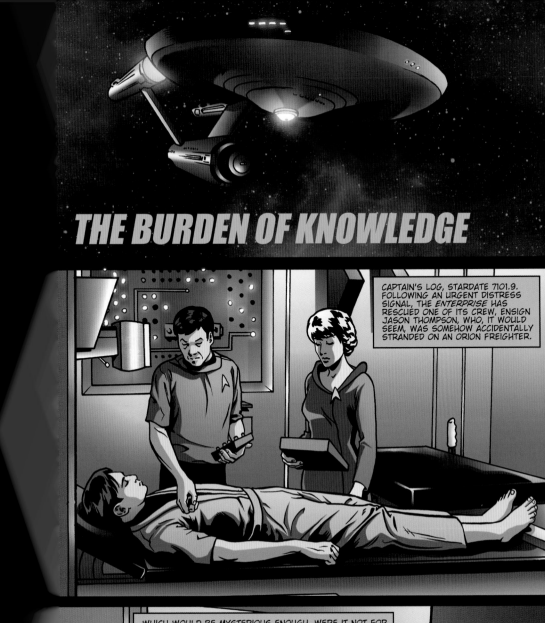

CAPTAIN'S LOG, STARDATE 7101.9. FOLLOWING AN URGENT DISTRESS SIGNAL, THE *ENTERPRISE* HAS RESCUED ONE OF ITS CREW, ENSIGN JASON THOMPSON, WHO, IT WOULD SEEM, WAS SOMEHOW ACCIDENTALLY STRANDED ON AN ORION FREIGHTER.

WHICH WOULD BE MYSTERIOUS ENOUGH, WERE IT NOT FOR THE FACT THAT ENSIGN THOMPSON WAS AT HIS STATION ON THE BRIDGE WHEN THE DISTRESS SIGNAL CAME IN...

I DON'T UNDERSTAND, CAPTAIN.

NEITHER DO I, THOMPSON. PERHAPS THE DOCTOR CAN PROVIDE US WITH SOME ANSWERS.

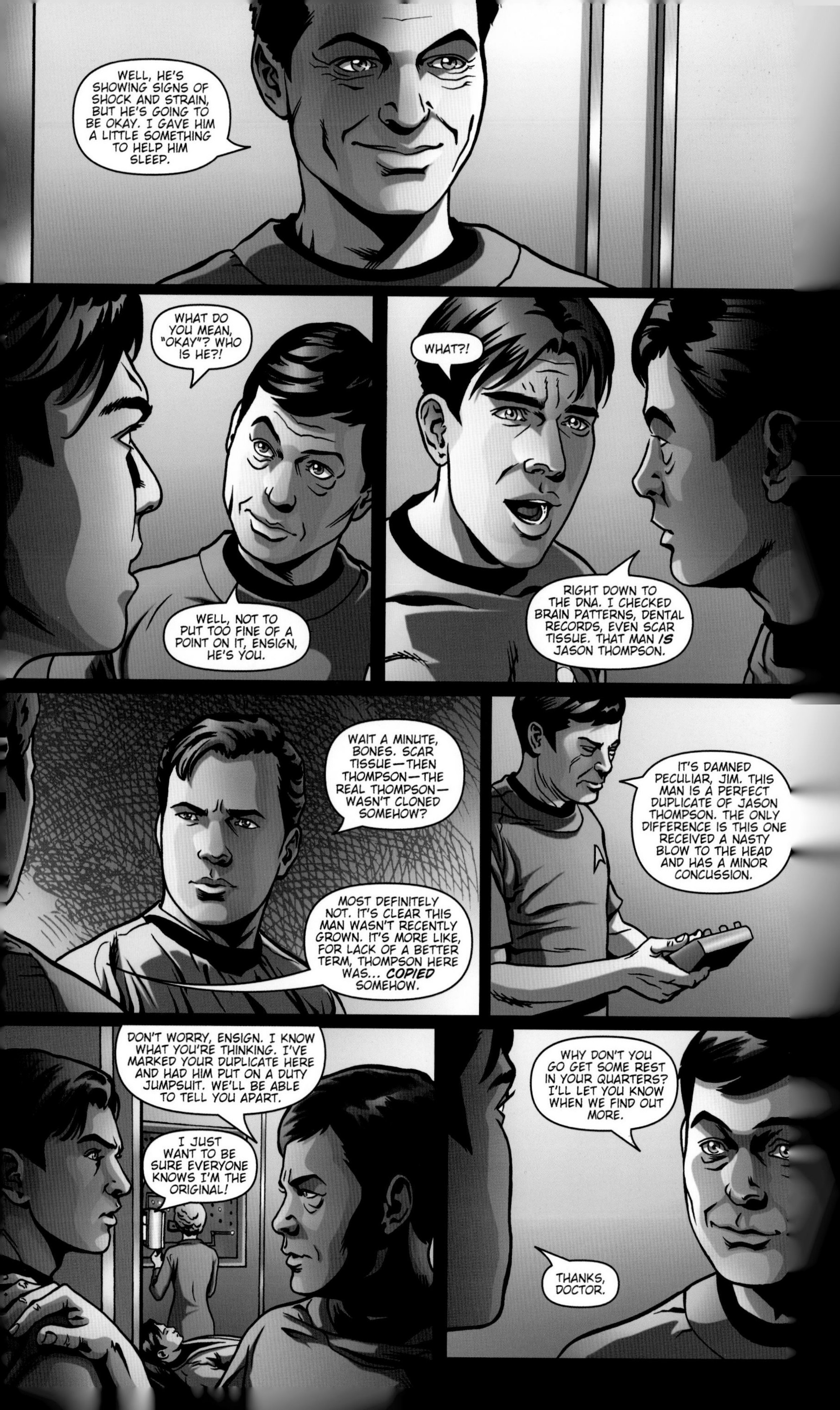
WELL, HE'S SHOWING SIGNS OF SHOCK AND STRAIN, BUT HE'S GOING TO BE OKAY. I GAVE HIM A LITTLE SOMETHING TO HELP HIM SLEEP.
WHAT DO YOU MEAN, "OKAY"? WHO IS HE?!
WELL, NOT TO PUT TOO FINE OF A POINT ON IT, ENSIGN, HE'S YOU.
WHAT?!
RIGHT DOWN TO THE DNA. I CHECKED BRAIN PATTERNS, DENTAL RECORDS, EVEN SCAR TISSUE. THAT MAN IS JASON THOMPSON.
WAIT A MINUTE, BONES. SCAR TISSUE—THEN THOMPSON—THE REAL THOMPSON—WASN'T CLONED SOMEHOW?
MOST DEFINITELY NOT. IT'S CLEAR THIS MAN WASN'T RECENTLY GROWN. IT'S MORE LIKE, FOR LACK OF A BETTER TERM, THOMPSON HERE WAS... COPIED SOMEHOW.
IT'S DAMNED PECULIAR, JIM. THIS MAN IS A PERFECT DUPLICATE OF JASON THOMPSON. THE ONLY DIFFERENCE IS THIS ONE RECEIVED A NASTY BLOW TO THE HEAD AND HAS A MINOR CONCUSSION.
DON'T WORRY, ENSIGN. I KNOW WHAT YOU'RE THINKING. I'VE MARKED YOUR DUPLICATE HERE AND HAD HIM PUT ON A DUTY JUMPSUIT. WE'LL BE ABLE TO TELL YOU APART.
I JUST WANT TO BE SURE EVERYONE KNOWS I'M THE ORIGINAL!
WHY DON'T YOU GO GET SOME REST IN YOUR QUARTERS? I'LL LET YOU KNOW WHEN WE FIND OUT MORE.
THANKS, DOCTOR.

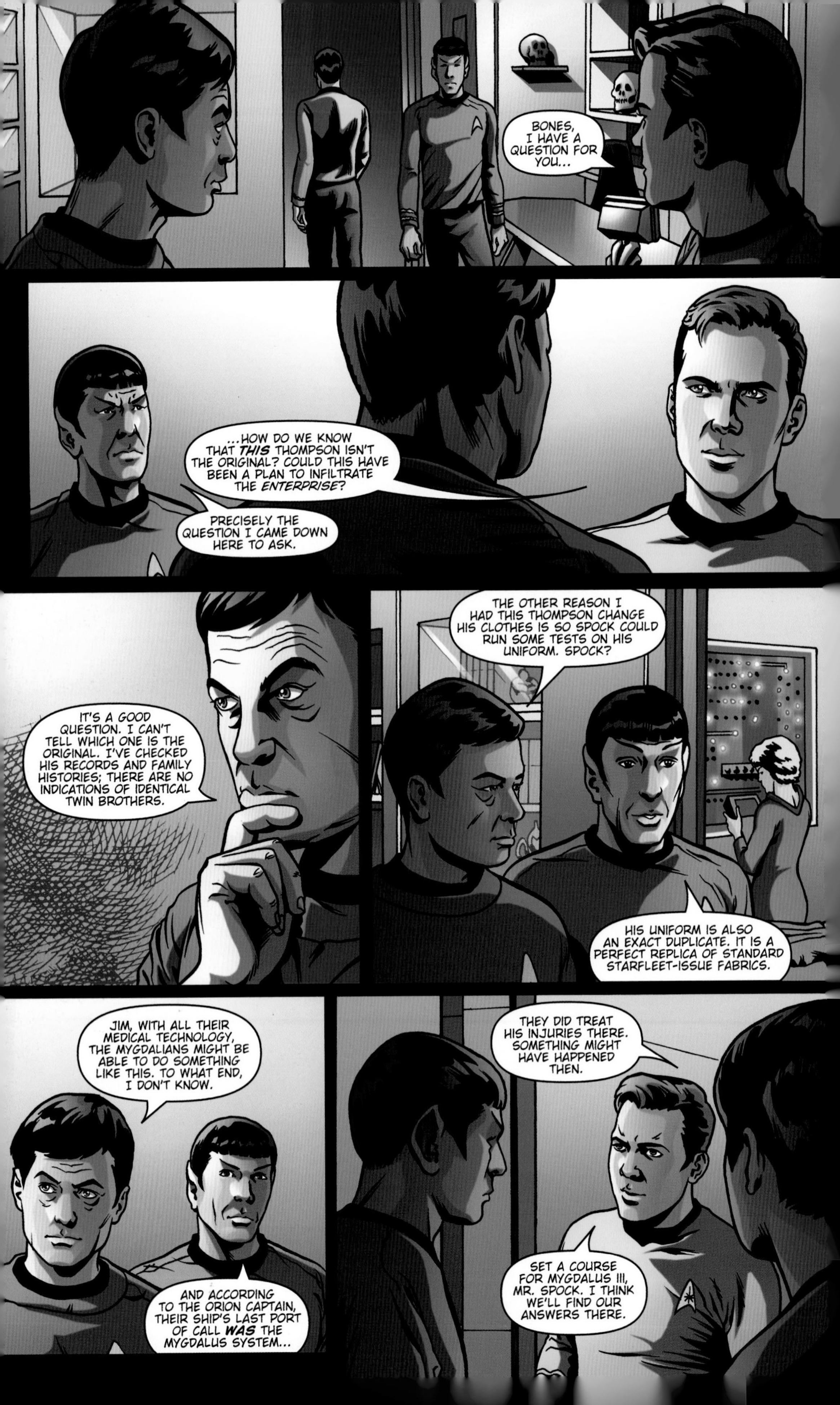
BONES, I HAVE A QUESTION FOR YOU...
...HOW DO WE KNOW THAT *THIS* THOMPSON ISN'T THE ORIGINAL? COULD THIS HAVE BEEN A PLAN TO INFILTRATE THE *ENTERPRISE*?
PRECISELY THE QUESTION I CAME DOWN HERE TO ASK.
IT'S A GOOD QUESTION. I CAN'T TELL WHICH ONE IS THE ORIGINAL. I'VE CHECKED HIS RECORDS AND FAMILY HISTORIES; THERE ARE NO INDICATIONS OF IDENTICAL TWIN BROTHERS.
THE OTHER REASON I HAD THIS THOMPSON CHANGE HIS CLOTHES IS SO SPOCK COULD RUN SOME TESTS ON HIS UNIFORM. SPOCK?
HIS UNIFORM IS ALSO AN EXACT DUPLICATE. IT IS A PERFECT REPLICA OF STANDARD STARFLEET-ISSUE FABRICS.
JIM, WITH ALL THEIR MEDICAL TECHNOLOGY, THE MYGDALIANS MIGHT BE ABLE TO DO SOMETHING LIKE THIS. TO WHAT END, I DON'T KNOW.
AND ACCORDING TO THE ORION CAPTAIN, THEIR SHIP'S LAST PORT OF CALL **WAS** THE MYGDALUS SYSTEM...
THEY DID TREAT HIS INJURIES THERE. SOMETHING MIGHT HAVE HAPPENED THEN.
SET A COURSE FOR MYGDALUS III, MR. SPOCK. I THINK WE'LL FIND OUR ANSWERS THERE.

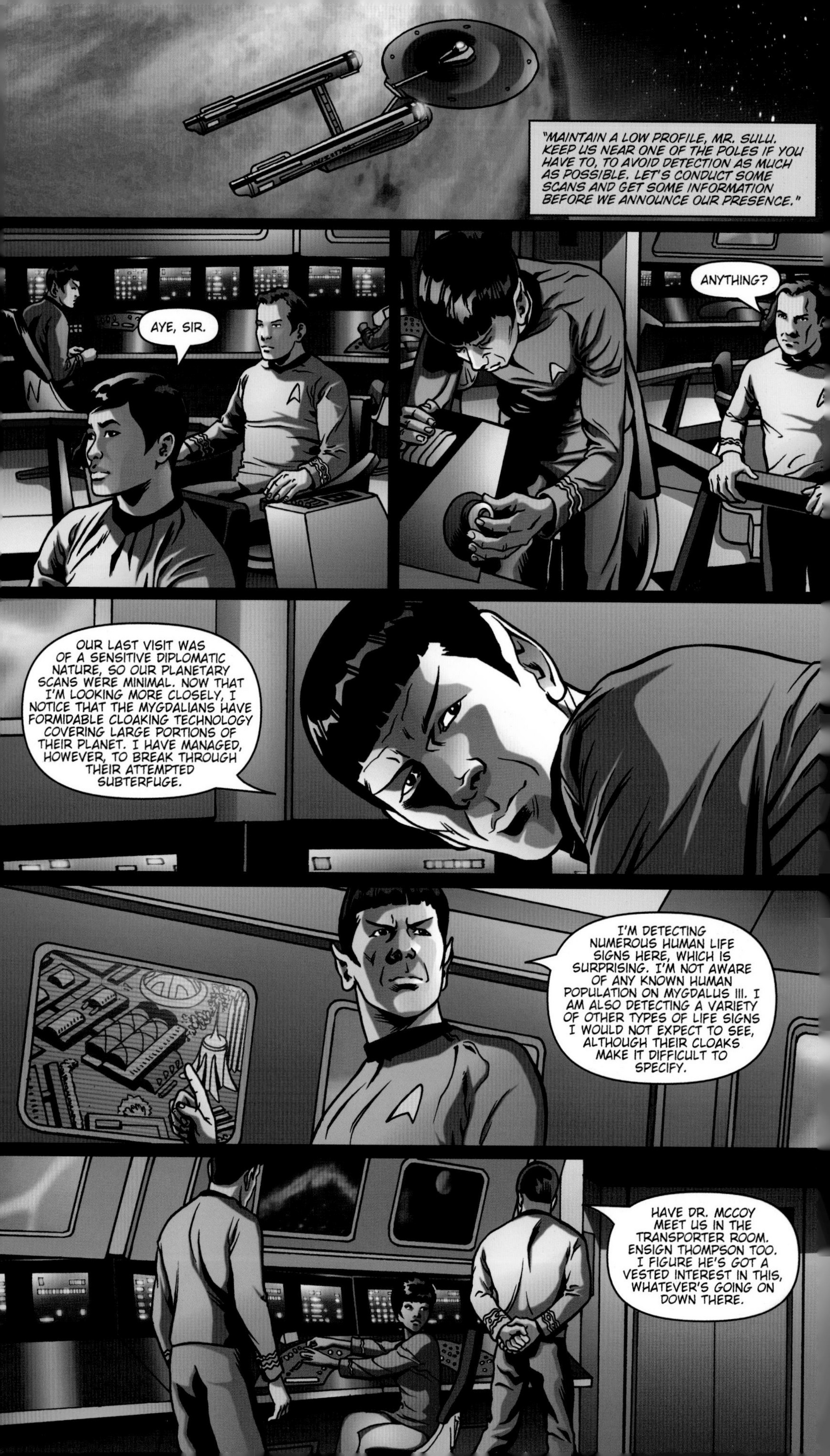
"MAINTAIN A LOW PROFILE, MR. SULU. KEEP US NEAR ONE OF THE POLES IF YOU HAVE TO, TO AVOID DETECTION AS MUCH AS POSSIBLE. LET'S CONDUCT SOME SCANS AND GET SOME INFORMATION BEFORE WE ANNOUNCE OUR PRESENCE."
AYE, SIR.
ANYTHING?
OUR LAST VISIT WAS OF A SENSITIVE DIPLOMATIC NATURE, SO OUR PLANETARY SCANS WERE MINIMAL. NOW THAT I'M LOOKING MORE CLOSELY, I NOTICE THAT THE MYGDALIANS HAVE FORMIDABLE CLOAKING TECHNOLOGY COVERING LARGE PORTIONS OF THEIR PLANET. I HAVE MANAGED, HOWEVER, TO BREAK THROUGH THEIR ATTEMPTED SUBTERFUGE.
I'M DETECTING NUMEROUS HUMAN LIFE SIGNS HERE, WHICH IS SURPRISING. I'M NOT AWARE OF ANY KNOWN HUMAN POPULATION ON MYGDALUS III. I AM ALSO DETECTING A VARIETY OF OTHER TYPES OF LIFE SIGNS I WOULD NOT EXPECT TO SEE, ALTHOUGH THEIR CLOAKS MAKE IT DIFFICULT TO SPECIFY.
HAVE DR. MCCOY MEET US IN THE TRANSPORTER ROOM. ENSIGN THOMPSON TOO. I FIGURE HE'S GOT A VESTED INTEREST IN THIS, WHATEVER'S GOING ON DOWN THERE.

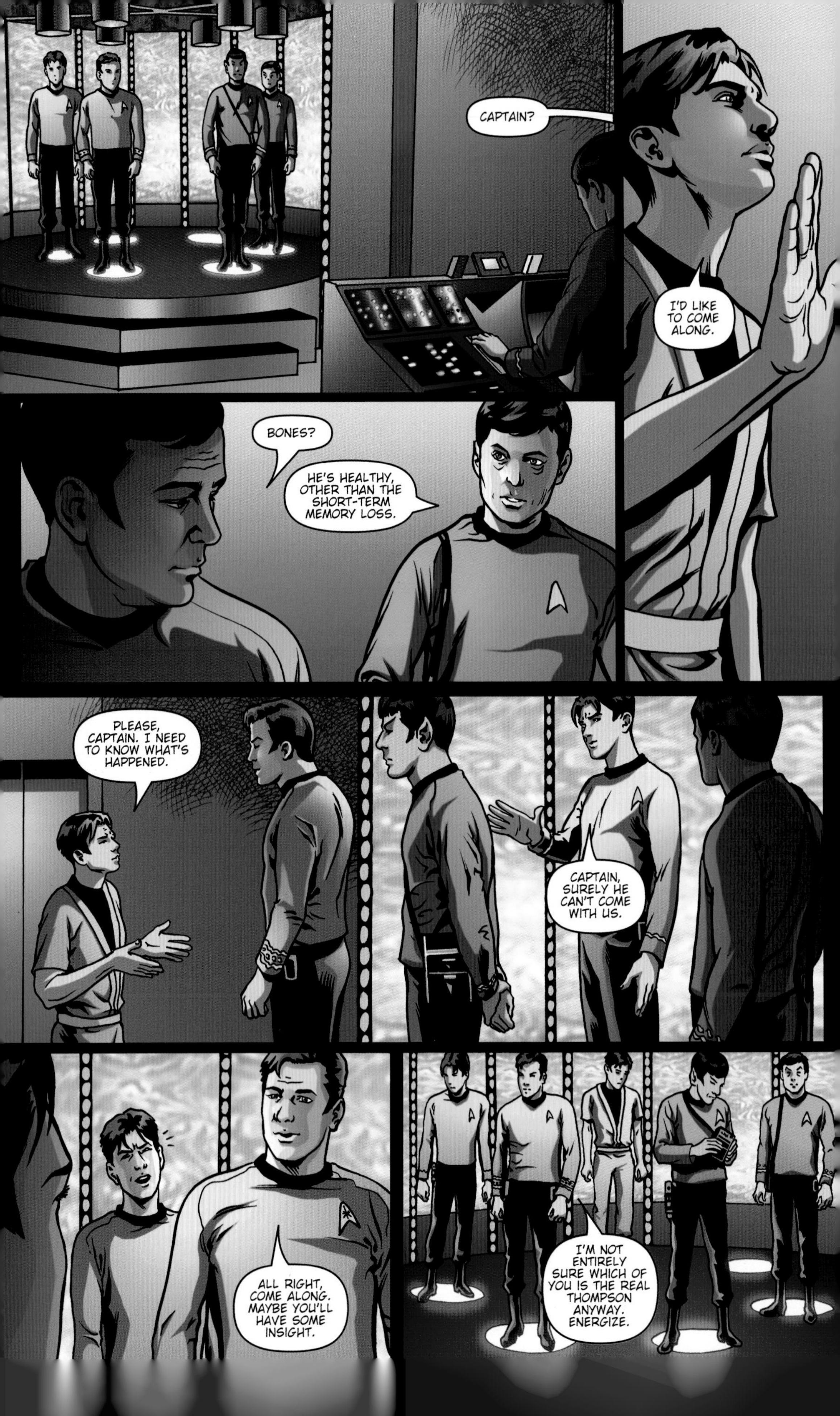
CAPTAIN?
I'D LIKE TO COME ALONG.
BONES?
HE'S HEALTHY, OTHER THAN THE SHORT-TERM MEMORY LOSS.
PLEASE, CAPTAIN. I NEED TO KNOW WHAT'S HAPPENED.
CAPTAIN, SURELY HE CAN'T COME WITH US.
ALL RIGHT, COME ALONG. MAYBE YOU'LL HAVE SOME INSIGHT.
I'M NOT ENTIRELY SURE WHICH OF YOU IS THE REAL THOMPSON ANYWAY. ENERGIZE.

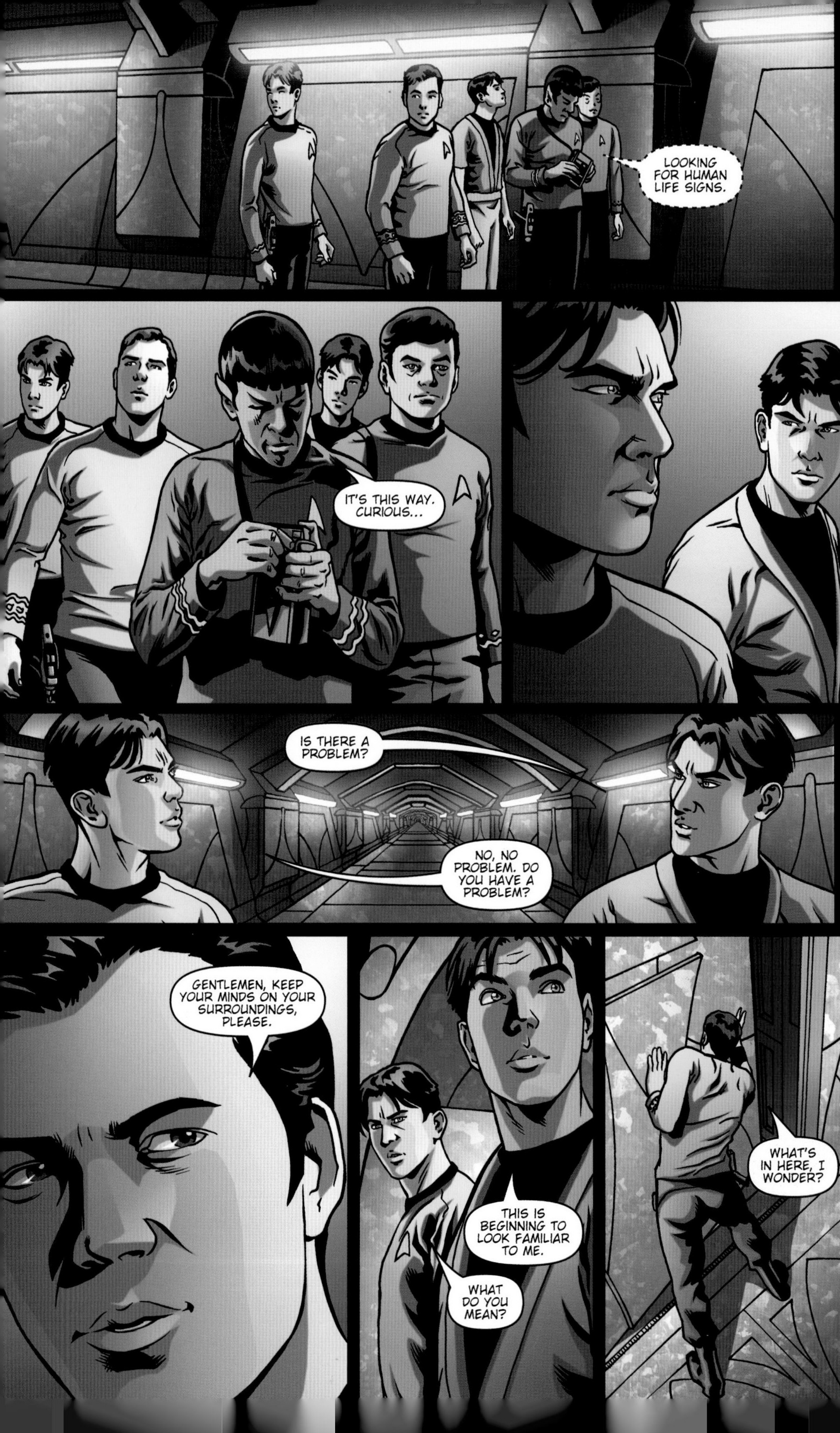
LOOKING FOR HUMAN LIFE SIGNS.
IT'S THIS WAY. CURIOUS...
IS THERE A PROBLEM?
NO, NO PROBLEM. DO YOU HAVE A PROBLEM?
GENTLEMEN, KEEP YOUR MINDS ON YOUR SURROUNDINGS, PLEASE.
THIS IS BEGINNING TO LOOK FAMILIAR TO ME.
WHAT DO YOU MEAN?
WHAT'S IN HERE, I WONDER?

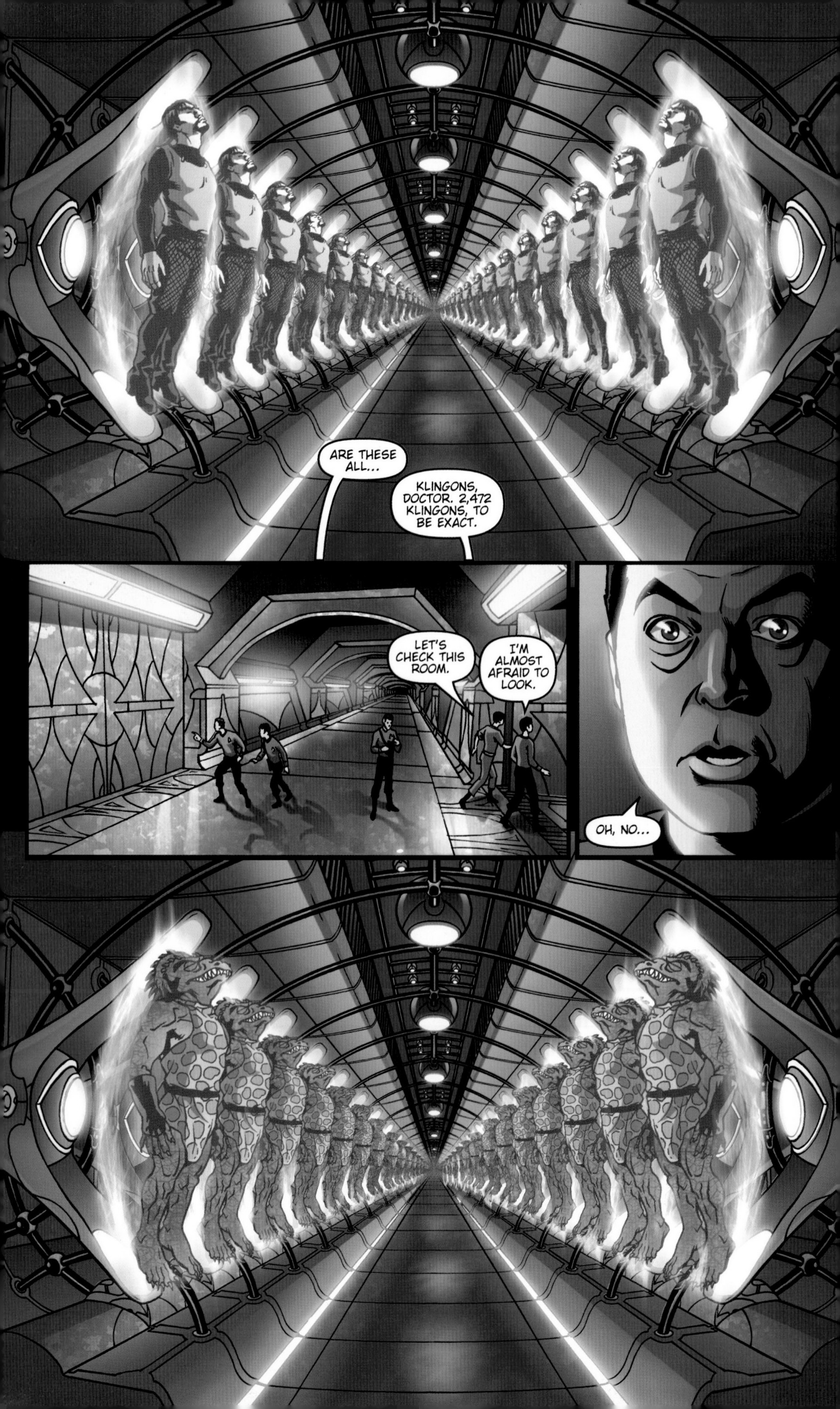
ARE THESE ALL...
KLINGONS, DOCTOR. 2,472 KLINGONS, TO BE EXACT.
LET'S CHECK THIS ROOM.
I'M ALMOST AFRAID TO LOOK.
OH, NO...

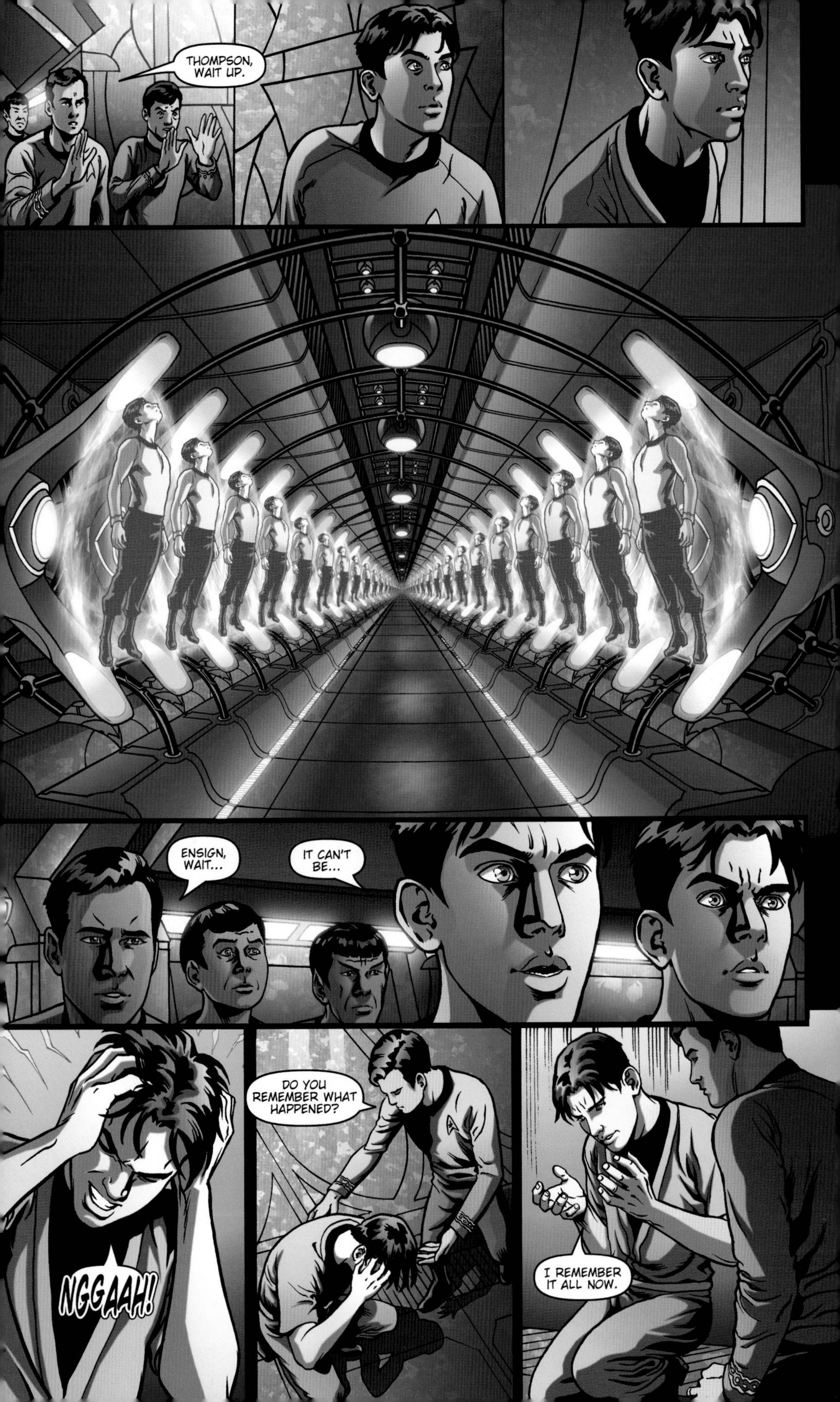
THOMPSON, WAIT UP.
ENSIGN, WAIT...
IT CAN'T BE...
NGGAAH!
DO YOU REMEMBER WHAT HAPPENED?
I REMEMBER IT ALL NOW.

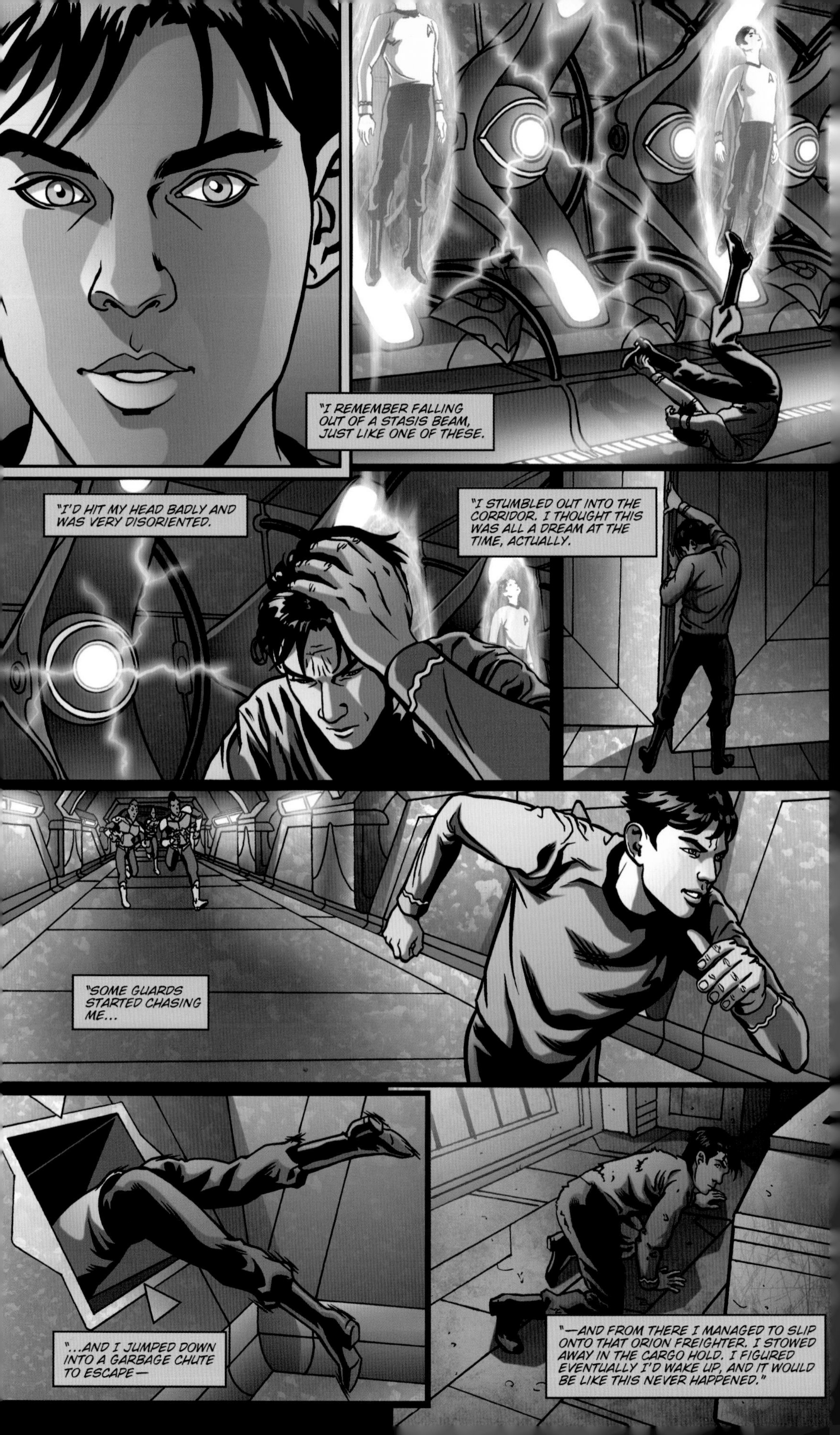
"I REMEMBER FALLING OUT OF A STASIS BEAM, JUST LIKE ONE OF THESE.
"I'D HIT MY HEAD BADLY AND WAS VERY DISORIENTED.
"I STUMBLED OUT INTO THE CORRIDOR. I THOUGHT THIS WAS ALL A DREAM AT THE TIME, ACTUALLY.
"SOME GUARDS STARTED CHASING ME...
"...AND I JUMPED DOWN INTO A GARBAGE CHUTE TO ESCAPE—
"—AND FROM THERE I MANAGED TO SLIP ONTO THAT ORION FREIGHTER. I STOWED AWAY IN THE CARGO HOLD. I FIGURED EVENTUALLY I'D WAKE UP, AND IT WOULD BE LIKE THIS NEVER HAPPENED."

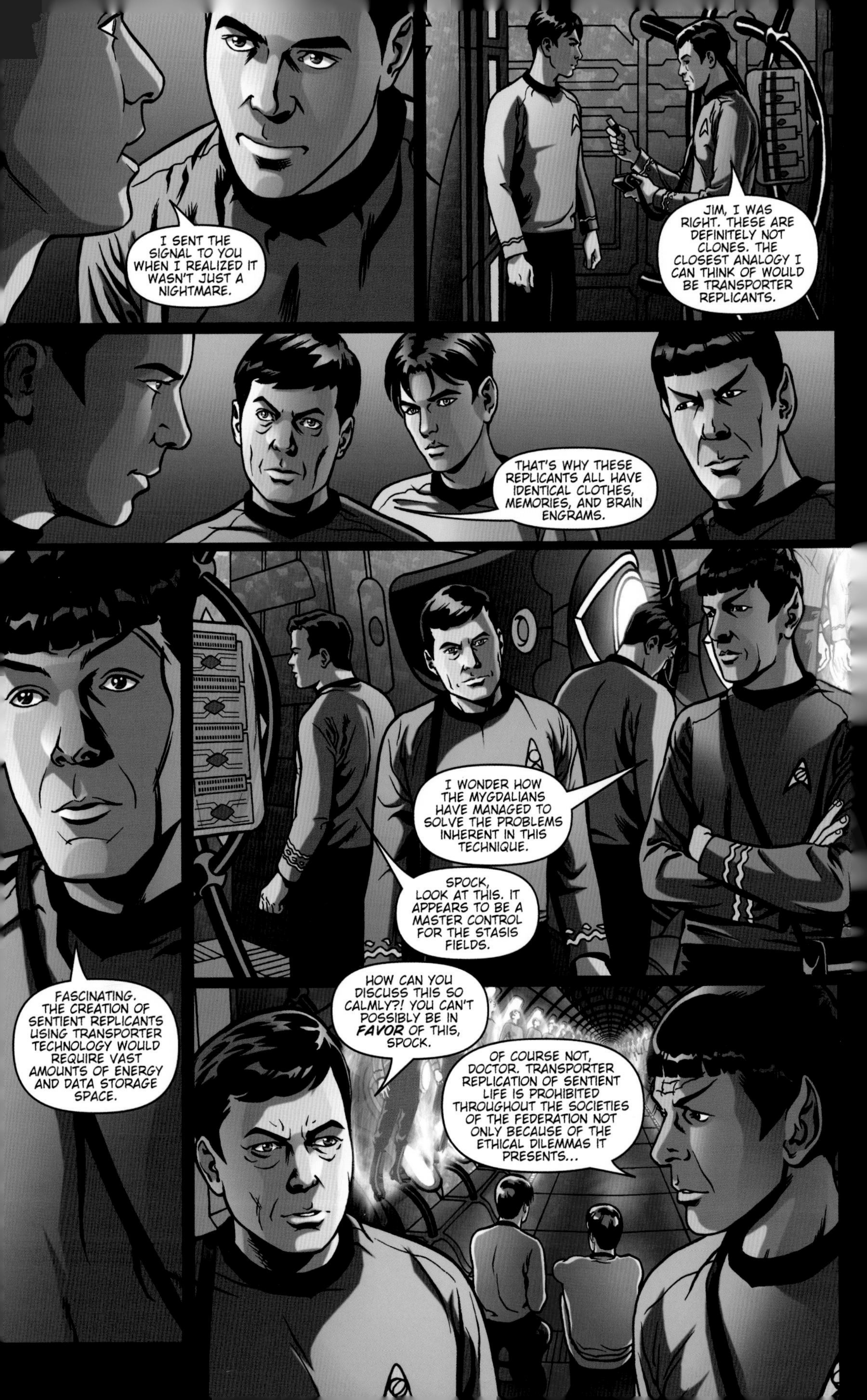
I SENT THE SIGNAL TO YOU WHEN I REALIZED IT WASN'T JUST A NIGHTMARE.
JIM, I WAS RIGHT. THESE ARE DEFINITELY NOT CLONES. THE CLOSEST ANALOGY I CAN THINK OF WOULD BE TRANSPORTER REPLICANTS.
THAT'S WHY THESE REPLICANTS ALL HAVE IDENTICAL CLOTHES, MEMORIES, AND BRAIN ENGRAMS.
I WONDER HOW THE MYGDALIANS HAVE MANAGED TO SOLVE THE PROBLEMS INHERENT IN THIS TECHNIQUE.
SPOCK, LOOK AT THIS. IT APPEARS TO BE A MASTER CONTROL FOR THE STASIS FIELDS.
FASCINATING. THE CREATION OF SENTIENT REPLICANTS USING TRANSPORTER TECHNOLOGY WOULD REQUIRE VAST AMOUNTS OF ENERGY AND DATA STORAGE SPACE.
HOW CAN YOU DISCUSS THIS SO CALMLY?! YOU CAN'T POSSIBLY BE IN ***FAVOR*** OF THIS, SPOCK.
OF COURSE NOT, DOCTOR. TRANSPORTER REPLICATION OF SENTIENT LIFE IS PROHIBITED THROUGHOUT THE SOCIETIES OF THE FEDERATION NOT ONLY BECAUSE OF THE ETHICAL DILEMMAS IT PRESENTS...

...BUT ALSO BECAUSE OF THE PHILOSOPHICAL AND EXISTENTIAL BURDEN PLACED ON ANYONE SO REPLICATED.

I WISH I HAD NEVER KNOWN THIS HAD HAPPENED.

SO WHAT'S THE POINT? WHY DO ALL THIS?

YOU'RE NOT GOING TO LIKE THE ANSWER, JIM. SUCH REPLICATION WOULD SUPPLY THE MYGDALIANS WITH AN ENDLESS SUPPLY OF BODY PARTS, READY FOR USE IN TRANSPLANTS, MEDICAL GRAFTING AND EVEN EXPERIMENTATION.

WHO KNOWS WHAT ELSE THEY ARE DOING WITH THESE POOR SOULS? THE POSSIBILITIES ARE ENDLESS, IF YOU CAN STOMACH THE MORAL IMPLICATIONS. NOW I UNDERSTAND THE SECRET TO THE MYGDALIANS' SUCCESS.

I AGREE WITH DOCTOR MCCOY. THIS WOULD CERTAINLY EXPLAIN THE MYGDALIANS' SEEMINGLY MIRACULOUS MEDICAL ADVANCES.

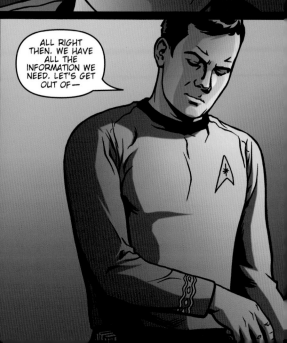

ALL RIGHT THEN. WE HAVE ALL THE INFORMATION WE NEED. LET'S GET OUT OF—

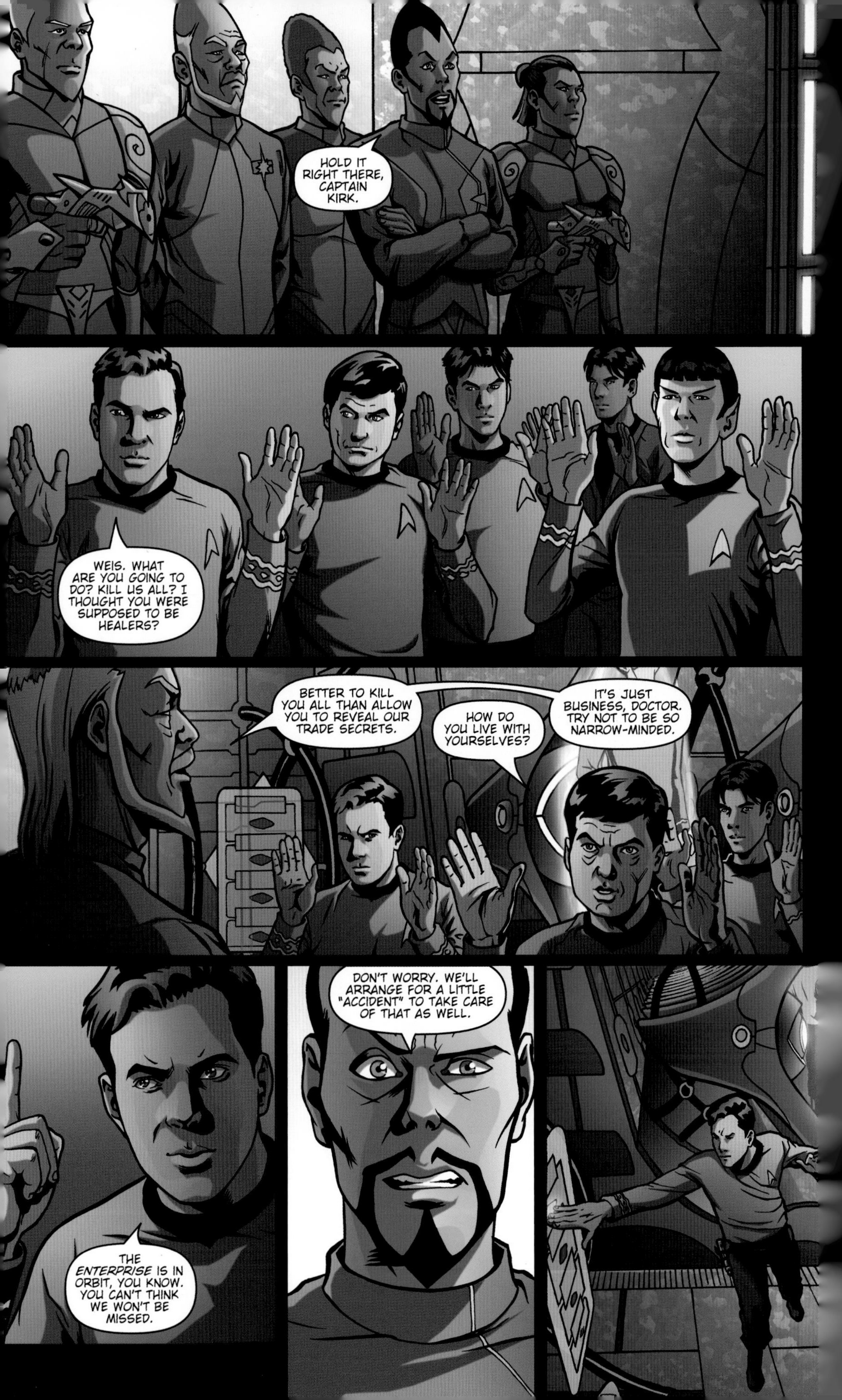
HOLD IT RIGHT THERE, CAPTAIN KIRK.
WEIS. WHAT ARE YOU GOING TO DO? KILL US ALL? I THOUGHT YOU WERE SUPPOSED TO BE HEALERS?
BETTER TO KILL YOU ALL THAN ALLOW YOU TO REVEAL OUR TRADE SECRETS.
HOW DO YOU LIVE WITH YOURSELVES?
IT'S JUST BUSINESS, DOCTOR. TRY NOT TO BE SO NARROW-MINDED.
THE *ENTERPRISE* IS IN ORBIT, YOU KNOW. YOU CAN'T THINK WE WON'T BE MISSED.
DON'T WORRY. WE'LL ARRANGE FOR A LITTLE "ACCIDENT" TO TAKE CARE OF THAT AS WELL.

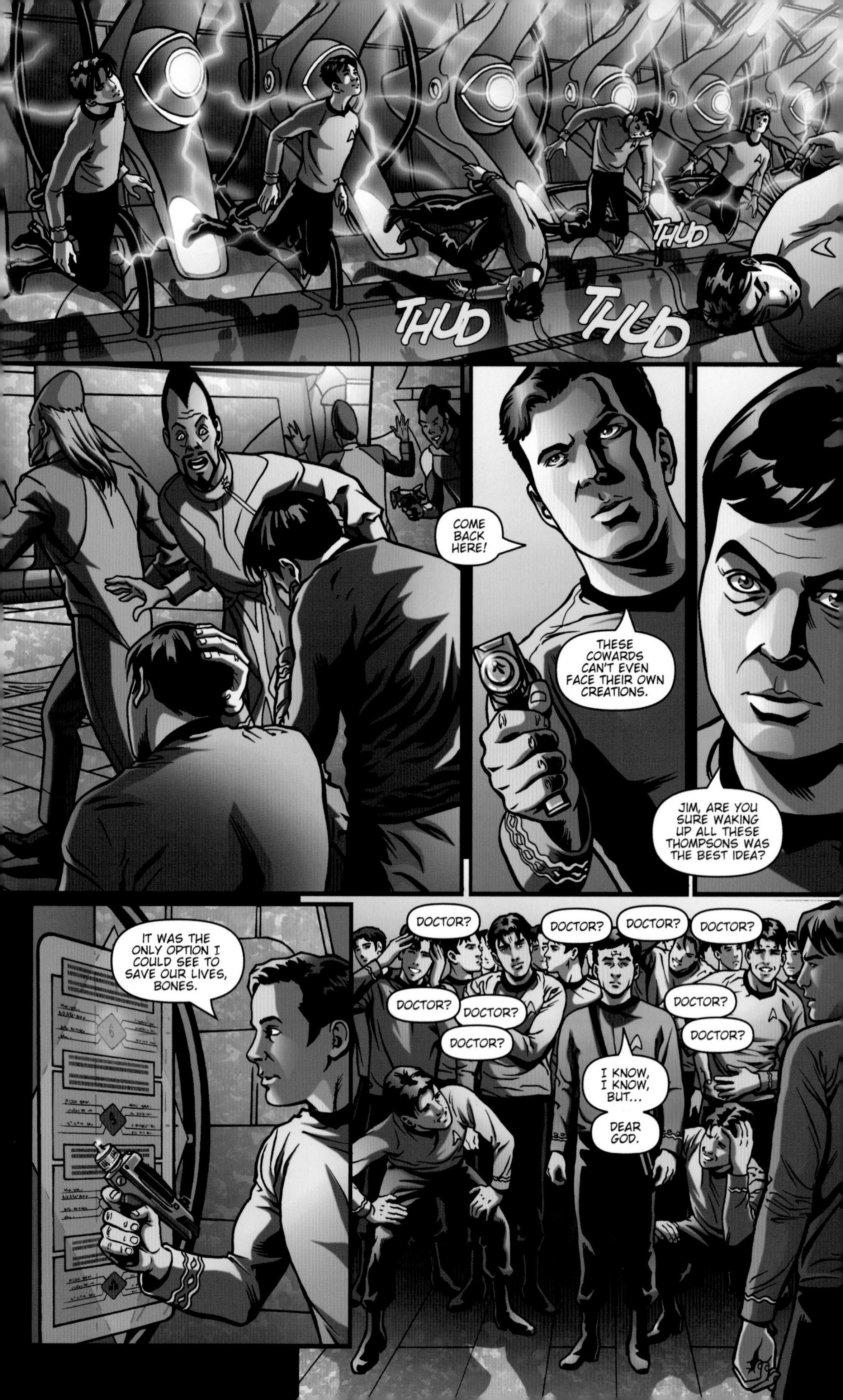
THUD
THUD
THUD
COME BACK HERE!
THESE COWARDS CAN'T EVEN FACE THEIR OWN CREATIONS.
JIM, ARE YOU SURE WAKING UP ALL THESE THOMPSONS WAS THE BEST IDEA?
IT WAS THE ONLY OPTION I COULD SEE TO SAVE OUR LIVES, BONES.
DOCTOR?
DOCTOR?
DOCTOR?
DOCTOR?
DOCTOR?
DOCTOR?
DOCTOR?
DOCTOR?
DOCTOR?
I KNOW, I KNOW, BUT...
DEAR GOD.

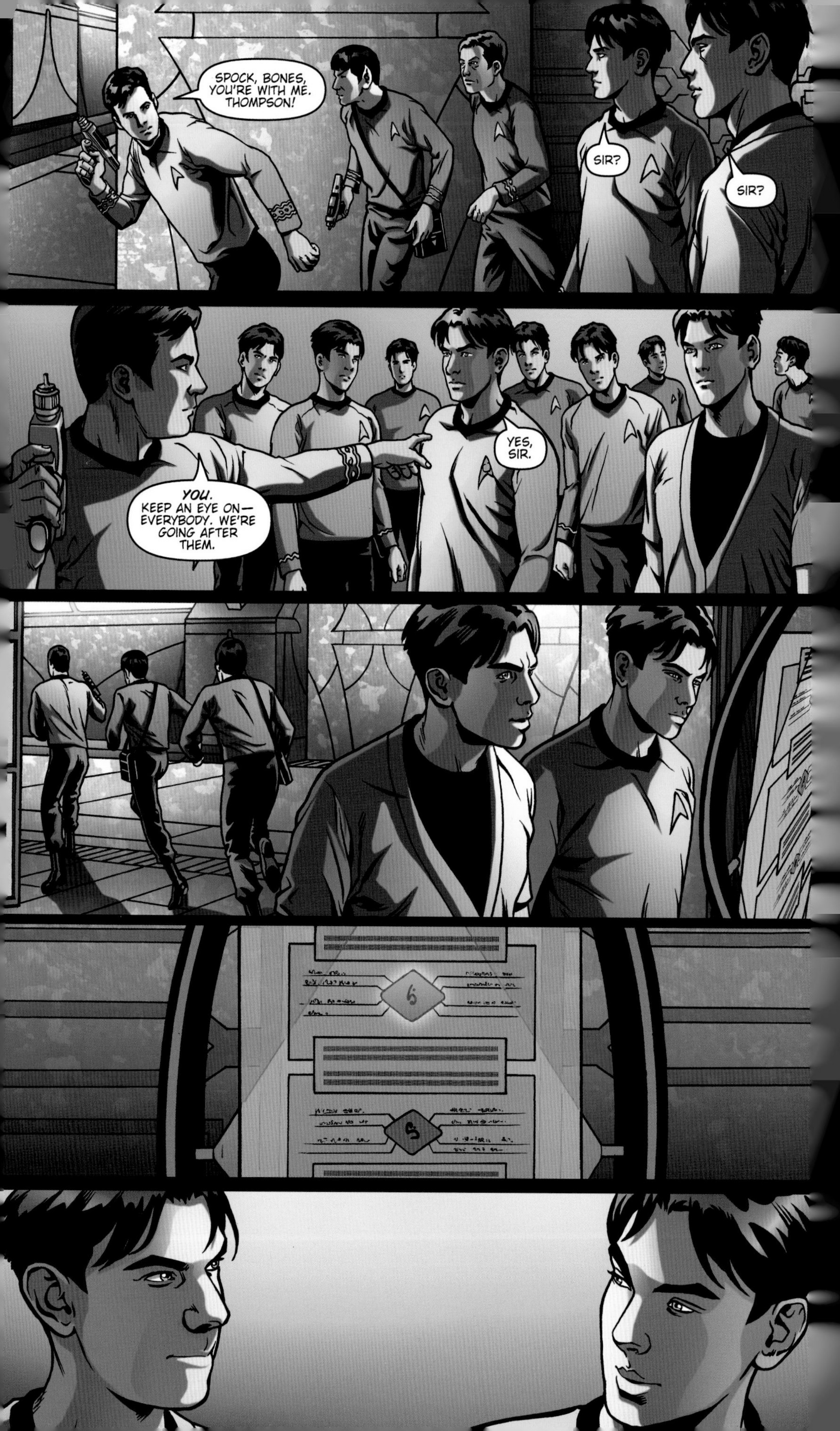
SPOCK, BONES, YOU'RE WITH ME. THOMPSON!
SIR?
SIR?
YOU. KEEP AN EYE ON— EVERYBODY. WE'RE GOING AFTER THEM.
YES, SIR.

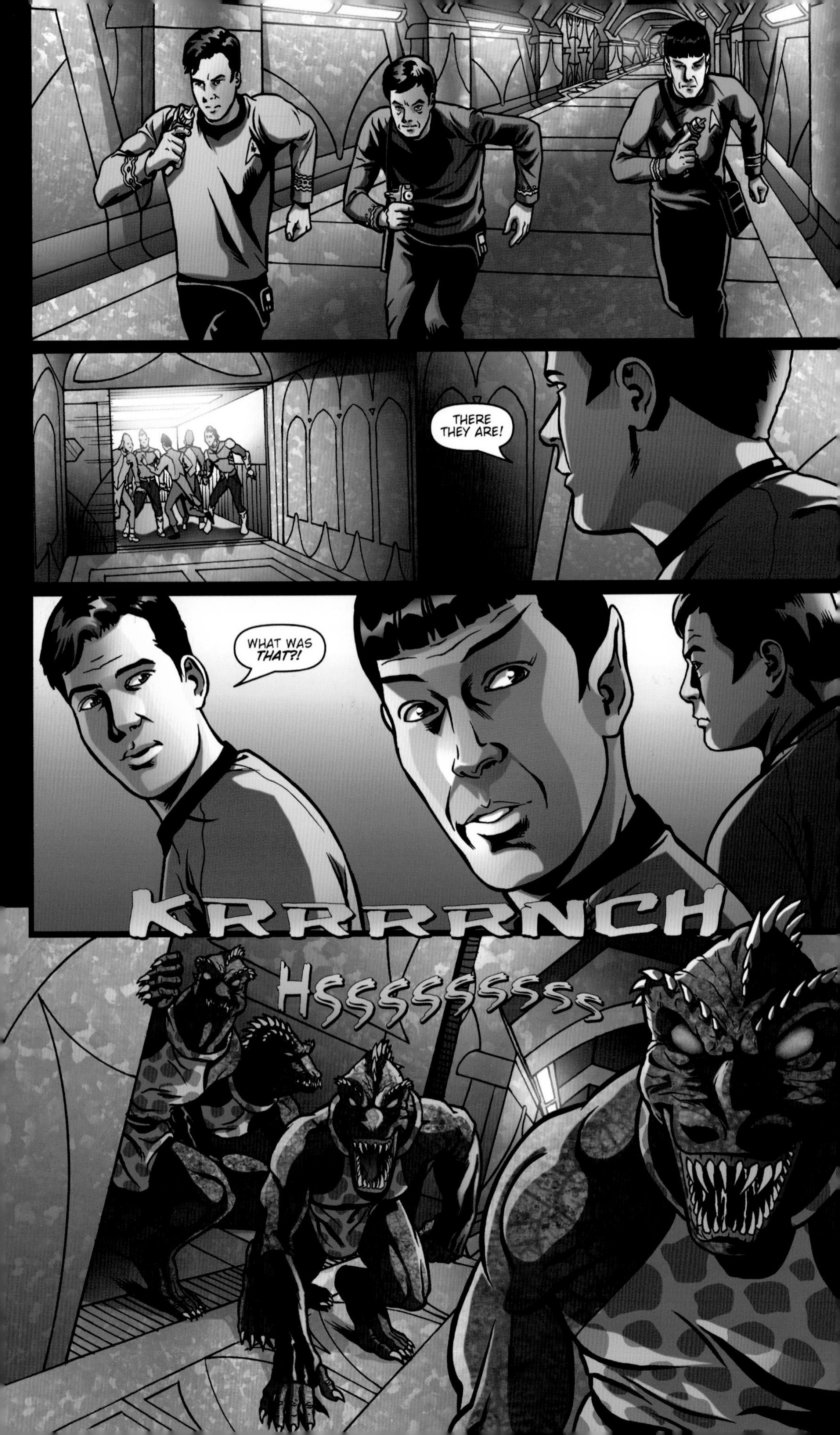
THERE THEY ARE!
WHAT WAS THAT?!
KRRRRNCH
Hssssssssss

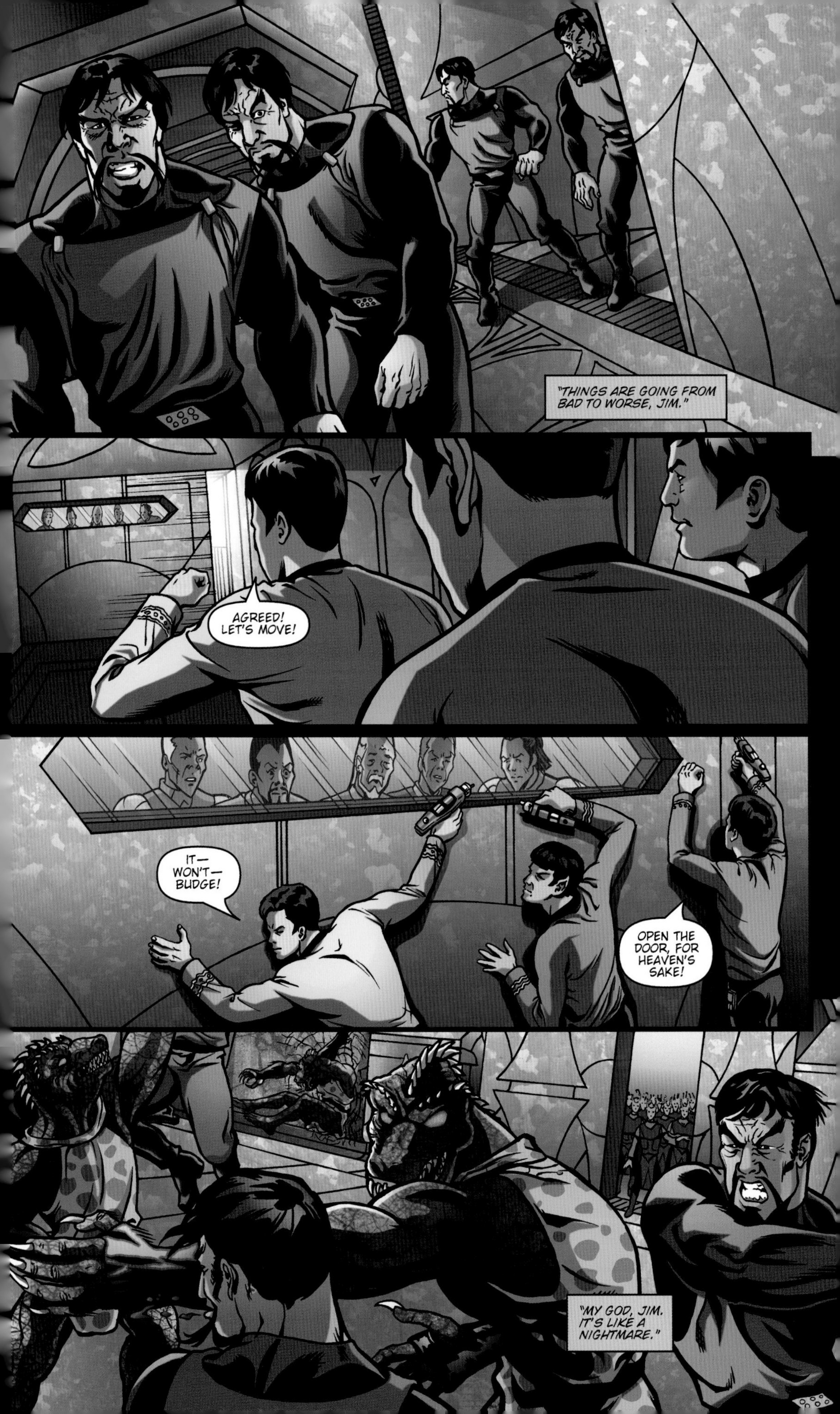
"THINGS ARE GOING FROM BAD TO WORSE, JIM."
AGREED! LET'S MOVE!
IT— WON'T— BUDGE!
OPEN THE DOOR, FOR HEAVEN'S SAKE!
"MY GOD, JIM. IT'S LIKE A NIGHTMARE."

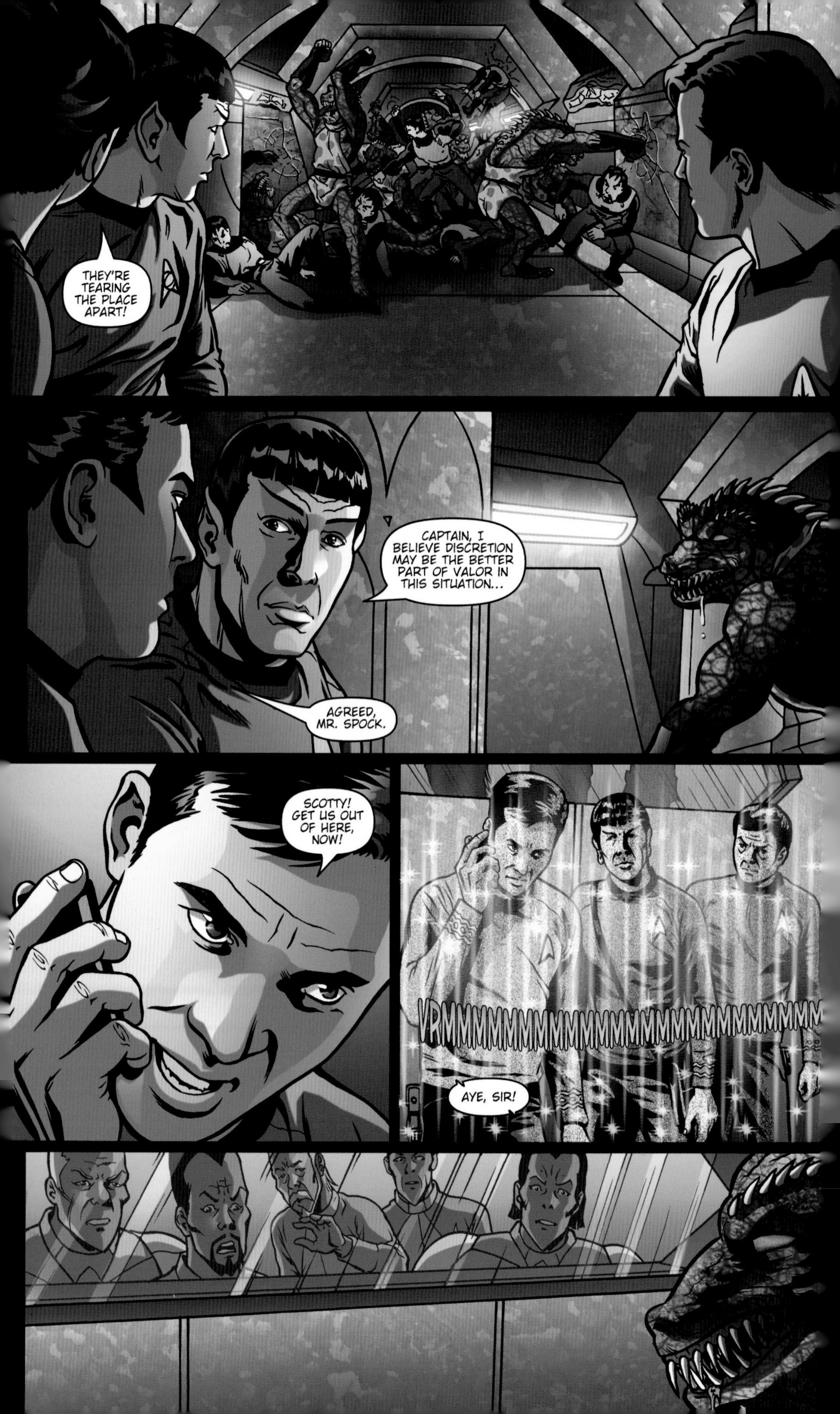
THEY'RE TEARING THE PLACE APART!
CAPTAIN, I BELIEVE DISCRETION MAY BE THE BETTER PART OF VALOR IN THIS SITUATION...
AGREED, MR. SPOCK.
SCOTTY! GET US OUT OF HERE, NOW!
VRMMMMMMMMMMMMMMMMMMMMMMMMMMMMM
AYE, SIR!

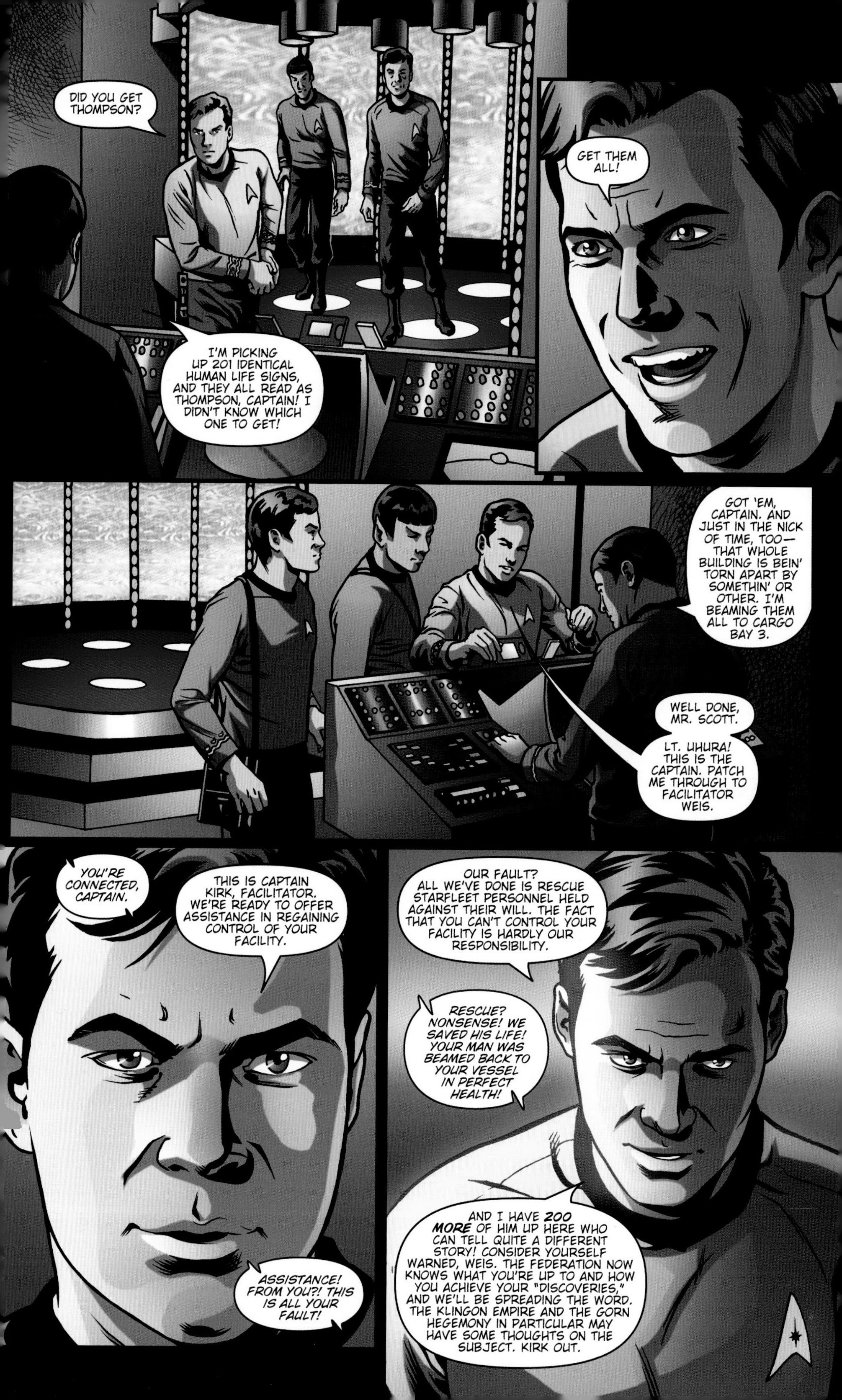
DID YOU GET THOMPSON?
I'M PICKING UP 201 IDENTICAL HUMAN LIFE SIGNS, AND THEY ALL READ AS THOMPSON, CAPTAIN! I DIDN'T KNOW WHICH ONE TO GET!
GET THEM ALL!
GOT 'EM, CAPTAIN. AND JUST IN THE NICK OF TIME, TOO— THAT WHOLE BUILDING IS BEIN' TORN APART BY SOMETHIN' OR OTHER. I'M BEAMING THEM ALL TO CARGO BAY 3.
WELL DONE, MR. SCOTT.
LT. UHURA! THIS IS THE CAPTAIN. PATCH ME THROUGH TO FACILITATOR WEIS.
YOU'RE CONNECTED, CAPTAIN.
THIS IS CAPTAIN KIRK, FACILITATOR. WE'RE READY TO OFFER ASSISTANCE IN REGAINING CONTROL OF YOUR FACILITY.
ASSISTANCE! FROM YOU?! THIS IS ALL YOUR FAULT!
OUR FAULT? ALL WE'VE DONE IS RESCUE STARFLEET PERSONNEL HELD AGAINST THEIR WILL. THE FACT THAT YOU CAN'T CONTROL YOUR FACILITY IS HARDLY OUR RESPONSIBILITY.
RESCUE? NONSENSE! WE SAVED HIS LIFE! YOUR MAN WAS BEAMED BACK TO YOUR VESSEL IN PERFECT HEALTH!
AND I HAVE 200 MORE OF HIM UP HERE WHO CAN TELL QUITE A DIFFERENT STORY! CONSIDER YOURSELF WARNED, WEIS. THE FEDERATION NOW KNOWS WHAT YOU'RE UP TO AND HOW YOU ACHIEVE YOUR "DISCOVERIES," AND WE'LL BE SPREADING THE WORD. THE KLINGON EMPIRE AND THE GORN HEGEMONY IN PARTICULAR MAY HAVE SOME THOUGHTS ON THE SUBJECT. KIRK OUT.

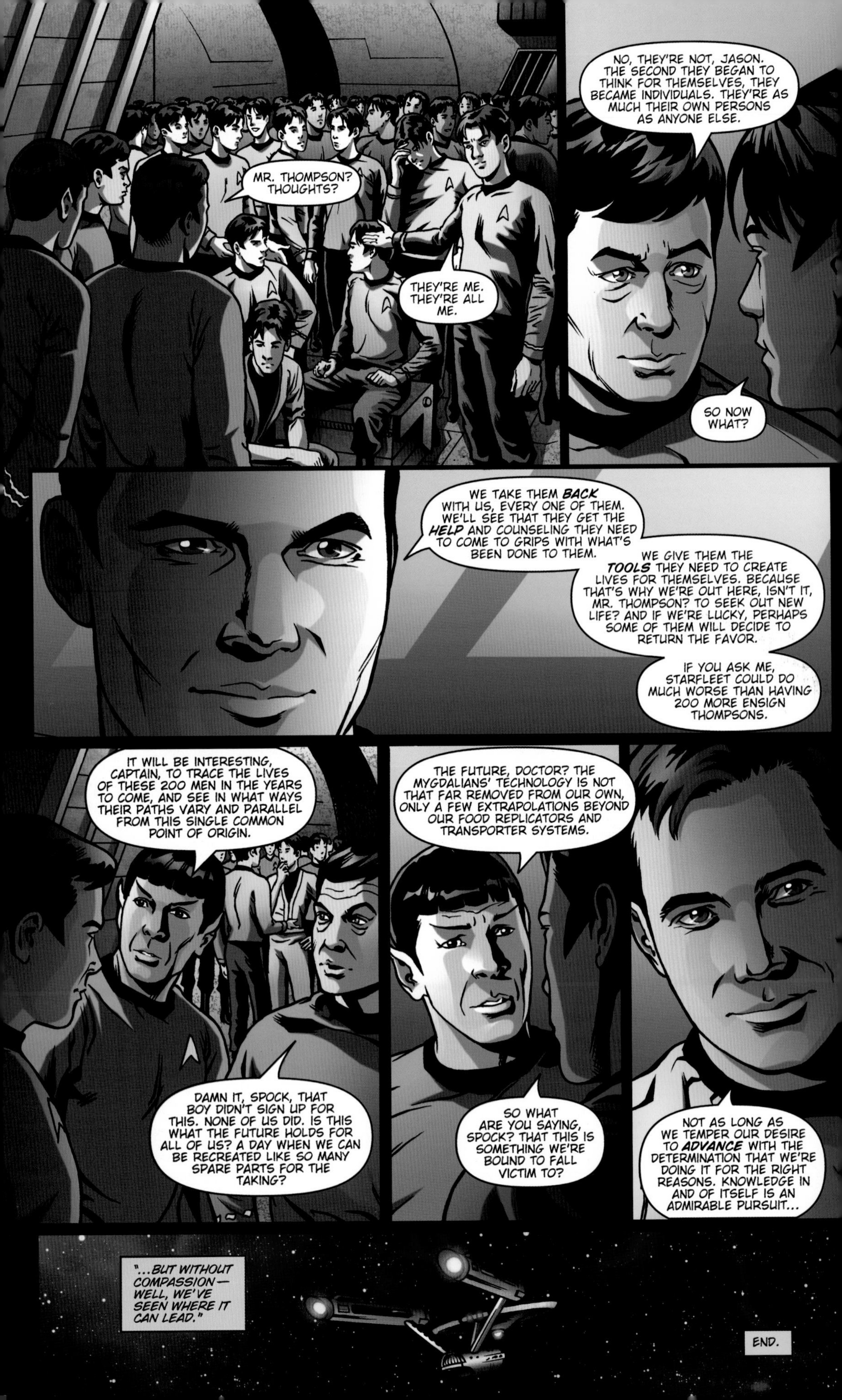
MR. THOMPSON? THOUGHTS?
THEY'RE ME. THEY'RE ALL ME.
NO, THEY'RE NOT, JASON. THE SECOND THEY BEGAN TO THINK FOR THEMSELVES, THEY BECAME INDIVIDUALS. THEY'RE AS MUCH THEIR OWN PERSONS AS ANYONE ELSE.
SO NOW WHAT?
WE TAKE THEM BACK WITH US, EVERY ONE OF THEM. WE'LL SEE THAT THEY GET THE HELP AND COUNSELING THEY NEED TO COME TO GRIPS WITH WHAT'S BEEN DONE TO THEM.
WE GIVE THEM THE TOOLS THEY NEED TO CREATE LIVES FOR THEMSELVES. BECAUSE THAT'S WHY WE'RE OUT HERE, ISN'T IT, MR. THOMPSON? TO SEEK OUT NEW LIFE? AND IF WE'RE LUCKY, PERHAPS SOME OF THEM WILL DECIDE TO RETURN THE FAVOR.
IF YOU ASK ME, STARFLEET COULD DO MUCH WORSE THAN HAVING 200 MORE ENSIGN THOMPSONS.
IT WILL BE INTERESTING, CAPTAIN, TO TRACE THE LIVES OF THESE 200 MEN IN THE YEARS TO COME, AND SEE IN WHAT WAYS THEIR PATHS VARY AND PARALLEL FROM THIS SINGLE COMMON POINT OF ORIGIN.
DAMN IT, SPOCK, THAT BOY DIDN'T SIGN UP FOR THIS. NONE OF US DID. IS THIS WHAT THE FUTURE HOLDS FOR ALL OF US? A DAY WHEN WE CAN BE RECREATED LIKE SO MANY SPARE PARTS FOR THE TAKING?
THE FUTURE, DOCTOR? THE MYGDALIANS' TECHNOLOGY IS NOT THAT FAR REMOVED FROM OUR OWN, ONLY A FEW EXTRAPOLATIONS BEYOND OUR FOOD REPLICATORS AND TRANSPORTER SYSTEMS.
SO WHAT ARE YOU SAYING, SPOCK? THAT THIS IS SOMETHING WE'RE BOUND TO FALL VICTIM TO?
NOT AS LONG AS WE TEMPER OUR DESIRE TO ADVANCE WITH THE DETERMINATION THAT WE'RE DOING IT FOR THE RIGHT REASONS. KNOWLEDGE IN AND OF ITSELF IS AN ADMIRABLE PURSUIT...
"...BUT WITHOUT COMPASSION— WELL, WE'VE SEEN WHERE IT CAN LEAD."
END.

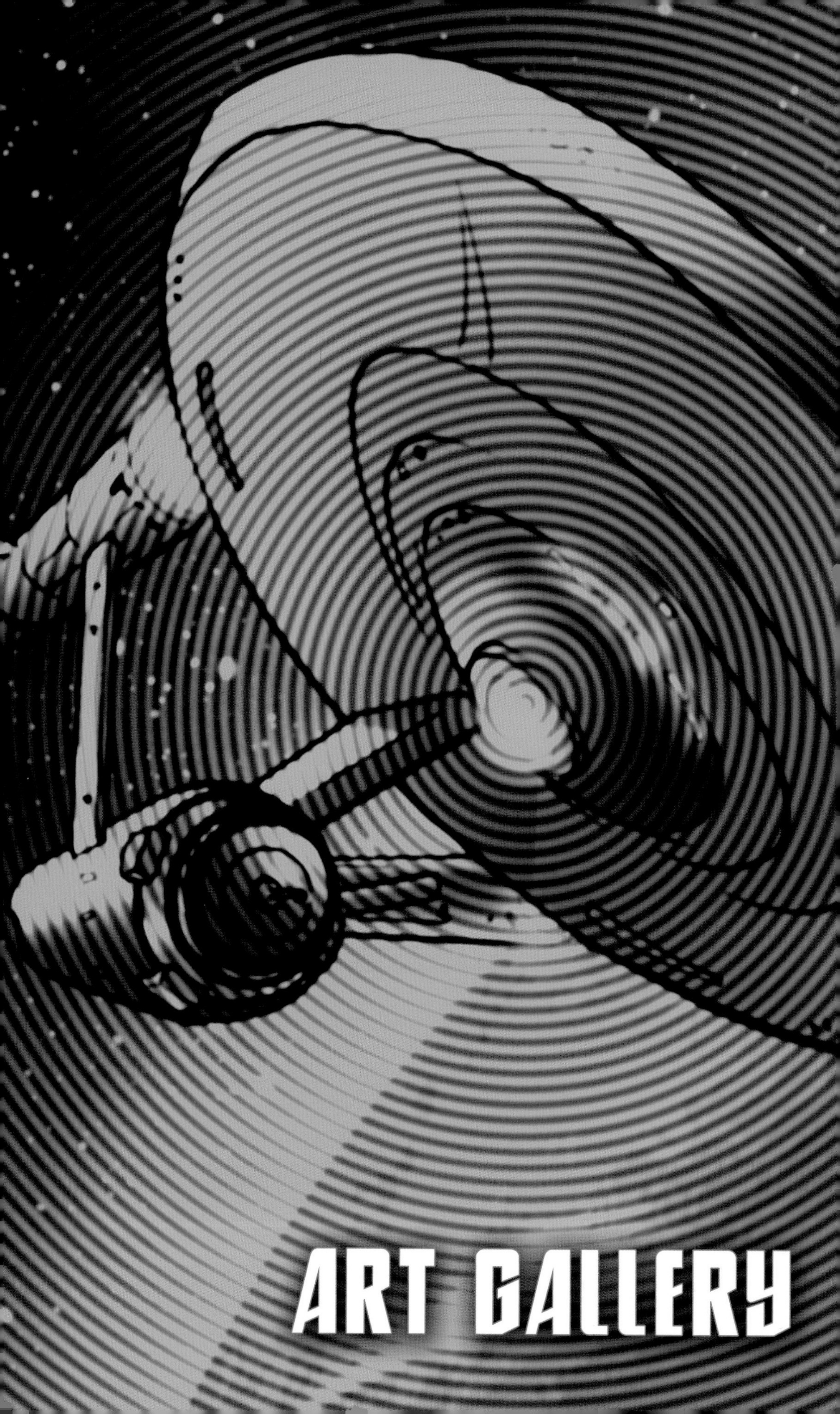
ART GALLERY

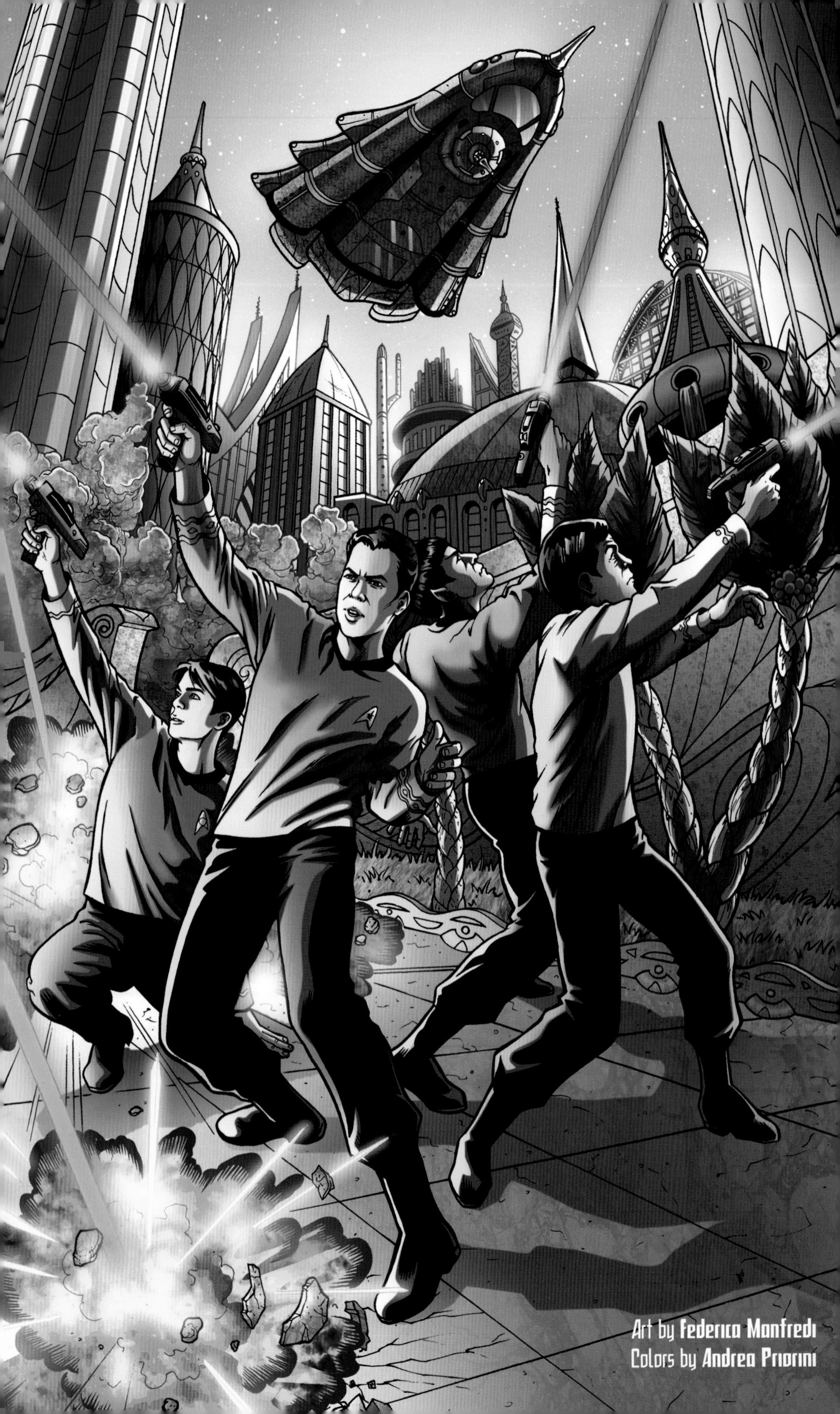
Art by Federica Manfredi
Colors by Andrea Priorini

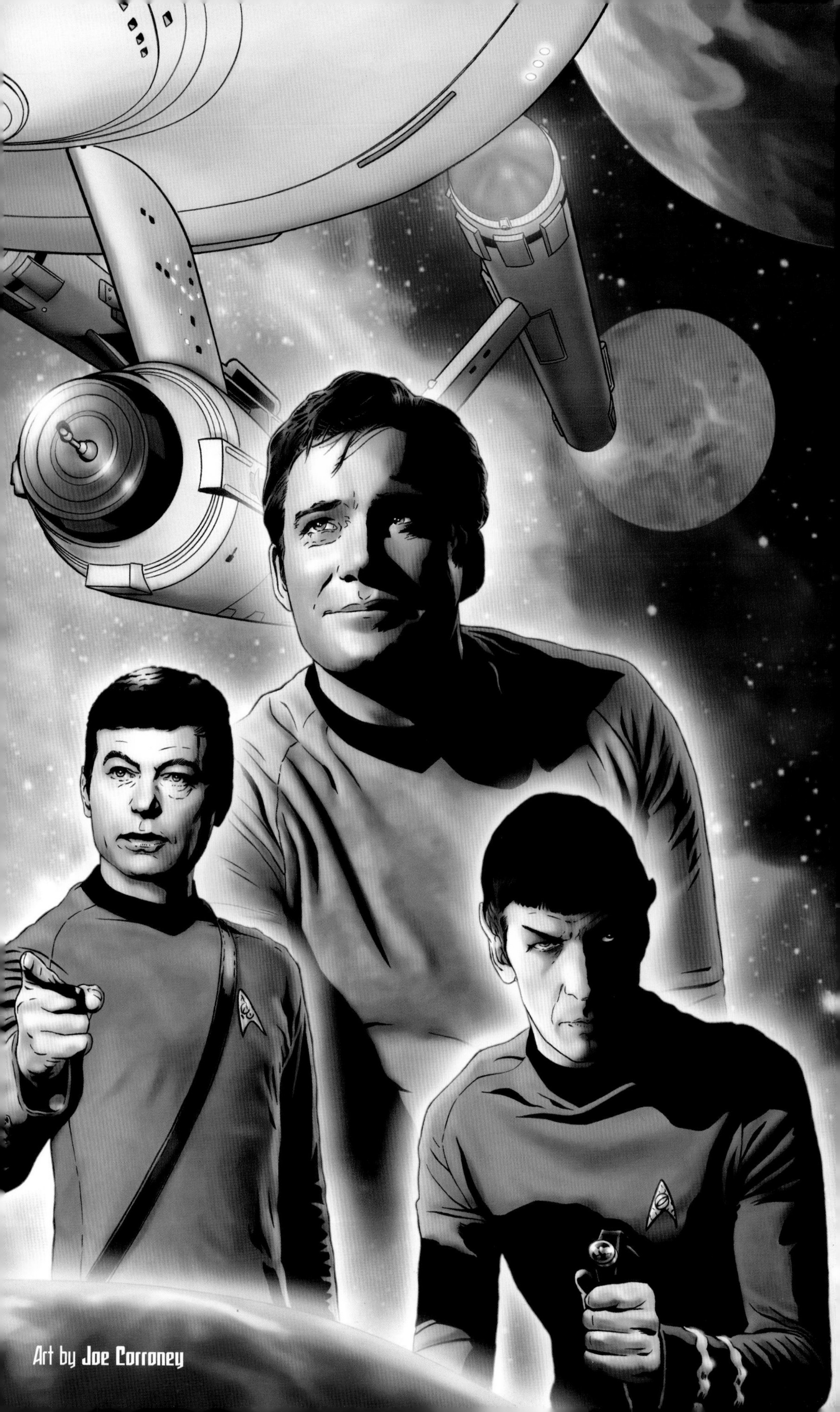
Art by Joe Corroney

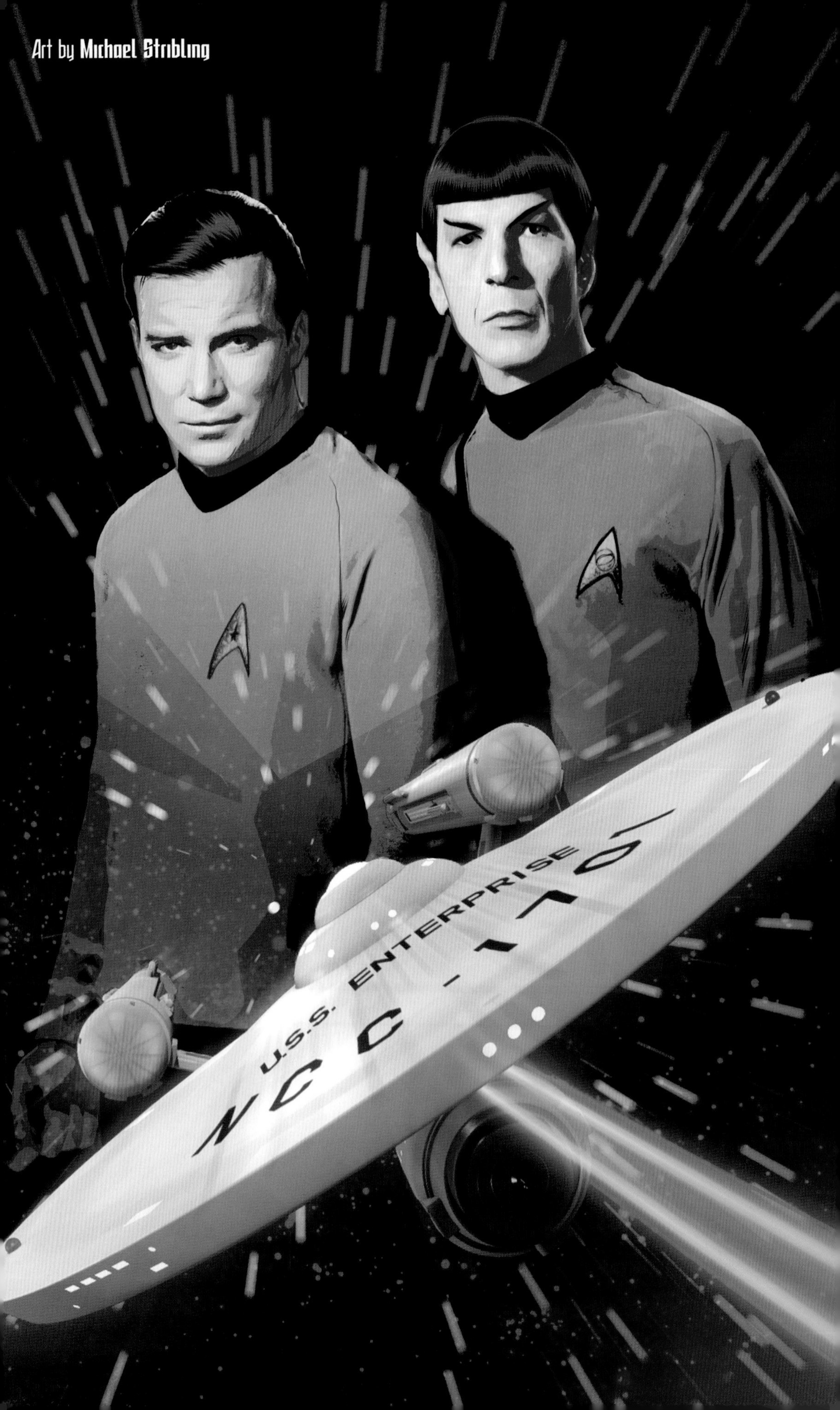
U.S.S. ENTERPRISE
NCC-1701
Art by Michael Stribling

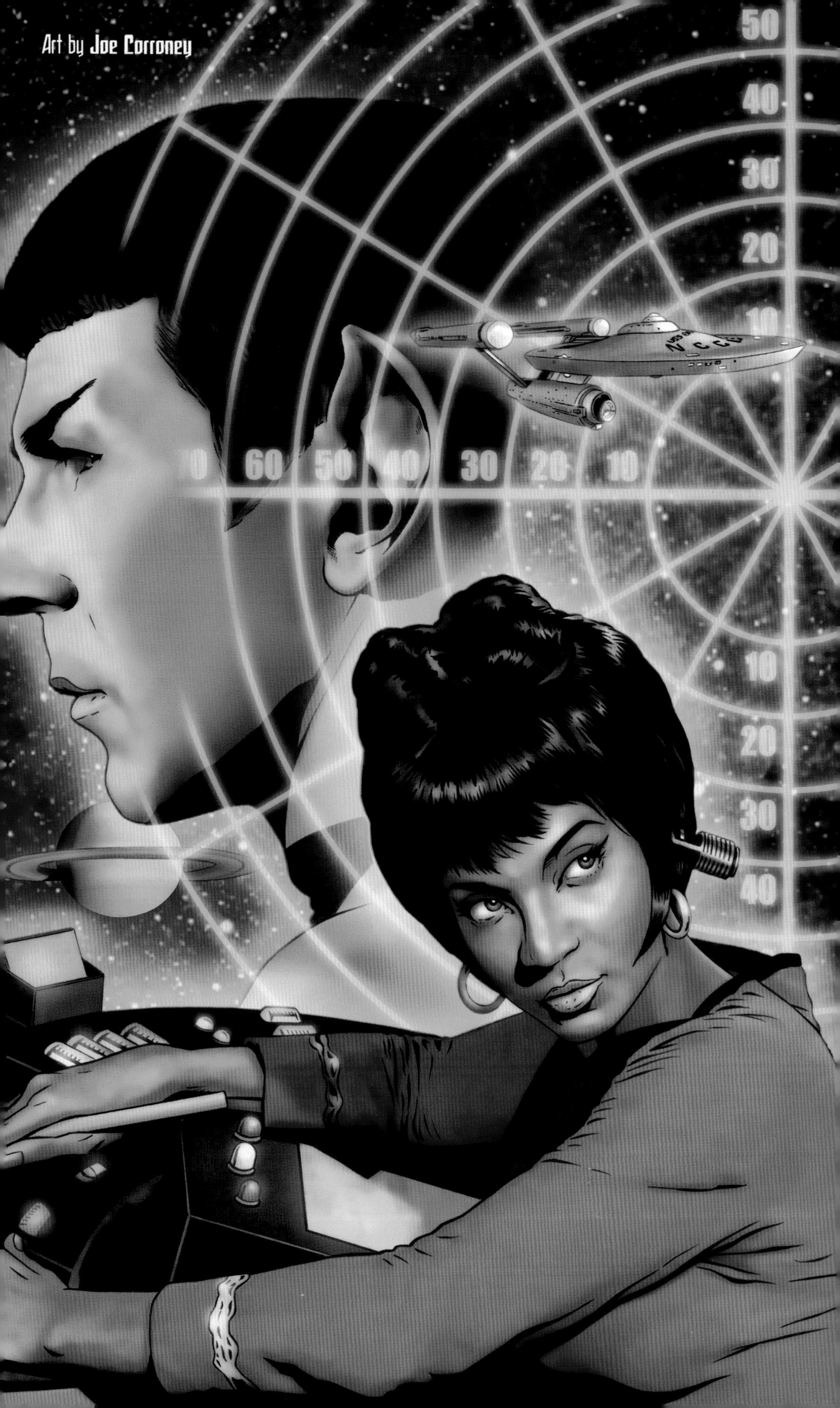
Art by Joe Corroney
50
40
30
20
60
50
40
30
20
10
10
20
30
40

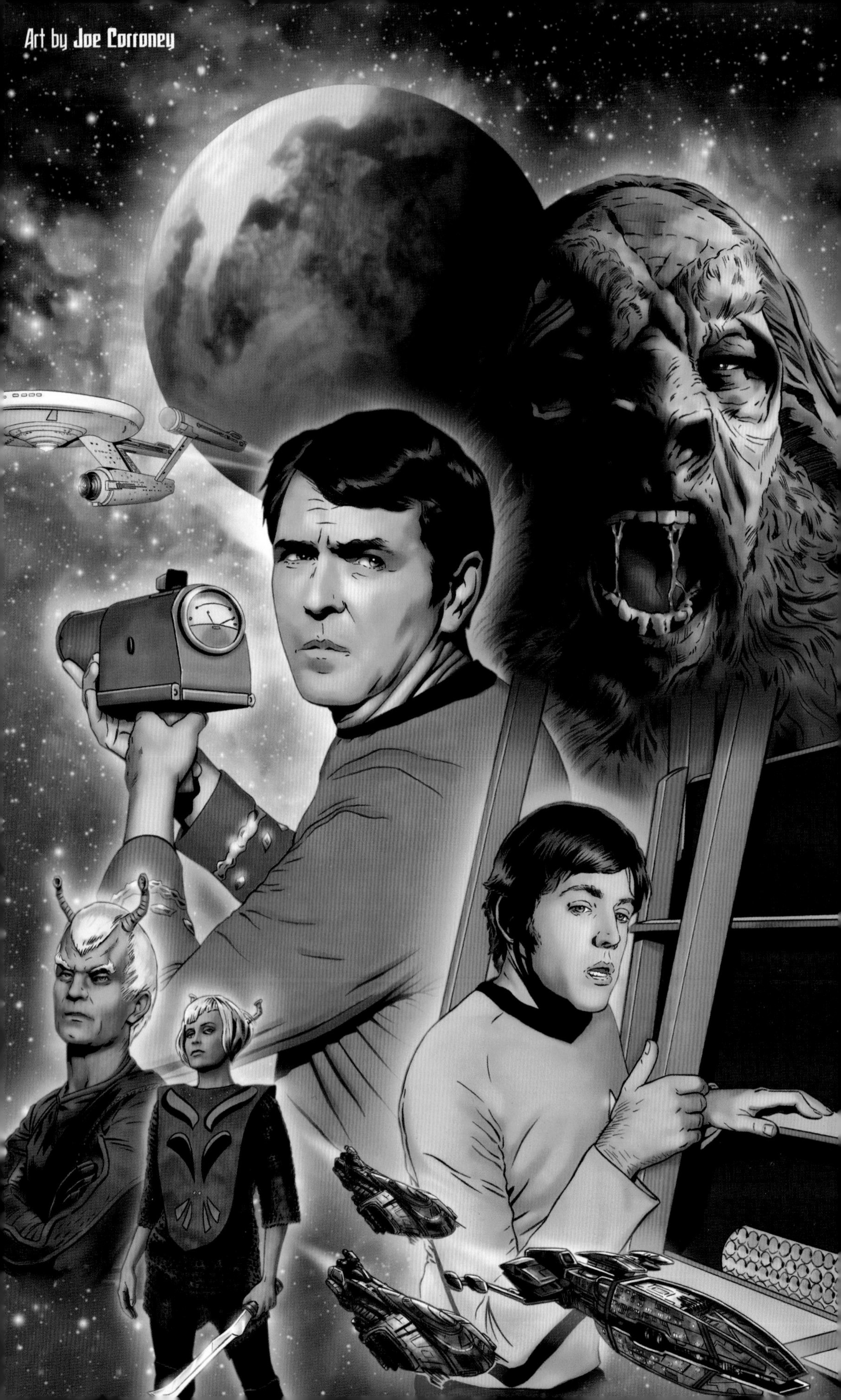
Art by Joe Corroney

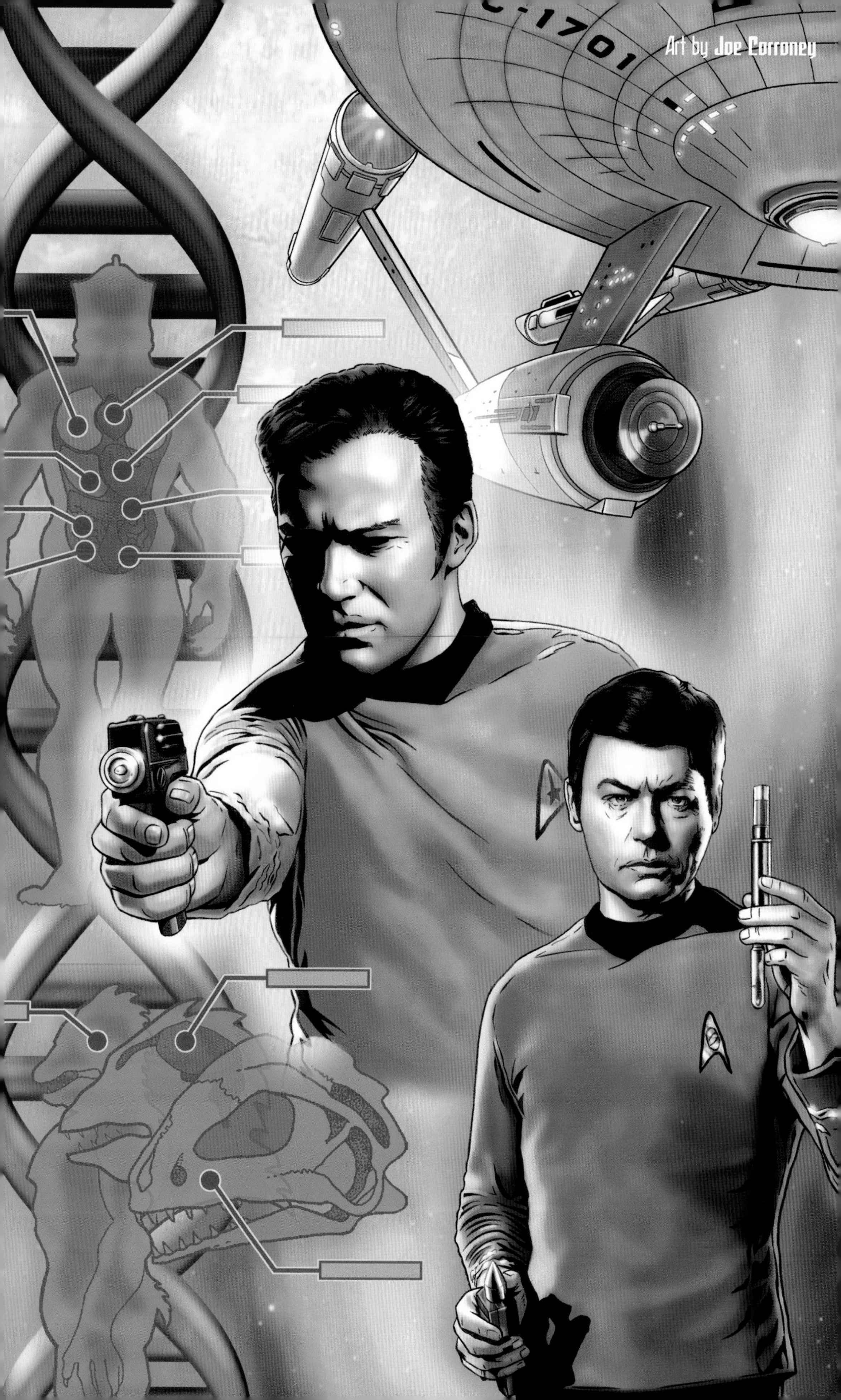

Art by **Joe Corroney**

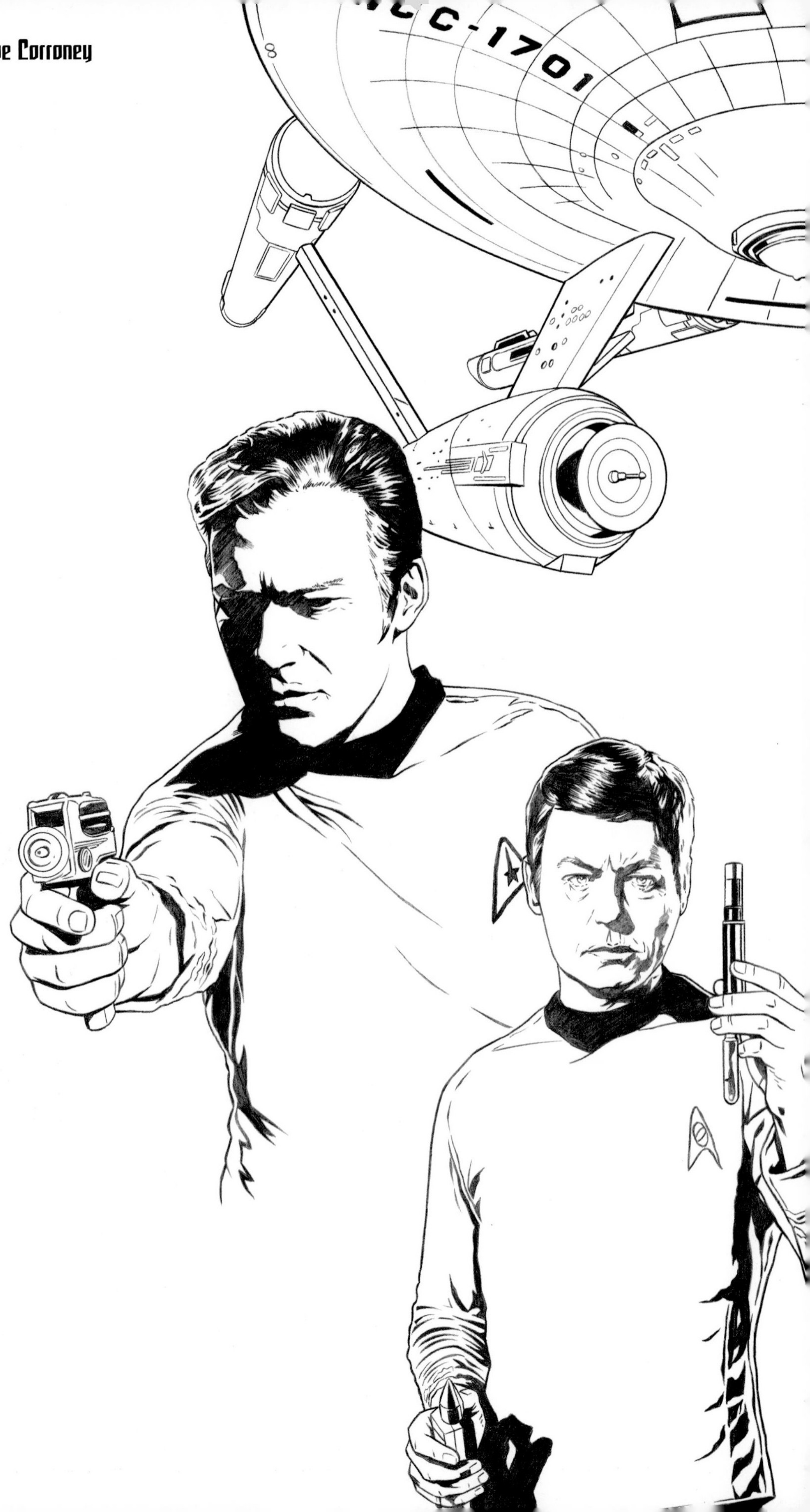
NCC-1701

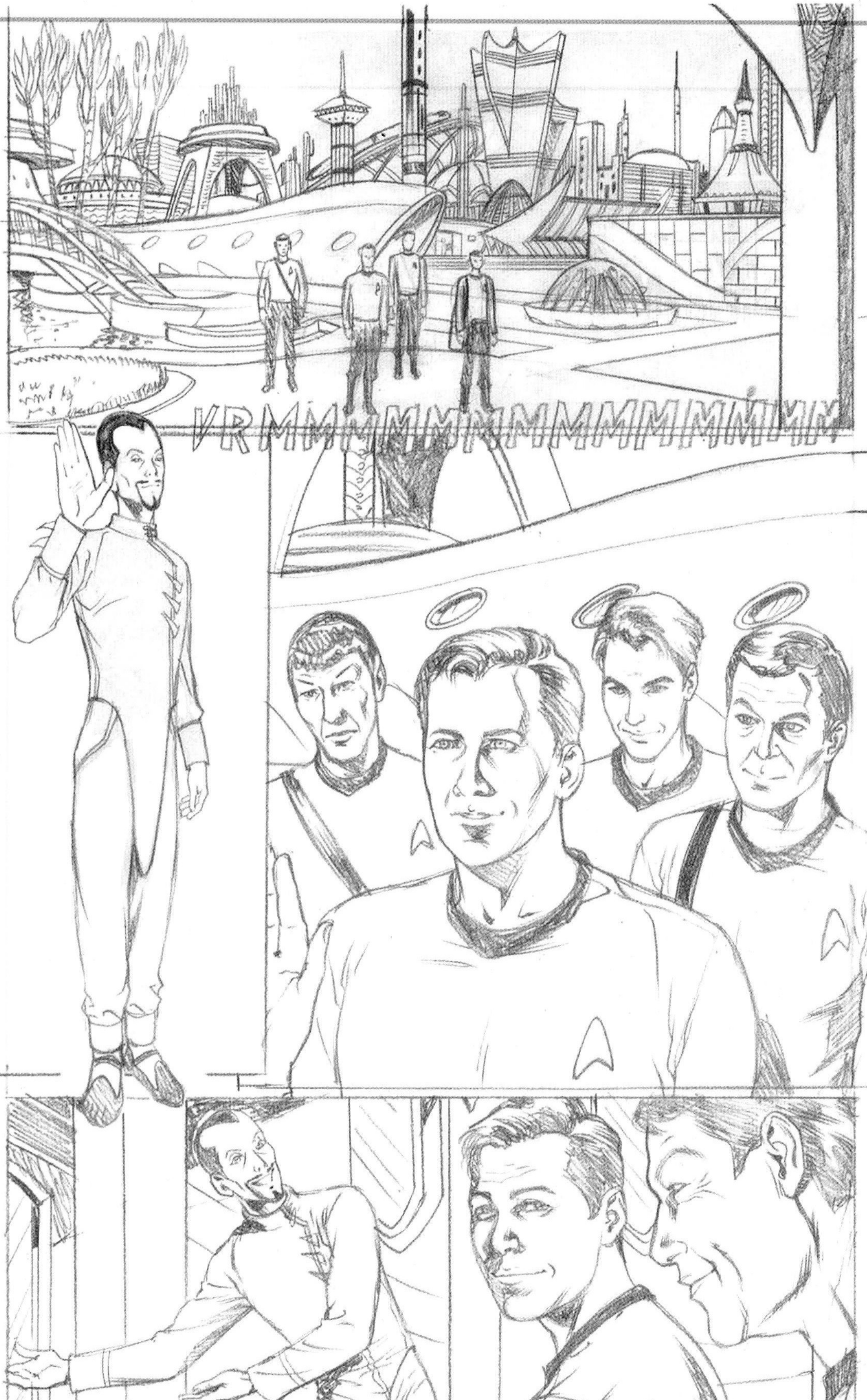
VRMMMMMMMMMMMMMMMMMM

Art by **Federica Manfredi**

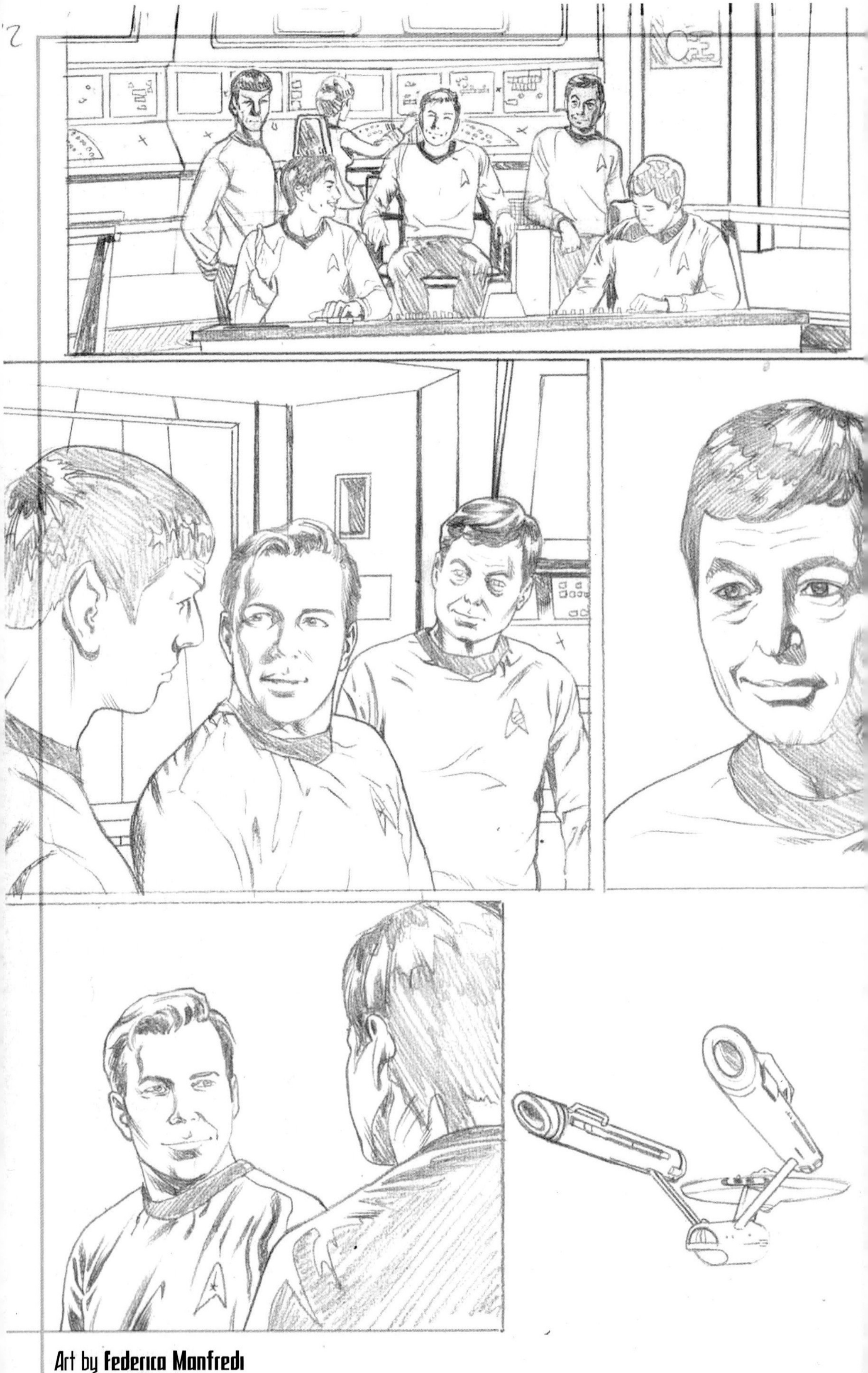

Art by **Federica Manfredi**

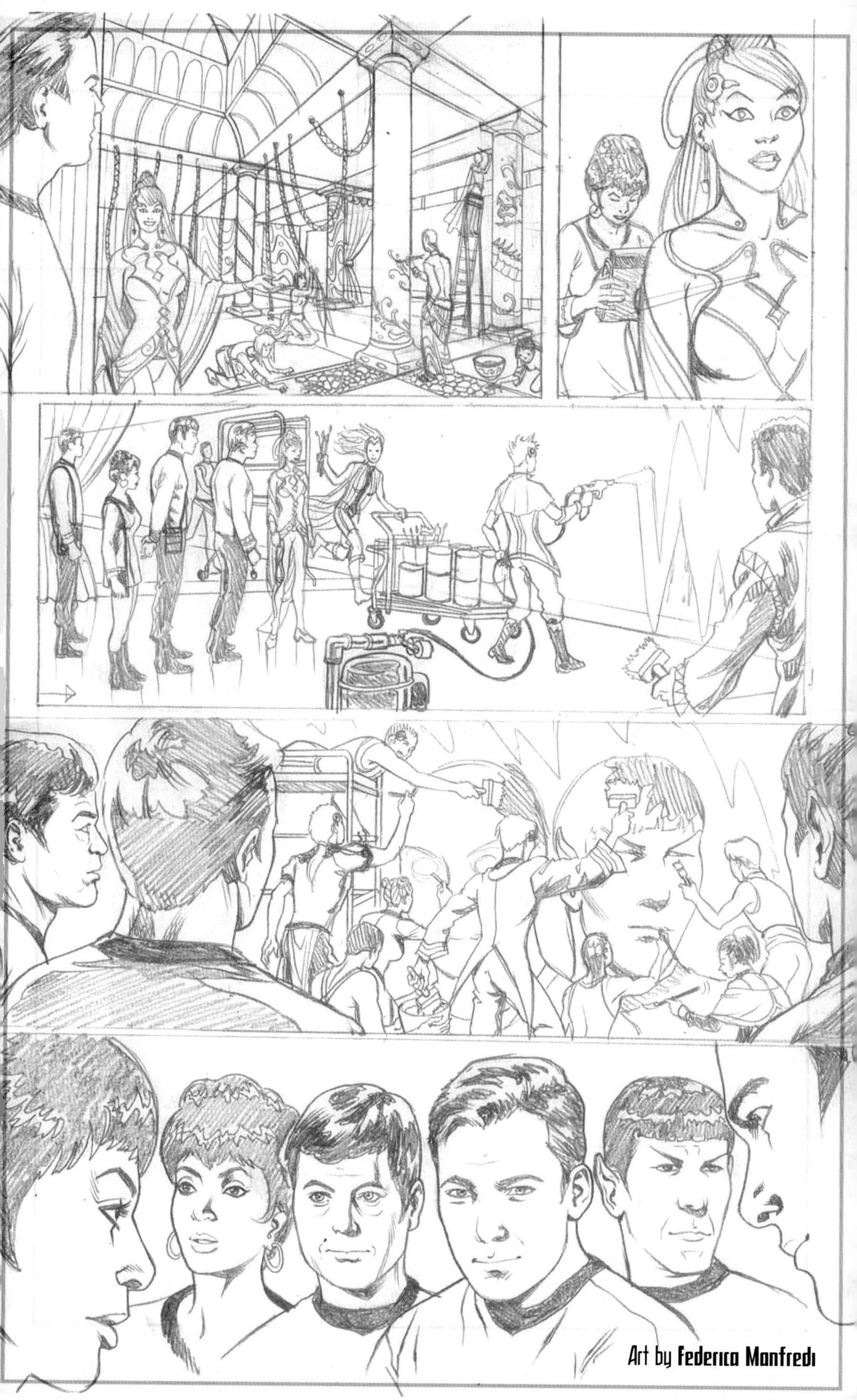
Art by Federica Manfredi

Art by Federica Manfredi

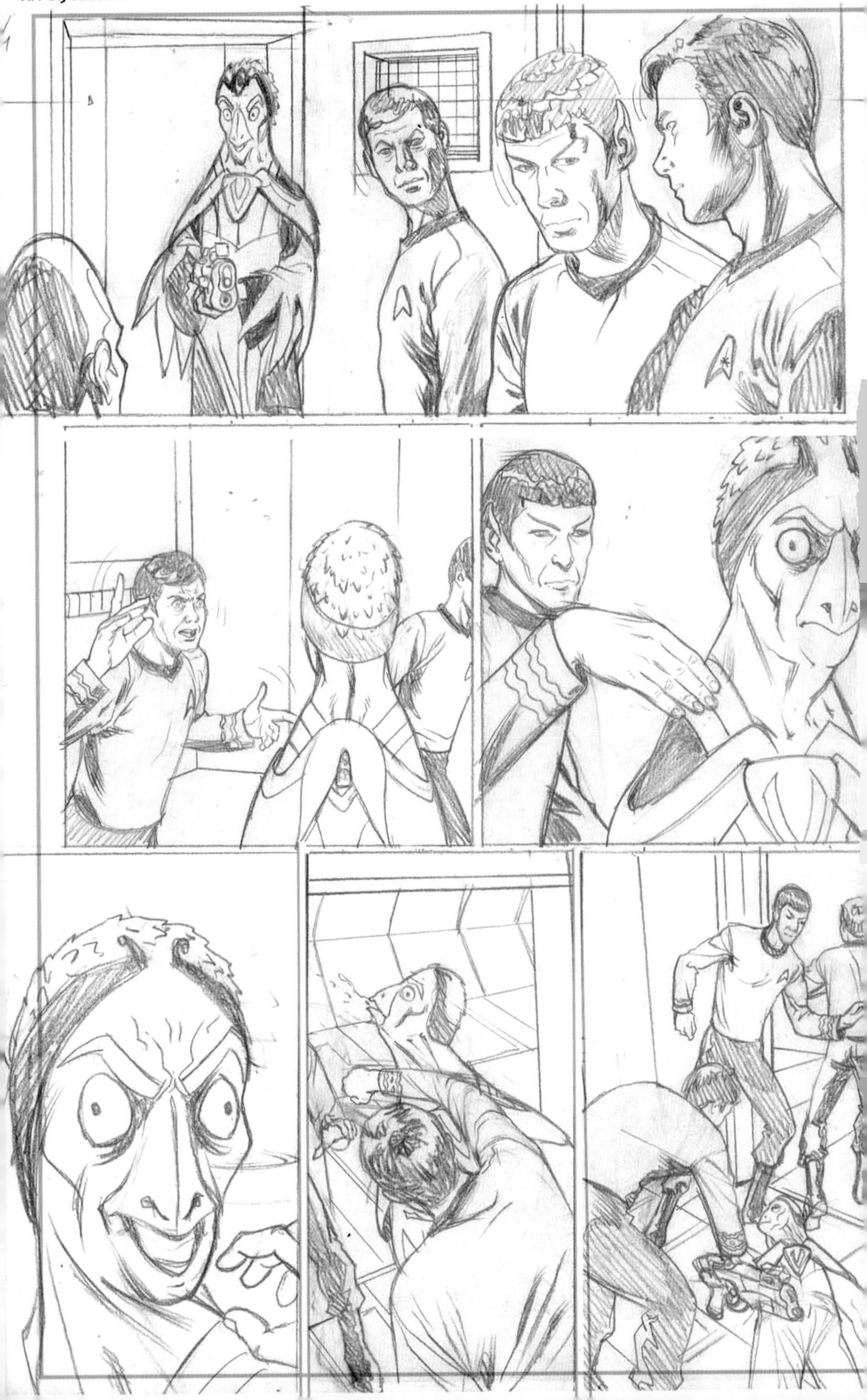

Art by Federica Manfredi

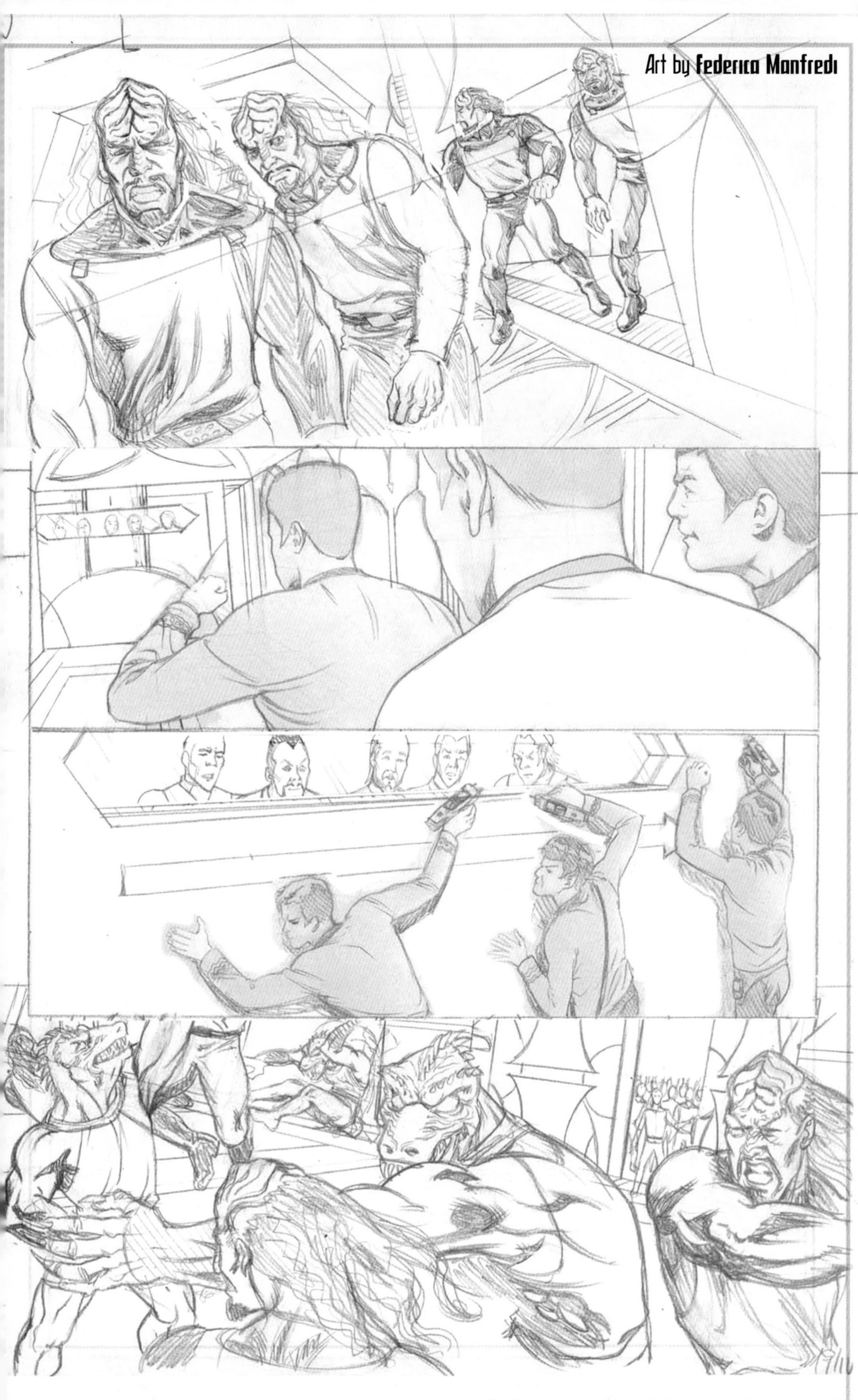

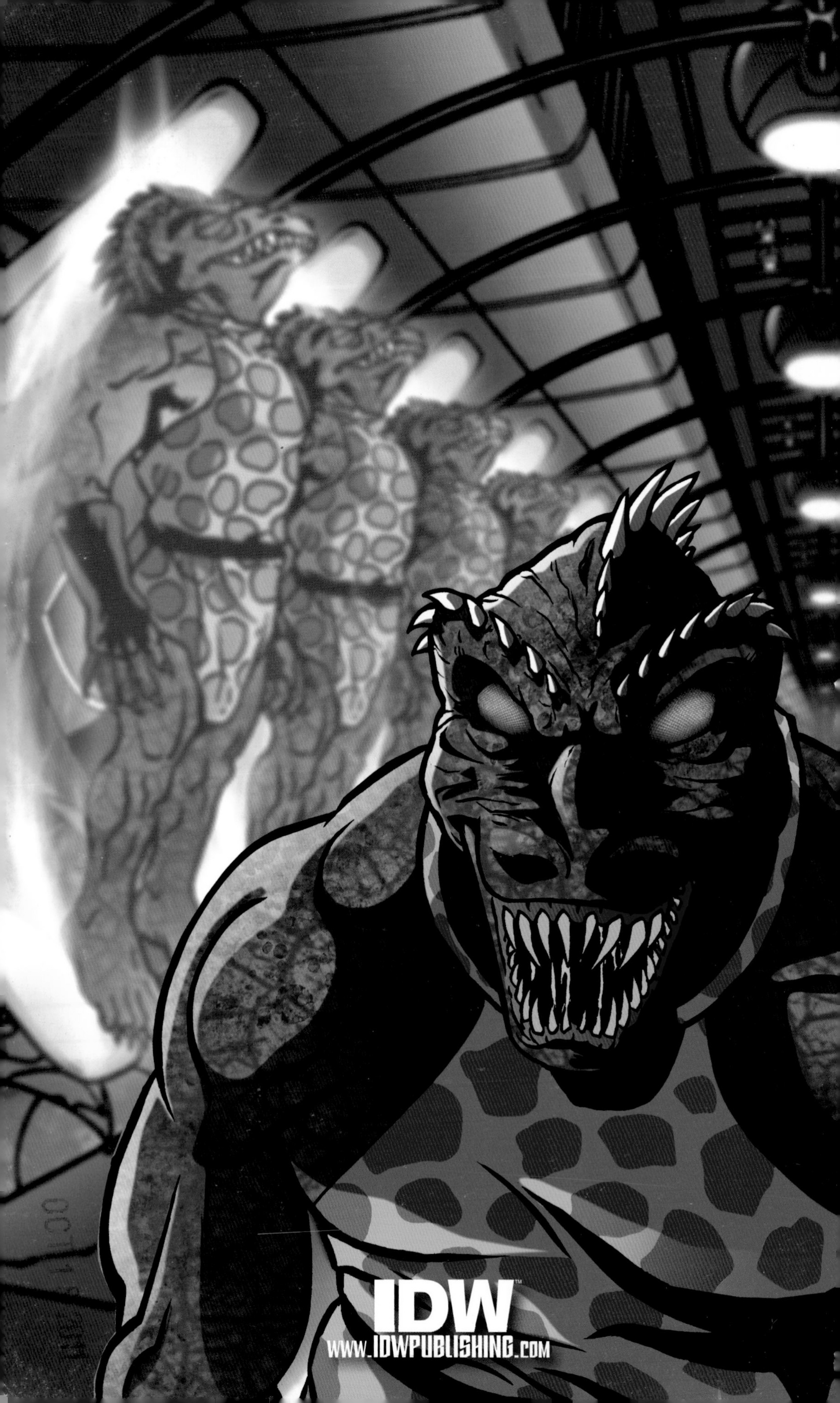
IDW
WWW.IDWPUBLISHING.com